BARBARA ERSKINE

Sleeper's Castle

HarperCollins*Publishers*

HarperCollins*Publishers*
The News Building
1 London Bridge Street
London SE1 9GF

www.harpercollins.co.uk

Published by HarperCollins*Publishers* 2016
1

A catalogue record for this book
is available from the British Library

ISBN: 978-0-00-751316-1

Set in Meridien LT Std by Palimpsest Book Production Limited,
Falkirk, Stirlingshire

Printed and bound in Great Britain by
Clays Ltd, St Ives plc

MIX
Paper from
responsible sources
FSC **FSC C007454**
www.fsc.org

Time

*The past, present and future regarded
as a continuous whole*
Collins English Dictionary

*A space of continued existence, as the interval between two
successive events or acts, or the period through which
an action, condition, or state continues*
The Shorter Oxford English Dictionary

Oneirology

*The science or subject of dreams,
or of their interpretation*

Oneiromancy

Divination by dreams

In the never-ending battle between the principalities of Wales and their aggressive, acquisitive neighbours, the victorious king, Edward I of England, having subdued the native princes had banned the bards, recognising their power, their ability to remember, their position in society as the keepers of memories of freedom and power. To be a bard was to be the inspiration of a people; to be the instigator of longing for freedom; it was a position of enormous influence.

To be a bard was now punishable by death.

Bards had come back of course. Or never gone away.

For two hundred years the Welsh people lay under the English yoke, their impatience growing, their dissatisfaction ever increasing, their bards and poets studying the dream of independence. They were waiting for Y Mab Darogan, the Son of Destiny, who would come to liberate them and make them a great nation once more.

In the middle of the fourteenth century such a man was born, his arrival heralded by a comet in the sky. By the year 1400 he was ready for his destiny.

Prologue

In their dream they smelt smoke. Far below the hillside where they stood the castle nestled within the angle of the great river, a black silhouette against the green of flood-meadow grass. The keep stood four-square, the stone walls massive cliffs pierced by slit windows, lit from without by the dying sun and from within by fire. The moan of the wind and the yelp of circling kites were broken by the occasional thunder of cannon fire and they thought they could hear the screams of injured men. Creeping closer to the edge of the wood, heart in mouth, they watched the topmost battlement crumble and heard the crash of falling stone. The cannon fell silent and there was a roar of cheering, though from here they could see no men, no banners, no rippling standards. The smoke grew thicker as the green-cut oak of the ceiling beams began to burn, the smell sweet on the air until, slowly, insidiously, it was flavoured with a rancid undertone of smouldering fabric and burning wool, as ancient dusty wall hangings and cushions, banners and silks from a bygone age flared and collapsed into the conflagration. Then, a sharp thread winding through the smell, the scent of cooking mutton and beef as the animals, herded into the shelter of the

1

curtain walls, began to roast alive; and with the burning flesh of animals outside the walls was mingled the scent of the burning flesh of men.

Horrified, they watched, hidden in the trees, hands clutching the mossy trunks, fingernails clawing at the lichen-stained bark. Far below they heard the crash as the roof of the keep fell and they saw the sparks fly up in the wind, a curtain of shimmering red against the smoke-filled sky.

When they woke, suddenly, with the sweat of fear icy on their bodies, they lay staring up at the ceiling in the dark and then slowly moved their heads, still hardly daring to move, to look towards the window where the sky was growing light behind the shoulder of the hill. They climbed from bed and padded to the window, leaning on the cold stone of the sill, looking out between the mullions, shivering, knowing that it had been a dream, seeing the sky clear, watching the silver crescent of the moon lying on its back above the trees.

Two women.

Two ice-cold silver dawns, centuries apart.

One endless nightmare.

1

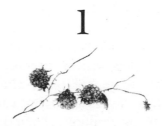

The present day
Towards the end of September

'Take care of Pepper! Tell him I love him!'

Sue handing her the keys. Laughing. Giving her a quick hug then running down the steep uneven stone steps to the gate and her waiting car. 'You remember where everything is? Enjoy.'

The engine revs. She is gone.

Andy stands listening as the car takes the succession of Z bends down the steep single-track lane with its high banks and its wild hedges until the sound of the engine is swallowed by the silence. She is alone.

Slowly she turns and surveys her new home. A year, rent-free, in exchange for looking after an ancient house with mullioned windows and a moss-covered slate roof and an old and grumpy cat called Pepper. Overwhelmed with unexpected happiness she begins to smile.

'He's too old to go into a cattery, Andy. It would kill him. He needs to stay at home. He needs someone to feed him regularly and make sure the house is warm. That's all. He won't need anything else. He's his own man. Well, his own cat! And he knows you.' Sue's voice was pleading, though she had already known that Andy would say yes.

Yes, the cat had met her. Once. For a couple of weeks when she and Graham had stayed here with Sue four summers ago. Andy's smile faded at the memory, then it returned. In her head, for a moment, the house was full of the sound of Sue's irrepressible laughter and Graham's deep guffaws.

Exhausted after the long drive, she sat down on the cold stone slab of the top step and, hugging her knees, stared down over the almost vertical wild rock garden which fronted the ancient stone building, down towards the parking space, no more than a lay-by really, off the narrow lane, occupied now only by her old Passat. She could see the low sun glinting on its dark blue roof, almost hidden by the tangle of autumn flowers. The car contained almost all she owned in the whole world.

She hadn't expected this – to be suddenly and irrevocably homeless.

'It's your fault he died!' Rhona Wilson, Graham's widow, shouted at Andy. 'If he had never met you we would have been happy. He would be alive now.' It took Rhona's sister, Michelle, to drag her away as Andy stood there, numb with shock, too over-whelmed with grief to move.

'Get out of our house!' Michelle almost spat the words at Andy. 'Go. Haven't you done enough damage here, stealing Graham away from us? Killing him!'

Andy backed out of the room, turned and ran down the stairs. She shouldn't have been surprised. She knew Rhona hated her. The woman had left Graham long before Andy had come into his life, run off with another man, left him as well and moved in with a second, followed that one to the States, come back with someone quite different, but never had she lost

4

her sense of ownership. She didn't want Graham, but she didn't want anyone else to have him either and she obviously didn't intend to let anyone else benefit, if that was the right word, from his death. In the past she had contented herself with the odd vitriolic phone call, occasional nasty letters and postcards, but in the past Graham had been there to protect Andy. Now he was gone and Rhona had found allies in her war of attrition.

Andy's life had been idyllic. She had lived with Graham for nearly ten years in his beautiful detached house in the quiet tree-lined street in Kew. She wrote her column for the local paper. She illustrated his books, fulfilling her contractual duties as his co-author by providing exquisite, tiny watercolours of the exotic rare plants he wrote about. That was how she had met him; his publisher had contacted her with a suggestion that she might be the person to illustrate his next book. She was happy. He was happy. Then the cancer came, swift and deadly, diagnosed far too late.

Within days of his death his ex-wife, technically still his wife, and her family had made it clear that Andy had no place, no rights, no security, no home.

She didn't even know they had keys to the house; they were in before she realised it. They tried to stop her taking even her own things, this vicious greedy cabal of women, his wife, her sister, her friends. They had supervised her packing, had checked everything as she threw her cases and bags into her car. They grabbed her sketchbooks and paintings. Graham had paid for them, they screeched, though technically they had not yet been paid for; she was contracted to his publisher. She didn't argue. Didn't fight back. Did not care. He was gone. She doubted she could live without him anyway.

But then the phone calls had started and the threats had continued even though Andy had left the house. Rhona was sure she had stolen things. But, if there had been theft it was not on Andy's side. Graham's will, and Andy had seen his will, leaving his house and garden and books and manuscripts to her, had disappeared. The solicitor, Rhona's sister's husband, as it happened, said he had no copy and knew nothing of it. Andy gave up. She wouldn't, she couldn't, fight them.

To escape Rhona's vicious calls she kept her phone switched off. She slept on sofas and floors and drank a great deal of wine with her mother and her wonderful loyal friends as she tried to come to terms with the fact that she had no home, very little money, no future and, it seemed, no past. Without her friends to steady her, replace the rock which had been Graham, she would have been a wreck, if she had survived at all.

Then Sue had phoned. She had heard what had happened on the grapevine. 'I'm not sure if this would be a port in a storm, Andy. If you like the idea it would surely help me. I planned this trip to Australia to go to my brother's wedding and then spend time visiting the folks, blithely assuming I could get a tenant in time. I'd much rather it was you than a stranger, and Rhona will never find you in Wales.'

And so, here she was. Rubbing her face wearily Andy stood up, conscious of the roar of water from the brook that ran along the edge of the garden, plunging over rocks and between deep overhanging banks thick with moss and fern, under the bridge in the lane and on down towards the valley.

The house, with its wonderful romantic name of Sleeper's Castle, was in the foothills of the Black Mountains, a few miles from the nearest town. The countryside was huge and empty and the contours on the map had been, as she reminded herself on her way here, suspiciously close to each other, a clue to the presence of steep hills and deep secluded valleys. Sue called it her retreat. She had no neighbours. None close by, anyway.

Andy turned her back on the endless view of misty hills and the turbulent sky and she made her way towards the front door, past the rough wooden bench which stood with its back to the stone wall, facing the view.

Sleeper's Castle was not, never had been, a castle, but it had once been a much bigger house. The name Sleeper's, Sue had told her vaguely, came from something in Welsh. It didn't matter. It was perfect. Wild, unspoilt, magical, built on the eastern fringe of the Black Mountains, the remote, mysterious range at the north-easternmost end of the Brecon Beacons National Park, on the Welsh side of the border between England and Wales. Andy took a deep breath of the soft sweet upland air and infinitesimally, without her noticing, the first of her cares began gently to drop away.

Nowadays the downstairs of the house comprised only four rooms, the largest by far, which had once been the medieval hall, paying lip service to its duties now as a sitting/living room only by the presence of an enormous baggy inelegant sofa and a couple of old, all-enveloping, velvet-covered armchairs. Smothered with an array of multi-coloured rugs they had been arranged in a semicircle around a huge open fireplace built of ancient stone, topped by a bressummer beam, split and scorched from countless roaring fires over many centuries. At the moment the fireplace was empty and swept clean of ash but the sweet smell of woodsmoke still clung in the corners of the room and hung about the beams. The rest of the room, with its oak table, bureau bookcase, ancient kneehole desk and scattered multi-dimensional chairs served Sue as a potting-shed-cum-office. Andy gave a wry smile. She had lived with a plantsman for years, but never once had he allowed his garden to encroach on the elegance of his home. His wellies – and hers – stayed firmly in the utility room at the back of the house. Where hers still were, she realised with a pang of misery. Here, judging by the state of the threadbare rug, Sue still wore hers indoors. The fact that there was a mirror on the wall was somehow counter-intuitive.

Andy caught sight of herself and briefly she stood still, staring. Her shoulder-length wild curly light brown hair stood out round her head in a tangled mass, her eyes, grey and usually clear and expressive, looked sore and reddened with exhaustion and misery. Her face, which Graham used to describe as beautiful, was drawn and sad. She was not a pretty sight. She stepped back with a grimace, turned her back on the mirror and with a last, affectionate glance round the room made her way through to the kitchen.

It took several seconds to absorb the shock of what she saw there. When she and Graham had stayed with Sue four years ago the kitchen had more or less matched the living room. Used. Scruffy. Barely, to be honest, even remotely hygienic. She remembered the ever-watchful cat strolling along the worktop to lick the butter when someone left the top off the dish, and Sue laughing at Andy's consternation when the same dish turned up on the table at lunch. But now it had all changed. Sue's kitchen had transformed, to Andy's astonishment and disbelief, into the epitome of every woman's dream. There was a butler's sink with brass taps, a large scrubbed refectory table and, joy of joys, an Aga like the one she and Graham had had in his kitchen in Kew, with next to it, a rocking chair, the only concession to comfort in the room and on the chair a large tabby cat.

'Hello, Pepper,' she said. Pepper, short for Culpepper, the herbalist.

He narrowed his eyes briefly then closed them, his expression bored but proprietorial. She got the message at once. His chair, his kitchen, his Aga.

She smiled as she walked slowly round the table, admiring every detail. On the dresser were two bottles of Merlot with a note.

To be taken x 2 daily with food. Enjoy. Sue xxxxx

It took several trips to drag her belongings up the steep steps from the car. Rhona's family had not been interested in her clothes, or the books she had time to rescue or, in the end, most of her painting gear. She had little jewellery, but what there was – seeing which way the wind was blowing – she had hidden in a flower pot, to be tipped later straight into the boot of her car, and after that into a drawer in her mother's house. Only two or three of those pretty things had been gifts from Graham; he didn't see the point of jewellery when a live flower tucked into Andy's hair was so much more perfect. The rest of the rings and bangles had come from her family, but she doubted the Wilson clique would listen and believe her.

'Go to the police!' her friends had said, or 'For God's sake find a solicitor,' but she had shrugged and shaken her head and now, please God, hidden away here in the Welsh borders she would at last be free of Rhona and her family. Only three people knew where she was and they had sworn to keep her secret: her mother, obviously, and two of the friends who had come to her rescue, James Allardyce, a former university pal of Graham's, and his wife, her former school friend, Hilary, to whom Andy had introduced him. Oh, and her father, but he lived far away in Northumberland.

The thought of her mother and father sent her reaching into her pocket for her mobile but then she pushed it back. She was on her own. This was her new life. She had promised the others she would stay in touch, but she was not going to ring the second she got here. She had to establish herself, make herself at home and somehow retrieve her confidence and her sense of identity. The unaccustomed and overwhelming wave of happiness and relief that had swept over her on her arrival had been a first step in the right direction.

Andy's full name was Miranda Annabel Dysart. *Don't Go out of Sight, Miranda* had apparently been the title of one of her grandmother, Petra's, favourite books and when her mother, Nina, was a child, Petra had read it to her repeatedly. Nina had in turn read it to her daughter after saddling her with the name of the heroine. Andy couldn't remember the story at all – maybe she had blocked it, but the name Miranda had left her with a sense of overwhelming melancholy. Not a good reason to endear it to her. Someone at school had named her Andy (after experimenting with Mandy and, even more unfortunately, Randy) and it stuck. She liked it. And so did her father. It was a neutral name, slightly ambiguous, rugged. Strong. It distracted people from the fact that her initials spelt MAD, something which her scatty parents had not considered at her christening but which mercifully she had learned to enjoy.

She couldn't remember either the time her parents had split up. It had been while she was very small and they seemed to have managed it without rancour or complications. They had remained friends as far as she, their only child, could tell. Her mother lived in Sussex, her father, long ago remarried and father to three more children, had settled in Northumberland. Perhaps the distance between the two counties made it easier for them.

The knock at the back door took her by surprise. She had just poured herself a glass of wine as prescribed and was wandering round the kitchen, finding her way around, touching things lightly, proprietorially, opening and shutting drawers, shuffling through the books on the dresser – all cookery or herbs – when the sound broke the intense silence of the house.

Nervously she glanced at the cat. He hadn't moved. If this was an unexpected or threatening sound surely, like her mother's cat, he would have bolted off upstairs to hide. She set down the glass and went to the door.

The woman on the step was of middle height, slim, middle-aged, she guessed, with a rugged wind-burned complexion and greying hair. She was wearing a heavy pullover against the autumn chill and muddy rubber boots with shabby cords. She stared at Andy in surprise. 'Sue around?'

'She left for the airport a couple of hours ago. I'm sorry.'

The woman sighed.'Ah, I saw her car wasn't there. Australia, right? Hell and damnation! I hoped she wasn't going for a while yet.' She half turned away, staring up at the racing clouds as though seeking inspiration, then turned back. 'I don't suppose she left anything for me, did she?'

'You being . . . ?' Andy let the question hang.

For the first time her visitor smiled. She held out her hand. 'I'm Sian. Sian Griffiths.' In spite of the Welsh name her accent was English. She paused as though expecting the name to mean something. 'I live over in Cusop Dingle.'

'Ah?'

Cusop Dingle, Andy remembered vaguely from their holiday, was a narrow, thickly wooded valley to the east of the range of hills where Sleeper's Castle nestled, separated from it by a high ridge and then a vertiginous plunge down to a fast-running brook. It was on the outskirts of the nearest town, Hay-on-Wye, and seemed to consist of a long winding country road, heading up towards the open hillside and lined with houses, a few of them large, secluded behind high hedges and ancient trees. They had visited someone there with Sue on that wonderful summer holiday, but not, as far as she could remember, this woman.

'Come in.' Introducing herself, Andy held the door open.

Kicking off her boots and leaving them outside, Sian accepted a glass of wine and pulled up a chair at the table.

'I'd better explain,' Andy said, reassured that Pepper seemed to know her visitor and had still not moved from his chair. 'This was a last-minute piece of serendipity. As you probably know, Sue hadn't found a tenant and was beginning to think she would have to cancel her trip, and I was in need of a roof. I'm self-employed with no immediate ties . . .' Her voice wavered but she managed to go on. Just give enough information to explain her presence here, no more. 'We made a lightning decision. I didn't give myself time to think.'

'Brave.'

Now she was inside and sitting opposite her, Andy could see that the woman was probably in her mid to late fifties, older than she had first thought. Her face was weathered with deep laughter lines at the corners of her eyes, eyes that were bright Siamese-cat blue. 'I'll leave you my phone number,' she said. 'If you need anything, you have only to ring. This house is pretty isolated if you're on your own. Your nearest shops and signs of civilisation are in Hay, did she tell you? You'll get most things you need there.'

'I'm looking forward to exploring.' Andy took a sip of wine. 'I have been here before, for a holiday. But it was in the summer.'

Andy had a momentary flashback to those warm, seemingly endless days strolling on the hills and mountains, happy evenings in local pubs, excursions down into the local market town of Hay, attractive, compact, famous for its bookshops and its castle and of course for the majestic, beautiful River Wye which cradled it in a constantly changing backdrop. It had been a glorious summer.

Now it was late September, with winter already a hint in the air, and she was on her own. She didn't say it out loud. It made her sound pathetic and needy, which she was not. She glanced towards the window where high clouds were streaming across the sky. 'What was it Sue was going to leave for you? Maybe it's here and she forgot to tell me.'

'Maybe.' Leaning back in the chair, Sian was watching Andy with an interested, narrowed gaze. 'Is she still planning to stay away for a year? She was afraid she would have to cut the visit short.'

'A year is what she told me,' Andy agreed. 'I hope Pepper can cope with that.'

Sian smiled. 'I'm sure he can. She had two main concerns when she was planning this trip: Pepper and her car. Last I heard, the idea was that she would leave the car with a friend who lives down south. He was going to pick it up from Heathrow and take care of it for her. And you have clearly solved the Pepper problem.'

Andy smiled as a spatter of rain rattled against the window. 'So no worries then. I can just imagine her saying those words! She was gone the second I arrived. I think she had more or less resigned herself to changing her plans then someone told her I might be in the market for a new home urgently, she rang and we settled it then and there. She got a cancellation on a flight. There was virtually no time to discuss anything.'

'The gods were with you both.' Sian gave a thoughtful smile. 'There are very few people she would entrust Pepper to.'

They both looked at him. As if overwhelmed by the unexpected attention he stood up, stretched and jumped off his chair. He walked to the door and with great dignity pushed out through the cat flap. 'I hope she's left food and instructions for feeding him,' Andy said. 'We didn't even have time to talk about that. It took longer than I remembered driving here, so I was very late. She was terrified of missing the plane.'

'I'm sure she made it.' Sian smiled again. She stood up, walked over to the dresser and pulled open one of the drawers. Inside were boxes of tuna and rabbit biscuits, little trays of gourmet cat food and a couple of cartons of cat milk.

'So Pepper is catered for.' Andy was relieved.

'And here are your instructions.' Sian had found a piece of paper on the worktop. *Pepper*, it said. *Breakfast, lunch and supper.* 'Quite the spoiled brat, our Culpepper.'

Andy took the paper, grateful that her visitor seemed to know her way round. 'This kitchen has changed so much since I was here last. I couldn't believe it when I saw it.'

Sian gave a snort of laughter. 'She was left some money by an ancient relative and she couldn't decide what to spend it on. Sue is one of those incredible people who has everything she wants in life. Her herbs are her life. She is extraordinarily self-contained. I think she consulted Pepper, who decided an upgrade of kitchen would be good.'

'I can believe that.'

'And you're not regretting coming up here, now you've had time to reconsider your impulsive decision?'

Andy shook her head. 'Hardly. I've barely been here a few hours.'

'Not everyone is as independent as Sue.' Sian hesitated. 'Old houses can be a bit spooky.'

'It's certainly atmospheric,' Andy reached for her glass and took a sip.

'And utterly beautiful.'

'But you find it spooky?'

'Sorry, that was a silly thing to say. I meant, it's a bit isolated if you're on your own. No, I don't think it's spooky. If there ever was a ghost here I think it would have been far more afraid of Sue than she would be of it. She would swear roundly in Australian and tell it where to go.' Sian laughed again and ran her finger round the rim of her glass. 'So, do you believe in them?' The question was almost too casual.

'Ghosts?' Andy pulled a noncommittal face. 'Actually, I made a bit of a study of them once.'

Once. She caught herself using the word with something like shock. Before Graham. So much that she had once thought important in her life had been before Graham. Their life together had absorbed her totally, taken up every second, monopolised her existence. She hadn't been aware of how much. For the first time since his death she realised that in every sense she was free now. Was she frightened or exhilarated by the thought? She wasn't entirely sure.

Sian was still studying her and Andy looked away, embarrassed that her face had betrayed too much. 'One of those things one pursues frenziedly in one's youth and then life and perhaps a certain cynicism kick in and the books get put away.' She gave a rueful smile.

Ghosts had been her father's passion and she had grown up enjoying his stories, his theories, the frissons they had shared on ghost-hunting trips. She had never been quite sure whether she believed in them herself, but the study of phenomena of a ghostly kind had absorbed her for a long time. Those books had been left with her mother. Graham had not liked ghosts. They gave him the creeps and therefore could not be discussed even in the abstract. Ghosts and meditation and psychology and anything he considered even remotely out of the ordinary on the paranormal scale of things had been out of bounds.

Sian nodded sagely. 'It's sad how one's early enthusiasms wane.' She changed the subject abruptly. 'That's Sue's strength and blessing. She has retained her childlike passion for her herbalism.'

That was how Andy and Sue had met originally. Sue was an old friend of Graham's, a plant contact and fellow author. Andy and she had liked each other instantly and become great friends. Although they had only ventured here, to Wales, once, Sue used to stay with them whenever she was forced to visit London and they had exchanged many long phone calls over the years.

Andy gave a wistful smile. 'I'm surprised she can bear to leave her garden. Especially to me. I paint flowers, I don't grow them.'

'You won't have to. She has someone to help her; I would imagine he will still be coming?' Sian glanced up at her again. 'Didn't she tell you?'

'No.' Andy felt ridiculously cross. She had thought she would be here alone; safe. Unbothered.

'Maybe I got it wrong.' Sian was backtracking hastily again. She seemed to be able to read Andy's every thought.

'No. I hope she has. I am not fit to be trusted with her garden. When the subject came up she just said it could look after itself for a while.' It was Andy's turn to study her visitor's face. 'Was it a herbal potion she was making for you?'

'For my dogs.'

'If I find anything, I'll let you know.'

Sian seemed to take the words as a dismissal. Draining her glass, she stood up. 'I should be on my way. It will start getting dark soon and I've a long walk home.'

Andy watched from the window as the woman ran down the steps and out of sight. The rain shower was over as soon as it had come. Sian's dogs, she saw, had been waiting for her outside, a border collie and a retriever. She wondered what Culpepper made of them.

Andy decided against taking over Sue's bedroom even though it had obviously been made ready for her. She and Graham had shared that room on their holiday and she didn't think she could bear to sleep there again, alone. A small neat indentation on the counterpane showed where the cat had made himself comfortable earlier in the day, unaware that his beloved Sue was about to abandon him for a whole year. Instead she chose one of the spare rooms. It was in the oldest part of the house, dark with ancient beams, its window mullioned in grey stone, facing across the valley where the sun was setting into the mist. There was a brightly coloured Welsh blanket on the bed and a landscape on the wall of the hills she could see from the window, the racing shadows picked out in vermilion and ochre and violet. She looked round the room with a sense which she realised after a moment was a feeling of coming home. The room felt relaxed and safe; it smelt of wood and something indefinable – herbs and polish and maybe, a little, of dust. Circling once more, and giving a final glance out of the window, she laid her hand on one of the crooked beams in the corner, then she trailed her fingers across the ancient stones of the wall. What memories they must hold.

It took for ever to lug her cases and boxes upstairs and spread some of her belongings on the chest and along the shelves. Finally she threw her jacket on the chair, an almost symbolic gesture to take possession of the room before she went back downstairs, hungry for the first time in ages. Tomorrow she would drive down to Hay and stock up the fridge. For now Sue had left her milk and bread and a pasty with salad. Outside it was dark. She drew the curtains and turned on the light. Behind her the cat flap opened and closed with a swish and a click as Pepper pushed his way through and leapt onto his chair. He sat and gazed at her. She felt that mentally at least he was tapping his wristwatch to make sure she knew that the hour for supper was approaching. She smiled at him broadly. 'I think we're going to get on fine, Culpepper, my friend. But if I make mistakes, you will have to tell me.'

On her past experience with cats she was sure he would.

She tossed and turned, unable to sleep. Climbing out of bed she pushed open the small casement in the mullioned window. Through it she could hear the sound of the brook hurtling over the rocky ledges at the side of the house and cascading down towards the road. Staring out into the dark she was very aware of how black the night was. She was used to streetlights and the headlights of cars probing through the curtains and crossing the walls of the bedroom she'd shared with Graham.

She had left her door open a crack so that Pepper could come and sleep on her bed if he felt so inclined, but when she turned off the kitchen light he had stayed where he was on the chair beside the Aga. If she had been at home in Kew she would have crept out of bed, careful not to wake Graham and gone out into the garden. She could do that now but she felt strangely intimidated at the idea. The garden here was huge and full of noise and wind and water; she hadn't got her bearings there yet.

Climbing back into bed she sat, propped against her pillows, her hands clasped around her knees, gazing into the darkness. In her mind she let herself travel back to Kew. She knew she shouldn't. She should put Kew behind her, but she couldn't stop herself. She pictured herself opening the French door which led from the kitchen and walking down the short flight of wrought-iron steps onto the decking of the terrace where they so often used to sit in the evenings or at lunchtime to drink wine and eat and talk and laugh.

The garden below the terrace had a pale reflected light from the lamppost in the road, diffused through the branches of the trees. It smelt fresh and cool and it was very still. In her imagination she stood for a long time looking round, listening. In the distance she could hear the faint drone of traffic on the nearby A307 and, once, the closer sound of a car engine as it turned into their road. It stopped nearby and after a minute a door slammed. She took a step or two onto the lawn, which was wet with icy dew. It soaked into her shoes. She was aware, as she always was at night, of how close Kew Gardens was, dark and deserted behind its high walls. From there sometimes she could hear the call of owls.

Behind her a light came on in the house. It was in one of the spare rooms on the first floor. She watched as the curtain twitched and moved and the silhouette of a head and shoulders appeared peering down into the garden. How strange. Was Rhona living there? She shivered and in her imagination she turned away and strolled towards the high wall at the back of the garden where a collection of shrubs and climbers wove their magic of autumn colour, leached to silver by the lamplight.

She heard the window behind her rattle upwards. 'Who's there?' Rhona's voice echoed into the silence. 'I can see you!'

The vision vanished and abruptly Andy opened her eyes. Her memories had been interrupted and spoilt by the intrusion of Rhona's harsh voice; Rhona had no place in her daydreams, Rhona whom she had only ever met once before that awful day when she had walked into Andy's life and blown what was left of her composure apart. She was someone best forgotten as soon as possible.

Andy grabbed her dressing gown and made her way downstairs and into the kitchen. The rocking chair was empty; there was no sign of Pepper. Pulling the back door open she overcame her misgivings and stepped outside. The contrast to the silent enclosure in the moonlight in Kew could not have been more marked. This garden was full of noise; the rustle and clatter of autumn leaves, the howl of the wind and always, above all else, the sound of rushing, thundering water. Shivering she stepped away from the comparative shelter of the back door and felt the push of the wind, the furious tug at her hair as she turned to face it. It was exhilarating, elemental, exciting. Deep inside herself she felt something stir, something that in her ordered, neat and organised life with Graham had not surfaced for a long time. It was a sense of freedom.

When, breathless and cold, she let herself back into the kitchen she found herself laughing. There was still no sign of Pepper. Well, he could look after himself. She put on the kettle and made herself some tea, leaning against the Aga rail as she sipped from the mug, cupping her hands around it for warmth.

She did not sense the silent figure in the corner of the room, watching her from the shadows, the figure which between one breath and the next had faded into nothing.

2

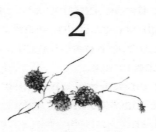

March 1400

The door banged shut in the wind, the latch rattling with the force of it, the draught sending up showers of sparks in the hearth. 'I made sure Betsi had locked up the hens.' Catrin kicked off her pattens, pulled off her shawl and hung it on the back of the door. She was a delicately built young woman with fine attractive features and grey-green eyes. Her hair, swathed in its linen coif, was rich chestnut. 'Is my *tad* still working?'

'He's not come out of that room all day.' Joan was bending over the pot hanging from the trivet over the fire, her face red from the heat. Sturdily built with muscular arms, she padded her hands against the hot metal of the handle with a cloth and unhooked the pot, thumping it down on the table. 'Did she find any eggs?'

'Two.' Catrin produced them from her basket and set them carefully in the wooden bowl on the table. 'I'll go and see if he'll come and eat. He'll get ill if he goes on like this.' Another gust of wind shook the house and both women looked towards the window. Sleeper's Castle stood full square and solid on its rocky perch beside the brook but when the wind roared up the *cwm* like this from the north there was nowhere to hide. The shutters were rattling ominously. Only weeks before one had torn free and gone hurtling off into the brook. It had been days before they could find one of the men from the farmstead down the valley willing to come up and fasten it back into place. She hated this time of year. Even the patches of snowdrops growing in the lee of the stone walls could not make up for the wild gales screaming over the mountains and the patches of snow still lying on the high scree. There were no real signs yet of spring; the deep impenetrable cold of winter was still implacable within the stone of the house.

Crossing the large empty hall and pushing the door open, Catrin peered into the shadows of her father's study. The candles on his desk guttered and spat throwing shadowed caricatures of his hunched figure over the walls. 'Go away!' He did not look up. His hand was racing across the page, the pen nib sputtering as he wrote and crossed out and wrote again. 'I need more ink,' he added.

Catrin sighed. 'I'll fetch it from the stillroom. Please, could you not stop to take some pottage? Joan has made your favourite.'

He did not bother to answer. She turned away. At the door she hesitated and looked back. He was seated on a high stool in front of his writing slope, bent low over his work, his weary figure illuminated into flickering highlights by the candles. He had a thin ascetic face with dark lively eyes, narrowed now with exhaustion and eyestrain. His hair was white, long and tangled. 'What is it, *Tad*?' Again he was furiously scratching out with his knife the words he had just written, almost tearing the thin parchment in his agitation. He ignored her. With a sigh she left him.

Joan glanced at her. 'Is he still working?'

'And still irritable. I need to fetch him more ink.'

They called it the stillroom, but it was really the buttery. That and the pantry led off one side of the hall, the main living space of the house, while her parlour and her father's study led off the other. The kitchen had originally been built separately, behind the house, but now it was joined into the main fabric of the building as a solid extension with behind it the bakehouse with its stone oven. Beyond it lay the high castellated wall of the yard.

Drawing her cloak around her against the cold, Catrin went into the buttery to find the ink. Besides overseeing the storage of their ale and beer and cider casks, she made her simples and receipts and remedies in this room. They were a small household; she and her father with their cook housekeeper Joan, Betsi the maid of all work and Peter the outside boy and scullion. Joan did her best but she was worked off her feet in the old house, which had grown increasingly shabby and neglected over the years.

When Catrin's father and mother had first come here there had been a steward and other servants and farmworkers but one by one they had been sent away. Catrin's father did not tolerate people around him; they distracted him from his poetry and from his dreams. And they cost money. Now all that was left of the livestock were a few sheep, a pig and a cow and they still had two horses and a mule. They were all looked after by Peter, who added to his long list of duties that of fisherman, keeping Joan's kitchen stocked with trout and grayling and crayfish, which he pulled from secret pools in the brook. He also had made himself responsible for training the two corgis – the short-legged cattle dogs that followed him everywhere – and, from time to time, cosseting the barn cats; her father did not tolerate cats or dogs indoors either.

The buttery was Catrin's special domain, full of the rich smell of herbs and the precious spices she brought back sometimes from the market. The stoppered jug which contained the ink she made several times a year was stored on a high shelf. Carefully she set the candlestick down and reached for one of the spare inkhorns, filling it from the heavy jug. The black liquid glistened in the candlelight. She glanced at the basket of oak apples on the shelf and next to it the jar of precious gum arabic and the dish of blue-green copperas crystals bought from a pedlar who called in from time to time as he travelled between the fairs and monasteries. If he didn't call again soon she would have to make the long arduous journey to Hereford to visit the only mercer there who stocked the items she needed. Her father was particular. He wanted his ink to be the best quality and he wanted it to last on the page. Early autumn was the best time to make the ink, the galls strong and full of acid after the worms had crawled out and left them empty. She had thought she had collected plenty; now there was but half a small basket left.

When she returned to her father's workroom he wasn't there. The candle flames guttered as she made her way across to his desk. The page he had been working on was still lying where he had left it, the lettering cramped and heavily crossed out. She set down the inkpot and leaned closer, squinting in the flickering light, reading what he had written. It was the draft of a poem. She loved her father's poetry. It was clever, intricate, perfectly written with the complex rules on metre and rhythm and rhyme as laid down by the bards of old, exactly as he had taught her but, as she looked at the page, her eyes widened in dismay. This was no poem.

BLOOD   *FIRE*   *DEATH*

The words were scratched angrily across the page. The point of the quill had split and splayed with the force of his hand and had spattered ink everywhere. She could see where his knife had tried to excise the words, angrily scraping the surface of the parchment scrap on which he was writing until it thinned so much it tore. At that point he had obviously thrown down his pen and walked out of the room.

'*Tad*?' she called. 'Where are you?' With another horrified glance at the page she turned to run back into the great hall. The front door of the house was standing open and, despite the heavy screens set up to keep it at bay, the large room was full of the wind. Sparks and ash flew in all directions from the fire. There was no sign of her father.

The garden was dark and reverberated with the noise from the trees beyond the high walls thrashing in the gale. As she stood on the step looking round she could see nothing. The sound of the brook hurtling down over the rocks vied with the wind and the trees to drown out any sound her father might make. She peered round desperately and then as her eyes grew used to the fitful starlight she thought she could see him, a darker shape against the shadows. She made her way cautiously down the path. He was indeed there, staring out across the *cwm* towards the mountains.

'*Tad*?' She came to a standstill beside him and timidly she reached out and touched the sleeve of his robe. He didn't react. 'Please, talk to me. I saw what you had written.'

He turned abruptly and stared blindly down at her. Her father was a tall man. She barely came up to his shoulder and he seemed to be looking out over the top of her head into the distance. 'You saw nothing.' His voice was dull and heavy. 'Do you understand me, Catrin? You saw nothing at all.'

'But, *Tad*—'

'No!' He seemed to awaken as though the dream of which he had written had slipped like a heavy burden from his shoulders. He straightened and stepped away from her. 'It was nothing. It's gone. I will burn the page. It was the result of an ague. Tell Joan her food is too rich. It lies on my stomach like a stone; make me something in your stillroom to settle it.'

She watched his dark shape as he strode back towards the house and disappeared through the door. It closed with a bang and she was left outside alone.

She drew her cloak round her. Her beloved father had been trembling. She had felt it in those few seconds as she touched his arm before he shrank away from her. He had been trembling not because he was cold but because he had been afraid.

Sleeper's Castle had been her mother's inheritance. She had been the only daughter of a wealthy well-connected local Welsh family – *uchelwyr* was the Welsh word for their class – and her grandfather had settled the old fortified manor house on her when she had married, with its farm and its supplement of servants. What he thought of her choice of an itinerant bard, albeit of impeccable descent, as a husband, Catrin never knew. Perhaps his decision to give them an isolated, ancient house hidden in the mountains and already the custodian of years of legend about its magical past and far from his own fertile acres in the Wyc Valley, was a witness to his hidden thoughts. When Marged died in childbirth the house remained with Catrin's father, who bit by bit had sold off what land it had until very little remained. What moneys they owed each year he paid from the earnings he brought home from his summer tours around the houses of his rich patrons.

Bards were popular. The people loved them and their visits were eagerly awaited. They were poets but they were so much more. As well as the genealogies of the principalities and the history of the land of Wales, the myths, the legends, the ancient stories, they also knew all the latest gossip. That had made them dangerous once, in the reign of King Edward I, passionate supporters of their princes as they were in their desperate battle for independence from England; and that could make them dangerous again. The bards sang and played the harp. But their business was words. Words are powerful; words can soothe or inflame. Words can inspire loyalty or treason. Words can incite revolt. Edward may have recognised their power and ordered their execution, but they had never been exterminated.

They toured the houses and castles of the land, staying a week here, a month there, eating at the table of anyone who would pay them with food and shelter. Some had no homes of their own, no roof save the roof under which they were staying. They owed their allegiance to the man who fed them. Thanks to his marriage, Catrin's father was one of those who had a home and he had both a family and a bloodline of which he was intensely proud. But Dafydd was the most dangerous kind of bard of all. He was also a seer, a soothsayer; he saw the future in his dreams.

A succession of nurses and housekeepers had reared Catrin. They had mostly proved loyal and kind to their small charge, but when she was old enough her father dismissed them, taught her himself and left the running of the house to the few servants who were trusted with the remaining farm animals, their ponies, the vegetable gardens and the kitchen. Catrin did not seem to notice. She loved this place. It was in her blood. She did not know or care that her mother's family had turned their back on her father and forgotten her.

This land in the border Marches of Wales was a place of beauty and magic and danger. Successive Marcher Lords, supported in their greed for land by their king, had built their great castles and made dangerous or at best uncomfortable neighbours to the local Welsh families over the centuries, but hidden away in this fold of the hills, cradled in the crooked elbow of a torrential brook and lulled by the cry of the birds, Sleeper's Castle, *Castell Cysgwr*, had seemed safe to Catrin. Until now. For her father's dreams of late had been frightening and full of ominous clouds.

She knew her father's fathers had been bards and soothsayers from the days of the ancient Druids. Poetry was in his blood, the inheritance of his family, the gift of his ancestors. His name was Dafydd ap Hywell ap Gruffydd ap Rhodri – his line stretched back through time like a bright ribbon of silk. And there she was, Catrin *ferch* Dafydd, Catrin, the daughter of Dafydd, the latest born and perhaps the last of that line.

She didn't remember her mother, Marged, but in her dreams, those dangerous sparkling dreams she never mentioned to her father, she could see her clearly, her eyes the colour of smoke, her face gentle and loving as she smiled at her little daughter, the daughter she had never met, the daughter who had inherited all her father's talents and more.

Dafydd taught his daughter all he knew. She could read at the age of four; she could play the harp at the age of six; she could recite the long histories of her father's family and their patrons and princes by the age of eight. She could write poems and stories of her own and at her father's dictation, and from the age of twelve she had been sufficiently confident to sing to the harp in front of her father's patrons. Once or twice, in the solar of an indulgent group of women, she had sung her own poems, cautiously diffident, embarrassed by their applause. The poems were a secret and even now she was a woman she had not confessed to her father that she wrote and dreamed just as he did. She sensed he would not approve. He was proud of his daughter's talents but subtly and firmly he had made it clear he would not tolerate competition, especially not from a woman. Things might have been different had he had a son.

There were other secrets in her life. After her mother died, in his first frenzy of grief and anger, Dafydd had hidden or destroyed everything that would remind him of his beloved wife. When the nurse who was taking care of this new scrap of life had seen what was happening she had rescued the one thing Marged had treasured above all else and which the loyal woman was sure would end up in his vengeful pyre: a small coffer in which was stored Marged's tiny, beautiful book of hours, another book of poetry and a collection of notes and recipes for herbs and cures and remedies, copied for her from the family of healers who lived in the village of Myddfai, on the banks of Llyn y Fan Fach on the far side of the mountains. Each successive nurse had been sworn to secrecy and promised to keep the coffer safe until Catrin was given charge of her mother's legacy by the last of the women employed to look after her. Her father now felt she had no need of female company beyond the servants and cooks who remained. By then Catrin already knew this small coffer and its contents was something else she had to keep hidden.

Her second secret she had found for herself. Half a mile up the valley, through a wood and across a brook she had stumbled upon a small cottage, lost in a tangle of wild herbs. The widow who lived there, Efa, was motherly and kind, full of stories of her own. Catrin told no one of her friend. It seemed important that she should be as secret from her father as the coffer full of her mother's treasures.

Woven into the stories Efa told were ancient legends and magic spells. Sometimes when Catrin climbed the bank towards the cottage she saw gifts which had been left outside, a skinned rabbit, a jar of cider, a pot of honey, and when she asked, Efa told her about the service she rendered to the community. She magicked the weather. It seemed natural for her to teach the wide-eyed child some of the simple spells. She knew where Catrin lived, she knew the stories about Sleeper's Castle. She guessed the girl would have a natural aptitude, and so it proved.

The farmers who came to see Efa needed fair weather for ploughing and harvest, they needed rain and then sun for ripening the crops; their wives came to seek good weather for markets and fairs and festivals. And then for fun Efa showed her some of the more powerful magic, the magic that would command the elements, conjure thunder and lightning over the high tops of the mountains, rites which commanded the mist and fog to wrap itself around the trees and drift into the *cwm*. It was all secret. When men or women came and asked for lightning to strike a neighbour dead or for weather to cause their cattle to sicken and die, Efa refused. Such magic was black and a mortal sin, but she taught Catrin that it could be done and how. That was the greatest secret of all.

'He has called for new candles.' Joan looked up as Catrin walked into the kitchen from the garden next day. She was chopping onions and leeks and tossing them into the pot.

'I'll take them in to him.'

Joan straightened her back, tucking a wisp of her blonde hair under her hood. The house was full of the smell of her rich fish stew. 'He's not well. You must make him eat.'

Catrin nodded.

'I heard him shouting again in the night.' Joan held her gaze challengingly before looking away. She reached for a dishclout and wiped her hands.

'I know. I know he's worried.' Catrin pulled a stool from under the table and sat down with a heavy sigh.

Her relationship with Joan was a difficult one. The two young women were of a similar age with but two years between them, and in the lonely valley with few neighbours they had become friends. But Joan was her servant; she was paid to cook and clean.

Joan's father, Raymond of Hardwicke, was a wealthy yeoman farmer and such work should have been beneath her, but his farm had struggled to survive over the last decades like so many others after the last great wave of pestilence had swept across nations far and wide, destroying towns and villages, leaving land depopulated and barren. Raymond had two sons, the eldest had married and was slowly taking over the running of the farm; his second son had also married and had left home with the idea that he would one day take over part of his wife's father's land. Raymond's only daughter, Joan, was expected to marry and marry equally well. But she had stubbornly refused every suitor her father picked for her. In the end, in a fit of vindictive spite, he told her to go and live off someone else's charity. She did.

Working for Dafydd ap Hywell had a cachet all of its own – besides, he paid well. His patrons were generous and he had realised almost too late that if he dismissed every servant on the place he and Catrin would be left to cope alone. Joan liked it at Sleeper's Castle. It had once been far grander, a fortified manor house in a scattered parish in the hills above Hay. Some of the walls had crumbled and it had little land left, but it still had a fine slate roof, Catrin was educated and her gowns had been made by a skilled seamstress. They were serviceable and these days Catrin patched them herself with neat clever stitches, but nevertheless they were of good expensive cloth, and her cloaks were warm and lined with miniver. Joan liked her and was sorry for her. She must be lonely. She needed a friend.

Joan glanced at Catrin, who was sitting at the table with her head in her hands. 'He's had these moods before,' she said. Her voice was gentler now. 'He'll come out of it. You'll see.'

Catrin looked up. 'I know.' Wearily she stood up. 'I'll go and see if he wants to eat. Perhaps if you throw more logs on the fire in the parlour and serve us there it will cheer him up.' She didn't notice Joan's tightened lips or her exaggerated sigh. Usually they all ate together in the great hall, or she ate here in the kitchen with Joan and Betsi and Peter after placing her father's food on a tray and taking it to him in his study. That was the way he liked it.

It was as she left the kitchen and walked back into the shadowy hall she thought she caught sight of a woman's figure standing near the window. Behind her the kitchen door banged and the draught sent a wave of cold air across the room, scattering ash, blowing out the candles. She blinked and stared and rubbed her eyes and the figure had gone.

Andy woke with a start. The morning sun was shining into the room and she lay quietly staring at its path across the black-painted floorboards. She had been dreaming, a gentle homely dream about cooking and putting logs on the fire downstairs, and then in the dream a door had banged and all the candles had blown out, leaving her in darkness. She had woken, aware that somewhere a conversation had been left unfinished, the words still echoing in the quiet of the room.

Sitting up, she groped for her slippers with her feet and pulled on her dressing gown. Pushing her hair back off her face she made her way downstairs to the living room. The bang of the door slamming shut in her dream had seemed so loud and so real it was as if it had been in here.

The room looked huge and shadowy at this time of the morning, living up to its title of great hall. She smiled, remembering that was the way Sue referred to it, her only concession to the house's medieval antecedents.

The sun hadn't come round yet to any of the windows. The papers on Sue's desk by the front-facing window with its ancient mullions had been blown onto the floor. Had that happened last night when she came in? She couldn't remember. She gathered up the papers and as she did so she noticed two tightly stoppered bottles of dark brown liquid standing there. Tucked under them was a torn sheet of paper which said simply: *For Sian.*

Neither she nor Sian had thought to look on Sue's cluttered desk the night before. Andy surveyed the chaos with a smile. If she had been going away for a year she felt sure she would have tidied her desk at the very least. She groped in her pocket for her phone and turned back to the kitchen to look for the note on which Sian had written her number.

'You don't look as though you slept much.'

They had arranged to meet in The Granary in Hay. Sian's dogs lay quietly under the table as Andy brought the two cups of coffee from the counter and set them down.

Andy gave a rueful grin. 'I suppose I didn't. I was exhausted, but my head was whirling all night. The silence is so different from London.'

She must have slept though. After all, she had dreamed.

'Silence? Didn't you hear the brook?'

'It is a bit noisy, I admit, but it's not cars and planes. My house – where I used to live,' Andy amended hastily, 'was under the flight path to Heathrow.'

'Ah.' Sian took a sip from her cappuccino and licked the froth from her top lip. 'Not in the same league, noise wise.'

31

'There are people who use the sound of water to send them to sleep,' Andy smiled again, 'but this is a constant roar. Not all that soothing. I'm sure I'll get used to it though.'

'I think you will soon find it wonderful in comparison to the early morning jet to New York.' Sian laughed. She watched as Andy rummaged in her shopping bag for the bottles she had found in the house.

Sian reached for one; unscrewing it, she sniffed the liquid and grimaced. 'As far as I can tell, that's the right one. Rosehips and nettles with burdock, plus one or two other secret ingredients no doubt. To build them up before the winter.'

Andy looked down at the dogs under the table. 'They look pretty fit to me.'

'They are. Thanks to Sue.' Sian sipped her coffee again. 'Was Bryn there this morning?' She reached down and scratched a dog's ear.

'Bryn?'

'The gardener.'

'I didn't see anyone.'

'I expect he will come when he's good and ready.' Sian looked at her thoughtfully. 'Remember, a lot of Sue's herbs are what you probably call weeds. Don't go rooting about without checking with him first.'

'I'm not going to touch the garden.' Andy picked up her spoon and stirred her coffee. 'That was part of the agreement. I'm in charge of the cat and keeping an eye on the house, that's all.'

'So, what are you going to do up there all day on your own?' There was a long pause. 'Sorry. None of my business.'

'No. It's not that.' Andy sighed. 'The truth is, I haven't really thought. I'm a professional illustrator. I specialise in painting flowers, so I suppose I will go back to doing that.'

Go back.

It made it sound as though she had stopped.

But she had. She had worked with Graham for years. They

had been a partnership in so many ways, kindred spirits, lovers, flower geeks. She smiled quietly as she recalled the term given to them by one of her half-brothers.

And now all that had gone.

Sian reached over and touched her hand. 'Sorry. I can see I'm treading on painful ground.'

Andy took a gulp of coffee. 'I have to get used to it.' She took a deep breath. 'I illustrated the books my partner wrote. He died two months ago. That part of my life is over and I have to rethink myself. I thought . . .' She paused. 'Sue thought coming here would be a good way of doing that, and I agreed with her.'

'It will. A complete change of scene is the best possible medicine.'

Andy laughed. 'Painting nettles and burdock would be a tonic on its own. I was painting rare orchids for Graham's last book.'

A woman at the next table stood up and began to manoeuvre her child's buggy out of the narrow corner. Andy and Sian grabbed for their table as their coffee cups rocked and slopped into the saucers. They waited in silence for the woman to extricate herself and then settled back down. 'You'd think she would have apologised,' Sian said quietly. She poured her coffee back into the cup from the brimming saucer.

Andy was chewing her lip. Babies were another thing to tug the heartstrings. Graham had not wanted any. She did not even have a child to comfort her in her loss.

Sian accompanied her back to the car park then waved goodbye. She had walked down to Hay from her house and firmly refused the offer of a lift back. 'Good for me and the dogs to walk.' She smiled. 'I'll ring you. You must come to supper soon.'

For a few minutes Andy stood staring wistfully after the retreating figure as Sian set off across the car park, through a gate in the far corner and into the field behind it, her dogs racing round her in delight as soon as she let them off their leads. Andy watched until she had vanished through a hedge on the far side of the field then she turned back to unlock her car.

There was an old mud-splashed Peugeot van parked in her spot outside the house. She edged her own car in beside it and ran up the steps to the front door. Letting herself in she glanced round. Presumably the mysterious gardener had at last put in an appearance and she wasn't sure if he had a key. There was no sign of him indoors however. Nor could she see him from the kitchen window.

He was digging in a bed at the far end of the garden. She watched him for several minutes before approaching him, aware that Pepper was sitting on the path near him, apparently intent on studying his digging technique. About six feet away from him she stopped. He went on digging, seemingly unaware of her presence. Losing patience she cleared her throat. 'Bryn, I presume?'

He paused in his work then, thrusting the fork into the ground, turned to face her. He was tall, his hair an unruly tangle, his eyes clear light grey, almost silver, his face weathered. Over a dark plaid shirt he wore a leather waistcoat. He didn't smile nor did he say anything. He surveyed her in silence, presumably waiting for her to speak again. Determined not to be wrong-footed, Andy narrowed her eyes. 'You are Bryn?' she repeated firmly.

He pushed his sleeves up to the elbow, revealing muscular arms, one of which bore a small tattoo. She couldn't see what it was from where she was standing. He nodded in answer to her question. 'I'm Andy Dysart,' she went on. 'I presume Sue told you I was coming to stay here for a few months.'

'A year, she said.' His voice was strong with a slight lilt.

'A year,' she confirmed.

'She left me instructions on how to run the garden,' he said. 'I won't need to bother you.'

'Would you like to come in and have a cup of tea while we

talk about how it is going to work?' From his expression she could already guess his answer and as she expected he declined.

'I have a flask, thank you. As I said, I won't need to bother you.' And with that he turned away. He pulled the fork out of the ground, and swinging it over his shoulder he walked off towards what looked like an orchard on the far side of the herb beds.

Andy glanced at Pepper, who was looking inscrutable. 'So, that went well,' she said out loud. The cat raised a paw and cursorily swept it over his ear. 'You're right,' she added. 'My fault for even starting the conversation.'

Heading back towards the kitchen she let herself in and pulled off her jacket. If she had been looking for the occasional chat to relieve the solitude of this house she would not find it in Bryn, whose second name she didn't even know and whose timetable she would no doubt find out by seeing which days he turned up. She felt a flash of irritation.

She spent the afternoon unpacking. Tidying the desk and putting all Sue's papers in a drawer out of sight, she surveyed the empty space with satisfaction before turning to lay out her paints and brushes and sketchbooks on the large table. It was a gesture to stake her claim on the house, she realised, as she lovingly touched the tools of her trade. Up to now she had not been able to bear even the sight of them; somehow she had felt she could never paint again without Graham's encouragement, his compliments, his quiet certainty in her skill but seeing them lying there on an unaccustomed surface in a different setting, she felt the lure of the paint again. When the time came her brushes would feel right in her hands once more.

Leaving them in place, ready for action, she turned away and began a tour of the house, slowly visiting every room, reminding herself of her previous visit with Graham. The house hadn't changed since that summer, except for the wonderful cat-inspired kitchen. The great hall downstairs was large, the walls of whitewashed stone, the ceiling white-painted between old rugged beams. The kitchen led off it in the far left-hand corner, while to the right were two smaller rooms, one of which was laid out as a dining room overlooking the front garden. It felt unused and slightly damp. Behind it was what Sue called the parlour, a small living room with its own inglenook fireplace, also unused. In the far right-hand corner of the main living room in the alcove beside the hearth, the broad stone-built staircase climbed to the first floor behind the huge chimney, a heavy rope doing the job of a banister. Upstairs, to the right, above the parlour were two bedrooms, one of which she had claimed as her own, and to the left was the much bigger room which was Sue's – Pepper's, she corrected herself – and the modern bathroom. At the opposite side of the landing were two more bedrooms. She lugged her remaining bags and boxes into one of those spare rooms. She would unpack the rest of her stuff as and when and if she needed it. As she closed the door on it all, her phone rang.

She groped in her pocket and warily eyed the screen. To her relief it was her mother.

'Hi, Mum.'

'Have you arrived safely, darling? How is it going?' Her mother was obviously outside in the garden of her home in Bosham in Sussex. She could hear the scream of seagulls in the background and the lonely whistle of an oystercatcher.

'It's fine. A lovely place, just as I remembered.'

'And the cat?'

They had discussed the cat at length before Andy set off for Wales. Her mother's cat was a wild, unsociable and slightly vicious Siamese whom her mother, unaccountably, doted on. He was the complete opposite of Culpepper in every way. 'He's enigmatic and I think a little puzzled as to why I am here. But he has graciously accepted all his meals so far.'

Her mother laughed. 'That's what matters. Have you stocked up with lots of food for you as well?'

'Of course. And Sue has left me plenty of wine.' Besides the two bottles on the dresser, Andy had found a wine rack in a pantry off the kitchen.

'And you're not going to be too lonely?'

Andy thought for a second before replying. 'No. I've already met one neighbour who seems very nice. We had coffee in Hay together this morning, and there's a gardener here as well.' Her eye was caught by the sight of Bryn through the window. He was walking back to the bed where she had first accosted him. He began to fork the ground again and as she watched she saw Pepper reappear to sit in almost the identical spot on the path to watch him. 'This house has a wonderful feel. I'm going to be very happy here.' To her relief her mother didn't ask about the gardener. They exchanged brief family news and then she hung up.

Andy did not find out what, if anything, Bryn did for lunch. After establishing that he was still digging round the back she opened the front door and went out to collect flowers from the front garden. Bringing them back indoors almost guiltily she put them in a glass and took them through to leave on the table. Later she would sketch them as an exorcism of the orchid period and a welcome to the new, wild, herbal Miranda Dysart experience. The thought of outwitting Bryn pleased her enormously. She doubted he would have minded her picking a few flowers, but she was not going to give him the chance to comment either way. He left at about five o'clock. She heard the engine of his van start up as she was sitting painting by the light of a powerful desk lamp which she had found in a corner of the room.

Bryn threw his tools into the back of his van, climbed in and sat back, closing his eyes with a sigh. Part of him had been dreading meeting the new tenant. He replayed his last conversation with Sue in his head. 'OK. I've found someone to look after the house, so I'll be off tomorrow.' She had looked at him with a quizzical smile. 'Now don't you bully her,' she said with feeling. 'She's been through a tough time. All she needs is peace and quiet.'

Bryn had given a snort of laughter. 'Wrong place to come then, I would have thought.'

'Yeah, well luckily you're here to dig, not think!' She had punched him affectionately on the arm. 'Look after the place, Bryn.'

When he arrived this morning there had been no sign of a car outside the house and Bryn had felt his spirits rise. Perhaps the new tenant had not materialised after all. He had been hoping in a way he would find a message: *Sorry, Bryn. She couldn't make it. Can you look after Pepper.* Obviously that wasn't going to happen. When he had heard a car pull in later he had felt real disappointment. He studied Andy's car thoughtfully. It was a dark blue VW Passat. At least ten years old. He sighed. Sue had given him nothing to go on. 'Been through a tough time' could mean anything. It was typical of her to give him the minimum of information. She wasn't interested in the detail of people's lives. He doubted if she even knew where he lived. She never asked questions, she gave instructions. In another person he might have assumed she was shy or maybe arrogant, but neither word applied to Sue. Single-minded described her best. She was focused. Small talk did not form part of her DNA, but that suited him. He had been through tough times too and a gossipy, gushing woman was the last thing he needed. He pictured the new arrival again. Appearing in the garden when he was digging over the beds she had given him a shock. She had moved quietly, almost creeping up on him. She was tall, slim, no, perhaps thin described her better; on the edge of gaunt. She was an attractive woman, or had been, her clothes casual, no make-up, her hair wild in the wind. He wondered why she was moving here to the deep country, seemingly alone.

She hadn't pushed him for information, although he could see she was curious to know about him. How much had Sue told her? Probably nothing. Presumably they were both as in the dark as each other. He opened his eyes and stared ahead across the lane towards the hills, then with a sigh he reached forward and turned the ignition key.

Andy gave him ten minutes to drive down the lane and then cautiously went outside and checked the parking space. Her car was now alone. She felt an overwhelming sense of relief. The next hour she spent exploring the back garden, every inch of it. The terrace outside the back door sported huge tubs of rosemary and lemon verbena and scented geraniums, plants which she guessed would have to go into the greenhouse come the really cold weather. Beyond the terrace was the first of the patches of grass. The garden rose quite steeply behind the house, just as it fell away steeply in front. It was large, unorthodox, laid out to favour Sue's herbs rather than any aesthetic plan. There were small areas of lawn and borders with what might be described as flowers rather than herbs, but on the whole the paths wound between islands of medicinal plants. The bed on which Bryn had been working was now neatly dug and raked. Other beds were obviously stock beds for herbs which Sue used often: marigolds, their flowers almost luminous in the fading light, and trimmed lavender. Beside these were more decorative beds, with old roses, and there was a vegetable garden, neat and well stocked. There were two sheds, one for garden tools and the other Sue's drying shed. As she opened the door Andy was swamped with the rich scent of herbs. Bunches hung from lines of hooks on the ceiling and there were drying racks ranged against the walls. The racks were empty, but the hanging herbs looked fresh.

Culpepper accompanied her on her tour and she found herself addressing him again. 'Look, I don't want you telling him I came out the moment he had gone, do you understand? We'll work something out once I know which days he comes.' She stopped in her tracks. 'Oh God, I hope he doesn't come every day. That would be the pits!'

Culpepper did not reply.

Andy went indoors at last and, making herself some tea, sat at the kitchen table with a newspaper she had picked up in Hay that morning. Unexpectedly the aching loneliness that had overwhelmed her after Graham's death began to envelop her again. It wasn't being alone that she minded, it was being here without him. He would have loved the life here. He would have enjoyed every aspect of this house: the architecture, the history, the garden, even her discomfort with the presence of a gardener who, let's face it, had intimidated her. He would have hooted with laughter and turned the whole episode into a huge joke.

Putting the paper down, she sat back in the chair and closed her eyes. Almost without realising it she found herself thinking again of Graham's garden; their garden in Kew.

Rhona Wilson woke with a start. She was still sitting in her chair by the window but it had grown dark outside and she was very cold. She sat there, her head back against the cushions, trying to work out why she was there. She had been tidying the room, going through the drawers of Graham's desk. She was a tall woman, well built, attractive still. She had looked after herself: her carmine-dyed hair cut into elfin spikes, which, satisfactorily, made her look years younger than her actual age; her manicured nails always immaculate; her complexion carefully preserved from the sunlight; her muscles toned from an hour a day at the gym. Why then did she feel so utterly exhausted and old? Then she remembered. She had been methodically going through his desk, pulling out drawer after drawer, staring at the contents, slowly allowing her rage to build. She remembered this desk. It had been given to them by her aunt shortly after they had married. She had thought of it as a hideous old-fashioned blot on the landscape. She hated old furniture. She wanted to fill their house with modern designer items which she had envisaged choosing with Graham on weekend forays to Habitat or Heal's or even New York. They did weekend forays all right. To places like Stow-on-the-Wold and Burford, and they returned to Kew with car boots full of yet more ghastly old stuff which he crooningly referred to as antiques.

She had already had a man in from the auction house in Richmond. He had looked round at Graham's stuff and almost visibly shuddered. 'Brown furniture,' he had said, as though it was contaminated with the plague. 'Valuable once, but worth almost nothing these days, I'm afraid.' She gave a grim smile, wishing Graham could have heard those words. How they would have annoyed and hurt him!

Their first quarrel had been over furniture, and probably their last as well. He would stroke it with those long sensitive fingers of his as though it was alive, touching it in a way he never touched her. 'Think where this has been,' he would say. 'Think, Rhona, how many generations of people have sat at this desk and written down their thoughts and their dreams.' She shivered at the memory. Well, that desk was due for a whole lot of new memories. When the auctioneer sent in his valuations she would tell him to take it away with all the other furniture, whatever it was worth. They could burn it for all she cared, as long as she was left with a clean, empty house. She hadn't had any choice with buying the house either. Graham had inherited this large Edwardian monstrosity from an old aunt. However she shouldn't complain too much about that now. The estate agent had told her the house was worth well over two million pounds. She licked her lips.

She had tipped the contents of the desk drawers out into a heap on the carpet and that was when she had grown so angry this afternoon. It was full of *her* stuff. Miranda's. After all that, there was nothing of Graham's in the desk to speak of. *Her* letters, *her* sketchbooks, *her* pencils. There were old lists, Christmas cards addressed to them both: *Graham and Andy; Andy and Graham; Andy and G*. Who the hell called him G? There was no trace of anything addressed to Graham and Rhona. Nothing of Rhona's anywhere in the house. In her own mind she had blanked details of the day long ago when she had walked out on her husband. In her mind she had elided the years of absence into a monochrome period of loss and mourning for a marriage which had in reality gone sour soon after it had begun – and who was going to contradict her now, when she claimed to be the grieving widow, wronged and cheated by the bitch of a mistress?

Since she had left, Graham had converted the top floor of the house into his office. It was a large room, with windows facing both directions, always full of light. In there, strangely, he did have modern furniture. A serviceable desk, bookshelves, a large table covered in neatly arranged piles of papers and proofs, large old books, too large for the shelves, full of hand-coloured plates of flowers and plants, which the auctioneer said might be worth a bit. He would need to bring in an expert to look at those, he had said. Books were not his speciality. *She* – *Miranda* – had a studio on the first floor. Again, a large room, with double aspect. She had taken most of her paints and stuff when she had left. Rhona and Michelle could see they were not worth anything on their own. The drawings and paintings for his book she had left behind and Rhona had told his publisher to come and take them away. A girl had come and collected them, tight-lipped and barely polite as she went methodically through the portfolios and shelves, separating each illustration with sheets of tissue as though they were something infinitely valuable and special. Rhona shuddered at the memory and glanced down at the heap of stuff on the floor. She planned to burn it all.

With a groan she hauled herself up out of the chair and walked over to the window, raising her hands to draw the curtains against the dark. It was then that she froze. There was a bright half-moon in the sky and the garden was flooded with light. A figure was standing on the grass again, staring at the house. It was a woman; at first she couldn't see her clearly. A tall, slim figure, a tangle of unkempt hair. How the hell had she got in? Rhona was sure she had bolted the side gate. Overwhelmed with anger, she turned and ran through to the dining room. Fumbling with the key she pulled open the French doors and ran out onto the veranda. 'What are you doing here? Who are you? Get out!' she screamed. Her whole body was suffused with rage. The doors swinging behind her, she leaned over the wrought-iron railings, her knuckles white as she gripped the icy metal and scanned the garden below her. There was no sign of anyone. The garden was empty, the grass, wet with dew, showed no footmarks in the moonlight.

Andy pulled herself out of her reverie, startled. The telephone was ringing. She groped in her pocket for her mobile and then realised it was the landline.

Sian had come up with a plan for a dinner party. 'On Friday, if that suits you. I'm asking a few people who I think you would like.'

Replacing the receiver, Andy smiled. The cat flap rattled and Pepper appeared. She was no longer alone.

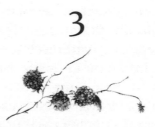

3

That night Andy dreamed again.

Catrin's father once more seemed his usual self. The storm had cleared away, the day was bright and he walked across the hills, swathed in his heavy cloak, leaning on his staff, returning to write and eat with a new calm.

When Catrin went into his study later there was no sign of his anguished struggles on the page. He had been as good as his word. She had found the ashes of the parchment in the hearth.

Now he was full of plans and he distracted her from her worries with reminders that time was growing short. In May they would be departing on their annual progress through the border counties betwixt and between England and Wales to visit his various patrons, and they needed to plan their route.

Usually they left on or around the Feast of St Glywys, relishing the lovely May weather, riding sometimes a few miles a day, other times staying a week or more in one place, but this year there was a problem from the start. Roger Miller would not go with them. The son of Dafydd's former steward had for the last few years accompanied them, leading their pack mule and acting as escort as they traversed the wild, often dangerous and inhospitable roads and trackways between the towns and villages and lonely manors and castles on their route. Since his father's dismissal it seemed he was no longer available and for several weeks Dafydd pondered the situation. He could not abandon their trip, that was out of the question, and he was growing increasingly worried and irritated until Joan made a tentative suggestion. Her younger brother Edmund could accompany them.

A few months before, it seemed, Edmund's wife of only a year had died in childbirth, as had their little son. His father-in-law had made it clear that with three sons of his own there was no longer a place for Edmund under his roof; another pair of hands to help was the last thing he needed, and an extra mouth to feed was an unnecessary burden. With daughter and grandson gone and no ties to hold them together, sadly but firmly he had sent Edmund home to Hardwicke.

It would do him good, Joan said with a combination of sisterly bossiness and devotion, to spend the summer far away; the money he earned would be invaluable as their father had told him there would not be a long-term future for him at Hardwicke either. The farm could not support two sons indefinitely. The elder son, Richard, and his wife were anxious for Edmund to go away and decide on a future career. The tour up the border March as Dafydd and Catrin's escort would give him the perfect opportunity to escape family pressures for a few months.

Dafydd and Catrin had known Edmund since he was a boy – he was the same age as Catrin, both of them two years younger than Joan. They hadn't seen him since his short-lived marriage, and the idea seemed sound. He was fit and strong, always an advantage in a bodyguard, and he was well mannered. He would do. Catrin had never particularly liked him, but she shared her father's opinion that he was trustworthy. And it was not as though they had any choice. There was no one else who would be able to abandon their work to travel around for the next five months.

The day of their departure was not as pleasant as they had hoped. Thick cloud had descended over the mountains and a soft rain was falling as Catrin and her father mounted, she on her hill pony, he on his old Welsh cob, and rode away from the house to begin the long journey northwards. Edmund strode behind them, a staff in his hand, his hunting bow on his back, a sword and dagger at his waist, leading the pack mule. Joan and Betsi had promised yet again to tend Catrin's herbs and Joan had unbent enough to hug her brother as she bade him farewell.

Their first planned stop was Painscastle. They passed outside the town walls of Hay, carefully forded the broad River Wye, rode past Clyro Castle and on up the steep wooded track towards the high wild hills and moorland of The Begwyns.

The wind was cold, whispering through the bracken and heather. Once or twice the mist lifted, showing distant hazy views towards the Black Mountains and the distant Beacons, then it drifted back, enclosing them once more.

It was midday when Dafydd's cob stumbled and nearly fell. The horse's hoof had slipped on the stones of the downward track towards Painscastle and almost at once it was obvious that the animal couldn't go on. Climbing stiffly from the saddle, Dafydd stared at it in helpless frustration. They were miles from anywhere. The wet mist clung to their hair and faces; they could see no more than a few yards ahead.

As Edmund bent to run his hands down the cob's leg Dafydd eyed the young man critically. 'Do you know what you are doing?' he asked brusquely.

Edmund glanced up at him from under his cap. It was still raining. 'Aye, Master Dafydd. It's only a sprain but she can't carry you further for a day or so.'

On her own pony Catrin shivered violently. She glanced around, trying to see through the mist. It was only the cloud, lying low over the higher ground, but it was cold and it was wet, penetrating her cloak, settling on her hood, dripping from the loose strands of hair which had escaped her coif. She transferred her gaze to Edmund, watching his hands run up and down the mare's leg. The animal nuzzled him. She could hear him crooning gently in his throat to soothe it, his long strong fingers almost coaxing the heat from the swollen pastern joint. She shivered and looked away. For a moment, just a moment, she had imagined how those hands would feel on her own body. The thought infuriated her. 'Well, what are we going to do?' Her voice was sharper than she intended.

He glanced up. He was a handsome enough young man, tall, broad-shouldered, his weathered face still marked with the ravages of grief. It was, after all, barely four months since his wife and child had died, leaving him bereft. He gave Catrin a rueful smile. His eyes were hazel, their expression gentle as he turned his attention back to the horse. 'We can't do anything. She needs a day's rest. How far are we from our destination?' He had been employed as an escort, not a guide.

It was Dafydd who replied. 'A mile or so, no more.'

'Then I suggest we transfer your saddle to the mule, Master Dafydd, and you can ride him,' Edmund said calmly. 'I will put the panniers on the cob here. She can manage that easily and I will lead her.'

Catrin was watching the horse rub her head up and down his shoulder. She seemed to have complete faith in him even if, judging by his face, her father didn't. They had no option though. Dafydd stood beside his daughter's pony and watched as Edmund deftly lifted the saddle from the injured animal and replaced it with the panniers containing their worldly goods. He put the saddle on the mule, who tossed his head in irritation but did not object further when Edmund offered his knee for Dafydd's foot and boosted him onto the saddle.

Catrin glanced round as the men fussed with stirrups and harness. There could be an army of footpads out there in the mist; Elfael was famous for its highwaymen, its outlaws. She shuddered.

Edmund sensed her unease. As he settled the other two

47

horses he glanced across at her. 'We are safe here,' he said. 'I don't sense danger and nor do the animals.'

She felt herself frowning at him. 'And can you talk to the animals then, to know that?'

He gave a cheery grin. 'In a way. I understand them and they understand me. Don't be afraid. We are safe here and your father says we are not too far from our goal.'

She scowled.

She had no faith in her father's estimate of where they were any more than in anything else he had said about this trip. How could he know which part of the path they were on when the mist enfolded them like a shroud? She was tempted to try to command the mist to lift. Efa had taught her well. The magic worked. Usually. But the woman had warned her never to do it in front of others and Catrin was nervous of ever letting her father see. She knew instinctively he would be angry. She picked up her reins reluctantly.

Edmund moved back to the injured mare and quietly coaxed her into a walk. Dafydd urged the mule on behind him and Catrin had no choice but to move into line.

She gave another glance round, still shivering. The mist was white and cold and opaque; there was no sign of life out there, at least for the moment. Even as the thought crossed her mind a wild scream echoed towards them out of the fog. Catrin gasped with fear. The horeses stopped, their ears back, staring round. Edmund soothed the injured cob and glanced back. He caught Catrin's eye and smiled. 'Only the cry of an eagle,' he said.

Andy woke with a start, her heart thundering under her ribs. She lay staring at the window. She had left the curtains open and she could see the moonlight shining on the leaves of the climbing rose on the wall outside. The room was silent. She couldn't even hear the brook now, but that unearthly shriek had shaken her awake from a strange, otherworldly dream. She tried to grasp at it, bring it back, but as she woke she sensed it sliding away out of reach. Whatever it was, it had gone and part of her was relieved. It had left her feeling unsettled. Then she heard it again. The lonely eagle's eldritch cry in her dream was nothing more than the husky scream of a barn owl.

4

'Had you never wondered why it was called Sleeper's Castle?'

Sian's supper party was going well. Andy looked round the table in contentment as her hostess put a steaming dish before them. The question had been asked by Roy Pascoe, who was sitting next to her at the scrubbed pine table in Sian's kitchen. He and his wife Ella lived several miles away, apparently, and ran a history bookshop in Hay. He was a gentle, intense man of middle height, his hair thinning, his round spectacles reflecting the light from the candle in the centre of the table. His wife had a slight build; she gave the impression of being overwhelmed by her long linen skirt and blue sweater offset by a heavy agate necklace.

'I am sure Sue must have told me,' Andy replied as Sian passed round plates of spicy casseroled lamb. Ella laughed. 'Wrong answer, Andy. What you should have said was, "No, Roy, I've no idea, do tell me!"'

'Shut up,' Roy retorted good-naturedly. 'Anyone would think I like to display my knowledge.'

'Well, you do, dear,' Ella put in.

'I would like to hear it,' Andy chipped in quickly. 'If she did say anything, I've forgotten. It's a fascinating old house. Sue isn't all that interested in history, as far as I can make out. I don't remember her saying anything much about it beyond how very old it was. She is passionate about her herbs, but when I asked her about the ruins in the garden she just rolled her eyes and said they made a perfect place to grow valerian.'

They all laughed. 'That sounds like Sue.' Sian was passing round bowls of creamy mash and roast vegetables.

'Well,' Roy went on patiently, 'since you asked, and as the others are so anxious to hear what I have to say, I will expound upon the history of the place!' He paused as his wife punched him on the arm, then went on, 'It was once a fortified manor house and quite an imposing building, judging by the bits that are left. Fortified because, like us here, it's on the Welsh–English border. You're in Wales, up your valley, Andy; we're in England down here in the Dingle. The Dulas Brook marks the border. The border March is dangerous country, never at peace, always a bit edgy.' He laughed. 'Sleeper's Castle is medieval of course, and what is left of the building is remarkably unchanged, I should imagine. Outside it's stone-built – which is always hard to date – slate-roofed and beautiful. Inside, there was a central great hall. As in all bigger medieval houses the hall was the main living space, but, probably early on in its history, it was divided – quite crudely, in my opinion – with oak studs and lathe and plaster, to partition off two smaller rooms: the dining room and the parlour behind it. That made the great hall less great, but it's still impressively large as a living room.

'The kitchen is interesting too. The free-standing early medieval kitchen and bakehouse were in later medieval times incorporated into the main house. The pantry and the buttery are original, and upstairs the two smaller end bedrooms with the lovely mullioned windows would have been the original solar, or private quarters of the house owner. There was a catastrophic fire at some point in its history and I suspect it was abandoned for a while after the outer walls fell. But, and this is what is so intriguing' – he leaned forward, his eyes sparkling enthusiastically – 'all that, ancient as it is, is relatively modern stuff according to tradition. The story of Sleeper's Castle goes back hundreds and hundreds, even thousands of years to the ancient Druids, who used the place for sacred dreaming. Hence Sleeper's Castle.' He took off his glasses and polished them, waiting for Andy to comment. She was staring at him.

'Sacred dreaming?'

He nodded. 'It's mentioned in ancient Celtic chronicles and poems. A seer would wrap himself in a bull's hide and sleep to dream, to foretell the future. Sometimes he would place a heavy rock on his chest.'

'Enough, Roy,' Ella interrupted. 'Pass Andy the vegetables.'

'A rock?' Andy echoed him in astonishment. 'What on earth for?'

Roy picked up the dish and held it for her. 'To help concentrate the mind, I would think. Isn't it fascinating? I don't know when the rest of the house was demolished or who lived there more recently – most likely a yeoman, or a tenant farmer – but in the end it became part of the Hereford Estates, and it was then sold off by Viscount Hereford in the 1960s. That's about it, isn't it, Sian?'

Sian began to pour the wine. 'Goodness knows, Roy. You're the expert. You've covered it pretty well, I'd say. Best not to overwhelm Andy with too much history to start with.' She set down the bottle and reached for the vegetables. 'You'll find, Andy, that Roy is passionate about history. He can bore for England on the subject! So, tell him to shut up if he overwhelms you with detail.'

'I'm not bored, I promise you,' Andy put in hastily.

'I'm surprised you didn't ask Meryn over to meet Andy,' Roy said a few minutes later. He glanced at Sian. 'If Andy is interested, he would know more about the Sleeper's side of the story. And he's a neighbour too, in a manner of speaking.'

'I did try to ring him a couple of times,' Sian said. 'No reply and no answer machine. You know what he's like. He's probably away somewhere on one of his mad escapades.'

Andy looked from one dinner guest to another. 'That sounds intriguing.'

'He is,' Ella put in. 'He's a real Druid. Or soothsayer. Or something. Quite a character round here, but he does tend to keep himself to himself, and he goes over to the States quite a bit, I think. He lives up on the mountain, a mile or so beyond you. He'll turn up one of these days, then you'll meet him. I think the pair of you would get on.' She smiled. 'He's a really interesting man, and if you're not into Druids, he does herbs as well, which might be more up your street.'

The conversation flowed on, away from the house, and slowly Andy began to find out about her new neighbours. Roy and Ella were self-evidently passionate about history and books. It had been their shared interest in history that had brought them together. Roy's other passion was hill walking. 'You may well see me from time to time strolling along on the footpath behind Sleeper's Castle,' he said. 'It's one of my favourite walks.' Ella had shaken her head eloquently. 'You won't see me there. Roy walks. I read.'

And then there was Sian herself, who, Andy discovered, had originally been married to a London businessman. He adored the City life and she had hated it. This house had been their second home, destined to be a place to wind down. But, it appeared, her husband had never actually wanted to wind down and Sian had come to Herefordshire more and more often on her own. 'It was inevitable,' she said with a sigh, 'and quite amicable. I had far more in common with people here than I did with his friends' wives in the City. I bought the dogs, who also preferred it here to London, and one day when I was due to drive home to Clapham I just rang him and told him I wasn't coming. I didn't intend to never go back, but I had inadvertently created a vacancy. There's always someone waiting to jump into the empty place at a successful man's side.' She gave a small self-deprecating shake of the head.

'He didn't deserve you, darling,' Ella said. 'You're better off without him.'

There was a moment of silence and then Andy realised they were waiting for her to speak. Story for story. It was only fair.

She cleared her throat. 'I suppose in some ways I was in the opposite corner,' she said. 'My partner was married, but his wife had left him quite a bit of time before we met; she had moved on to another man and showed no signs of ever wanting to come back. I'd been introduced to him with a view to illustrating his books and we began as a business partnership, but in the end we fell in love and I moved in. We were together for ten years, then he died.' She managed to keep her voice steady.

'That's tough.' Ella leaned across and touched her hand.

Andy sighed. 'And at that point his wife decided to turn up and reclaim the house, which was why I was suddenly homeless. Sue saved my sanity by offering me Sleeper's Castle.'

'That's awful, Andy,' Ella said softly. 'I'm so sorry.'

'But you do like it here?' Roy's voice was full of doubt. 'I didn't realise you'd been parachuted into the area.'

Andy laughed. 'I love it here. Graham and I had been to stay with Sue in the past, so I knew what it was like.'

Did she though? Seeing it now through their eyes, she thought of the empty house, the endless sound of the water thundering over the rocks, the void where Graham ought to be. The silence lengthened and she realised that the others were all looking at her again.

Sian broke the silence. 'Help me collect the plates, Andy,' she said, getting to her feet. 'I've made an apple-and-blackberry crumble for pudding. Roy, can you find another bottle of wine? You know where they are.' As they stacked the plates in the sink, she glanced at Andy. 'I'm sorry. We didn't mean to touch on a nerve. Are you all right?'

Andy sighed. 'A moment of tristesse. They come and go. But I am enjoying myself, Sian. Thank you so much for asking me tonight.'

'Good.' Sian glanced over her shoulder at the table. 'They're a nice couple.'

'Right, a change of subject is in order, I think,' Roy said as they sat down again. 'So, Andy, is everything peaceful at Sleeper's Castle? Have you seen any ghosts up there? It's a spooky old place.'

'Roy, that's hardly tactful,' Ella put in. 'The poor woman is living there all on her own.'

Andy laughed. 'I don't mind. I loved the idea of ghosts when I was a child – the whole concept of who and what they were, or might be. My father was interested and I suppose I followed his lead. But it was all theory. I never saw one, as far as I know. I went on studying them and reading about them even when I grew up, but Graham was very anti. He didn't like the idea at all, so I dropped the subject.'

'That's men for you!' Ella put in. 'Why is it we always have to subsume our interests and passions in the face of their sensibilities? Does it ever work the other way round? Never. Women get dragged off to watch sport and play trains and God knows what and never query it.'

There was a short silence. 'Was that tirade directed at me, sweetie?' Roy said meekly.

Ella laughed. 'No. Luckily you are the perfect husband.' There wasn't a hint of irony in her voice. 'But it is true as a general rule, I think.'

'It certainly was for me,' Andy confirmed. 'And I'm only slowly beginning to realise how much of myself did get subsumed by our relationship. But that doesn't mean I'm hoping to go back to Sleeper's Castle and find it populated with ghosts. As Ella says, I'm there alone and I don't want to scare myself!'

'Well, if you do,' Roy put in, 'Meryn is your man. He's the local ghostbuster as well as a Druid. Fascinating chap. As Ella said, you'd like him.'

The memory of that conversation came back as Andy let herself into the house later. It was well after midnight and a bright moon was high in the sky, throwing shadows across the garden. She paused on the threshold and waited, trying to sense the atmosphere inside the house. As before it seemed benign.

She had left the light on in the kitchen and she went in, looking round. There was no sign of Culpepper, but every self-respecting cat in the world would be outside on a beautiful moonlit night like this.

She found herself surveying the kitchen with new eyes. Now it had been pointed out she could see that half the room was much older than the other half; the stone walls, the shape of the window, the beamed ceiling. The modern fitments had distracted her. Even the flags, though skilfully matched, were obviously from different eras.

Upstairs, she opened the window in her bedroom and leaned with her elbows on the sill, looking out into the garden. It was an ancient window, she now recognised, obviously medieval, with stone mullions. The small leaded panes of glass were Victorian, she guessed. The window can't have opened originally, but now it had a slightly bent metal frame with latch and handle, and swung open behind the mullions as a casement. Outside she could hear the brook. The water seemed quieter, gentler than on the previous night. Moonlight threw the garden into silver relief with deep shadows beneath the trees and bushes and for a while she stood, staring out contentedly, aware of an owl hooting in the distance and another answering it with quick short calls that echoed against the house walls.

It was a long time before she pulled the window shut and crept into bed, shivering. She lay there, all desire for sleep gone. The company and happiness of the evening had left her with a feeling of anticlimax and loneliness. In spite of herself she found her mind travelling back to Kew, and this time she didn't fight it.

Throwing the last of the letters and cards into a cardboard box Rhona looked round the room one last time. She didn't want there to be one single sign of Miranda Dysart left. She had to accept that the whole house reflected Miranda's choices, her taste; she could see her hand in every room but, much as she would like to, she could hardly burn every stick of furniture. The sale people would come soon enough and take it away. In the meantime there was all this . . . she hesitated as she tried to think of a word . . . all this *stuff* imposing Miranda's personality on everything. She added a couple of notebooks full of delicate watercolour sketches, which she had found on top of a bookshelf, to the box and lifted it with a groan, heaving it over towards the French doors and out onto the terrace. In the far corner of the garden a wisp of pale smoke drifted up from the earlier pile of *stuff* she had thrown into the incinerator. The sketchbooks went on the fire first and she gave a grim smile. She hadn't expected to feel such malicious joy at destroying things that Miranda and Graham would have treasured. The books were followed by a pile of postcards from friends who appeared to have travelled all over the world. She glanced at one: *Andy and G – truly truly wish you were here. Andy, you could paint this place for a thousand years and not grow tired of its beauty, love Sal and Sam.* It came from Hawaii. Rhona sneered as she tossed it after the sketchbooks. 'Goodbye, Sal and Sam,' she whispered. It wasn't just Miranda she was trying to hurt, she realised as she stared down into the flaming bin, it was Graham as well. Graham had deserted her; Graham had dared to be happy with this woman; Graham had enjoyed his life while she, she had been miserable and abandoned. She stood back, watching the conflagration. She had long ago forgotten or buried the truth, that she had left Graham for another man,

a relationship that had foundered as had all the others that had followed it. Everything was Graham's fault. And Miranda's.

She tensed and turned to look behind her, half expecting to see the woman in the garden, watching. There was no one there, but she could feel her skin prickling. It was as if Miranda knew what she was doing. She stepped forward into the intense heat, dropped the rest of the contents of the box into the incinerator and turned away, dusting off her hands.

Miranda was standing on the step outside the kitchen, staring down at her.

Rhona stood transfixed, unable to move; the next moment the woman had vanished and she was alone in the garden with the bitter pall of smoke engulfing her.

In bed, Andy groaned and turned over, unable to endure the cruel drift of the dream. In her sleep she had pushed away the duvet and her hand brushed the wall, coming to rest against the cold stone.

With the touch of the stone came older, more powerful memories.

Rhona was gone; in her place came darkness, then Andy could hear the clash of swords, smell burning, feel the ground shake beneath the hooves of heavy horses ridden by men in full plate armour and now she could see a company of archers drawn up on a hill. Someone must have shouted a command. The men were reaching down into their arrow bags. They set their arrows to the string. As one they drew the great long-bows and paused for the order to rain death on the ranks below. The whistling sound of the arrows flying through the air was deafening and the screams of those below, as every barbed head met its mark, were hideous. Men and horses alike writhed and fell, and Andy in her dream could do nothing. In her sleep she groaned and wrestled with her pillows. She lashed out with her arm again and struck the wall. The pain woke her.

She stared round in the darkness, nursing her bruised knuckles, aware that she had been shouting. She was, she realised, drenched with sweat. She was shaking with real terror. She lay staring up at the darkened ceiling, trying to recall the nightmare. It was about death. That much she remembered. She was watching men die. And she was not alone. There was another woman with her, a woman wearing a dark cloak with the hood pulled up over her hair. They were standing next to each other in the shelter of the trees and they were both frozen to the spot by their horror and their helplessness.

Dragging herself out of bed, Andy switched on the light and looked at her watch. It was just after 3 a.m. She had been asleep barely two hours. Reaching for her dressing gown she pulled it on and stumbled downstairs to the kitchen. Exhausted though she was, she didn't think she could go back to sleep. Her head was too full of the horror of what she had seen. It was a battle, that much she could remember now. A battle between two armies. She had seen men die, writhing in agony on the bloodstained mud of a battlefield. Sitting down at the kitchen table she put her head in her hands and closed her eyes.

Something she had eaten at the supper party must have disagreed with her; her mother always used to say food made you dream. But this was a house of dreams. Her eyes flew open and she caught her breath as she recalled Roy's explanation of the house's name. Surely not! No, this was something she had read about or seen on TV, regurgitated by her tired brain as a protest against the rich food and wine. She had lost the habit of eating and drinking late over the last few months, that was all. She would have a hot drink and go back to bed. Wearily she dragged herself to her feet and put the kettle on, then she searched through the cupboard. In the house of a herbalist surely she would find some camomile tea. She did. A perfectly ordinary commercial brand. So, even Sue needed a quick fix at times. With a weary smile she pulled a teabag out of the box and put it in a mug, then she turned to take the kettle off the hob. As she retraced her steps to the table she glanced towards the door. A figure was standing there. A woman, huddled in a dark cloak. They stared at each other in astonishment for barely a second, then the woman was gone.

5

Catrin woke and looked round in the dim light of a flickering fire. Her heart was pounding from the horror of the dream. The dream she had shared, did she but know it, with another woman, a dream she had dreamt recently, at home in Sleeper's Castle. But she wasn't at home. She pulled her cloak around her, shivering, confused as to where she was. Then she remembered. It was the first night of their summer tour. They had arrived at Painscastle after dark, the limping horse between them, afraid there might be some kind of curfew which would consign them to a barn or an outhouse until the next day. But the constable was at home and they found they had been half expected, looked for. 'You always come around this time of year, my friends,' he had said with a smile. He had taken their hands and brought them to the great fire in the central hearth; his wife had hugged Catrin like a lost daughter. Visitors were not so frequent in this lonely place that they would not be welcomed royally. Their wet clothes were taken for drying, they and their horses were given warm shelter. Edmund ate with the small garrison and the servants at the lower table in the hall, Dafydd and Catrin with the constable and his wife at the high table, differentiated in this small castle only by its proximity to the fire. After supper they would sing or tell a story. That would earn their night's keep and perhaps a silver coin or two before they rode on in the morning.

Later Catrin found her way outside to make sure the injured horse had been taken care of. She found Edmund gently rubbing salve into the animal's leg by the light of a lantern. He glanced up at her as he heard the rustle of her skirts in the straw as she approached him. 'How is she?' she asked.

'She'll do. It's not a bad sprain. Rest is all she needs.' The smell of the salve floated in the air. She sensed there was lavender there and peppermint and perhaps juniper.

'Did the grooms give you that ointment?' she asked. She had seen them huddled round a brazier in the yard; they had told her where to find him.

He shook his head. 'I always carry a pot of this with me when I travel.' He straightened, rubbing his hands together and then rubbing them up and down on the front of his doublet. 'Good stuff. I make it myself. It does for men as well as beasts.'

She raised an eyebrow. 'Only men?' she found herself asking pertly.

He laughed. 'I dare say it would do for ladies as well,' he said. 'There is nothing there to harm them. You like it, don't you, my love.' He had turned back to the horse, his voice a low croon. The horse rubbed her muzzle on his arm and nibbled his sleeve.

Catrin watched fascinated. 'I'll bear that in mind,' she said at last. 'Do you have all you need out here?'

'I have plenty, thank you.'

'Then I'll bid you goodnight.' She hesitated then turned and retraced her footsteps to the keep.

Her father had noted her absence and guessed where she had gone. 'Is the boy all right?'

She sat down beside him on the bench at the table. 'He's fine. He's with the horses.'

Dafydd nodded. 'They have asked us to sing again.' He glanced at their host and hostess, who were watching them eagerly. 'Shall we give them a lullaby or two to send us all to bed?'

She smiled. 'I will fetch my harp.'

As she unwrapped her instrument, set it on her knee and began to tune it, her fingers finding the little pegs with accustomed ease, she felt extraordinarily happy.

But that night the nightmares came back. Awake with painful suddenness, she stared up into the darkness, her heart heavy. It was a warning, of that she was certain, but of what? There was always skirmishing in the March. There was war in Scotland too. Edmund had told her and her father something of that as they rode and she had learned that he was tempted to join a company of archers. 'The pay is good as an archer.' He had glanced up at Dafydd's face as he walked at the horse's head near her. 'I no longer have a place with my wife's family, God rest her soul' – he crossed himself sadly – 'but now I am back at Hardwicke, I have no place there either. My brother Richard will inherit all that there is to inherit. Joan is safe with you. So I am free to go wherever fate sends me.'

To go to war. Catrin shivered under the warm covers of the truckle bed she had been given in the women's chamber, high in the keep. Was it Edmund's war she foresaw? The war with Scotland or perhaps in France? He had talked a little of such matters as they had walked through the mist earlier and grudgingly she had had to admit to herself that he was an intelligent man, intrigued as he was by the politics of kings. He had told them of the treaty with France and of the repeated demands by the king for money to fund his excursions into Scotland.

Sleepily she pictured her father's study, his much rubbed-out parchment, the words of horror he had written there. She was not the only one to have premonitions of death. He had tried to keep his fears from her and she had kept hers from him, but they were going to have to discuss it one day; to try and discover what the walls of their house were telling them of the future and who it was who was being forewarned.

Sitting up with a sigh, she pulled her cloak around her for warmth and sat gazing into the heart of the embers of the fire. The women servants of the castle slept on truckle beds near her. The room was warm and safe but it was not her own little bedroom. She thought back to the dream. How strange that something so intimate, which belonged to Sleeper's Castle, could follow her here.

She wasn't sure when in her dream she had realised she was not watching the battle alone. Another woman was with her, as horrified and afraid as she was. Away from the mêlée, sheltered by a belt of ancient oak trees, they moved closer to one another in their terror; they were higher than the men they watched, not in her own *cwm* but on a hillside somewhere, witnessing the horror unfolding beneath them.

Then between one breath and the next Catrin had awoken and the dream had faded as dreams always will and with it her companion, but not before she had noticed that the woman had light brown hair, wild and unkempt, with no coif or veil. As they looked at one another in horror at what they had seen, she saw the woman had clear grey eyes. For a moment they had held one another's gaze, then she had gone with the dream into the mist.

The next day it was raining and cold.

Andy yawned and, dropping her paintbrush, stretched out her fingers to relieve their stiffness. After ringing Sian to thank her for the supper party she had settled down at the table in the living room and had been painting for several hours. She gave a wry smile, noticing the plants she was painting – a small posy of hastily gathered yellow tormentil and St John's Wort – had drooped slightly in their glass of water. Instead of looking cheerful, they seemed exhausted and depressed, which was pretty much what she felt too.

She sat staring into space, allowing herself to think again about the figure from her dream the night before, the figure she'd imagined seeing standing in the kitchen doorway. Almost without realising she had done it, Andy pulled her sketchpad towards her, reached for her pencil and began to touch in the details of the woman's face. It was clear in her mind: sharp, fine-featured with expressive grey-green eyes, her hair hidden by a hood, her hands strong and capable. The rest of her clothes were indistinct. Andy remembered only the long heavy cloak, which swept the ground. The woman had been a remnant of a dream that had been particularly vivid, easily explained after months of stress and unhappiness. Hadn't she?

Pushing back the chair, she stood up and walked over to the hearth.

Apart from the pool of bright light focused on the table where she had been working, the room was full of shadows. She looked round as the curtains stirred in the draught from the windows which were streaming with rain. A puff of ash shifted from the long-dead fire. This was the oldest part of the house, its great hall, she now realised. She thought back to what Roy had told her last night about its ancient and historical origins. The heavy ceiling beams emphasised its age, solid, brooding, throwing off the light from the lamp with something like disdain as the weight of ages overwhelmed the room. She felt the hairs on the back of her neck stir. There had to be ghosts here. How could a house this old, steeped in history, lived in by generations of people long gone, not have ghosts? Ghosts, whatever they were, would be in the DNA of ancient plaster and oak; they were part of the fabric of time, as real as the pegs that held the joints of wood together.

She didn't feel afraid at the thought. The house was friendly; it seemed to welcome her, but it was easy to imagine a sense of its former life, watching, waiting, comfortable she hoped in the knowledge that she was here as the new caretaker.

She sat down on the edge of the sofa and closed her eyes,

wondering if she could conjure up anything of the house's past. She used to do this with her father when she was a child, always hoping something would happen. Nothing ever had, but maybe this time it would. She was hoping, she knew, that the woman from the kitchen would appear again.

She thought back to her father's explanation and the theories she had read so often in her books, the ones she liked best, that ghosts were memories, moments in the past which had caught in the fabric of a house like a moth in a spider's web, clinging, fluttering briefly then gone back into the dark. Sometimes it was more than that; sometimes someone had left a trace of themselves anchored by their emotions, and those would be the strongest impressions. She remembered once or twice, ghost-hunting with her father, when there had been a subtle shift in the air as though someone or something had moved on stage while they watched from the darkened auditorium, prompting her to open her eyes, frightened and excited, clutching at her father's hand. Sometimes a slight flicker of light would catch their attention, but that was all that happened.

As far as she recalled there were solid scientific explanations for all this stuff, something to do with quantum physics, but she never became an expert. Graham had come along and scoffed and shuddered and mocked, and she had put it all behind her.

She hadn't encountered any of these memories, fragments of the past, in the old days when she had been so keen on doing this, but maybe there was something here, in this house with its dreams and its shadows and its memories.

Slowly she emptied her mind, allowing it to rest, open, receptive, ready for any impressions that might come as the silence of the room wrapped itself around her.

Five minutes later she tensed. Was that a change in the atmosphere? She could feel someone there watching her. Someone was ready to communicate. Her eyes flew open.

Culpepper was sitting in the doorway gazing at her in silence, his expression enigmatic.

She laughed out loud. 'You caught me,' she said. 'I'll bet you can see them, the people who used to live in this house.'

The cat's expression remained unchanged.

The knock at the front door made her jump. The sound of the rain on the flags outside had muffled the noise of the car engine as an old muddy Volvo drew up outside the gate. Holding her coat over her head Sian ran up the steps and huddled under the stone lintel of the porch until Andy pulled open the door.

'Had a wonderful thought,' Sian spluttered, running her fingers through her rain-soaked hair as they headed into the warmth of the kitchen. 'Let's go and find Meryn. Not only does he know about the history of this house and this area in general, but I think he's writing a book about herbs. Maybe you could illustrate it for him. I'm going to drive you up to his cottage, show you where he lives and we will see if there's any sign of him.'

Andy stared at her, shocked at this sudden explosion of energy. 'Are you sure?'

'Of course I'm sure. He might even be there! Do you want to come?' Sian was laughing.

Andy thought for a moment then she smiled. 'That sounds good to me. I've been cooped up all day painting and I could do with a bit of fresh air.' She cocked an eye towards the window. Rain was streaming down the panes, rattling on the flags outside. 'Does he never answer the phone?'

Sian shook her head. 'Often not. He's an amazing character, Andy. I think you would like each other. He may not be there – he does travel a lot – but it's worth a look. If the cottage is all locked up then we'll just have to wait until he returns. But if it looks as though he's around I can leave a note and get him to ring me. Then I can engineer a meeting.' She was studying Andy's face. 'You do look very tired.'

Andy bit her lip. 'I've been dreaming a lot.'

'Ah.' Sian went to lean on the Aga.

'You sound as though you were expecting me to say that,' Andy said slowly.

'This house is not called Sleeper's Castle for nothing, as Roy told you. People do dream here.'

'Did Sue ever mention it to you?'

'I think she had nightmares occasionally.' Sian's reply was cautious.

'About Catrin?'

'Who's Catrin?'

'A woman who I think might have lived here once. I've heard her name in my dreams.'

'I don't remember Sue telling me what the dreams were about.' Sian frowned. 'She just shrugged them off. Are you telling me you're dreaming about a ghost?'

'No.' Andy reached for her coat. 'No, not a ghost. It doesn't matter. You know how some dreams linger. And I don't think I'm sleeping very well, if I'm honest. It's odd, but I suppose I'll get used to the silence. The brook is a strange bedfellow. I'm beginning to see how it works. Now it's raining it will start to roar over the rocks again; when the weather has been dry for a day or two, the roar will subside to a pleasant ripple. I like it.'

'Good.' Sian looked round. 'I love this house. Sue was so lucky to find it. It belonged to an old man who lived here for years and years. He had a bit of a reputation as an oddball – a bit fey, you know? Local girls used to come up and ask him to do magic spells for him to make sure they caught the lad of their dreams.'

'You're joking!'

'No. I know one of the guys at an estate agent in Hay and he told me there was a problem with the house after the old man died because no one knew who had inherited it. For ages they thought he had no relations, then at last someone turned up, a great-nephew, I think, who had been living in Canada. He wanted nothing to do with the place luckily, so it went on the market and they rang Sue who had been hunting for a cottage for a few months and she came down and bought it within days. Well, I expect you know that.'

'She told me about it at the time. The house was in an awful state, as I remember.'

Sian nodded. 'He was old and living on his own. But he was completely sane, and he had designed the herb garden. He must have been nearing one hundred when he died and he had never been to a doctor in his life. He used the herbs as taught to him by his granny.'

'He didn't have the services of Bryn, I take it.'

There was something in her tone that made Sian smile. 'You've met him then.'

'Not so as one would notice. He grunted at me and more or less told me to mind my own business – in fact I got the impression he would prefer it if I kept out of the garden altogether.'

'That sounds like Bryn.'

'It's not just me then?'

Sian hesitated. 'Let's say he seems to take a while to get to know people.' She headed towards the door. 'Give him time. Come on, let's go and see if Meryn is at home. If nothing else it will get you out in the fresh air.'

Thick cloud lay low over the mountains. As Sian drove up the steep winding lane, crossed a cattle grid and forked onto an even narrower road, the visibility narrowed to a white wall around the car. From time to time she braked and steered round a sheep sitting at the edge of the road, seeking the comparative warmth of the tarmac. The animals gazed at them with blank yellow eyes, expressionless in the rain. 'They hate this weather, poor things,' Sian commented as they stopped for the fourth time.

'Does he really live right up here?' Andy was vainly peering through the windscreen hoping to be able to see where they were going.

'It seems a bit bleak now,' Sian answered. 'But it's beyond beautiful when you can see the view. We're right up below Hay Bluff here. One can see several counties spread out below.'

They came to another fork in the road and she swung the car onto an even narrower track, which after a few hundred yards disappeared beneath a swiftly running ford, then reappeared to climb steeply again. Abruptly the mist began to thin and there were glimpses of blue in the sky ahead. 'We've climbed above the cloud,' Sian said. She changed down into second gear.

They turned through an open gate, passed a sheltered stand of thorn trees and then they were there. A white-painted stone cottage appeared at the top of the track, its garden surrounded by a thorn hedge. There was no sign of a car outside.

Sian turned off the engine and opened her door. The blast of cold air almost took Andy's breath away as she followed suit, pulling up the hood of her jacket.

She hadn't expected Sian to head round to the shed at the back of the cottage and push open the door. She re-emerged with two parcels and a key. 'I'm afraid he is still away. These have been here a while. They're quite damp. The postman leaves them for him on a special shelf.' She led the way back to the front door and inserted the key. The door was swollen and she struggled before pushing it open, leading the way into the cold dark interior. It smelt of long-ago apple logs and stone.

'I take it he doesn't mind people coming up here?' Andy asked cautiously. 'It feels wrong coming in when he's not at home.'

'He has let a few people know where he keeps the key,' Sian said cheerfully. 'That way if any of us are up on the mountain we can pop in and make sure everything is all right. No one seems to have been here for a while though.' She put the two parcels down on the table. 'I'll check if there are any clues as to when he's coming back.' She disappeared through a door in the back wall.

Andy stood where she was, looking round. She could sense the man who lived here very strongly. It was as though a part of him was still here, watching them. She bit her lip, remembering her own strange new ability to daydream herself back to the house in Kew. That had been such a powerful experience it was as though it was real, as though if anyone had looked through the window of the house into the moonlit garden they would have seen her standing there. She took a deep breath as the thought of Rhona calling out to her in the darkness came back to her. From what she had heard of the man who lived here, he would be more than capable of watching her from afar. Hastily she followed Sian through the door and found herself in a small neat kitchen. 'He's turned off the water,' Sian announced, spinning the cold tap in the sink. 'That's ominous. He wasn't expecting to come back before the deep frosts.'

'Pity.' Andy was feeling more and more uncomfortable. It was silly to feel him watching them; it had to be her imagination. Just as it must have been her imagination thinking Rhona was watching her that night in Kew.

She shivered. 'It's cold in here.'

Sian gave another quick glance round the room and then headed back into the living room. 'I'll leave him a note. He's bound to come back sooner or later.'

Walking over to the table by the window she found a spiral-top pad and reached for a pen. As she was writing there was a sudden bang outside. They both looked up. 'What was that?' Sian exclaimed.

'It sounded like a door banging,' Andy said nervously. 'Perhaps you didn't shut the shed properly.'

'I'll check before we leave.' Sian tore off her note and left it prominently on the centre of the table.

Andy felt an overwhelming wave of relief as they let themselves out and locked the door behind them. When Sian headed round the side of the house to return the key to its hiding place she followed closely behind her. The shed door was indeed hanging open, swinging in the wind. The cloud was dispersing as they watched, the landscape opening up before them, revealing a panoramic view across the countryside below.

'It's breathtaking, isn't it,' Sian said as she latched the door firmly in place.

Andy was speechless with delight as she stared down. Cloud still laced the green of the valleys and foothills below them, white and fluffy as sunbeams spotlit different areas in turn.

'I'm glad you like my view.' The voice behind her made Andy spin round to see who had spoken.

There was no one there.

'Did you hear that?' she gasped.

'What?'

'A voice. A man's voice. Meryn's voice? He said he was glad I liked his view.' Andy turned round, scanning the garden behind them, her wild hair flying. 'No. No, I'm sorry. I'm hearing things. It must have been the wind. There's no one here.'

Sian gave a cryptic smile. 'I thought you two would get on. Perhaps he'll come back now he knows there is someone interesting up here for him to talk to.'

When Andy let herself back into Sleeper's Castle later she found the message light blinking on the telephone. It was her mother. 'Darling, ring me back when you get a chance. I've had an idea which I hope you will like.'

Andy sat staring at the phone for several minutes before she complied. She used to think that she and her mother had a special telepathic link, but over the years she had lived with Graham it had gone. Now her mother resorted to the phone when she needed to speak to her daughter exactly like anyone else.

'Mum? How are you?'

'I'm fine. I wondered if you needed anything from the stuff you've stored here. Now you've moved in, you might want a few of your books around you.' Nina hesitated. 'I know you didn't have time for your old interests when you were living with Graham, but now, maybe they will come back and, if you like, I could drive up and spend a weekend with you and bring anything you need. Only if you would like me to, of course.' Her mother's voice was rapidly losing its confidence in the face of Andy's silence.

'How did you know?' Andy said at last.

'Know?'

'Never mind. Yes please. I need any books I've got about dreaming; my mind, body and spirit books; my ghost books. And I would love it if you came to stay. Whenever you like. As soon as possible.'

6

Nina Dysart arrived the following Friday evening. She stood for a few moments staring up at the house after she climbed out of her car then she made her way towards the front door.

'Mum!' Andy had heard the car. 'Come in. It's so good to see you.' They exchanged a long warm hug.

Mother and daughter did not resemble one another. Andy was tall, her eyes grey, her hair light brown, shoulder length and curly. Her mother's hair was white, cut short and neat, and her eyes an intense brown. While Andy's clothes inclined towards the colourful and artistic, Nina was always immaculately dressed in carefully matched neutrals. She wasn't as tall as Andy and her figure was petite, but there was no mistaking the fact that they were mother and daughter. Their mannerisms were similar, their voices blended, they both talked at once and then paused and laughed and both started again.

'Oh, Mum, it's so good to see you!' Andy caught her mother's hands and squeezed them. 'I have missed you.'

Nina pulled free and gave her daughter a quizzical look. 'You can't have missed me so soon, darling. Not possible. So, what's wrong? Have you made a ghastly mistake coming here?'

'No!' Andy's denial was adamant. Then she paused. 'No,' she said again, less sure this time.

'So, what's wrong?'

'Nothing.'

'Supposing you show me round,' Nina said. 'Then you can give me an incredibly strong cup of coffee after that horrendous drive, then we will talk.'

Unloading the books almost defeated them. They brought in half a dozen cartons and stacked them in the living room. Andy stared round helplessly. 'I'd forgotten I had so many. I hadn't thought about shelves. I will have to have some made I suppose.'

'Rubbish. Not in someone else's house. Buy flat-pack. Have you got a handyman who can put them up for you? I think you mentioned a gardener?'

Andy gave a hollow laugh. 'I don't think I would dare ask him.'

'Why?' Her mother paused in the middle of what she was doing and stared at her.

'He doesn't seem to approve of my presence here. Don't worry.' Andy straightened her back with a groan. 'I am capable of assembling a flat-pack. It can't be that hard. In the meantime let's pile the books round the walls in here.' She glanced help-lessly out of the window. There were at least four more boxes in her mother's car.

It was like meeting old friends. Every few minutes she stopped to look at the book she'd just unpacked and run an affectionate hand over the cover. 'I have missed all the mind, body and spirit stuff. It was such a passion of mine for so long.' She gave Nina a wan smile.

'Not everything about Graham was good for you,' her mother put in tartly. 'I know you loved him to bits and you worked well together, but he rode roughshod over so much that was you, my darling. He moulded you into his ideal woman.'

Andy wasn't sure whether to be angry and amused. 'You make me sound like a Stepford wife!'

'No. But it was odd for you to cut such a large part of your own personality out of your life. He didn't like animals, did he? So you didn't have any pets. He wasn't interested in history or old buildings. You used to do such wonderful paintings of ruins in landscapes, do you remember? And you loved visiting them. You used to cook; you adored cooking. With Graham, I know because you told me once, you ate out all the time or had snacks because he didn't see the point of wasting time in the kitchen.'

Andy nodded ruefully. 'Do you know, I've lost the instinct to cook. I have this beautiful Aga here and I haven't done more than boil the kettle or heat up a can of soup.'

'QED!' Her mother stared round. 'This lovely kitchen going to waste. Now that I know what I'm destined to have for supper I will insist tomorrow we go shopping and stock the larder, then you can start cooking. I want decent food while I'm here and you can practise on me.'

Andy sat up a long time after her mother had gone to bed, thinking over everything she had said. She was right. So much of what made Andy Andy was on hold, battened down somewhere at the back of her head. She thought about that wonderful feeling of freedom she had experienced on her first night here, the joy of going out into the garden and feeling the wind in her hair and the raindrops on her face. For a few moments she had become a wilder version of herself; a more authentic version. Then she had slid in her daydream to the garden in Kew, drawn inexorably back to civilisation.

She was sitting at the kitchen table, her back to the Aga, feeling its warmth a solid comfort gently enfolding her. She was thinking about her father. Her interest in the supernatural came from him. The solid acceptance of the weird and wonderful being a normal part of an amazingly varied and extraordinary world. She remembered as a child exploring old castles and abbeys with him. He was the one who had discouraged cameras and made her sketch instead. 'That way, Andy, you capture the heart and soul of a place.' Even when he remarried he found time to go on encouraging her. Nina, who had showed no bitterness at the break-up and seemed to accept the status quo with extraordinary equanimity, would pack her off on the train north where she would be welcomed into her father's new family by his lovely Northumbrian wife, with first one then two then three new siblings, all boys, and all of whom she adored. They still got on well. She had missed them too. She had seen very little of her father in the last ten years. Perhaps Graham had taken his place. A father figure. She frowned. That was not a pleasant thought. She would get in touch with Rufus soon, re-establish ties, maybe go and see him.

Behind her the cat flap clicked and Pepper appeared. He trotted over to his empty food bowl, examined it and turned to look at her reproachfully. She smiled. 'You are not going to try and persuade me you haven't had your supper, my friend. I remember distinctly giving it to you because my mum watched me and she thinks you get too much to eat.'

Pepper turned his back on her, sat down and began washing his face. She was sure he understood a lot of what she said. Nina was right there too. She had missed having dogs and cats around her. It was wonderful to have a cat again, even on loan. And as Pepper had reminded her, she was here to look after him. If she was going to see her father again he would have to come down to see her.

Pepper yawned and without realising it she did too.

Still exhausted from their long ride Catrin lay back in another unaccustomed bed, staring up at another stranger's ceiling and drifted off to sleep. Her dream was different this time; in it she was back at home; the violence and the shouting were gone. Sleeper's Castle was quiet. In the silence she could hear the sound of the brook outside the window, enveloping her, wrapping her in the comfort of the darkness. For a while she lay without moving, then as the first birds began to sing across the *cwm* she rose from her bed. Her eyes were still closed as she walked towards the stairs. Her father was asleep in his own bed, for once snoring gently on his pillow stuffed with dried hops to soothe his dreams. Sleepwalking down the stairs and across the hall, she went towards the kitchen. The other woman was there, asleep at the table, her head cushioned on her arms.

In her dream Catrin stood looking at her for a long time without moving, then slowly she crept across the flagged floor towards her. Andy moved uncomfortably and reached out an arm without waking. Catrin stepped back sharply, watching. Andy didn't move again, her breathing slow and regular. Once more Catrin approached and cautiously stretching out her hand she touched the corner of the table with the tips of her fingers. The table was plain scrubbed pine. The table in Catrin's kitchen, the table where Joan prepared their meals, was made from a huge chunk of solid oak, criss-crossed with cuts from her cleaver as she prepared their meat and vegetables. Catrin stood still, holding her breath, then she turned and tiptoed back out of the kitchen.

Andy didn't stir but somehow she was aware of the shadowy figure, seeing it cross the great hall and walk slowly up the stairs. In her dream Catrin climbed slowly back into bed and lay down. As she snuggled once more onto her pillow she gave a small sigh. The room was Andy's room, the bed in the corner where Andy's bed stood, the window the window Andy looked out of down to the moonlit garden below. She could see the mullions, trace the lines of the stone, the smooth curve of the chisel, the rough edges where the man who made them had drained his tankard of ale, smacked his lips and returned to work slightly the worse for wear.

Andy woke suddenly and sat upright, staring towards the window. There was a faint glimmer of daylight filtering into the room. There were curtains now, but the mullions were the same.

She had staggered up to bed only four hours ago after waking to find herself in the kitchen, her head cushioned on her arms. There had been no sign of Pepper and her neck was agonisingly stiff. She had forced herself to stand up, turn off the lights and head next door towards the stairs, then she had stopped, aware of a presence in the house. Her mother. Of course, her mother was asleep upstairs in Sue's room.

She paused on the landing, listening. There was no sound from the other bedroom. Making her way to her own bed she slipped off her shoes and lay down under the duvet fully dressed. In seconds she was asleep.

She remembered the dream after a shower and a change of clothes next morning. The Catrin of her dreams had been standing staring down at Andy as she was asleep in the kitchen. She could see herself, unconscious, vulnerable, unaware, the young woman creeping towards her, extending her hand as if to touch her, then gently stroking the corner of the table instead. It had been so real. Catrin was younger than she had realised, perhaps seventeen or eighteen. She was slim beneath the bulky clothes, with rich chestnut hair slipping from beneath her linen coif and gentle concerned eyes.

'You're up early.' Nina was already in the kitchen when she went downstairs. She was listening to the *Today* programme as she made breakfast. The table was laid. Pepper was sitting on the windowsill watching the proceedings with what looked suspiciously like approval.

Andy approached the table and held out her hand to touch it, stroking the corner lightly with her fingertips.

Nina turned off the radio. 'What's the matter?'

'I dreamt there was a woman in here. I fell asleep where I was last night after you went to bed and she was standing watching me. She reached out to touch the table near my hand.' Andy shivered. 'It was strange. Very real. It was as if she was studying me; watching me. She's called Catrin.'

Nina put the coffee pot on the table. 'Get some of that down you. You were so exhausted last night I'm not surprised you dreamt vividly.'

'I can't help wondering if I was actually awake.' Andy reached for the coffee.

'Dreams can be incredibly real sometimes.' Her mother produced two slices of warm toast and put butter and marmalade on the table.

'I know. I've been having some truly violent dreams since I arrived here. Battles.'

'That sounds like stress and exhaustion to me.' Nina sat down opposite her. She surveyed her daughter's face. 'You don't have to stay here, darling. I've told you before, you can always come home with me.'

'No! No, I love it here!'

'Are you sure?'

'Absolutely sure.' Andy hesitated. 'It never even occurred to me that the house might be haunted until someone mentioned ghosts at a supper party I went to last week. Even then, I wasn't worried. You know me.' She smiled at her mother. 'Catrin is part of my dreams, but I think she is a ghost as well.' She paused. 'If she is, if there are ghosts here, it's interesting. It doesn't bother me.'

'You're sure it doesn't frighten you?'

'No, it doesn't.'

Nina screwed up her face. 'As I reminded you, darling, this is not my department. I am impervious to ghosts. If you want to discuss it, you should ring your father. But my instinct is to leave well alone. Living up here completely alone is going to be quite enough of a challenge, I would have thought, especially as winter sets in. Have you thought about that? What you will do when it snows?'

Andy smiled, glad of the change of subject. 'Sue left me a book of instructions. She has actually been a bit more organised than I thought. I suspect she wrote it all out when she first decided to let the house. She left it in the drawer with the cat

80

food. She talks about stocking the freezer, getting an extra couple of months' supply of logs, contacting the farmer who lives up the lane and who will plough it through with his tractor if it gets closed with snow. It all seems very efficient, and if dear old Sue, whose natural habitat is Bondi Beach, can hack it here, so can I.'

'That all sounds very organised, as you say,' Nina said, reassured. She leant forward purposefully. 'Now, talking of being organised, what have you done about your job?'

Andy reached for a slice of toast. 'Nothing.'

'Why not?'

'In case you hadn't noticed, Mum, Graham is dead.' Andy gripped her mug tightly with her fingers.

Nina ignored the comment. 'You didn't always work exclusively for Graham,' she said crisply. 'There are plenty of other people out there who would love you to illustrate their books. Thank God that's a job you can do, even out here. Have you been in touch with Krista?'

Andy shook her head wordlessly. Speaking to her agent was something that hadn't even crossed her mind.

'God, Andy! You need a kick up the backside, darling.' Her mother was incredulous. 'Money doesn't grow on trees. You're going to have to live. I bet Sue isn't paying the bills for this house. Even if you're getting it rent-free – you are getting it rent-free, aren't you?' – she barely waited for Andy to nod before proceeding – 'you're going to have to pay the bills, pay for food, petrol, everything. And if necessary a solicitor. No!' she raised her hand as Andy opened her mouth to protest. 'You are not going to let that dreadful Rhona woman ride roughshod over you. You've had a couple of months to get over Graham's death, and I know you feel you never will, but you have to pick yourself up and dust yourself off.' She stopped. 'Did you ever hear such a string of clichés! But I've always found that clichés are what people need when they're in crisis. That is what they are for. One hasn't time to think of bons mots. One needs a good cliché.'

Andy managed a laugh. 'If anyone is riding roughshod, Mum it might be you.'

'That's what I'm here for. And is that your gardener outside? Who's paying for him?'

'Gardener?' Andy looked, startled, at the window.

'Tall, devilishly attractive man, carrying a spade over his shoulder.'

Andy suppressed a smile. 'Bryn. That's him.'

'So, you had noticed he's attractive?' Her mother raised a quirky eyebrow.

'Not till you said it just now,' Andy protested. 'I actually find him rude and unpleasant. He doesn't like the look of me either, so I'm avoiding him.' She bit her lip. 'And you're parked in his space so he'll be even more rude and unpleasant. I wonder where he's left his van. I don't suppose there's room for three out there.'

'Perhaps he walked. It is a lovely day. Where does he live?'

Andy was silent while she thought. 'Do you know, I haven't a clue. I don't even know his surname.'

Nina pulled a face. 'I don't much like the idea of someone like that wandering round the garden up here with you when you're alone.'

'Don't be silly! I may not know him, but Sue obviously does. And so do my neighbours, so there's nothing to worry about. And for goodness' sake don't rush out there and antagonise him or he will walk out on me and I'll be left in the most awful hole!'

'Literally,' her mother commented with grim humour. 'I won't say a word, darling. But asking him about how he expects to be paid will give you an excuse to go out and have a word with him. Why not take him a coffee?'

'I offered before and he said no.'

'He might not say no this time.' Nina was in management mode. She stood up, reached for a clean mug. 'Does he look like a man who takes sugar? No. I would say not.' She pushed the mug towards Andy. 'Go.'

It wasn't worth arguing. Andy pulled open the door and

walked out into the wind and sunshine. 'Bryn?' He was pruning a hedge on the far side of the nearest bed to the house. She walked towards him and pushed the mug into his hands without giving him the chance to refuse. 'I'm sorry if my mother is parked in your space. We weren't expecting you. I have no way of knowing which days you come unless you tell me.'

He stared at her as if debating whether to reply or walk off, then he cupped his gloved hands round the mug and blew on it. 'I don't have a regular day. I come when the weather is right,' he said. 'If that bothers you, we can arrange something I suppose.'

'Do you garden for other people round here?' Andy asked curiously. 'Is that the way you work it out with them?'

He nodded. He took a sip from the mug. 'I work two or three days for Sue, then two days for Colonel Vaughan up at Tregarron Farm and one for the Peters on the far side of Capel-y-ffin. None of them mind when I turn up.'

'Then I don't either.' Andy ventured a tentative smile. 'I was just worried about your parking.'

'There's plenty of room, no problem. If people park carefully.' Draining the mug, he handed it back to her. 'Thank you.'

'It's a pleasure.' She turned away then remembered. 'By the way, I'm not sure what the arrangement is about paying you?'

'Don't worry about that either. Sue pays me by direct debit.'

She laughed. 'I might have known she would be efficient. Good, I'm glad that's all taken care of.'

'So you should be. I'm expensive.' He almost smiled, then he turned back to the pruning.

'There,' Nina said as she went back indoors. 'That didn't seem to hurt too much.'

Andy sat down at the table. 'No. Not too much. Sue pays him by direct debit.' She couldn't contain another peal of laughter. 'He's probably a limited company!'

Catrin enjoyed that summer more than she would have thought possible. They had moved on as soon as the horse was sound, riding slowly and carefully now, sometimes through gentle well-tended farmland, sometimes through wilder hills, each evening stopping at a farm or manor house or a castle, sometimes moving on daily, sometimes staying a week or more in one place.

Realising that Dafydd often rode in a daze of inattention, rehearsing new rhymes and ideas in his head, Edmund took to leading the pack mule beside him, watching where the cob put her feet; sometimes though there were tracks where the going was easy and he would drop back beside Catrin and they would fall into stilted conversation. She was intrigued by his knowledge of healing, his way with animals. They discussed herbs and the making of salves and potions, something that was more often than not the job of the women in a household. At each outpost on the road guard dogs would race out barking and snarling but within a short time they would be clustering round him, making friends, tails wagging, begging for his attention, all hostility forgotten. It was a boon. Catrin remembered only too well previous trips with the hapless Roger Miller when she had cowered on her pony, terrified of the dogs until they had been called off.

'How do you do it?' she asked after yet another greeting by animals who seemed to think of him as an old friend.

He laughed. 'Ignore them; don't show you are afraid. Greet them when they come to you as you would a friend. Then ignore them again. They must learn you are not creeping into their house. You are here by right, to greet their masters, and you greet them as well.' He fondled the ears of the huge wolf-hound which was standing in front of him. Catrin smiled. She was not sure it was quite that easy, but she was prepared to try.

As they moved north up the March her dreams had moved with her. At night as she climbed into yet another strange bed under yet another unfamiliar roof she slipped almost gratefully into the darkness, aware that she would return in her dreams to Sleeper's Castle. But once there her dreams were not always kind. Insistently, again and again she found she could hear the distant call of the drums, the blast of war trumpets and the scream of horses. The ground would shake beneath heavy hooves and in her sleep she would toss and turn and whimper in the dark, and she would wake and sit up, and gather her cloak around her shoulders and try to still the anxious thudding of her heart.

It was not meant to happen. On a well-organised journey it would not have done so, but one night in June they found themselves too far from their destination as night fell and Edmund insisted that, rather than travel on in the darkness, luminous as it was, they find a sheltered spot to stop. The high moorland was deserted; with light still persisting in the north-west as he tethered the three animals, Edmund removed their saddles and the packs and lit a fire in the shelter of a steep gulley.

Catrin glanced around nervously. 'Are you sure we will be safe?'

'As sure as I can be.' Edmund watched as Dafydd wandered off a little way, trying to ease the stiffness in his bones. Even here, in the dark, they saw him reach for the tightly stoppered inkhorn and quill at his belt and scribble something on the scrap of parchment he pulled from his pouch. 'Better this than have a horse trip or your father fall from his saddle with exhaustion. We'll move on early in the morning. Come, sit here.' He patted the ground near him. 'I have oatcakes and cheese enough for us all and we have warm cloaks. We'll be fine.'

Hesitantly Catrin lowered herself onto a flat rock near him and watched as he coaxed a fire into life. He produced the food and horn mugs from one of the saddlebags.

Catrin smiled. 'Do you always travel prepared for every eventuality?'

He nodded. 'On a journey like this it is sensible. See, I have put the saddles here in the shelter of the rocks. You and your father can lean against them to sleep and be reasonably comfortable. I have ale which we can mull if you wish.' He had unpacked a leather flask.

The horses were already grazing the short sweet mountain grass; as it grew darker Catrin looked round for her father. 'Where is he?' she cried. He had been sitting some distance from them, squinting down at his notes in the firelight, but now as the moon rose slowly on the horizon she realised he had disappeared.

Edmund scrambled to his feet. 'You stay here. Don't move. I will go and find him.'

She peered after him into the darkness, relieved as the moon rose higher to see the soft light flood the broad valley below. There was no sign of anything moving, but she was still nervous. They shouldn't have stopped. It would have been safer to continue to their next destination; the moonlight would have kept the trackways safe, safer than this, anyway, camped here in the mountains with her father missing. She stood up and stepped away from the fire, scanning the countryside. There were great black pools of darkness where the moonlight couldn't reach, shadows, ravines, deep hiding places behind rocky outcrops. In the distance she heard the lonely whistle of peewits from the high moors and she shivered. There was no sign of Edmund, no sound at all apart from the birds. She glanced at the animals. If there were anyone out there, close at hand, they would hear. In Elfael they had heard wolves in the distance once. They were relaxed, happy, nibbling the grass. Then as she watched them all three stopped eating and raised their heads, ears pricked as they looked down towards the shoulder of the hill where the track disappeared into the deep shadow. Catrin took a step backwards and pulled her cloak more tightly round her shoulders, straining her eyes to see what it was the horses had heard, then she saw two figures appear in the distance. She breathed a sigh of relief.

Her father was not happy. 'I needed to be alone,' he grumbled as Edmund handed him a mug of ale. 'I cannot think, always in company! Either we sit in busy halls or I am with you two and your endless chatter, chatter, chatter!'

Edmund and Catrin glanced at each other, both aware that they never chattered, that there was more often than not an uneasy silence between them as they traversed the lonely roads. Edmund winked at her and Catrin found herself responding with a smile. 'I am sorry, *Tad*, but you should have told us, then we wouldn't have worried. I thought you might have been lost in the dark.'

Dafydd threw himself down on the ground beside her and accepted a hunk of cheese and an oatcake from Edmund, who then went and sat at a distance away from them, near the horses, which had resumed grazing. The moon faded into darkness behind a wall of cloud and the only light came now from the embers of the fire. Edmund did not attempt to revive it.

'Edmund and I will not say a single word now, so you can think in peace,' Catrin said after a long pause. 'Goodnight, *Tad*.'

Her father grunted. He hunched himself deeper into his cloak and sat with his back to her.

It was several hours later when Catrin awoke. The moon had moved across the sky and there was a line of light on the eastern horizon. The fire, she realised, was burning again and a hunched figure sat beside it. She was stiff and cold and the ground felt very hard as slowly she sat up and dragged herself to her feet. She went across and knelt near the warmth, holding out her hands.

'Did I wake you?' Edmund was huddled in a horse blanket, sitting cross-legged, his eyes on the flames.

'I'm glad you did. I am frozen.' They were both speaking quietly. The hunched figure of Dafydd lay with his back to them without moving.

'It will soon be light,' Edmund went on. 'Then we can get back on the road.'

'Are you sorry you agreed to come with us?' Catrin asked after a short silence.

'No.' There was a short pause. 'I am enjoying it.'

'Really? Two mad poets with no sense of time or direction!'

He laughed softly. 'Two talented people who need me to set them right. But it was no one's fault we were delayed yesterday. The road was hard and steep and the horses are tired. If we rest for a while at our next stop we will be back on schedule. Your father wants to travel all the way up the March beyond Oswestry and Chirk.' He glanced up at her. 'Has he mentioned to you that he wants to go so far?'

Catrin nodded. 'We always go that far. We usually visit the same people each year, so he doesn't have to tell me. One of his chief patrons is the Lord of Glyndŵr, whose lands lie in that direction. His family have been friends to us and beg us to return each time we go and see them.' She smiled. 'This is a good way of life.'

'In spite of the trouble between Wales and England?' He hugged his knees, staring into the smouldering ashes.

'There is always unrest somewhere. We manage to avoid it.'

She heard him sigh. He rested his forehead on his knees. 'Have you heard different?' she asked after a moment.

'As you said, there is always something; one lord takes offence at another; the Welsh are treated badly by the English – even I can see that; the laws against them are prohibitive.'

She smiled. 'You don't consider yourself Welsh, Edmund?'

He shook his head. 'I was born in England and I am loyal to King Henry.'

'Joan told me you plan to join his army to fight the Scots.'

He didn't reply.

'If you were called to arms by your liege you would have no choice,' she prompted.

She saw his shoulders tense, then relax. 'I am a good archer,' he said at last. 'I've trained since I was a child. I believe I am good enough to join an elite band, make a name for myself; make money.'

'My father's family, my family, have always had Welsh allegiance,' she said quietly. 'Though living as we do in the March it pays to be reticent about one's politics.'

'That would always be wise. Especially now, as your father visits the houses of both Welsh and English. I see even the most ardent supporters of King Henry enjoy your father's Welsh songs.'

'Which he carefully sings in English for their ears.'

'It is like walking a tightrope as the acrobats do.' He sat back and took a deep breath. 'Maybe we should think about packing up our camp and moving on. It is growing lighter now.' He turned and faced her. 'While we are on the road my allegiance is to you and your father, Catrin, in whichever house we find ourselves.' He gave her a reassuring smile. Before she could react he had scrambled to his feet, heading towards the horses, leaving her staring after him.

7

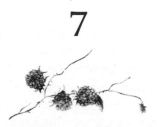

Nina dropped her bombshell as they were wandering round Hay next morning. 'I'm so sorry, darling, but I'm going to have to go back tomorrow.'

Andy felt a lurch of disappointment. 'Why?' It was too soon. She had thought they would have plenty of time to talk and explore; time to settle into Sleeper's Castle, knowing there was someone else there at night, along the landing, someone real and strong and reassuring.

'I've had a text. It's a pupil I've been coaching. She's been asked to go and play as part of an interview and she's very nervous. I promised I would help her with her party pieces.' Nina smiled fondly.

For as long as she could remember, Andy had heard the tentative notes of the piano echoing through the house, becoming less and less tentative and more and more competent as her mother's pupils progressed. Even better had been the occasional glorious sound of her mother playing alone in the sitting room of the cottage in the evenings, filling the place with music. Andy would turn off her radio or the TV and sit staring into space listening, transported by the beauty of the sound.

'I'm sorry, darling.' Nina touched her arm, sensing the wave of devastation which swept over her daughter.

'No, don't be silly.' Andy shook her head fiercely. 'That's what is so special about you. You're always there for people.'

'And I wanted to be here for you.'

'You are. You have been. After all, you can come back.' Andy swallowed hard. 'Perhaps we can book a nice long holiday for you to come up, when none of your pupils are likely to need you?'

Nina gave her a thoughtful glance. 'You're strong Andy,' she said. 'And I can see you're loving it up here. Those moments of doubt will come less and less often as you get used to being without Graham. I promise you, darling.'

Nevertheless, one of those moments of doubt hit her the following day after she had waved Nina out of sight down the lane and she was once more alone. The day was cold and grey. A soft mizzle of rain lay like a damp blanket over the valley and the house felt very empty. There was no sign of Pepper when she went back inside, closed the door and headed for the kitchen; through the window the garden looked sodden and messy, the first leaves already off the trees and lying yellow on the lawns. No doubt the brook would be gathering strength to roar through the night and keep her awake. She sighed and began to gather their lunch plates and put them in the sink. She was too downhearted to do more. Wandering through the house she listened to the silence. Once she stopped and looked round. 'Catrin?' she called. 'Are you there?' But there was no answer. There wasn't even any wind in the chimneys to drown out the sound of the steadily falling rain on the flagstones outside the windows.

Huddled under the duvet in her bedroom she put on the bedside lamp and reached for one of her favourite books. Later she would turn on the TV or perhaps start to plan a supper party to return Sian's hospitality. Anything to distract her. She didn't want to think about Kew. She didn't want to think about Rhona there in her home, Graham's home, desecrating the place, taking ownership of everything Andy treasured and loved. She didn't want Rhona invading her memories. Better to try and forget.

But it was no good.

'Graham,' she whispered. 'Where are you?' The loneliness was unbearable.

On that last sunny day she and Graham had spent at the house in Kew before he had had his terrible life-shattering diagnosis they had wandered out onto the terrace with a jug of Pimm's and two glasses and the Sunday papers. She was barefoot; she remembered clearly the wood of the boards warm under her feet. Graham of course would have been wearing shoes. She didn't ever remember seeing him without shoes in the garden. In her mind she put down the paper and her glass and she walked down the steps onto the grass, which was soft and warm beneath her toes.

As she walked across the lawn the sun went in and a cloud crossed the sky, blotting out the blue. The first drops of rain began to fall.

She turned and looked back at the house. It had changed. The season had changed. It was raining hard now; Graham had gone. The table on the terrace was deserted, raindrops bouncing off its surface. Before going in he had tipped the chairs against it so the rain ran off their seats. It was the last time they had sat outside together.

Running up the steps she put out her hand to the door. 'Let me in, Graham,' she called. But the door was locked. There was no Graham there.

Rhona shivered as she walked down the passage towards the back of the house. It was a dull wet day and the building felt empty and cold and sad. Pushing open the door and switching on the lights she walked into the kitchen and stopped short.

There was a figure outside on the terrace, peering in through the glass of the French doors. Miranda. She could see her clearly. With an exclamation of utter fury she turned and ran back into the hall. With only the smallest hesitation she picked up the phone in the living room and dialled 999.

There was a clean wash of cold sunshine across the garden next morning as Andy walked into the kitchen and switched on the radio. There was no sign of Pepper but she filled his bowl with biscuits, rather hoping the familiar rattle would bring him bouncing in through the cat flap. There was still no sign so after a minute she put it on the floor anyway; he was probably celebrating the return of the sunshine and would come in later. She reached for the jar of muesli and was stooping to take the jug of milk out of the fridge when there was a knock at the back door.

The policeman was tall and fair-haired and accepted a cup of tea with alacrity. 'I just need to establish your whereabouts last night, Miss Dysart.' Sitting at the kitchen table he smiled at her as he reached for his notebook.

She stared at him, confused. 'I was here. Why?'

'Can you prove it?'

She frowned. 'My mother was here until about four o'clock. She'd been spending the weekend with me. I saw her off down there in the lane.' She had glanced down at the parking space when he arrived and seen the blue-and-yellow squares of the police car with the Welsh word *Heddlu* inscribed across the doors parked in the space where her mother's Citroën had been.

'And your mother could vouch for your presence here and the time she left?'

'Yes, of course she could. Why? Is she all right? Oh my goodness, she hasn't had an accident?' Andy was suddenly frantic.

'No. No. Nothing like that.' He smiled at her reassuringly. 'I'm sure there's nothing to worry about. It must be a case of mistaken identity. There has been a complaint that you were harassing someone in Surrey last night.'

'Oh no. Not Rhona.' Andy looked at him in despair. 'Rhona Wilson? In Kew?'

'So you do know the lady?'

Andy sighed. 'Oh yes, I know the lady. She's the former wife of the man I lived with for ten years. She can't forgive him, or me, for being happy together after she left him. She's a vindictive bitch.' She smiled at him apologetically. 'Sorry, I probably shouldn't have said that. But really . . . No, I wasn't harassing her last night. I was here. I can't prove it, though; there wasn't anyone else here to back me up.'

'Your mother left at about four o'clock, you say?'

Andy nodded.

'Well, the complaint was made at six fifteen last night. So unless that car out there is a great deal faster than it looks . . .' he looked up and gave her an apologetic grin, 'I don't see how you could have driven to Surrey in the time. Would your mother confirm the time she left?'

Andy nodded again. 'I'm sure she would. She's very accurate about things like that.'

'Perhaps you could give me her address and one of my colleagues can take a statement from her. Then we can put Mrs Wilson's mind at rest. Have you any idea why she should think you were at her house yesterday evening?'

Andy gave a groan. 'If anyone was being harassed it was me. She drove me away after Graham died a couple of months ago. He left me the house in his will, but the will disappeared.' She paused. 'I can't prove that either. She just upped and moved in. I decided it was better I leave the area, and I was lucky that Sue, the lady who owns this place, was going away and needed a house-sitter. So I quietly faded out of Rhona's life. Or I thought I had.'

He was staring at her, his elbows on the table, his yellow jacket crackling slightly as he lifted his mug to drink. 'That's Sue Macarthur? She's gone to Australia?'

Andy nodded. 'You know her?'

He smiled even more broadly. 'Everyone knows everyone round here, you'll find.'

'Do you mind me asking how you knew where I was?' Andy shivered. 'Rhona was very unpleasant after Graham's death. She rang me constantly and made life very unhappy for me. I was anxious she shouldn't know where I was living after I came to Wales.'

He flipped the page back on his notebook. 'Mrs Wilson said a James Allardyce would know where you were. He was contacted and he gave your address to the constable in charge of the case.'

'James,' Andy whispered. One of the trusted few who had sworn not to tell Rhona where she was. 'Will the police have told her I'm here?'

He hesitated. 'They will tell her that we have proved you couldn't have been in her back garden. I will mention to my Surrey colleague that you want your whereabouts protected. I'm sure they would keep it confidential anyway.'

'I hope so. James shouldn't have told anyone where I was. I thought I was safe here.'

'Mr Allardyce had no option but to tell the police,' he replied reproachfully. 'But I will make sure they understand the situation. They're used to dealing with domestics.'

Andy gave a small laugh. 'A domestic? Is that what this is?'

'Well, I admit it is unusual. And the fact remains, if it wasn't you banging on her kitchen door, then who was?' He glanced up at her again. 'Perhaps she was dreaming.'

His quick look had been casual, but she could see him trying to read her mind, double-check, form a judgement.

He pushed away his mug, standing up at last. 'Well, I'm sorry to have disturbed you so early. I will report back and make sure they understand the situation. Obviously Mrs Wilson was mistaken. I'm sure we won't have to bother you about this again.'

Andy watched from the window as his car reversed out of the parking space and turned down the lane. She sighed and glanced at her watch.

'James? You swore you wouldn't tell anyone where I was!' She was clutching her phone as she stared out of the window a few minutes later. The watery sunlight was throwing a pale wash of colour across the garden.

'Oh God!' she heard James's voice so clearly he could have been in the room. 'I am so sorry, Andy. The police came over late last night. They insisted on knowing where you were. I gather Rhona told them I knew you and would know how to get hold of you. What's happened? They wouldn't tell me.'

'She's accused me of harassing her. A policeman has just been here to check on my whereabouts.' Andy scowled. 'I think Mum can give me an alibi. She's been here for the weekend, and although she'd gone by the time Rhona thought she saw me, the policeman pointed out I couldn't have driven from here to Kew in that time.' She heaved a deep sigh. 'I wish that woman would leave me alone, James. I hope to goodness the police don't tell her where I am.'

'I explained the situation to the chap who came here. I emphasised that she was paranoid and had threatened you,' James said. 'I am sorry, Andy. God, Graham would be so angry if he knew what was happening!'

Andy nodded sadly. 'Well, thanks for making it clear what the situation was. Hopefully that will be the end of it. Come and see me, James. Bring Hilary.'

'We might well do that, Andy.' She could hear the smile in his voice. 'I'm due some holiday, so perhaps we can work something out. And if we come, I promise we will drive round in circles to make sure we're not followed.'

She stood for a while, continuing to stare out of the window after they had ended the conversation. She should have known that James would not have given her whereabouts away willingly. He and his wife Hilary were the most trustworthy people she knew and she missed them dreadfully, she realised, as she missed so much of her previous life. She sighed with a rueful smile. So, who had been looking into Rhona's window last night? She thought back to her solitary daydream. Had Rhona been right? Was it her? She remembered the last time she had thought about the garden; Rhona's angry shout, her pointed finger. She shivered. If Rhona could see her back there in Kew, could she also somehow see Andy here, where she was now, in Wales?

She looked round thoughtfully. This was a house of dreams. For generations it had had the reputation for being a magical place where Druids and poets dreamed of the future. Did it have the power to make dreams of the past real as well?

Slowly, carefully, Dafydd, Catrin and Edmund wound their way northwards from house to house and castle to castle, following ancient trackways and drove roads, newer cart tracks and roads. Over mountains and along river valleys they made their way from Presteigne to Bryn y Castell, near Knighton and on towards Newtown, then spent a week at the great castle at Welshpool. By the end of July they were at Oswestry then Chirk. After a discussion they decided to avoid Wrexham, where on their previous trip Dafydd had encountered the town's resident bard who had vociferously resented their arrival. Instead they turned west towards Llangollen, where in past years they had found a far more favourable reception in the houses of one or two richer merchants and in a farmhouse on the hillside. From there they planned to travel south across the Berwyn Mountains towards Sycharth, the home of Dafydd's most generous patron, the Lord of Glyndŵr. From there they would continue south, heading back towards home.

It had been a good summer. On the whole Catrin had enjoyed herself. Her father's health had improved with good food and the stimulating company. He had blossomed and put on weight. They had visited old friends, made new ones and earned good payment; buried in the panniers on the pack mule was enough in gifts and coin to keep them over the following winter. Only their outward appearance of poverty and Edmund's trusty sword kept them safe from being robbed, but this year they had been lucky and seen little of footpads and thieves, and those they had witnessed had been but shadows in the distance, on their way to accost other more wealthy-looking travellers.

But the time had come to think of home. It was imperative they reach the end of the journey before the weather broke and the roads became impassable. Besides, Catrin was finding it increasingly difficult to hide her dislike of Edmund from her father.

It had started with a disagreement over the places they were to visit. They were sitting beneath the shade of a copse of trees, resting the horses, and Dafydd was dozing, his back against the trunk of an ancient rowan.

'You must wake him.' Edmund had led each of the horses in turn down to a mountain brook and allowed them to drink. He had grown impatient, his eye on the horizon and the huge clouds piling up in the west. 'There is a storm coming and it would be nice to be safely under cover before it breaks.'

Catrin stretched lazily. 'Not yet. Let him sleep. He so seldom manages to find rest.'

'He is always resting!' Edmund snapped. 'You wear yourself out running after him and he sits and allows you to wait on him hand and foot. You earn as much as him; you are as good a poet as him. Give yourself a little leeway for once.'

She scrambled to her feet. 'Don't you dare talk about him like that!'

'Why not? It's the truth. And you will be the first to worry and fret if he gets wet in the storm. Then it will all be "Hurry, Edmund, *Tad* mustn't get soaked. Hurry, Edmund, *Tad* is shivering, we must find him shelter!"' His voice slid into a falsetto parody of hers.

'He's right, Cat.' Their raised voices had awoken Dafydd. He stretched and with a groan dragged himself to his feet. 'I do not like getting soaked and that storm is obviously coming this way.'

'I just wanted to allow you a few more moments of sleep,' Catrin retorted.

'And then you wake me with your shrieking,' Dafydd grumbled. 'Get the horses saddled, Edmund, and let's be on our way.'

He stamped away from them and stood gazing out across the waving grasses of the sunlit moorland towards the mountains, where already they could see the occasional flash of lightning against the black of the western sky.

Catrin turned on Edmund furiously. 'Now you've upset him!' she snapped.

'I've done nothing of the sort. He can see that storm as easily as I can. I'm amazed you don't seem to understand it's coming this way. You will be soaked too. Your cloak will be sodden. Your belongings in those bundles will be drenched as much as your father's, and we will arrive looking like drowned rats!' He turned away and reached for one of the saddles, humping it onto Dafydd's horse. 'What if your father's books and scrolls get wet again?' he called over his shoulder as he reached under the horse's belly for the girth. 'And your harp. It won't be my fault if they are ruined one of these days!'

'It will be your fault. It's your job to pack them properly and look after us!' she cried. She began to stuff all her own things into her saddlebag and turned to pick up her cloak. She had been sitting on it and it was creased and grass-stained. She shook it angrily. Edmund left Dafydd's cob and turned to her pony. He lifted her saddle with ease, cinched it into place and then took the cloak out of her hands. 'I'll roll this for you and you can carry it in front of you. You will need it when it rains.' His face was set with anger.

Her fury flared to meet his. Without giving herself time to think, she stepped away from him and turned to face the storm. A gust of wind caught her skirt and pulled it out behind her as she raised her right hand and whispered the words of command that would chase the storm away. Silently she breathed a thank you to Efa and knew that the woman would hear. It was ancient magic and powerful, invoking the gods of thunder. As she watched she saw the lightning slice across the horizon, a vicious spark, resentful of her command, but the next flash was further away. Turning back, she smiled.

Edmund had seen her. She saw the shock on his face. Weather magic was witchcraft.

She glared at him defiantly.

He said nothing.

It took only minutes to put the three of them on the road once more, the two riders following Edmund as he led the mule down the steep track. Catrin did not glance over her shoulder towards the retreating storm. Somehow it seemed important not to acknowledge its existence.

Andy hadn't wanted to wake up. She had lain still, her eyes tight shut, grasping for the dream, but it had gone. With a sigh she went downstairs into the living room, and stood there looking at her piles of books. Her head was resonating with the story. So was it the house itself which was the custodian of Catrin's narrative? And perhaps Rhona's as well. If so, how? The idea was too exciting to ignore. House as an echo chamber. House as receiver of messages. House as medium for contact, not only with the past, but with parallel present existences.

Sitting cross-legged on the rug on the floor in front of her book collection, Andy began to shuffle through them, pausing every now and then to greet an old favourite, sorting them into different categories, discarding a few as not relevant to her present sphere of interest, piling others closer to read again soon. She had forgotten so much of this stuff, the fascination of combining serious scientific theory with the completely subjective nature of the actual experience.

What she needed was a couple of notebooks to start writing

down the experiences so as not to lose the freshness of describing the moment. Even the best scientist must find it hard sometimes to resist the urge to improve on an account of things that had come up in the course of an experiment. She wanted to keep her record accurate.

She sat back at last, pushed her hair out of her eyes, then scrambled to her feet. Scooping up an armful of books, she carried them back to the kitchen and stacked them on the table. She was tempted to go down to Hay now, to buy a notebook. She eyed her car keys, lying on the dresser.

But she was desperate to go back and see what happened to Catrin and Edmund. They were so real in her head. That spark of anger between them had been so spontaneous, his shock as she murmured that spell to divert the thunderstorm so obvious she couldn't bear to leave them like that, on the road in the middle of nowhere. Where were they going? What happened next? She had to find out and maybe she had had a long enough break to be able to go back to sleep?

But, did she have to be asleep? Could she just retreat into some sort of meditative state as she did when she visited Kew? This was what her books could tell her. Or her father. It was the sort of thing he would probably know. She reached for the phone.

'How are you, pet?' Her father's second wife, Sandy, was a lovely Northumbrian woman who had taken Andy to her heart. 'When are you going to come and see us?'

Her father it appeared was away at a conference. Sandy promised to make sure he rang as soon as he got back. They chatted for a while and Andy found herself immersed in news of her half-brothers' school exploits, the adventures of their two border terriers and Sandy's mother's operation. When at last she laid down the phone she stared at it sadly, astonished at how lost and lonely she felt.

She sighed. They were far away and part of another life and Catrin was here, waiting for her. Without her father's help it was up to her to work out a way of travelling back to that thundery Welsh mountain.

Aware that Pepper was sitting on the windowsill watching her with apparent interest, his paws tucked sleepily into his chest, she sat down and closed her eyes.

And found herself in the kitchen of her old home. The room was tidy, the only sign of occupation a carefully rinsed mug upside down in the draining rack beside the sink. She stared at it with a painful pang of nostalgia. It was a mug Graham had bought for her when they visited Chartres Cathedral together. It was decorated with the pellucid blues and reds of the beautiful medieval windows.

Looking down at it, Andy was overcome with anger. She reached out to the mug, intending to throw it on the floor and smash it; it was then she realised that she couldn't see her hands. She tried to pick up the mug but nothing happened. Her hand, if it was there at all, made no contact with the cold china. Her anger was replaced by irritation and then by a strangely analytical sensation of interest.

Rhona was sitting on the sofa in the living room going through yet another box of papers. Andy's papers. She looked up with a start as she found herself staring at Andy. For a split second the two women remained unmoving, holding one another's gaze, then the vision was gone. In the silence of the room someone screamed.

Andy jerked back to reality. Pepper had vanished through the cat flap. Moments later there was a knock at the door. 'Are you OK?' Bryn opened it without waiting to be invited. He glanced round. 'I heard you scream.'

Andy stared at him, confused. 'I didn't. At least, I don't think I did.'

'Then who was it?' He closed the door behind him. 'I saw

102

Pepper running through the garden as though the hounds of hell were after him.'

'Well, one hound, perhaps,' Andy muttered sourly. 'Or if we want to be technical, a bitch.'

'I beg your pardon?'

She shook her head. 'Sorry. It must have been me, mustn't it? I must have been the one who screamed. There's no one else here. I must have been dreaming. I've not been sleeping well and I fell asleep.' She was embarrassed at her stammered explanation and found herself avoiding his gaze. She could feel him studying her.

'Well, if you're sure you're OK,' he said at last.

'Yes, I'm OK.' She gave a weak smile. 'But thank you for looking out for me.'

He hesitated for a few seconds more, then without a word he turned and let himself out into the garden.

Andy's mobile rang. She picked it up. The phone had recognised the number. It was her old number. Graham's number. Kew's number.

Rhona's number.

She sat staring at the screen, her heart thudding, then she laid the phone down on the table before reaching out and switching it off. She sat without moving, waiting dry-mouthed for it to ring again. It didn't.

Andy was furious with herself. She hadn't intended to go back to Kew. Rhona had caused her enough embarrassment and misery to last a lifetime without aggravating the situation. She had wanted to see what happened to Catrin, not stir up a hornet's nest.

It wasn't until later, after she noticed that Bryn had gone home, that Andy realised she hadn't seen Pepper since his swift exit out of the cat flap. Anxious, she went out into the garden and began to call. There was no sign of him anywhere. The evening was soft with low slanting sunlight and, sure for once that she had the place to herself, she wandered out towards the far end of the garden. It was an irregular shape, roughly trapezoid, one side defined by the brook, the other by the ruins of the old wall and beyond them a high bank topped with wild hedgerows strung with hips and haws and sloes. At the far end of the garden there was an orchard of old gnarled trees, still laden with apples, some already standing over a carpet of windfalls. Behind that was an acre or so of wild meadow, which she was sure would be rich in herbs. The far corner above the brook was a rocky area that climbed steeply into something which would qualify, she reckoned, as a small cliff. She wandered towards it, still calling. She had realised almost at once that she would not be able to find Pepper unless he wanted to be found. This was his home. Hopefully, in spite of whatever eldritch screams had startled him, he would find his way back before too long.

She followed a narrow path towards the cliff, noticing an abundance of unusual plants on either side, thinking how much Graham had loved this place; would have loved to explore it now, at leisure, with her. No wonder he and Sue had been friends. The low sun was throwing deep shadows across the rock face, giving it a texture and shape that she found herself longing to paint. As she drew near she spotted a large fissure in the rock. Intrigued, she crept closer. It was broad and deep enough to allow her to edge sideways into the dark crack in the rock. At once she found herself in a small cave, faintly lit by the last rays of the setting sun. Pepper was sitting on the stony floor, washing his face. He paused in his ablutions for a full second, scanning her carefully, then he went on washing.

'I don't suppose you heard me calling,' Andy commented. She crept further into the cave. It was small, barely a foot above her head in height and perhaps ten feet across, but the far end was out of sight in the darkness and she found herself curiously reluctant to make her way further in to find out how far it went. She glanced up, expecting to see bats hanging from the ceiling. If there were any, would they still be there with Pepper sitting below them? She didn't know. She couldn't see well enough to tell. The cave had a strange silence, an atmosphere all of its own which was both intriguing and slightly unnerving. As she stood there it was growing darker as outside the sun sank lower into the haze. Turning, she retraced her steps. The sun was almost gone now behind the hills and as the sky flushed crimson, a line of dark shadow crept across the garden. With a shiver she made her way back towards the house. At least now she knew the dimensions of the estate and she had discovered Pepper's secret retreat. She let herself back into the kitchen and turned on all the lights. She glanced at the phone. No more missed calls.

Making her way to the desk in the living room she stood studying the watercolour sketch she had been working on: delicate fronds of fern, threaded with small pink heads of cranesbill. Sitting down, she picked up her brush.

Suddenly she didn't want to risk falling asleep again. It was too uncontrollable, too full on, too frightening.

8

There had been a long discussion about whether to change their plans and go north to Ruthin. Sir Reginald Grey, the Lord of Dyffryn Clwyd was not a popular man in the area and especially not with his southern neighbour the Lord of Glyndŵr with whom he had a long and festering legal dispute.

'But Lady Grey specifically invited us!' Catrin argued. The Lady of Ruthin had been a guest at the last manor house they had visited and she had taken to Catrin. The two women had talked and laughed and Catrin had played her harp long into the night when the ladies had withdrawn to their hostess's chamber. As was usual, Catrin was regarded as a fount of information. News and gossip was the mainstay of the travelling community's stock in trade, each household's occupants, as they moved on, eager to hear the latest information from the last. Catrin had long ago realised that this conversation was enjoyed as much by the ladies in their solars and bowers as was her harp playing. She was not entirely comfortable with this process but she recognised it was a way of paying for their food and board as much as her father's news and songs and poems were valued down in the main hall.

On this occasion she had felt her father's eyes watch her as the womenfolk left the hall. Of late he had seemed less than happy to see her so much accepted in her own right for her talent and now he was actually frowning.

When they left the manor a few days later, she asked him why.

'I do not want you to associate with the Greys,' was all he said.

'But why? I liked her enormously.' Catrin flashed to her new friend's defence.

'I am sure she is a commendable woman,' was his response, through tight lips. 'Her husband is not.'

'Her husband is rich and powerful. We would be well rewarded if we went to Ruthin Castle,' she retorted.

'Her husband is the mortal enemy of the Lord of Glyndŵr, who we go to see next.' The legal wrangle between the men had not been addressed in the courts in London, where it had been deemed of no importance, and Lord Glyndŵr had ridden back to Wales in a fury. Dafydd had picked up the news along the way; his daughter had obviously missed it.

Catrin paused. Lord Glyndŵr was one of her father's most generous and kind patrons. They had planned to spend a week or more with him and his family before turning south on the long weary trek home.

'We needn't tell them where we had been,' she said at last, on the defensive. 'He would never know.'

'No, Catrin.'

'I promised,' she muttered. 'I gave her my word. I liked her.' She glanced at Edmund, but if she thought she would find support there she was mistaken. He and she were barely talking and now as he tested the cob's girth and held the stirrup, waiting for Dafydd to mount, he was staring out of the gate towards the distant hills, seemingly uninterested in their conversation.

'One day at most,' Catrin pleaded. 'It is almost on the way.'

'It is a day's ride in the wrong direction.' Her father set his jaw.

'She promised me a bag of silver coins.' Catrin hated herself for her wheedling tone. 'And it would be wrong to break my word.'

Dafydd swung up into his saddle. 'It would be disloyal to the Glyndŵrs to keep it.'

'Then perhaps I can go there on my own. What is he supposed to have done to them, anyway?' She nudged her pony alongside his and with a last wave to the servants who were seeing them off they rode out under the courtyard archway with Edmund following behind.

'It is a long story,' Dafydd said.

'We have plenty of time.'

Her father sighed.

She won the argument and the welcome they received from Lady Grey made their furious quarrel and the arduous journey worth it.

As their weary horses skirted the town walls of Ruthin and they made their way towards the castle, set on a high ridge above the river valley in its own rich parkland, the thought of food and rest and of a dry, comfortable bed was foremost in all their minds.

The castle was huge. They drew to a halt to gaze up at the vast red stone walls and towers, above the largest of which hung Sir Reginald's blue, silver and red banner, rippling in the wind.

Edmund led them over the bridge which crossed the deep grassy moat, to the main gate in the outer wall. Accosted at once by a guard he glanced back uncertainly at Catrin. She rode up beside him. 'I have come at the personal invitation of Lady Grey,' she announced. As he led them under the raised portcullis and into the shadowy outer bailey she saw her father shiver.

*   *   *

That night she slept well. She had played and sung late, digging deep into her repertoire of ballads in Welsh and in English, playing her harp until she was exhausted and her fingers were raw. Her lodging was in the family's private quarters where she shared a bed with two of Lady Grey's maidens.

It was a comfortable bed and warm even though it lacked a tester and hangings. The Greys were moving south within the next few days, they were told, and already the private chambers of the lord and his wife were being stripped ready to be packed on the sumpter horses and heavy carts and transported to their next destination.

Waking at first light she lay still, staring up at the vaulted ceiling above her head, looking forward to the day ahead. There would be more stories and singing later and when they all gathered in the great hall for the main meal of the day maybe she would get the chance to sing to the whole household. She wasn't sure how long they would stay, maybe a day or so more, and then they would turn south again to ride back towards the Glyndŵrs' home at Sycharth. She snuggled down into the bed. It had all gone as she had hoped.

She couldn't get back to sleep and as she lay there, trying not to move for fear of disturbing her bedfellows, she found herself going over in her head her father's explanation of his reluctance to come here.

The Lord of Ruthin, was, according to her father, aggressive and acquisitive and had appropriated lands from his neighbours. Above all he had targeted the Lord of Glyndŵr, whose lands bordered his. 'The man has lied and cheated and woven tales about Lord Owain at the king's court,' Dafydd had said angrily. 'If you had been listening to the talk in the halls where we have stopped you would know the whole March is speculating about the situation. And on top of all that, Sir Reginald has now lied to the king, accusing the Lord Owain of being a traitor because, when the king summoned the men of the area to muster for his fight against Scotland, something Lord Glyndŵr had faithfully taken part in in the time of the old king, Grey deliberately failed to pass on the message so that Lord Owain is now held in contempt for not appearing on time! And Grey laughs up his sleeve at a trap cunningly laid and Lord Owain, who is a good and honourable man, is condemned.'

Catrin sighed. She had first met Lord Owain when her father had taken her to the Glyndŵrs' home at Sycharth near Llansilin in the valley of the River Cynllaith three years before when King Richard had still been on the throne. It was one of the first times Dafydd had taken Catrin on his travels, and at only fifteen years old she had been full of nervous excitement. On that occasion too, it had been early September when they had found themselves riding wearily down the track that led to the home of the Glyndŵrs.

It was a beautiful timber-framed manor house, on a motte within a protective moat, elegant and well furnished, with a separate great hall built within the outer bailey. It boasted gardens and orchards and fish ponds, lying in a broad basin in the hills, sheltered by a steep wooded ridge to the east, and she and her father had spent several wonderful weeks as the family's guests. She had sat with Margaret, the Lady of Glyndŵr, and two of her daughters, Catherine and Alys, talking and sewing and laughing, and she had sung to them accompanied by her own little harp and, to ensure the sun stayed shining, she had taught them one or two of her weather spells. She told them how to keep the sun steadfast in the sky, and how to make it rain and how to summon the mist down from the mountains. They had spent hours reciting her spells, flicking water drops at each other and fanning the roiling steam from water heated over the fire with special incantations and carefully chosen herbs to draw in the fog, giggling as they reached for their spindles or sewed by the fire, putting the formulae to the test. Sometimes it worked, sometimes it didn't. Either way it had been one of the happiest times of her life, her first experience of a loving close family. Their own house, Sleeper's

Castle, much as she loved it, had seemed poor and rough by comparison.

That summer had been full of happiness, a happiness that for the Glyndŵrs had now been broken by the massive injustice done to Lord Owain by the Lord of Ruthin, the same Lord of Ruthin in whose castle she now slept. And she had brought them here. Her impetuous liking for the man's wife and her insistence on the chance to display her talents to a new audience had overridden her father's loyalty to his greatest and most devoted patron. The realisation made her feel like a traitor. She turned over in bed and closed her eyes.

She remembered Lord Owain as tall and handsome, a strong man of middle years with enormous charm who had taken her hand and smiled at her and listened to her when, overcome with shyness, she had stammered one of her own poems to him before the entire household in his hall one evening. They had cheered and whistled when she had finished and he had given her a plaited silver ring as a present. She had worn it ever since. She raised her hand up from beneath the covers to look at it now and felt another twinge of guilt. It was easy to understand why her father had not wanted to come here.

But on the other hand this was their livelihood. They could not afford to turn down invitations to perform for their rich patrons and she had liked Lady Grey so much. Like Margaret Glyndŵr she was kind and motherly and warm towards the lonely girl. With a groan she turned over again and punched her pillow.

Beside her Mary, one of Lady Grey's personal maids, stirred and opened her eyes. She looked towards the window and seeing the wash of blue sky outside sat up, dragging the covers off the other two girls. 'Catrin, Anne, wake up. It is morning. We must get dressed.'

Washing in ice-cold water carried up the winding staircase by a scullery maid, the three young women dressed amid much giggling, then the girls led the way to the solar on the first floor of the tower where their breakfast was laid out on a table. Lady Grey was there already. Her face was white and strained, her eyes puffy with lack of sleep.

'I'm sorry, Catrin, but you have to leave as soon as you've eaten.' She groped on the table for a small pouch and pressed it into Catrin's hands. 'A small recompense for your kindness in coming so far. I realise it was out of your way.' She gave a tight smile. 'God bless you, child.' Without another word she turned and left the room.

Her maids looked at each other in dismay. 'What's happened?' Mary, the younger, asked out loud. 'Is something wrong?'

Catrin stared from Mary to her companion, hurt and frightened. 'Perhaps I had better leave now,' she said uncertainly.

'She said to break your fast,' Anne, the eldest, said firmly. 'At least take a morsel of bread and a mug of small ale, then we'll go down to the hall and find your father.'

There was no sign of Dafydd in the great echoing hall, nor in the private chambers of the tower. As Catrin grew increasingly worried, Anne and Mary searched for news of him. The place was empty. A few servants scurried to and fro, replenishing the fires in the two enormous fireplaces, scrubbing the trestles before stacking them at the side against the walls, until at last Catrin heard her name called.

'Over here. We are leaving now.' Edmund was standing in the doorway, clearly agitated.

'What is it? What has happened?' She ran over to him.

'Your father has been taken ill.' He saw Mary approach with two serving boys who were carrying Catrin's saddlebags and her harp, hurriedly stowed in its protective bag. 'Leave those. I'll take them.' He relieved the boys of their burden.

'What's wrong? Where is he?' Catrin cried.

'He's with the horses, ready to go.' Edmund bowed to Mary. 'We take our leave, mistress.'

Mary smiled at him coyly. She stepped forward and gave Catrin a hug. 'I hope your father is better soon.'

Catrin scurried out after Edmund. The outer bailey was busy, full of men and boys, horses and dogs, and she looked round for Lord Grey but there was no sign of him. Then she saw her father, already mounted, sitting slumped on his cob near the main gate.

'*Tad*, what is it? What's wrong?' She ran towards him, with Edmund carrying her bags behind her.

'Be quiet!' It was Edmund. He turned on her furiously. 'Say nothing. We are leaving now.' He threw her packs over the mule's rump and tucked the harp gently into one of the panniers, then he boosted her unceremoniously onto her pony's saddle. Beckoning her to follow, he went to the head of her father's horse and, taking the lead rein of the mule in his other hand, he led the way out beneath the great portcullis.

Catrin felt her cheeks stinging with embarrassment at his unceremonious treatment of her, aware of men watching and grinning as she rode across the cobbles. She looked back at the steps up to the tower doorway but there was no sign of Mary there.

'South. We have to go south,' Dafydd commanded hoarsely. 'To Sycharth. I need to speak to Lord Glyndŵr.'

'That's where we planned to go next, anyway,' Edmund retorted, his voice terse. 'I have already ascertained the best route. We need to go back towards Llangollen first, then south through Glyn Ceiriog, to the east of the mountains. We should be there before dark.'

Dafydd turned on him, his eyes wild. 'You told them where we were going?'

'I wasn't aware it was a secret, Master Dafydd,' Edmund was on the defensive.

'Not even when you heard the way the English were talking about Lord Owain last night?'

113

'Edmund wasn't with us last night,' Catrin put in sharply. 'If you remember he slept in the stables with the horses.'

Edmund grinned. 'Not quite as basic as that. I was given a straw mattress and a *brychan* above the stables with the horse boys. It was warm and we fed well. I was comfortable, at least until I was called in to see to you—' he broke off as he saw Dafydd's face.

'What is it, *Tad*, what is wrong?' Catrin repeated.

'What is wrong is that this part of the world seems to be on the brink of war,' Dafydd snapped. 'And that was my dream!' He gathered his reins. 'Or at least part of it.' He kicked the cob into a trot.

The other two followed him in silence as they headed south across the treed parkland. It was a while before they spoke again. Catrin kicked her pony alongside the men. 'So, are you going to tell me what happened? Why did we have to leave? Lady Grey had guests coming today. I was to play for them.' Trying to swallow her disappointment she reined in her pony. 'Stop!' she shouted in frustration. 'Tell me what has happened!'

Edmund halted the horses. He looked at Dafydd, who was slumped in the saddle, his face grey with exhaustion. 'Will you tell her or shall I?' His tone was bordering on the hostile.

Dafydd scowled at him. 'I remember nothing,' he said hoarsely.

Catrin slid from her pony's saddle and pulled the reins over its head, hitching it to a tree. She looked grimly at Edmund. 'You tell me.'

'He had a dream.' Edmund glanced at Dafydd.

Catrin's heart sank. 'What happened?'

'I was sleeping in the great hall with a couple of dozen other men. At least, I thought I was sleeping,' Dafydd said at last. 'I was wrapped in my cloak. It had been a good evening. Sir Reginald never appeared. Nor did most of his household. They said he was away, as was his steward. It didn't matter. There were others there. At first there was some hostility when they realised I was Welsh, but I sang in English and it went well.

114

They enjoyed it. I enjoyed it. We settled down. I slept. I remember no more.' He glanced at Edmund again.

Catrin's eyes were fixed on his face. 'That is not true, Father. You always remember your dreams,' she snapped.

'They told me he was snoring peacefully, but then he grew restless,' Edmund put in. 'Then he began to shout in his sleep. He was in great distress. They couldn't wake him so someone came to fetch me.' He hesitated. 'I have never seen anything like it.' He stopped again as if he were unable to go on. 'He was screaming. He sat up and threw off his cloak. His eyes were open, staring, but I knew he was seeing nothing. At least . . .' he waited as if hoping Dafydd would speak, 'he was seeing nothing outwardly. And he was yelling and shouting. Luckily he was speaking Welsh so they understood nothing. Lord Grey's household is English. I doubt there are any Welsh speakers there. I hope not,' he added fervently. 'He was seeing something in his dream, something so bad—' he broke off as Dafydd straightened his shoulders.

Dafydd looked at Catrin. 'I was seeing blood,' he said slowly, dragging the words out of the inner depths of his soul. 'I was seeing fire. I was seeing death. I was seeing this nation torn apart.'

Catrin felt a trickle of ice crawling through her body. Blood. Fire. Death. Those were the words he had written and then scratched out again and again on that scrap of parchment back in the spring.

'He woke everyone,' Edmund went on as Dafydd lapsed back into silence. He ran his hands through his hair. 'As I said, I doubt if many, or any of them spoke Welsh, but I'm pretty sure they got the gist of it.' With a sigh he looked round at the thick undergrowth in the distance. Alongside the road the cover had been scythed back, and there were sheep grazing on the shorter grass. Ancient oak trees sheltered the coverts where no doubt the Lord of Ruthin enjoyed good hunting. There was no sign of anyone else on the road.

Catrin was staring at her father's face in bewildered concern when abruptly Edmund put his hand on her arm. She jumped. His fingers tightened. 'Get back on your pony and ride slowly on,' he whispered. 'Now. Don't look round. There are horsemen in the shadow of the trees over there, in the distance. A lot of them. I don't know who they are, but I don't intend to find out. Just act casually. You too, Master Dafydd.' He looked anxiously at him. 'Follow her. I'll walk to the tree and relieve myself. It will serve as a reason we have stopped, and it will give me a chance to look round again, then I will follow on. I don't know if they have seen us, but with luck they won't do anything about it if they have. Hopefully they will know we were guests in the castle and leave us alone.'

Catrin obeyed him without argument. Her mouth dry with fear, she untied her pony, scrambled onto the saddle and turned back onto the road. Her father followed. Neither of them looked round. Catrin's fingers tightened on the pouch in her pocket that Lady Grey had given her. She hadn't even opened it. If it were stolen now she would never know what was in it.

She heard the click of hooves behind her. Edmund was following with the mule. Somehow she managed to keep herself calm. If the horses sensed her fear they would start to play up. She kept her eyes on the track ahead to where it curved out of sight between thick stands of trees.

She almost cried out in fear when she felt a hand on her stirrup. Edmund had caught her up. He pressed the lead rein of the mule into her hand. 'Ride on slowly. They can't see us now but they can probably hear the hooves on the stones. I'm going to double back and see what they're up to.'

'No!' Catrin reached out to him but he had gone, flitting like a shadow across the broad grassy verge and into the undergrowth.

'Stupid boy,' Dafydd muttered. 'He'll get us all killed.' He seemed finally to have gathered his wits. His eyes had cleared and he was sitting straight on his horse. He looked at Catrin.

116

'We have to go on. I have to speak to Lord Owain. This concerns him.' He shivered. 'This concerns him absolutely.'

There was nothing for it anyway but to ride on as though nothing had happened, first through soft loam under the scattered trees then onto a stony track, then on again, intensely aware that any moment a band of men might erupt out of the undergrowth behind them. There was no sign of Edmund.

'Perhaps he imagined it,' Catrin broke the silence.

'I don't think so. That boy is quite acute,' Dafydd said.

Catrin could feel her shoulders tense beneath her cloak as though expecting any minute to feel an arrow between her shoulder blades. Her stomach was tight with fear.

'It would be more normal to talk,' Dafydd said testily.

Catrin gave a wan smile. 'It would indeed. Are we on the right road?'

Her father nodded. 'We should be near Llangollen by noon. Edmund says Sycharth is another half-day's ride south from there.' He glared round. 'If we are spared.'

Catrin leaned forward to pat her pony's neck. 'They would have accosted us by now if they were going to.' She breathed a quiet prayer to the Blessed Virgin that her confident words were right.

'So, where is Edmund then?' Dafydd grumbled. 'He is supposed to protect us.'

'He hasn't done a bad job of it so far.' Catrin screwed up her nose. 'Perhaps he went to distract them before they saw us.' She was not going to admit how exposed she felt without his solid presence beside them. He might irritate her unbearably and drive her to distraction with his plodding gentleness with the horses and with her father, but now he was gone she felt bereft and very vulnerable.

'Keep going. You know what he said,' her father muttered beside her.

She did not realise she had allowed the horses to drift to a standstill. Her pony put its head down and tore at a clump of grass. She jerked at the reins. 'If he doesn't come soon we'll stop at the next brook to water the horses and wait for him for a while.'

Her father was squinting into the distance. 'We are coming out of the deer park here. The road will be more open soon. If they were going to attack us they would have done it by now,' he said.

She looked around nervously. In her heart she knew he was right, but even so she felt uncomfortable. She could feel a strange prickling at the back of her neck. They were being watched, she was sure of it. 'I wish Edmund would come back.' She regretted saying it as soon as the words were out of her mouth.

Her father gave a humourless laugh. 'So he's not so bad after all, eh? All your head-tossing and indignation and resentment, but you can't do without him when you get scared!'

'I'm not scared!'

'Well you should be. There are outlaws in these woods. They were telling me last night.' He gritted his teeth. 'In the pay of the Lord Glyndŵr, so they said.'

'And you guided us onto this road.' Catrin stared at him in horror.

'It is the way to Sycharth,' he protested. 'How else are we going to get there?'

She was speechless. The fact that her father could be so careless of their safety was beyond horrific.

'So, where is Edmund?' she said again. 'Surely he should have caught us up by now.' They both reined in their horses and turned to look back the way they had come. The road was empty but now suddenly Catrin knew with absolute certainty that someone was out there, watching them.

Andy stretched out and slowly she opened her eyes. She had been afraid of going to bed, of falling asleep and dreaming, but now she was reluctant to let go of the dream. It had been exciting, fascinating. She had been on horseback with Catrin and Catrin's father, hacking through the wooded hills. She could picture the trees, the sunlight shining down through the branches, smell the fresh scent of leaves and loam and grasses and even more immediate the rich savoury aroma of horse, a smell that took her back to her childhood. She raised her fingers to her nose, almost expecting to smell the horse sweat on them, the warm damp feel of the animal's neck under the coarse hair of its mane. There was nothing. She could still smell faintly the shower gel on her hands from the night before.

She pushed back the covers, swung her legs over the side of the bed and was about to stand up when she heard the voice again in her head.

Blood. Fire. Death.

She sank back with a shiver. Not all of the dream had been pleasant. She remembered now. Dafydd had had a nightmare, Dafydd the prophet. And that was what the old bards did, didn't they? They prophesied, be it glory or doom and destruction. Somehow they knew the future. She stood up, raising her hands to push her hair off her face, then groaned unexpectedly. She was aching all over. Her legs were in agony, her shoulders stiff. It was as if – she couldn't bring herself to acknowledge the fact – it was as if she had been on a long ride.

She stood for a long time under the shower, trying to ease the ache from her shoulders, then she went downstairs. Opening the back door she looked out into a garden wet with rain and smelling of autumn. Behind her Pepper was sitting by his empty bowl looking faintly reproving. Having fed him, she found a few scraps of paper in Sue's desk. While she made toast for breakfast she started to make notes about her experiences of the night before.

Dreams could be vivid. Dreams could seem very real. Dreams could leave you exhausted. All those things were well-known facts. Nothing to get excited about; nothing out of the ordinary. But definitely something to think about.

Another well-known fact: the more one recalled one's dreams, the more one could recall. It was a matter of practice. And it was important to write it all down at once. If possible, without thinking. Too much thinking and one's recall began to shift. A dedicated notebook began to look more and more imperative.

Another well-known fact: bits of paper got lost and out of order.

Andy ran into Ella Pascoe in the paper shop as she stacked two notebooks and a pack of pens onto the counter and fished for her purse. 'So, how are things?' Ella asked as they walked out of the shop together.

'OK.' Andy grinned at her. 'I'm being drawn into the history of the house. I would love to know a bit more about it some time when you've both got time.'

'I'm not the expert, that's Roy,' Ella replied. 'But if you've got a bit of time now, d'you fancy a coffee?' She had a newspaper under her arm. 'Roy and I take turns to take an hour off in the morning to read the paper. Coffee and cake is the order of the day, at least for me. A shocking and unhealthy habit, but I enjoy it. I would much rather talk to you and leave the paper until later.'

Andy led the way round the corner and into Shepherds overlooking the Cheese Market and the castle square. By the time they had collected their drinks and in her case a flapjack and in Ella's a piece of carrot cake, she had made up her mind to confide in her about her dreams.

They found themselves a table in the window. Ella rested her elbows on the table and scrutinised her face with interest as she listened.

'Is this delighting you or frightening you?' she said.

Andy smiled. 'Mostly delight. But a few of the dreams are quite violent.'

Ella looked shocked. 'Violent as in . . . ?'

'They're about war and the fear of war.' Andy leaned forward. Ella said nothing, waiting for her to go on.

'The latest dream was about a journey they're making on horseback up through the border March. It's all so real, so detailed; I woke thinking I must check out the facts to see if they are facts.' She paused, watching Ella cut her slice of cake into quarters. Absent-mindedly she gathered up the crumbs into a little pile, pressed her finger onto the pile, then licked it.

'Do you know what date you're dreaming about?'

Andy hesitated. 'I don't think they've mentioned any specific dates.' She kept her answer deliberately vague. 'They set off in the early summer.'

'Which any traveller would if they were planning a long journey on horseback.' Ella put one of her squares of cake delicately into her mouth and chewed thoughtfully. 'This sounds very intriguing. Do I gather you honestly think you're dreaming about something which might have actually happened?'

'I don't know. I don't see how I could be,' Andy conceded.

'Maybe you're reliving a novel you've read or a TV programme or a film?'

Andy gave a rueful nod. 'I suppose that's one explanation.'

'So, are you dreaming in episodes, like a serial? Does the story pick up where you left off each time you dream?' Ella went on, obviously intrigued.

'Pretty much. I came into town to buy a couple of notebooks so I could write down everything I could remember.' Andy pointed at her bag, sitting on the floor beside her chair, her purchases sticking out of the top.

'Sensible.' Ella smiled. She paused, looking out of the window up towards the castle, where its jagged silhouette rose black against the sky. A flock of jackdaws was swirling above it, noisily squabbling over the best perches on the bare branches of the surrounding trees. 'Have you seen Hay Castle in the dream?'

She shook her head. 'They've been to a lot of castles on their journey, but not Hay. The last one was called Ruthin.'

121

Ella put down her fork and stared at Andy. 'Ruthin? In the Vale of Clwyd? Are you sure? That's way up north of here. There's a hotel there. Perhaps you've stayed there? I'm sure one can find photos of it online.' She nibbled another square of cake. 'Are these the only dreams you have? About Catrin and her family? You don't dream about anything else?'

Andy paused for a fraction of a second. 'No.'

Andy saw Ella glance up at her hesitation, but she said nothing and Andy wasn't going to enlighten her. Her other dreams were her business alone. She wasn't ready to share information about her visits to Kew. She wasn't even sure they counted as dreams.

'Another coffee?' Ella's voice broke into her thoughts.

'That would be nice.' Andy was enjoying the other woman's company. She was lonely, she realised. It was a relief to sit in a warm, crowded little coffee shop with someone to talk to.

It took Ella several minutes to queue at the counter. When she returned Andy had taken out one of her new notebooks and begun to scribble in it. 'I'm going to make a note of anything I can remember. I don't think the dreams come from something I've read or watched. I've got a good memory, I would know,' she said firmly. 'I wonder if I've in some way plugged into these people's lives through the house. It all seems to fit, at least at the beginning it did.' She ignored the thoughtful expression on Ella's face. 'But now I wonder if Catrin or her father are driving the dreams?' She meant it as a serious question.

'You think Catrin is trying to tell you something?'

'Perhaps she is,' Andy said. She stared down into her cup. 'I think I may have seen her – or perhaps sensed her is a better word – in the house, when I was awake.'

'Not a ghost!' Ella sounded excited.

Andy smiled. 'I have always been interested in ghosts. I may not have seen one, but I do believe in their possibility.'

'I do too,' Ella said eagerly. 'Most people do, of course, whatever they say. In my case, it's probably as much a part of my interest in local history as anything else; I like to collect ghost stories. Sometimes they contain snippets of actual memories of past events. I'm sure they do.'

'I would love to think that is what this is,' Andy said. 'Two poets on tour and—' She broke off abruptly. 'I hope I'm not going to find out that their journey ended in tragedy.' She sighed. 'Sian took me up to see if there was any sign of your friend Meryn at his house,' she changed the subject.

Ella sat forward, her elbows on the table. 'And was there?'

'No.' Andy took a sip of coffee. 'What makes him such an expert on the paranormal?'

'What makes anyone an expert on anything?' Ella thought for a moment. 'Interest. Study. In the case of the paranormal, I suppose people feel they have a certain facility which is not given to everybody and when your name gets around then you become the local consultant of choice. Meryn claims to be something of an academic. He travels round giving lectures, although as far as I know he isn't attached to any university. His speciality is Celtic Studies but he also claims to be a spiritual man. Not too long ago a story went round that he was working with some people in the West Country and was involved in some sort of a haunting which involved Jesus's visit to Glastonbury.'

'*The* Jesus?' Andy said, startled.

Ella laughed. 'The one and only. Don't quote me. Perhaps one day he will tell you about it himself.'

'I am so looking forward to meeting him.'

'You will.' Ella hesitated, then pushed aside her cup. 'Be careful, Andy. Interesting as all this is, don't get drawn in too much. You've obviously got a good imagination. Don't let it get the better of you, will you.'

Andy drained the last dregs from her cup. 'Don't worry. If ever I wake up drenched in the blood of battle, you won't see me for dust. I shall be off back to London the same day!'

They both laughed.

Ella sighed, glancing at her watch. 'Much as I'm enjoying

123

this chat I have to go, I'm afraid. Roy will be cross if I'm late back to the shop. Keep me posted about what happens next to Catrin and her family, won't you.'

Andy watched her as she made her way to the door, greeting people as she went out, turning along Castle Street, threading her way through the morning shoppers until she was out of sight.

Why, she was wondering, hadn't she mentioned Owain Glyndŵr to Ella, the name that told her the exact date of Catrin's adventure – the early 1400s. Even she, as a mere Englishwoman, knew that Glyndŵr was one of Wales's greatest heroes, a freedom fighter and something of a King Arthur figure, half history, half myth. Instinct had stopped her talking about him, and maybe she had been right. She wanted to be a bit more sure of her facts before she talked about her dreams to anyone else.

She followed Ella out only a few minutes later, heading for the car park and home.

There was something she wanted to try.

Andy parked the car next to Bryn's van and sat glaring out of the window at it. It was wrong of her, she knew, but she couldn't help resenting his presence, turning up at odd hours, removing at a stroke her sense of privacy. Not that he was likely to bother her one way or the other. She got out of her car, glancing up at the front garden clinging to its precipitous perch above the parking area. The early morning rain had moved away towards the east and the sunlight was reflecting in a million raindrops, dazzling in their diamond brightness. She ran up the steps to the front door, let herself in and walked through to the kitchen.

Pulling off her jacket she hung it on the back of the chair. There was no sign of Bryn outside but even so his presence in the garden made her feel jumpy. She made her way up to her bedroom and closed the door behind her, then sat on the bed, settled back against the pillows and closed her eyes. She didn't want to sleep. She wanted to travel in her waking mind. Could she guide herself back in meditation or reverie and control what happened? One or two of her books seemed to think it was possible. It was worth a try.

Carefully and in as much detail as she could manage, she imagined herself back into Catrin's world. She pictured the trees, the horses and the mule with its long velvet-lined ears, the mist hanging on the horizons. She smelt the scent of the sweet grasses under their hooves as they rode.

It didn't work.

She kept her eyes closed and tried to make herself relax until she found herself struck with an unexpected pang of guilt. How Graham would have hated her doing this. She could picture his face, almost feel his cold scorn at such childish behaviour. 'Grow up, Andy!' His voice seemed to echo round the room. 'Get a real life!'

He was sitting outside on the terrace, a glass of wine at his elbow, a newspaper lying folded on the table beside it. He was leaning back in his chair, his eyes closed against the sunlight. She watched, holding her breath, noting every tiny detail of his face, the sunburned V revealed by the open neck of his shirt, the tiny fair hairs on the backs of his fingers gold in the sunshine to match his unruly hair. She felt herself smile.

'Graham,' she whispered. 'Can you see me?'

He didn't move.

She could see herself tiptoeing up the steps from the lawn and standing near him, but there was something not quite right in the picture. She moved uncomfortably on the bed and realised that she was still there, in her bedroom, that this picture in her mind was still just that, in her mind. She leaned towards him and reached out her hand, but she was casting no shadow as she came between him and the sun. He was smiling lazily now, the smile she loved so much, the momentary irritation gone, but it was a smile from her own memory. He wasn't real.

'Relax,' she murmured to herself. 'Let it come naturally. Graham, darling, I'm here, with you. Can you see me?' He smiled again, easing himself on the wrought-iron chair, his fingers tapping on the tabletop. The paper. What was the date on the paper? She leaned forward, trying to see.

'What the hell are you doing here? Can't even the police keep you away!' The shrill voice cut across her reverie like a knife. She heard the squeak of the kitchen door as it was pushed back and Rhona stepped out onto the terrace only six feet from her. She was dressed in a T-shirt and jeans with strappy sandals. She marched towards the table and pushed in the empty chair on which Graham had been sitting so hard that its legs grated on the boards. He had gone. He had never been there. Reaching into her hip pocket, Rhona brought out her phone and brandished it in Andy's face. With a grim smile she raised it and clicked a picture. 'Now we'll see if the police believe their own eyes. This time you will find yourself in a prison cell. Stalking is a crime, you know.'

Paralysed with shock, Andy couldn't move. She clenched her fists trying to regain control of herself, of her dream; she and Rhona were looking at each other, their eyes locked, for several seconds, or so it seemed, before she found herself back in her bedroom, wide awake, her heart thudding with adrenaline, her hands sweaty and hot.

She sat up, trying to steady herself. The room was spinning. Her mouth was dry and downstairs the phone was ringing.

Rhona stared at her phone. There was no answer when she tried Miranda's mobile. There never was. She pulled up the photo file and studied the last one. It was a picture of the table, the empty chairs, the house wall behind the terrace. There was no sign of Miranda on it at all. She shook it angrily and stared at it again then let out a string of expletives. The woman was there, in front of her and then she had gone.

She had imagined her.

Deep in thought, she stepped back into the kitchen and pulled the door shut behind her.

There had been no point in her threat to go to the police again; they had made it absolutely clear that they viewed her as a jealous, demented old bag. She tightened her lips. On the other hand, they had believed her enough to check up on Miranda's whereabouts at the time of her last visit and apparently she had an alibi. Her mother! As though anyone would believe a mother's word.

Her hatred of the other woman was increasing with every moment she thought about what had happened. Had her jealousy really deepened to the point where she was capable of imagining her rival in front of her? Because she was jealous, there was no denying that. She had reason enough after all. Miranda had stolen the best years of Graham's life and then she'd driven him to an early grave with her selfish demands. She was a murderer. Oh yes, they said it was cancer. They always said unexplained deaths were due to cancer, but Graham had been a fit, strong man. He wouldn't have dropped dead just like that in his fifties, and she was going to prove it. Then she was going to destroy the woman who had killed him.

She pulled out a kitchen chair and sat down heavily, her chin propped on her hands.

Either she was imagining Miranda's presence with a vividness which was terrifying or Miranda was really here, perhaps staying with a neighbour and somehow sneaking in with the express intention of tormenting her. But how could she? The gates and doors were locked.

The first thing was to establish where Miranda was supposed to be staying. Even the police were determined to keep Miranda's whereabouts a secret. That in itself was suspicious. She sat back in the chair and thought hard. Three people had Miranda's address. Her mother and the Allardyces. That had been a good guess. She knew they had been close friends. She scowled. Where did that get her? They weren't going to tell her. She

thought back to the embarrassed young policeman who had
come round to inform her that Miranda had an alibi and anyway
was too far away. Had he actually said that? She squeezed her
eyes tightly, trying to think. Yes, he had said those words.
Inadvertently he had given her a clue. She wasn't based in
London. She was far away.

She gave a slow triumphant smile. Now all she had to do
was work out with which of her friends she was staying, and
in the top drawer of the bureau bookcase, which would soon
be on its way to the auctions, Rhona had found an old address
book of Miranda's. She climbed to her feet and went through
into the next room. Most of Miranda's belongings had been
consigned to the incinerator, but this was one of the things she
had kept.

Slowly and methodically she began to go through the book
page by page. The majority of Miranda's friends lived in London
and for now she discounted them. She picked up her phone
and one after the other she began to dial the rest. After an hour
she was left with three names and addresses which she had not
been able to verify or discount for one reason or another. One
of them was Sue Macarthur. She dialled the number twice.
There was no reply. The name was familiar. Graham must have
mentioned it to her at some point. The woman lived in a remote
farmhouse and he had been to stay with her, that was it. He
had told her he couldn't meet her because he and Miranda
were going to Wales for the summer. Wales. She studied the
address in front of her. It was a definite possibility. So, all she
had to do was keep ringing. In the end somebody would be in
and pick up the phone and then she would know for certain.

She wasn't sure what she was going to do with the information once she had it, but the knowledge would be empowering.
With a small, satisfied smile she climbed to her feet and went
to fill the kettle. A cup of one of the special coffees she had
found in the cupboard would be a perfect way to celebrate her
newly honed forensic skills. If the distance between Miranda

Dysart's hiding place – even inside her head she gave the name a mocking emphasis – gave the woman an alibi, it could work in both directions.

Supposing Miranda had some kind of accident in her hide-away, be it in Wales or in any of the other addresses in this book. An accident to stop her in her tracks. An accident to pay her back for tormenting her and for being here, with Graham, and being happy. If something happened to the woman, nothing even remotely suspicious would be laid at her door; after all, the police knew she lived miles away on the other side of the country. It was a delicious thought. Rhona smiled to herself. Until this second she had not contemplated why she wanted to find Miranda so badly, but this last sighting of her had made one thing clear. She was never going to be rid of her as long as the woman was freely roaming round this house. How she had transported herself here and why she was making herself such a problem, Rhona couldn't fathom. All she needed to focus on was the fact that it must not happen again.

Wearily Andy walked over to the window and stared out over the garden. There was no sign of Bryn. A rain shower raced across the valley, splattering against the window, reducing the visibility to nil. Minutes later it had gone and bright sunlight spread across the herb beds once more. Behind her the phone rang again. She ignored it, clenching her fists in the pocket of a jacket.

'Graham,' she whispered. 'Oh God, I miss you so much. Why aren't you there for me?' Warm tears trickled down her cheeks. Miserably she wandered back upstairs. She paused in the doorway to Sue's bedroom where her mother had slept. The room was still full of her presence. She walked over to the bed. Her mother had stripped off the sheets and the duvet was looking naked and bereft without its cover. Without thinking clearly what she was doing Andy crawled under it and curled up to a tight ball.

Outside the window the sunlight dimmed and black clouds massed behind the hills. Shadows spread across the garden and with the shadows came the howl of the wind. Andy shivered. Somewhere out there beyond the mountains Catrin was waiting, staring into the distance, her ears strained for the sound of hoofbeats.

9

Catrin glanced up at the sky. Another storm was threatening; the wind had grown stronger, tearing at the clouds, fragmenting the sunlight into patches of light and shade. They had found a brook and she slid from her saddle, allowing her pony to drink as she looked nervously around her, narrowing her eyes against the wind. Behind her, her father sat slumped on the cob without moving. When she spotted Edmund she almost cried out in surprise. He was concealed behind the bushes at the side of the track quite a distance in front of them. He put his finger to his lips and beckoned them on and then he was gone, back into the shadows. Catrin looked at her father, who was sitting, arms folded, his rein loose on his horse's neck as it lowered its head to drink. 'Tad, I have seen Edmund. He wants us to move on quietly,' she whispered. 'There must be danger back there. Let's walk on slowly.'

For once he didn't argue. He gathered his rein as she scrambled onto her pony and they turned back onto the track, riding as casually as they could towards the shelter of a copse ahead. Her mouth had gone dry. As far as she knew they hadn't been seen yet, but any loud noise might draw attention to their presence.

Catching up with Edmund they followed him off the track and round into the copse. Only when they were a good distance further on did he stop. 'There are large numbers of men back there,' he said once he thought they were sufficiently concealed from the road. 'Men-at-arms, wearing Grey's blazon. I'm not sure what they are up to – a training sortie, at a guess, but I would rather they didn't see us. They must be in hiding for a reason.'

'Was he there?' Dafydd asked, frowning.

'Not that I could see. There was one knight in charge. They were fully armed. My guess is that they were mustering to join the king's army for his Scottish campaign, but any body of armed men on the move is bad news for a small group like us.' He glanced anxiously at Catrin. 'I want us out of this area as soon as possible.'

'Keeping in mind that Sir Reginald is no friend to the Lord Glyndŵr, so it would be little protection to say that was where we were headed,' Dafydd added with a nod. He pulled himself up onto his saddle. 'I will feel safer once we are safely under his rooftree. Kind though Lady Grey was to you, I fear I disgraced myself last night.' He shivered. 'I have no way of knowing what I may have said to betray our destination.'

Edmund and Catrin exchanged glances. Edmund moved to Catrin's side. 'Let me help you mount. We have a long way to go and the sooner we are on our way the sooner we can be sure of being safe.'

They arrived at Sycharth, the residence of Lord and Lady Glyndŵr, as the sun was beginning to set. The house was beautiful in the slanting light, the elegant manor house with its orchards and gardens and fish ponds lying still and tranquil in the gold of the autumnal evening sun. They were greeted by the Lord of Glyndŵr's wife Margaret, and her eldest daughters,

Alys and Catherine. To Dafydd's disappointment and intense frustration she told them her husband and their elder son, her husband's brother and their advisors and senior household staff were all at his other residence, half a day's ride away across the Berwyn Mountains at Glyndyfrdwy. Without knowing it, Dafydd and Catrin had ridden near it on their way south from Ruthin.

There was nothing to be done that night. They were exhausted, as were their horses, and Dafydd and Catrin gladly accepted her invitation to stay and await Lord Owain's return.

It was seventeen years since Owain Glyndŵr had married Margaret, his childhood sweetheart. It was in the household of Sir David Hanmer, Margaret's father, that Owain had first set eyes on her and fallen hopelessly in love. After the early death of his parents, Owain, a royal ward, had been put in the care of Margaret's father, a close family friend and neighbour and a kinsman. The older man was a member of parliament and a King's Bench judge at Westminster and he had sent his ward to university and then to London to study law at the Inns of Court. After that Owain became a squire to the Earl of Arundel, with whom he learned the art of war in service both at sea and on land. He was a talented and well-connected young man.

The match between the Anglo-Welsh heiress and the brilliant young Lord of Glyndŵr was met with approval on all sides and the marriage had been by all accounts a great success.

Margaret Hanmer was now the mother of eleven children, their parents' pride and joy. She had a handsome face with strong bones and a direct gaze, a powerful woman in her own right, enjoying with her husband his retirement from the army and the administration of his rich estates in Wales. With all her other duties she had an ever-watchful eye for people she thought needed her help and one of those was Catrin. She had become fond of the girl on her previous visits, shrewdly seeing that she was in need of motherly attention, overshadowed as she was by a domineering and selfish father. Quietly she had removed Catrin to the women's quarters and encouraged her undoubted talents, trying to instil some much-needed confidence. This visit would be no different.

Catrin found herself sharing a bedroom in the manor house with Catherine and Alys, her two special friends amongst the Glyndŵrs' daughters. And they greeted her with hugs and much delighted giggling. Once she had washed her dusty face, hands and feet in a basin of warm water, proffered by a household servant, the young women trooped back across the bridge over the moat to the great hall which was built against the perimeter wall of the bailey. There, they joined the household for the evening meal, after which Dafydd recited and sang for the assembled company, accompanying himself long into the evening on Lady Margaret's beautiful harp. It was as the household was settling to sleep that she beckoned Dafydd and his daughter back across the bailey and into the main house where they settled by the fire in her private solar and at last they had a chance to talk privately.

'I remember that you see the future, Master Dafydd,' she said. 'There are many men of your talents and my husband values all their opinions, but none so much as yours. As you may have heard, we are embroiled in many problems, most at the instigation of our neighbour Reginald Grey, who every man woman and child in the border March knows to be my husband's mortal enemy.' She sighed. 'The man has stolen our land and lost Owain the hearing in parliament at Westminster which should have restored it.' She paused, trying to contain her anger at the memory. His claim had been dismissed with the insulting comment, 'What care we for barefoot Welsh curs', an insult which could not be forgiven. Wiser heads than Sir Reginald's had tried to calm the situation with no success and her husband had returned to Wales in fury.

She took a deep breath and when she spoke again her voice was calmer. 'This man compounds the injustices the Welsh people suffer at the hands of the English authorities and now, as you no doubt have heard, he has betrayed and tricked us again by telling the king that Owain refused to answer his call to fight the Scots when Owain knew nothing of the summons because Sir Reginald had chosen to keep the muster a secret from him. That has led to my husband being declared a traitor!' Her dark eyes flashed with fury. 'You have heard about this, I see it in your faces.' She gave him a fierce look of encouragement as she intercepted Dafydd and Catrin's quick glance at one another. 'This is all too much! The feelings of the people of the whole of North Wales are running very high, Master Dafydd. We feel we are sitting on a tinderbox here. My husband is a popular man. Very little provocation now would set the country alight, Welsh against English.'

Dafydd nodded. 'The situation is grave and I have dreamed of the Lord Owain,' he said after a moment's hesitation. 'I had hoped to tell him in person.'

'The reason he and the majority of our household are not here to greet you, Master Dafydd, is because Sir Reginald is to meet Owain tomorrow to discuss the problems between them at our hunting lodge in Glyndyfrdwy.' She sighed again. She could not see the point of this meeting; no more could Owain's brother. No good would come of it, but her husband was, as always, fair and anxious to resolve matters without violence if it were at all possible. 'If you have anything relevant to impart, you should tell me.' Margaret waited, drumming her fingers on a small table where a servant had left them wine and a plate of marchpane cakes.

'I dreamt about him . . .' Dafydd hesitated, 'while I was a guest at another house north of here. Unfortunately I talked in my sleep and woke people, and my outburst led to us leaving rather hurriedly.'

Margaret's face grew even more tense. 'Another house?'

Dafydd threw another hasty look at Catrin. 'We were at Ruthin Castle, my lady.'

She stared from one to the other askance. 'You stayed with the Greys?'

'It was my fault,' Catrin put in. 'My *tad* told me Sir Reginald was your enemy, but I insisted. I liked Lady Grey.' She hung her head miserably. 'I am so sorry.'

'What did you dream?' Ignoring Catrin, Margaret Glyndŵr stood up and began pacing in front of the fire, increasingly agitated.

Dafydd hesitated again.

'Tell me.' She stood looking intently into his face.

'Sir Reginald was preparing for war.' He pursed his lips as Margaret stared at him. 'He had an army at hand. I dreamed of fire and slaughter.' He took a deep breath. 'Our own eyes seem to confirm my dream. On our way south to Sycharth we saw armed men in the deer park at Ruthin. It seemed to be some kind of muster.'

'Thirty men.' She nodded. 'That was what was agreed, to accompany Sir Reginald to the meeting with my husband and his advisors, to discuss their differences.'

Dafydd shook his head violently as the reality of what they had seen fell into place. 'No, no! On our way here our groom Edmund spotted a large quantity of armed men. Far more than thirty. They were gathering in the shelter of the woods in Sir Reginald's park. We assumed they were preparing to follow the king, part of the muster to fight the Scots, but now I am not so sure. There would not have been any need for such secrecy if they were to go to Scotland.'

'And your dream showed fire and slaughter?' Margaret's voice was tight with fear.

'I saw blood and betrayal.' He sighed. 'Your lord and husband should be very careful, my lady. I dreamed of his victory and his triumph over the greed of the English lords, but now, at this moment, he is in danger and he should flee. I dream true, madam, as you know.'

She looked at him hard. 'My husband does not flee,' she

retorted. She sat down abruptly. 'I knew Sir Reginald wasn't a man of honour, but I didn't believe he would go back on his word if there was a chance of sorting all this out.' Her tone wavered.

Dafydd continued to hold her gaze. 'He is not to be trusted.'

'You should have told me the moment you arrived here.' A flash of impatience crossed her face. 'So much precious time has been wasted.' She jumped to her feet again. 'Take fresh horses. Go to him now. It may not be too late. You will have to ride through the night.'

Having made up her mind she acted swiftly, calling out instructions to her steward, pausing only briefly to glance at Catrin. Her heart went out to the girl who was looking distraught. 'This is not your fault, child. It is thanks to your insistence that you go to Ruthin that we are warned, and I thank providence for that. But for now, you look exhausted. You should stay here with Catherine and Alys until your father returns. I know they were looking forward to seeing you. They are hoping you will give them more lessons in weather magic.' She gave a quick smile. 'Do you remember once you taught them to call down the mist from the mountains? They tried to teach their father, and he grows quite adept.'

Catrin smiled at the memory. She had so looked forward to this moment, but she had to stay with her own father. He would expect it. 'I will go with him, my lady.' She lowered her gaze. 'I too dream these days,' she added softly. 'My dreams too speak of Lord Glyndŵr's triumph. But he will wade through a river of blood.' She stopped abruptly, appalled at her own words. Looking up she saw Lady Margaret's face blanch. 'He is destined to be a great prince,' she went on in a whisper. 'His name will live forever as a hero of our people.'

'A prince!' Margaret Glyndŵr's eyes narrowed as she echoed the word.

'He is the descendant of princes is he not?' Catrin could have bitten out her tongue. She looked round for her father, who had already headed out of the door. She wasn't sure where the words had come from. She knew nothing of the Lord Owain's ancestry. Unlike her father, she had never had to learn the pedigrees of princes. With a hastily bobbed curtsy she turned and fled, leaving the older woman staring after her.

They rode through bright moonlight, escorted this time by four armed guides, men who had been born and bred in these mountains and could find their way blindfold through the trackways in the forest, along the drovers' roads over the high tops and down into the shadowed valleys between. They kept up a steady pace as the route climbed steeply ahead of them onto the bleak lonely moors where the bright colours of the bracken and heather leached pale in the cold moonlight and the wind keened through the heather, then they dropped down into the wooded valleys, where the rustling leaves of the trees were silvered and shaded as clouds crossed the moon.

They had been given sturdy mountain ponies, fresh and well trained, and Edmund was with them. He too had been given a horse and they were travelling fast, hooves thudding rhythmically on the peaty tracks, every now and then striking a hidden rock, the sound ringing out across the hills as they threaded their way up and over the passes towards the north.

Fighting her exhaustion, Catrin glanced nervously behind her now and then. Her father's words of warning were circling in her head. After all, she too had seen the men quietly mustering in the woods behind Ruthin Castle, and she had seen the intense worry in the eyes of Owain Glyndŵr's wife as she took in the possible meaning of Dafydd's warning, but the quiet confidence of their guides and the speed of their journey was reassuring. They would arrive in time.

The sky was lightening in the east when at long last they descended into the valley of the River Dee. The watchmen and the dogs at Glyndyfrdwy heard them coming. They saw the bright flare of sconces as a door opened and heard the rasp of swords being drawn. One of the men-at-arms with them called out and in minutes their small party had been admitted to the courtyard of the Lord of Glyndŵr's hunting lodge on the banks of the river. Their exhausted horses were led away and they were shown into the house where he was waiting for them. Obviously awoken from his sleep he was wrapped in a fur-trimmed mantle as he sat by a newly lit brazier. He called for refreshments for his guests then waited for Dafydd to speak, his face becoming increasingly grim as he heard what his visitor had to say.

A tall man of around fifty, his eyes as intent and piercing as those of his wife, he heard Dafydd without comment until he had finished, then he sat back, thinking, rubbing his beard. Several other men had joined them as Dafydd's explanation of their arrival and visit to Sycharth proceeded and they all looked at one another grimly in the firelight.

'I told you that you could not trust him,' a deep voice spoke from the shadows. 'You have no need of a stranger to prophesy for you when your own bards and seers have warned you of the dangers and urged you on to your destiny.'

Owain glanced towards the corner of the room and nodded slowly. 'You are right, Crach, my friend, and I have listened to you all, and now Dafydd comes to emphasise what you have told me, and with an eyewitness account of the men he has seen. But surely we must give Sir Reginald one more chance to prove himself an honourable man? We can't be certain what he intends for those men-at-arms, or indeed that there are as many as our good friends believe. In the darkness of the woods they could have been mistaken.' His gaze moved to Edmund, who was standing in the background.

Edmund straightened his shoulders. 'I was not mistaken, my lord. I crept very close through the trees.'

'And you don't think perhaps that Sir Reginald was preparing to hunt?' Owain asked, anxious to give the man the benefit of the doubt. He noted Edmund's shake of the head and glanced across at his brother, Tudur, who had joined them near the fire. The two men conferred quietly then Owain turned back to Dafydd, who stood grim-faced. 'I believe you, Master Dafydd, but I can't react without more proof. The important thing is, we have been warned. If we feel Sir Reginald has betrayed us yet again, then we will act.' He softened his words with a smile. 'You shall have food and rest, and your daughter too.' He directed a quick glance at Catrin who, though awed by the presence of these powerful men, was falling asleep on her feet. 'Later today, we will see what transpires when Sir Reginald arrives, and thanks to you we will be ready should he show any signs of treachery.'

Catrin slept huddled against the back of one of the serving women, in front of the fire in the kitchen. Glyndyfrdwy was nothing like Sycharth. This was no handsome manor house. More of a rugged lodge, the hall had been built on the banks of the River Dee below the high motte which had been the site of an ancient castle. This was a place where men met for the hunt. It was beautiful and basic.

Her rest was brief. Within a few hours the kitchen was bustling with preparations for the meeting which was to be held later in the day.

Her father told her what happened later. The hall had been transformed into a council chamber with the Lord Owain, his brother and advisors and his eldest son, Gruffudd, all seated at one side of the table. Dafydd was placed on a bench next to Glyndŵr's personal seer and prophet Crach Ffinnant who scowled at him throughout.

At the allotted time Sir Reginald Grey had arrived with his thirty followers as stipulated. He was a seasoned politician and warrior, but his hostility to the Lord Glyndŵr was barely concealed as he took his seat at the table. Dafydd studied him with care, aware that the man had not registered the presence of a travelling bard who, had he but known it, had graced his wife's own table only two days before. As it was he sat back, his fingers drumming silently on the table, his eyes fixed on Glyndŵr's face, his mouth a thin sneer as the proceedings began.

The chamber was silent save for the crackling of the logs in the hearth and the shifting of the men seated around the long table with the silent ring of followers standing behind them. As stipulated in their agreement, all the men had left their swords outside.

When the door opened to admit a latecomer, Dafydd felt his stomach tighten with fear, but it was a man he knew, one of Glyndŵr's neighbours and his own friend and colleague, the poet Iolo Goch, who bowed and made his apologies for arriving late to the meeting.

'Allow me to make amends for my tardiness, my lords,' Iolo said, still standing although he had been waved to a place at the table. He walked to the far end of the room and without giving anyone time to speak he began to sing, his powerful baritone voice rising to the rafters. Dafydd saw Sir Reginald glance heavenwards in disbelief, making it clear that the ways of these Welsh were beyond countenancing, but Glyndŵr nodded and smiled, relaxing back from the documents before him on the table. Iolo was singing in Welsh and Sir Reginald had already made it clear he did not speak the language. Nor it appeared did any of his men. There was an imperceptible shift in the atmosphere of the room as the song progressed and Dafydd realised that the poet was improvising. *There are men outside; men with swords; beware, my lord, and save yourself. Leave the house now. Go swiftly. Hide like a fleeing stag to fight later.* Iolo's smiling serene face gave no sign that he had deviated from the time-honoured form of the song as he drew to an end and bowed.

Around him there was a quiet ripple of applause as Glyndŵr stood and bowed back. He left his place at the head of the table and strode down the hall to where Iolo was standing, clapping him on the shoulder. 'Make yourself comfortable, my friend. Your words remind me that I have documents in my chamber

141

which I think will make my case more clearly to Sir Reginald.' He half turned and bowed towards Sir Reginald, who was looking more and more impatient, then he walked slowly and with dignity out of the hall.

There was a restless movement amongst the men left behind. Sir Reginald was chewing his lips, his face becoming more choleric by the minute as his men stood ranged uncomfortably along the wall behind him. Glyndŵr's followers, spread out down the opposite side of the hall, moved from foot to foot and, eyeing each other meaningfully, edged imperceptibly across the doorway. No one would leave the hall by the main doors without their say.

The Lord of Glyndŵr did not return. He had made his way through to the back of the house and slipped out through the kitchens onto the riverbank and thence up into the woodland beyond. In minutes he had vanished, but not before seeing that the warning of Iolo and of Dafydd had been well made. A large body of armed men was approaching across the water meadows. Sir Reginald had again proved himself a man of no honour.

When Glyndŵr's escape was discovered Sir Reginald's fury was immediate. With a howl of rage he threw the document in front of him onto the floor and stamped on it, and with a shout at his men to follow him he strode towards the door. The men of Glyndŵr, with a glance at Tudur, stood back, their faces grim, and let them go.

Outside, the extent of Sir Reginald's deceit was obvious. His thirty allotted followers were far outnumbered by the body of armed men milling about outside the gates. With Sir Reginald at their head they galloped away up the track towards the east.

The men left behind armed themselves and waited for the inevitable return of their foe, intent on revenge at being outwitted, but no one came.

As the scene faded, Andy became aware slowly that she wasn't in her own bed. She was lying under the duvet in Sue's bedroom.

142

She stretched out and stared up at the ceiling, her eyes closing again as she tried to return to the past. It was engaging and exciting and Catrin was there, in the midst of a piece of history. She wanted to know what happened next.

Then she remembered. Rhona. And Graham.

With a groan she lay back, the dream retreating, feeling the hot tears welling out from beneath her eyelids. She hadn't seen Graham, not properly. She hadn't felt his arms, nestled against his chest, heard his quiet chuckle as they talked into the night. Instead she had seen Rhona. Why always Rhona? It wasn't what she wanted. It was the thing she desired least in the whole world, the woman who had heaped misery on misery.

She staggered out of bed and went over to the window. Sue's bedroom overlooked the front of the house. It was raining again and the view of the valley was obscured by a blanket of cloud, white and all enveloping, drifting up between the trees, curling through their branches, clinging to the rocks, licking at the walls of the house. Opening the window, she leaned out, her hands on the cold wet sill.

Was it the house itself making her dream, switching something on inside her? Had it done the same for Catrin? That was a hugely exciting and at the same time frightening thought. But it was also empowering. In the past people had obviously learnt to control this gift the house gave them, and if other people had done it, surely it was potentially something she could do as well. She closed her eyes, her fingers clutching the stone as she tried to picture Catrin, not here in this isolated house where silence enfolded the memories, but out there on the banks of the River Dee, listening to her father, her eyes wide, her cloak clutched around her, her hood pulled up against a cold wind.

Rhona had two full, black rubbish bags on the kitchen floor. She turned as she heard a sound behind her. 'So, you've come back. I thought you might. Well, while you're here you can watch and see what I intend to do with your belongings. Perhaps you thought you would come back and collect them. Well, you're too late.'

Andy wasn't sure if Rhona could actually see her as she opened the door and pulled the bags out onto the terrace. It was raining in Kew as well. The boards were wet and slippery as the woman dragged them across the decking and pushed them down the steps onto the lawn. She ran down after them and pulled them onto the grass then dragged them towards the far corner of the garden. 'Come on then' – she turned back with a shrill laugh – 'don't you want to see?'

Andy hesitated. She didn't want to be here. She hadn't intended to be here. How had this happened? Were they both dreaming?

Somehow she couldn't stop herself moving down the steps and onto the wet grass. Rhona was ahead of her, dragging the lid off the old, singed incinerator in the far corner of the garden. She untied the first bag and dived in, pulling out handfuls of paper. She pulled a box of matches out of her pocket, struck one and dropped it into the bin, watching in satisfaction as the blue smoke spiralled into the air. 'See?' She bent over the bag again. 'Letters. These were all letters from Graham to you. Well, say goodbye to lover boy. They're gone.'

Andy let out a whimper of unhappiness. Rhona must have found the Victorian workbox in which she had kept all Graham's letters, tied up with ribbon.

'Don't!' she called. 'Don't. You can't!'

'Why can't I?' Rhona was laughing now. Another handful of papers fell into the burning cauldron as the wind and rain circled the fire, whipping the flames into a frenzy.

'No!' Andy ran the last few steps towards her and reached for the bag. 'Leave it! You can't! They are not yours.'

'They aren't anyone's now. If they meant so much to you, why did you leave them behind?' Rhona was exultant.

'You wouldn't let me take them!' Andy shouted.

'No, I didn't, did I.' Another handful went onto the flames.

Andy reached after them desperately, her fingers clearly visible this time near Rhona's as she reached into the smoke. She caught a handful in mid-air as the flames reached up to engulf them and for a fraction of a second she was holding a fiery torch that licked greedily at her hand. With a scream she dropped them and was once more in Sue's bedroom in Wales.

Tearing herself away from the open window Andy ran to the door and dragged it open. She fled down the landing to the bathroom, sobbing. Turning on the tap she thrust her hand under the cold water and held it there for several minutes until it was numb with cold then she pulled it away and stared down at it. There was no sign of a burn. She was, she realised, shaking violently. She turned her hand up and down, examining front and back, then stared down at her fingers. She could still smell the smoke. Couldn't she? She stood in front of the mirror and stared at herself. She was pale and her face was streaked with tears but there was no sign of smoke or soot. She grabbed a handful of her hair and pulled it to her nose. It smelt of shampoo.

Sian welcomed her in and sat her down by the fire in her chaotic small front room. Andy had grabbed a bottle of wine from Sue's rack as she fled out of the door and they opened it. Before Andy could bring herself to explain her arrival she had taken several gulps from her glass. 'I'm really sorry, I should have rung. I just couldn't . . .' She paused. 'I couldn't take it another moment. I keep having these awful dreams. Of home. Of my partner. Of his wife.' She clenched her fists and winced at the pain. She stared down at her hands and her eyes widened in horror. A livid red scar had spread across the back of her left hand.

Sian leaned across and touched her wrist. 'My God, Andy, how did you do that?'

Andy shook her head. She couldn't speak.

Sian waited as Andy swallowed another mouthful of wine and only then after a deep breath did she manage to tell Sian the whole story.

When she had finished she sat looking down into the fire in silence, waiting for Sian to say something. The flames had burned low and Sian pulled a couple of logs out of the basket, dropping them onto the embers. She reached for the bottle and topped up Andy's glass. 'You're right. It's the house. Sleeper's Castle. That old man I told you about, who told people's fortunes? One of the ways he was supposed to have done it was by dreaming for people. They would ask him something and he would tell them to come back the next day and he would give them an answer. It cost them, mind you.' She gave a sad smile.

Andy picked up her glass and stared down into it. 'Was he right in his predictions?'

'Oh yes.'

'And were people pleased?'

'Not always, no. They thought he was a wizard. Or a warlock. Once someone set fire to the house.' Sian's gaze went back to Andy's hand.

'You won't tell anyone what I've told you tonight, will you,' Andy whispered.

'No, of course not.'

'It is all so strange. So real.' She stared down at her hand miserably and her eyes filled with tears. 'My letters. I had kept them all. His love letters to me, spanning ten years.'

'You can hardly blame her for targeting them, I suppose.'

'I know.'

'None of this is real, Andy,' Sian said gently. 'It's a dream, you know. None of it really happened. It can't have done.'

Andy sniffed as she looked up. 'But that's it, Sian. It is real. Not just my hand. The police came.'

Sian stared at her.

'Rhona could see me as clearly as I could see her.'

Sian sat forward, her elbows on her knees, and studied Andy's face in silence for a while then she reached for the bottle. As she refilled their glasses she shook her head slowly. 'God, I wish Meryn was here. He would know what to do. Rhona must be freaking out if you're popping in and out of her life the way you describe.' She put the bottle down. 'This is all in your mind, isn't it? It has to be. You don't actually go back to Kew. Obviously. But then,' she paused, 'how did you burn your hand? How does Rhona see you? Is she asleep and dreaming too?' She climbed to her feet. 'Come into the kitchen. I think we both need something to eat. And you must stay the night here. By the time we've finished this bottle of wine you won't be in a fit state to drive back, and I think a night away from the mayhem and intrigue of your life over the mountain will do nothing but good.'

Andy followed her into the kitchen. 'So you do actually believe me,' she said as she sat down at the kitchen table.

Sian was rummaging in the fridge. She emerged with a box of eggs. 'Will an omelette do you?'

'That would be lovely.'

'I do believe you, yes. I'm a firm believer in Hamlet's little dictum about there being more things in heaven and earth.' She reached into the fridge for the butter. 'You haven't mentioned Catrin,' she went on. 'When we spoke before you told me you had been dreaming about someone called Catrin. Is she part of this story?'

Andy shook her head. 'Another set of dreams. Set in the past. Catrin lived in Sleeper's Castle hundreds of years ago.'

Sian stared at her briefly then she reached for a bowl and dug a whisk out of a drawer. 'No wonder you're tired, you poor love, with all this going on.'

'I sound crazy, I know.' Andy gave a rueful smile. 'Catrin's life is very exciting. She's a poet. She and her father are friends of Owain Glyndŵr.'

Sian was concentrating on breaking eggs into the bowl.

147

'Ella suggested I might be dreaming about some novel I read when I was a child.'

'You've been talking to Ella?' Sian looked up.

Andy nodded. 'We had coffee together. I met her when I was buying some notebooks to write down everything that happened in the dream so I could see if any of it checked out.'

Sian put down the whisk. She reached for her glass. 'Did you tell her about Rhona?' she asked cautiously.

'No. No, that's too real. That's private stuff.'

'Well, a word to the wise. Our friend Ella, God bless her, is not known for keeping secrets, so it's as well you didn't tell her. I love her to bits, but she can be a gossip. If you mentioned Glyndŵr and let on you were having dreams about him I don't think she could contain her excitement. You would have journalists on your doorstep. In fact, you would probably find yourself on national TV within the week.'

Andy stared at her, aghast. 'You don't mean that.'

Sian grimaced. 'I think I do, I'm afraid.'

'She mentioned that Meryn had been involved with some sort of haunting that involved Jesus.'

'Well, there you are. Heaven knows how Ella heard about that. I thought Meryn managed to keep a lid on it at the time.'

'But he talked to you?' Andy was wondering more and more about this mysterious man in whom Sian obviously had so much faith.

Sian grimaced. 'He knows I can keep quiet.'

Andy smiled. 'I only talked to Ella about Catrin and her father. I didn't mention Glyndŵr.'

'Well, remember Glyndŵr is a magic word in Wales. If you haven't said anything to anyone, leave it like that.' Sian began to whisk the eggs. 'I know I keep saying it, but I wish Meryn was here. Now that is a man you could trust with your life and your soul.' She set the bowl aside and fished salad and tomatoes out of the cold box and put them down on the table. 'Would you like to construct a salad? And there's a nice loaf of bread in the bin. One of the best things about Hay is that there seem to be more artisan bakers per square inch here than anywhere else on the planet. I hope you don't plan on staying slim.'

Andy smiled. She took another gulp of wine. 'I used to know all sorts of magic formulae for keeping evil at bay,' she said thoughtfully. 'But I'm not sure they would work for Rhona.'

Sian let out a yelp of laughter. 'Sorry. I thought for a minute you were referring to artisan bakers. OK. I suspect all you have to do is stop thinking about her, or is that too simplistic?'

'I think it may be. Inadvertently I seem to have stirred up a hornet's nest.'

'And does that go for Catrin as well, do you think? If she's been hanging around for six hundred years or so the odd bit of magic formula might not work.' Sian produced a knife and put it in front of Andy. 'Toms. Start chopping.' Turning to the cooker she lifted a heavy pan onto the heat. 'I'm sorry, Andy. I am finding this hard to get my head round. I know all these weird things happen at Sleeper's and I know people sincerely believe it. I wouldn't be Meryn's friend if I couldn't accept that he believes it all, but I've never had any of these experiences myself and it's hard to understand. Maybe that's why he talks to me. I keep him grounded.'

'No one really understands,' Andy put in. 'Isn't that rather the point?' She picked up the knife. 'I need to talk to my dad. He would know what to do. He was the one who made me interested in all this stuff when I was a child.'

'Have you spoken to him about all this?'

'I tried. He's away at a conference. If your friend Meryn doesn't show up, I'll phone him again.'

'Well, you could send a psychic email into the ether for Meryn. You never know, that might work. Where does your dad live?' Sian poured in the beaten eggs.

'Northumberland.'

Sian's eyebrow shot up. 'And your mum is in Sussex?'

'It works for them. He has remarried but they still get on.'

'So miracles do happen.' Sian slid the omelette onto a plate and set it to keep warm while she made the next.

They sat for a long time over their supper with Sian's two dogs asleep under the table and Andy almost asleep in her chair. When at last Sian showed her upstairs to her spare room, Andy turned to her in horror. 'What about Pepper? I haven't fed him this evening.'

Sian smiled. 'He won't starve in one evening.'

'But he'll be furious. He will never trust me again.'

'Of course he will.' Sian reached past her to switch on the light. 'Let me tell you a little secret. Sue spent more than one unscheduled night with me after we'd demolished the odd bottle of wine. Pepper got over it. I'm not saying he won't sulk – cats always sulk if they feel hard done by – but he will recover the moment you rattle his biscuit box. Grovel a bit and make a fuss of him.'

Andy was still smiling when she crawled under the sheets and closed her eyes. For a few seconds she wondered if Catrin or Rhona would disturb her dreams, then she was asleep.

It was after nine when she awoke to the smell of frying bacon.

'So, did you sleep well?' Sian was standing in the kitchen, reading the morning newspaper.

'I slept like a log.' Andy stared at the table, laid with cereal and toast and a huge pot of coffee.

'Here. Take this.' Sian thrust a plate of bacon and fried tomato and mushrooms at her. 'Sit down and tell me about your night. Did you dream?'

'If I did, I can't remember it.'

'Good. Well, I want you to remember one thing. If ever you get fed up with your dream factory over the hill there, I want you to come to me for a few nights' peace. Promise?'

Andy grinned. 'I promise.'

She meant it.

*   *   *

The evening before, Bryn had drawn up into his accustomed parking place outside Sleeper's Castle. He sat there briefly staring up at the house. Her car wasn't there. No matter. He didn't want to see her. Far from it.

In a moment of absent-minded aberration he had left earlier in the day without his canvas holdall. He was a man who looked after his tools; he had his own in the back of the van. At each of the houses he worked in he insisted on a basic set of the heavies, as he called them. Wheelbarrow, mower, roller and a few more of the things which were too heavy or bulky to cart around with him, but apart from that he had his own spades and forks and trowels, the smallest of which were in his holdall with his flask and his sandwich box. Slamming the car door behind him, he ran up the flight of steps and ducked round the back of the house to the outbuildings at the side, one of which was used for garden implements. Sue was almost as fastidious as he was when it came to one's personal tools. Hers were neat and clean and hanging on the walls of the shed in meticulous rows. 'You can borrow them when you like, Bryn,' she had chortled when they were going over the garden maintenance plan. 'I know you never manage to have all the tools you need.' He had grinned back. It was a long-standing joke of theirs that between them they had enough to stock a garden centre. Opening the door he picked up his bag, which was lying inside the shed. That was all he needed. He walked slowly back towards the path, the bag slung over his shoulder. Outside the back door to the house he stopped. Pepper was sitting on the windowsill inside. Bryn tapped the window. 'Hi, fella,' he said softly. He always spoke Australian to Pepper. It was another joke between him and Sue. 'Has she gone out without feeding you?'

The cat of course made it clear that she had. Bryn knew where the cat food was. If he were to nip inside he could give Pepper a handful of biscuits and no one would be any the wiser.

He tried the back door. It was locked. He frowned. Sue had

never bothered to lock the door even when she was going away for a few days. That way he could always get in if she rang and asked him to look in on the cat. He tried the handle again. There was a spare key hidden under a flower pot on the terrace; she had never mentioned it but he knew. It was kept there in case she ever got locked out, which as far as he knew she never was – largely because the door was never locked. If the key was still there he could go in. He glanced back at Pepper, who was now making a huge fuss about the possibility of being fed. The fact that he could easily come out through the cat flap did not seem to occur to him. It was a matter of principle. He wanted Bryn inside. Now. With a smile, Bryn found the key, pushed open the door, slipped off his boots and padded into the kitchen. A handful of cat biscuits pacified the starving wild animal in Pepper at once.

Bryn stood still and stared round the kitchen. It felt different. He tiptoed over to the table. Her laptop lay there amidst a sheaf of papers and piles of books. He glanced at the papers. Doodles. Sketches, some of flowers. He picked one up and scrutinised it. It was good. Accurate. And it had captured the personality of the plant. There were lots of jotted notes as well and two fat notebooks, one of which was unused, the other already a quarter-full of her handwriting. Those he ignored. He glanced round and listened intently. The house was silent except for the delicate crunching of cat biscuits. Quietly he walked through into the great hall. All Sue's furniture was still there of course, but the surface detritus was different. Her stuff had gone; another set of belongings was scattered around the sitting room. Pens and paints and brushes; sketchbooks. There was a strong smell of paint. He wrinkled his nose. The table was covered with sketchbooks and there were paintings clipped to a makeshift clothesline across the room. So, she was a working artist. The pictures were lovely; he hadn't realised she was a professional painter. That must be how she earned her living.

A throw on the sofa was quite definitely not Sue's, and a

sweater, lying across the arm of one of the chairs wasn't hers either. Andy seemed to have a slightly boho, ethnic taste, quite unlike Sue's. Artistic was perhaps one way of describing it. He touched nothing, circling the room silently, just looking. Books everywhere. One or two he did pick up and he frowned. Mind, body and spirit was how they classified these things in book-shops. Ghosts. Meditation. Healing. Dreams.

Dreams. Ghosts.

'So, Catrin,' he whispered. 'Have you been making a nuisance of yourself already?'

It was nearly eleven the next morning when Andy pulled into her parking place, blessedly empty, and made her way up the steps to her front door. Pepper was sitting in the hall.

'I'm sorry,' she said at once. 'I'm going to make up for it now. Double rations. How does that sound?'

As she opened the cat-food drawer she saw the message light blinking on the phone. Turning her back on it she reached for a fork and filled Pepper's bowl with the requisite dose of tuna. He danced across the room on his back legs as she went to put the bowl down on the floor in its accustomed place, sniffed the food and then turned to her with a look of disdain on his face. She grinned. 'I was warned you would do that, my friend. I expect you've been stuffing yourself with delicious little mice or something while I was away. Up to you if you eat it or not.' She turned her back on him in her turn and pressed the play button on the phone. There was a moment's silence then Rhona's voice rang out in the room. 'I thought you would like to know all the burning is done. There's nothing left.'

Andy felt herself grow cold. She forced herself to take a deep breath, then she pressed the delete button. So the woman had found the phone number to this house. She must have been reading through the letters before she burned them and tried all the numbers till she got the right one. Andy shivered, aware that the burn on her hand was stinging.

She turned away from the dresser. While she had been distracted by the phone call someone had emptied the cat plate and licked it clean. Pepper was sitting in the middle of the floor, washing his whiskers. When he saw her watching him, he stopped washing and glared at her. 'You old hypocrite,' she said fondly. He held her gaze for a moment then he stood up and headed for the cat flap. It wasn't easy, she realised, to look dignified when you were halfway through a cat flap with only your bottom left in the room, but somehow he managed it and the flap shut with a snap behind his retreating tail.

She took a deep breath. She was not going to allow Rhona to wind her up. This was her own fault for leaving her letters behind, and everything else that Rhona claimed to have burnt. There must have been a lot of stuff in that house which she'd not had the time or space to pack up and bring away. Ten years of mementoes. But Rhona couldn't touch the memories. They were indelible. All she had to do was sit down and bring them back to mind – and that was more than Rhona had. Over the last ten years Rhona had virtually no memories of Graham at all.

Thinking about it, Rhona couldn't have been sure that the number she had dialled was going to find Andy. It can only have been a guess, unless somebody had told her. She swallowed hard, trying to master her panic at the thought. Did it really matter if the woman knew where she was?

Nevertheless she rang her mother.

'Darling, you know I wouldn't give your number to anyone, let alone that dreadful woman! How could you even think it?' Nina was indignant.

Hilary was even more cross. 'She wouldn't get it out of either of us with thumbscrews. It's much more likely to be the police,' she retorted indignantly. 'She could have tricked that young man who came to see us. He wasn't the brightest light on the Christmas tree, bless him. She'll never come up there, though, Andy. Good grief! Why would she? She wants shot of you, not to keep in touch.'

That much was true.

Andy didn't dare admit it was all her fault. It was she who had inadvertently tweaked a tiger's tail, and now she didn't know how to let go.

10

At Glyndyfrdwy all was silent for a while. Those who had remained in the hall waited and held their breath. The day faded into night and there was no sign of Dafydd's host nor of Sir Reginald and his men. Lady Margaret and her daughters and younger sons with other members of the Glyndŵr family had arrived, grim-faced and anxious, others had slipped away with Owain's brother, Tudur, up into the mountains, no doubt to rendezvous with Owain. Up there, in a hideaway deep in the Berwyn Mountains, Owain Glyndŵr was holding a council of war.

Dafydd sat at a makeshift desk and scribbled notes and wrote lines of poetry. His dreams had stopped and for two nights he slept soundly by the great banked fire, but his poetic zeal was in full flow. Catrin, nervous and wary, followed Lady Margaret as she walked in the sunlight outside. They were all waiting; even the birds had stopped singing.

The Lord of Ruthin did not return.

Three days after the aborted meeting with Grey, Owain Glyndŵr came back to Glyndyfrdwy full of resolve. The time for talking was over. He had tried conciliation. He was the descendant of princes, a man of courage and honour, a man of passion and justice and loyalty and he had been traduced and betrayed. Grey's hostility and plotting and scheming had been the last straw, one insult too many, not only to him but against the Welsh people. However reluctantly, it was time to lay down his lawyer's pen and pick up his sword. The prophets had spoken long ago and his bards, Crach and Iolo and Dafydd and men like them, had reminded him of his duty and his destiny. They had reminded him of his princely blood. His people were suffering the same insults, the same taxes, the same disparagement as he was. It was time to call a halt. The people of Wales needed a leader in their fight for freedom and he was the man to lead them. He was a true Welshman with royal lineage, he would reclaim the title of Prince of Wales from the son of King Henry. This Prince of Wales would be worthy of the title by descent from his royal ancestors, by his qualities of leadership and by his support throughout the country. His leadership, his resolution, and his victory had been foretold by the seers.

There was no need for Owain to send out a call to the people of Wales to come to his banner. Within days word had spread throughout Wales, into England and beyond, and men were flocking to his standard from every side. The fight for independence had begun. They came from the mountains and the coast and the valleys, in groups and singly, as word spread like wildfire that the time for waiting, for talking, was over. The men of North Wales had found a leader, a figurehead for their dreams.

The sixteenth of September was Owain's birthday, a symbolic day and coincidentally also the birthday of that other prince of Wales, the imposter in King Henry's court. Around three hundred people had gathered around the ancient motte in the angle of the river at Glyndyfrdwy, as Owain stepped forward on its summit and gripped the lance to which the banner of the princes of Powys, Owain's ancestors on his father's side, had been fixed, raising it above his head to the cheers of the crowd around him. On one side of him stood his eldest son,

Gruffudd, and on the other his brother, Tudur. All three men were looking up at the flag as the rampant black lion with its vicious claws rippled and thundered in the wind.

Catrin was there, at the front of the crowd, by her father's side, her eyes fixed on Owain's face. Behind her, Edmund too was gazing up at this man who had transformed himself seemingly overnight from a country gentleman into a warrior prince. She felt it as a physical wave of energy, the determination and pride and excitement of the people around them. Their cheers rang out across the countryside and came back to them with the cry of the eagle and the raven from the distant cliffs and valleys.

There would be war. It was inevitable.

The next morning Owain called Dafydd and Catrin to the chamber he had set aside as his headquarters while his plans were laid and as they waited for more and more men to make their way to his standard. 'Dafydd, my friend,' he said quietly. He was standing in front of the fire, wearing his long gown and cloak, looking more like the lawyer he had been trained to be than the warrior in armour of the day before. 'You have done me a great service, and I thank you for it. And you, Catrin.' He smiled down at her. 'But now you must go home.'

Dafydd stared at him. 'No! Not now. Not just as things are falling into place.'

Owain sighed. 'They will not just fall into place, Dafydd. We will have to fight and fight bitterly for what we want, you know that as well as I do. There will be bloodshed – you said as much. You foresaw it in your dreams. The men of Wales are gathering behind me. Two arrived this morning who had ridden posthaste from Oxford University where they had thrown up their studies to join my standard. Word has travelled the length and breadth of the land like lightning. If you were on your own, Dafydd, I might ask you to stay with me, but you have your daughter to consider. I cannot ask you to risk her life by being in the vanguard of the fighting. I have my seers here, Iolo and Crach, and they will stay with me. So go, my friend, with my thanks and my blessing.' He pressed a bag of coins into Dafydd's hand.

'No!' Dafydd repeated. 'You can't send me away. Not now.'

Iolo and Crach had insisted Owain dismiss Dafydd. He was a disruptive presence, they said. His dreams were inconsistent. Owain had listened. He was used to petty jealousies amongst his advisors, but he too heard the wild unpredictability in Dafydd's declarations. 'I can send you away, Dafydd, and I command it. As your prince.' He turned to Catrin and reached over onto the table. 'I want you to have this, my dear. A necklace which Margaret thought you would like.' He picked up a smaller pouch and poured the contents into his palm. 'Let me fix it for you.' He stepped towards her and fastened the necklace round her neck. It was made of gold and hung with garnets.

Catrin raised her hand to the cold gems. It was a magnificent gift. 'My prince. No. I want to stay too. My father is right, we can't go now.'

He wagged his finger at her. 'You must. I will not be responsible for putting you in danger any more than I would my own wife and daughters. I am sending them back to Sycharth today. We ride out tomorrow to take the battle to Ruthin.'

He held her gaze. 'Do not be embarrassed that you went there, child. You and your father were able to warn us about Grey's treachery. You probably saved my life and all Wales will thank you for that.' He turned to the table and picked up a pen. 'Now leave me. Tell the men waiting outside that they should come in.'

Dafydd and Catrin looked at one another. She saw the devastation on her father's face. 'No. Please. You can't send us away,' she cried. 'I will go. I will go back to Sycharth with the Lady Margaret, but please, let my father stay. You need him. He is the best seer in the whole of Wales.'

He smiled. 'I am sure he is, Catrin. But he has a beautiful daughter and I would not want her to be hurt. I know what war is. I would not wish any woman to be needlessly present.'

'I wear your ring,' she said suddenly. She brandished her hand in front of him. 'You gave it to me three years ago and I have worn it ever since. You can't send me away.'

He glanced down at her hand and reaching out gave it a squeeze. 'When I am triumphant and the English are driven from the land and I have a royal court to entertain you, you will come to me and remind me of the ring you wear, Catrin. I will remember your loyalty, I promise.'

He stood and waited. There was nothing for it. They had to leave.

Outside in the courtyard Dafydd was furious. 'You could have gone with the Lady Margaret. Because of you, I am to miss all this!' His gesticulating hand took in the crowds of men and horses massing on the water meadows below the lodge. He clenched his teeth furiously.

'But I offered to go with her.' Catrin was stunned at the injustice of his remark. 'You heard me. I begged him to let you stay.'

'And he said no.' Dafydd stared round. 'And now we have to find our horses. And Edmund.'

'Edmund!' She looked round, stunned. She didn't remember having seen him since they had stood together and watched Owain raise the banner. How would they ever find him in all these crowds?

Prince Owain had, it appeared, thought of that. A messenger had been sent to find Edmund and their horses in the stables. Edmund was starry-eyed. 'I would fight for Prince Owain to the death,' he said as Dafydd called him over. 'I have sworn my allegiance. I am to be one of his bowmen.'

'I think not,' Dafydd snapped. 'You are escorting me and my daughter back to Brycheiniog.'

Edmund stared at him, his face white with shock. 'No,' he whispered. 'I can't. I have sworn allegiance—'

'And so you will obey his orders. He has told us that you will escort us back to Sycharth, where we exchange these horses

160

for our own, and then we have to return south.' Dafydd's own expression was bleak. Edmund made no move to bring the horses forward. 'Well, boy, go and find our bags!' Dafydd ordered testily. 'This pleases me no more than it pleases you, but Lord Owain has given the order. He needs to protect Catrin. If she hadn't come, this wouldn't have happened.'

'That's not fair!' Catrin exploded. 'You asked me to come on this journey with you and you have been pleased I was here. All the way! Prince Owain thanked me. He recognised my service.'

'And he saw you as a hindrance,' her father retorted. 'Hurry, Edmund. Fetch our belongings and we will go. We need to be on the road by noon or we will be caught again by the dusk. At least we can spread the word as we go and tell the people of Wales that their deliverance has come, even if we are to be no part of it.'

It was the fourth time the landline had rung, piercing Andy's dream, and each time she had ignored it, sinking back into a half-waking reverie as she sat dozing at the kitchen table. Opening her eyes she finally picked it up and answered. There was silence on the other end of the line. 'Hello?' she repeated.

There was another moment's silence and then clearly she heard a quiet laugh, a woman's laugh, before the caller hung up.

Andy sat still for several minutes, staring into the distance, her mind a blank until slowly her faculties began to work again. So Rhona knew where she was. So what? It was one hundred and seventy-odd miles from Kew to Hay. The woman was not going to travel all this way, just to be unpleasant.

She picked up her ballpoint and looked at the open notebook before her. Then she looked again. This was her writing all right, but pages and pages of it? When had she written all that? She could feel her chest tightening with fear as she turned the pages back one by one, noting words here and there which stood out clearly – Owain. Prince. Sycharth. Other bits of the text were so wildly scribbled she couldn't read them, or at least not easily, packed onto the pages with an urgency she couldn't recall at all.

Catrin and Edmund were not speaking. Catrin and her father were not speaking. They were riding fast southwards, stopping for only one night at a time, spreading the word of Glyndŵr's uprising, greeted in some places by excitement and enthusiasm, in others with horror and anger at the thought of war.

At a farmstead near Newtown they had gathered a piece of news which made them all pause. Owain had led his men to Ruthin. The castle had proved too much for the small band of bitter men, but they had overrun the town and burned it to the ground. Catrin gasped as she heard the account. Lord and Lady Grey and their family had not been there. They had already left for the south. But what of the others she had met? What of Mary and Anne? Had they been safely in the castle, peering over the battlements as the smoke rose from the burning buildings, or had they been out there in the town? There was no word of casualties. From Ruthin, Owain's men had marched on to Denbigh, Flint and Oswestry, amongst other places, targeting English strongholds to show them he meant business. Then as Catrin, Dafydd and Edmund moved on south, further and further away from the action, they heard, via a king's messenger, taking the news on a sweating horse back along the high road to Westminster, that Sir Hugh Burnell had mustered a huge army of local men and defeated Owain's small band near Welshpool. Catrin and Dafydd listened to the news with dry mouths and anxious hearts, but there the news stopped. Owain's men had withdrawn as swiftly as they had attacked. His little army had disappeared. He had vanished into the misty mountains.

Edmund was not dismayed. He grinned at them when he heard the news. 'I heard one of his bowmen say he is a magician. He can order the weather, command the clouds. The English will never catch him,' he announced. 'I can't imagine where he could have learned such arts.' He glanced at Catrin and she blushed.

Edmund went on: 'But now he has started on his campaign he will continue until he has secured Wales as an independent kingdom in its own right.'

Dafydd looked at him doubtfully. 'You think so, Edmund?'

'I know it.' Edmund turned back to them, readying them for the road. They had spent the night at a roadside inn and were preparing to leave as the messenger had ridden in. They still had a long way to go. 'Don't you think he will win?' the younger man swung back to face Dafydd, his arms full of bridles and halters. 'Didn't you dream of success for him? Didn't you tell him he was the son of the prophets, foretold in the ancient prophecies – the *Mab Darogan*.' For all he was an English speaker, Edmund could get his tongue round the Welsh language when he needed to.

Dafydd nodded slowly. 'I dreamed that, yes. But I dreamed of other things too. Of death and destruction.'

Catrin swallowed. She would never forget the notes in her father's study, the anguished nightmares, the fear, the taste of blood on the wind. He hadn't been the only one to forecast disaster as well as triumph.

'There is always death in war,' Edmund said cheerfully. 'The important thing is who wins in the end.'

'Indeed.' Dafydd's voice was dry. 'I suggest you put that bridle on the horse, Edmund. We have a few miles to go today yet.' He turned away, pulling his cloak around him and waited, arms folded, his eyes on the distant hills.

Andy jerked herself out of the dream. She had been reading the last page of her notes, trying to decipher her writing and then all at once she had been back in the past. She could hear the melancholy cry of a curlew in her head, smell the sweet grass and the heather on the high pass as the three travellers made their way south. It was late. They would have to camp again on the open hill unless they could beg or bribe an outlying farm to give them hospitality for the night, something which was getting ever harder as news of the fighting in the north spread and people grew more and more wary of strangers.

This time they were travelling fast. They were anxious to get home. As Andy watched, no longer conscious of herself as an eavesdropper but as an unseen member of the party, she saw everything as they gave up hope of reaching Painscastle before nightfall. Edmund guided them into a sheltered *cwm*, safe from prying eyes and from the cold wind that swept down from the bleak crest of the Hergest Ridge. He unsaddled the horses, lifted off the packs and tethered the beasts in a small glade where they could graze on grass, still relatively rich in a damp corner beneath the rocks. Then he returned to Dafydd and Catrin and lit a fire.

Dafydd had wrapped himself in his cloak. He sat down on a slab of stone and stared into the flames. 'We'll be back tomorrow or the next day,' Edmund murmured. He had found oatcakes and cheese and dried meat in one of the saddlebags and was distributing the food between them. 'Shall I heat water?'

He was looking at Catrin. 'Why ask me? You decided to stop here,' she retorted.

'We agreed it was too dark to continue,' he said patiently. 'It is sheltered here and relatively safe. I can make us a hot drink, or I can mull some ale.'

'We'll have ale,' Dafydd snapped over his shoulder. 'Don't ask her. She is as cross as a bag of weasels.'

Edmund rummaged for one of the stoppered jugs in the pack and found their three horn mugs. 'Do we know why she is cross?' Edmund asked softly. He was not addressing the remark at Dafydd.

'Because I am exhausted and cold and saddlesore!' Catrin

164

snapped. 'And I am tired of being ordered about by the likes of you.'

'The likes of me,' Edmund repeated, his voice even. 'And what exactly am I like?'

She pulled her cloak more tightly around her. 'You give me orders. You ignore my opinion. You decide where we stop. You don't listen to anything I say. You treat me as though I am but a servant.'

'A servant – like me – and not a great lady?' Edmund sounded puzzled. He stood before her, mugs in one hand, jug in the other. 'How can that be?' He set the jug down on the hastily improvised hearthstone. 'Forgive me my lady.' He swept a low bow. 'I am truly sorry if I have offended.'

Catrin blushed. Angrily she scrambled to her feet and walked off into the darkness. 'Ignore her, boy,' Dafydd called over his shoulder. 'She has an attack of the megrims! Give me some ale.'

Edmund poured it for him and handed him the mug, then leaving him still sitting on his stone he turned to survey the darkness, looking for Catrin. There was no sign of her. He frowned. It was all very well him saying it was safe but up here in the wilds of Elfael it was anything but. The countryside on the high moors was rough and desolate, and the rocky outcrops and steep river valleys were treacherous; the place was known to be a hideout for outlaws and thieves. He walked a little way away from the fire, allowing his eyes to become accustomed to the dark.

She hadn't gone far. He could see her outline against the stars, sitting on an outcrop of rocks. She was facing away from him, staring out into the night. Silently he approached her. He stopped several paces away. 'Will you come and have some food,' he said quietly.

He saw her shoulders stiffen but she didn't reply.

'Please,' he added. 'Let me mull a little ale for you. It will help keep you warm.' Again she ignored him. He stepped closer. 'Catrin—'

'Do you not understand!' She spun round. 'I will not have you address me like that!' She stood up and took a pace towards him.

He grabbed her arms, forcing her to look at him. 'Why?' he said. 'What else am I to call you? I have been calling you Catrin for the last three months!' As they stood staring at each other in the darkness he moved forward infinitesimally and kissed her lightly on the lips. He was still holding her and his grip did not relax. She said nothing so he leaned forward and kissed her again, more firmly this time, and this time she broke free, wrenching her arms out of his grip and ran a few steps away from him. He waited several seconds then at last he spoke. 'Well, aren't you going to call your father?' he asked. 'Aren't you going to tell me I am dismissed? Aren't you going to tell me you never want to speak to me again?'

She didn't reply. He stepped after her. 'Answer me, Catrin!' he ordered.

She made a little whimpering noise in her throat. She was crying.

He frowned, then he reached out for her and gathered her into his arms. This time neither of them spoke. When he had finished kissing her he smiled down into her eyes. 'So, all that anger was because you knew you could not resist me.'

She shook her head violently.

'No?'

'No!'

'I've seen you watching me when I touched the horses,' he whispered. 'You were wishing it was you standing there, under my hands.'

'No!' She pulled away from him.'

They both looked up suddenly as they heard a voice calling. 'Catrin?' Dafydd had moved from his seat. Now they could see his silhouette against the fire as he stood there looking round. 'Where are you? We should eat our supper and get some sleep. We need to leave at sun-up.'

Catrin dodged past Edmund and hurried towards her father. When she looked back from the safety of the circle of firelight there was no sign of Edmund. He was still standing in the shadows staring out into the dark.

11

Andy had thrown the kitchen door wide open to the sunshine. It was one of those glorious October days scented with damp earth and mushrooms and bonfires. She wondered where the smell of smoke was coming from. Not from her own chimney. She might light a fire later, but for now she was content to sniff the air. She stepped outside and wandered up the path between the herb beds. Had Bryn lit a bonfire? There was no sign of him. She hadn't seen him for several days now and there was no sign of Pepper either. Having scoffed his breakfast he was off about his own adventures. She gave a tolerant smile. She didn't blame him. It was a day for being outside. The early morning chill was already wearing off and the heavy dew was evaporating fast.

She turned her back on the brook and made her way through the garden towards the cliff face at the back, wandering through the herb beds, breaking off a leaf here and a flower head there, rubbing them between her fingers and sniffing the aromatic oils they released. She paused as she came to the shrubbery which concealed the cave. Someone, presumably Bryn, had piled a huge stack of pea sticks across the entrance, concealing it completely. She stood regarding it for several minutes. Why had he put them there? She looked round, carefully noting the surrounding flowerbeds, the orchard, the winding paths. There were dozens of other places he could have put them. Had he blocked off the entrance deliberately? Or hidden it? Didn't he know she had seen it already? She stared at the place where the entrance had been for a moment longer then she turned and wandered away.

Retracing her steps slowly through the garden she spotted Bryn at last. He was walking towards the far end of the stock beds, his back towards her, a canvas bag slung across his shoulder. She stopped and watched him, aware that she was partially concealed by a couple of large hypericum bushes. He stopped at the edge of the bed and stood surveying it for a full minute before throwing down his bag, and taking off his jacket, hanging it from the branch of a crab-apple tree, heavy with fruit. Quietly she retraced her steps following one of the other paths down towards the brook. The water cascaded over the rocks, catching the sunlight, and slowly she became aware of a small bird standing on one of the wet slabs. It surveyed the stream, head to one side, then dived straight in. A dipper. She smiled. Another of her father's passions – birdwatching.

When she glanced back she saw Bryn. He was standing watching her. She raised a hand to wave but he had already turned away.

She was tempted to do the same – go back inside and have breakfast – but then she paused. She was not going to be intimidated by this wretched man.

'Good morning, Bryn.' She greeted him cheerfully. 'Isn't it a lovely day.'

He looked up from his bag. 'Good morning.' He was fishing out several packets of seeds, a dibber, and a trowel.

'The cave at the back there, where you've stacked the sticks. It's an interesting feature,' she went on. 'Did you block the entrance deliberately?' Her eyes were fixed on his face.

He remained impassive. 'I always store the bamboos there over winter. It allows them to dry out.'

'But doesn't it stop the bats flying in and out?' She wasn't sure she had seen any bats, but it was a good bet they were there.

He looked taken aback. 'I'm sure they find a way round.'

'I would suggest you move them,' she said firmly. 'Don't make it so hard for the poor creatures. They're a protected species, aren't they? I'm sure there is somewhere else you can dry pea sticks.' She turned away and headed back towards the kitchen. She did not turn round. She could guess his expression without the pleasure of seeing it.

As though to emphasise her bid for control she paused as she crossed the herb beds to pick a handful of blooms. By the time she had regained the house she was smiling quietly to herself. She put them in a glass of water and set them on the work table in the living room beside her paints. They would form her next project.

There was something else to do while she was in the mood. She picked up the phone. 'Krista?'

'Well, hello stranger.' Her agent sounded pleased to hear her voice, which was a start.

'Sorry for the long silence. I need advice.'

They talked for half an hour, after which she hung up and sat staring into space. So, she was not as broke as she had feared. She still had an income, independent of Graham, she had royalties due any moment which Rhona would be unable to touch and she had one, possibly two offers on the table for commissions for illustrating further books. Besides that, Krista suggested blithely, it was time to consider an exhibition. Why not? Her name needed to be put out there again. 'I was only waiting for a sign from you, honey,' Krista had said. 'What do you say we meet up for lunch and discuss it all?'

'I'm not ready for London yet,' Andy replied firmly. 'Can you email me the details so I can think about them? I'll be ready for work soon, just not quite yet. I have things still to do.'

'OK, kiddo!' Krista laughed. 'Don't take too long. We're missing you. And, Andy? Welcome back to the world.'

What did she have to do? Really. Andy sipped at her mug of coffee. Well, Catrin for a start. She wanted to know so much more about Catrin. It was like having a film running constantly inside her head, a film she could turn on and off almost at will. She pulled her notebook towards her and glanced down at it. The storyline between Catrin and Edmund was developing nicely. She smiled. Perhaps she should be a novelist. *Chapter 21: The kiss!* She chuckled to herself. The kiss had not gone well. Catrin had not spoken to Edmund again that night and indeed not for the rest of the journey. If her father had noticed anything, he had not said; he was probably too self-obsessed.

She flipped back through the pages. There was definitely a strong attraction there. Edmund fancied Catrin – and who wouldn't, she was an attractive young woman – but was the feeling reciprocated? At first she had thought so. Andy picked up her pencil and rattled it against her teeth. Now, she wasn't so sure. She stared across at the dresser, not really seeing it. How old was Catrin? Eighteen? Perhaps nineteen by now? Perhaps more. So why wasn't she married? Surely all women in medieval times married early unless they were nuns or something. Nowhere in her dreams did she remember seeing or hearing if there was a suitor or an ex. Perhaps she had been married, like Edmund, and her husband had died. Was that likely? Or was it possible that Dafydd had forbidden her to marry; that he had kept his daughter at home to look after him? That seemed a distinct possibility, given his selfishness. But Catrin was a feisty woman. Surely she wouldn't have stood for that. She could have packed up her stuff and gone.

Gone where?

She seemed to have a lot of friends and fans. Her visit across Wales had proved that much. But neighbours? Andy had never seen or heard of any neighbours, save for the woman Efa who had taught Catrin weather witching. Andy reached for her mug again. Efa was an interesting person. She wasn't that old. She was far from being the archetypal witch in the wood. She seemed intelligent, educated even. Her spells and incantations sounded complex and powerful rather than just being simple rhymes. She invoked the elementals, the nature spirits who commanded the wind and the rain.

The knock at the back door made her jump. Bryn stood there, his hand cupped against his pullover. 'I thought you would like to see something,' he said. 'As you're interested in bats.'

Andy stepped back so he could come in, wondering fleetingly if this was payback time. Assuming he had picked up the body of a bat in the cave, did he expect her to scream and wave her arms about and tell him to take it away? As he opened his hand she saw the tiny creature, clutching his fingers with the minute claws at the edge of its wings. It wasn't dead as she had expected, but it was clearly stunned. 'I think it's OK,' he said softly. 'A victim of our Pepper, I'm afraid.'

'It's lovely,' she whispered. 'He is a bad cat. Are you sure it will be OK?'

'I can't see any injuries. He leapt at it as it flew out of the cave.' He glanced up at her. 'I was moving the pea sticks as instructed and it disturbed them.'

'So, it's my fault?'

'I didn't say that.' He gently touched the tiny creature with his little finger, stroking its back. 'It's a pipistrelle.' He didn't return her glance. 'I'll take it back to the cave. If you could call Pepper in and distract him for a bit.'

She gave a rueful smile. 'Since when has he come when called?'

'Try shaking his biscuit box. He's just outside the door. He wanted to know what I was going to do with his bat. He seemed a bit scared of it once he'd caught it. He put it down and looked faintly disgusted.'

Andy laughed. 'I know the expression. He doesn't expect his mice to have wings, I guess.' She turned to the dresser and found the biscuits. Almost at once Pepper appeared in the doorway looking supremely innocent. He ignored Bryn. As she reached for the bowl, Bryn slipped out of the door with his small scrap of rescued fur.

He did not return.

She went back to her notebook, closed it, and after a few moments began slowly to climb the stairs.

She allowed Bryn and his bat to slip from her mind. Her bedroom had been Catrin's bedroom. Where better to call Catrin back and find out what happened next.

Rhona was sitting at her desk staring at the road atlas. She had found Hay-on-Wye. Sleeper's Castle wasn't marked. Presumably it wasn't a proper castle anyway. She sat back thinking hard. She had the postcode from the address book and she had a satnav in the car. That was all she needed. But did she really want to go there and see the place for herself? She looked down at her hands, clenched into fists on the table in front of her. In the course of the last few days her jealousy and anger had tipped over into something far more unmanageable. She'd had no rest; no sleep. Every time she went to the window she expected to see Andy's face out there, pressed against the glass. She hadn't been able to go out into the garden for fear of meeting her again. Why? Why did the woman keep coming back to haunt her?

She leaned back in her chair. Haunt was the right word. She was a ghost, flitting back and forth between the flowerbeds and under the trees, drifting up the stairs and into the bedrooms. Once she had seen her standing in front of Graham's portrait, painted by a friend of his, staring at it. When Rhona came into the room she had turned and looked at her and then she had disappeared as if she had never been there. Rhona pushed back the chair and stood up, her hands still clenched into fists. Andy had destroyed her life with Graham, stolen her husband, hijacked her home and her marriage. Perhaps the figure was no more than a figment of her imagination, but whatever it was, she had to make it stop.

She walked slowly out into the hall and stared down at the doormat. A pile of post lay there from the morning. It would all be for Andy. Letters seemed to have stopped coming for Graham, but they still arrived addressed to 'Miranda Dysart'. She stooped and picked them up. Two pieces of junk mail and three envelopes, two official-looking, one a personal hand-written envelope. All for Miranda. She almost spat with rage as she carried them into the kitchen, tore all of them across the middle and tossed them into the bin. That was it. The last straw.

She stood and stared at herself in the mirror in the hall. Whatever she decided to do about Miranda, it would be justifiable; a *crime passionnel.* She smiled grimly. Whatever it was, it didn't matter. She had no intention of being caught.

To her extreme frustration and annoyance, Andy had no dreams about Catrin for two nights. As far as she could remember she had no dreams at all and her notebook, which she had left beside her bed with a pencil tucked between the pages in case she awoke in the middle of the night and wanted to write something down, remained untouched.

To temper her frustration she went down into Hay twice to poke around the bookshops and came back with several books on Owain Glyndŵr. At first she hadn't been entirely sure she wanted to know what happened to him, but now she couldn't wait to read them. Even Sian seemed to know more than her about his history, and surely it would help to understand Catrin's life if she knew what was happening.

Outside, the brief spell of sunshine was over and the room darkened as another rain cloud drifted up the valley. Even in here near the Aga she found herself shivering. She'd left her sweater lying over the arm of the sofa next door, so she got up to retrieve it, pulled it on, then returned to her chair near the Aga and began to read the introduction.

The great Welsh hero, Owain Glyndŵr, had fought to make Wales a sovereign state. He had been born in or about 1354 and had died some time around 1415; both dates, it appeared, were approximate. This was a man of mystery as well as fame. His rebellion had begun on that fateful September day in the year 1400 when, goaded beyond endurance by the behaviour of his deceitful neighbour, Owain had given up on being Mr Nice Guy and had raised his flag in rebellion. She looked up from the page. She had been there. She had seen him do it.

The background history was complex. Wales had been a target since the Normans began to peer over the mountains at it and Edward I had built his string of great castles; before that the Romans had done the same. After all, Wales had gold. Glyndŵr's own history too was complicated. The heir on both sides of his family to ancient Welsh principalities, he had the royal blood but for much of his career he had been a loyal servant of both the Earls of Arundel and King Richard II, learning his skills at guerrilla warfare while fighting on the king's side in the wars against the Scots. By 1400 Henry IV was in charge in England and Welsh border politics had become inextricably tied up with the Wars of the Roses.

The speed with which Glyndŵr's popularity had escalated was easy to explain once one had read the history. Two hundred years of resentment by the population of Wales, plus the man's undoubted charisma and talent as a soldier. And the incredible influence of the poets and bards. Again Andy paused in her reading. Crach and Iolo were real, famous men. They were the media personalities, the celebs of their day. The stories they relayed and the myths they recited had real power. She found herself thinking back to the two men she had seen through Catrin's eyes at Glyndŵr's momentous gathering that night at Glyndyfrdwy. Crach was a short, thin, wiry man with wild white hair and piercing dark eyes that missed nothing. His age was hard to guess. His face was weathered and he leaned on a staff but he was probably of no more than middle years. Iolo on the other hand had been elderly. Her book said he was born about 1328, which would put him in his early seventies. He had faded red hair and blue eyes. Unlike Crach, who wore a simple floor length black tunic with a leather belt, he was richly attired in doublet and hose with over them a gown and a fur-trimmed cloak. Mud-splashed from his hasty ride he neverthe-less looked every inch the gentleman. Iolo, the poet, had a powerful melodious voice. Crach, the prophet, had sat next to Glyndŵr and whispered in his ear and his hostility to Catrin's father had been impossible to hide.

The book she was reading quoted endless sources – letters, statutes, annals. It quoted a lot from a chap called Adam of Usk. After a while she began to skip the detail, looking for specific references to Glyndŵr the man rather than the toing and froing of the armies. It appeared to have been a vicious war of attrition. Both armies burnt and laid waste to towns and villages and land, trying to starve each other out as they rampaged up and down and across the land. Castles were a particular target – in-your-face centres of English power, which the Welsh slowly captured one by one. Glyndŵr had dreams – dreams of creating Wales's own university, of having its own archbishop, of negotiating with other nations like France and Scotland as an equal. And at first those countries encouraged his ambitions, lending their support.

For ten years the battle raged on, then almost as swiftly as it had arisen, the rebellion began to die. The English under Prince Hal, the other 'Prince of Wales', finally began to win the upper hand; the French and the Scots were distracted elsewhere, and, above all, the people of Wales, sick of all the brutality, starvation and suffering, began to lose faith in the man in whom they had invested such hope.

One final defeat, one more retreat by Glyndŵr into the

mountains, which had always been his friend, and it was over. He disappeared from history if not from myth.

Andy spent three days reading the first book, then at last she pushed it aside with a sigh. So, Dafydd's predictions had been right on both counts. There had been success, but there had also been blood, fire and death.

And what of Catrin and Dafydd in all this? What had happened to them? This house and garden were tied into the story of Glyndŵr through them, but what had happened in the end? Only her dreams would tell her the answer to that.

Had knowing the basic bones of what happened helped her understanding of what Catrin and Dafydd were going through? She wasn't sure.

She wanted to go back and see.

And found herself yet again back in Kew. In the dream she walked slowly across the garden towards the incinerator and peered sadly down into the ashes. There was no trace of what had been burned there. Lying on the ground near the bin was a long sturdy stick. Judging by its ash-covered charred tip it had been used to stir the ashes to make sure nothing remained. Andy turned away miserably. A few of Graham's favourite plants were flowering now, delicate autumn roses, chrysanthemums, Michaelmas daisies, but the garden was beginning to look overgrown and untidy. It would have broken his heart to see his treasured azaleas and sedum nearly hidden by weeds. Cautiously Andy climbed onto the veranda. The windows in the kitchen were shuttered and the curtains in the living room closed. The house felt empty. She wasn't tempted to go inside. Instead she drifted round to the garage and looked through the gate towards the front entrance. There was no sign of Rhona's car.

Rhona drove up the farm track to the B & B and parked beside two other cars in front of the old farmhouse. Reaching for her bags, she stood looking up at the front of the house. It looked old and beautifully mellow in the late afternoon sun, the stone facade hung with crimson Virginia creeper. As she stood gazing at it, the front door opened. 'Mrs Jenkins?'

Rhona smiled. It had been second nature to use an alias.

She joined the other guests in the sitting room once she had been shown her bedroom and had a chance to unpack. They were sitting in front of a table laden with Welshcakes and biscuits as their hostess poured the tea. 'I like to welcome my weekend guests with a proper tea,' the woman said with a warm smile. 'After that you're on your own food wise, I'm afraid. Apart from breakfast, of course.'

The other guests were more than ready to discuss their plans for the weekend. The older couple, white-haired, smart and American, full of enthusiasm and excitement, were here looking for their Welsh roots; the other pair, English, younger and intense, were going to spend the whole weekend in the book-shops of Hay.

Rhona had her story ready. 'I'm photographing old trees, poking round graveyards mostly, looking at yews.' It gave her an excuse to be out all day and to drive up into the hills to remote hamlets and isolated churches. Her prolonged scrutiny of the Ordnance Survey map she had bought at a roadside service station had finally pinpointed Sleeper's Castle. It looked impossibly remote, but not so far away she couldn't go there, straight away after tea.

It was not a sensible plan. The light was fading by the time she climbed back into her car with her bag and her camera. The sun was setting into a bowl of crimson mist as she headed down what passed for a main road along the bottom of the valley until she came to the turning. The lane was narrow and steep, the hedgerows hanging low over the car as she changed down to a lower gear, going more and more slowly as the road continued to narrow and wind as it climbed.

She had almost given up, assuming she had taken the wrong road, when she rounded a corner and saw Sleeper's Castle. The house stood up on a ledge above the road, with an almost vertical garden and steep steps leading up towards it from the parking space, which was occupied by the mud-spattered Passat which she recognised as Andy's, and, beside it, a small scruffy van. Stopping her car in the middle of the lane, with the engine still running, she stared up at the house. It was beguiling in its way, built of ancient stone, with attractive creepers and an exquisite old lichen-covered roof. There were no other houses in sight, as she had seen on the map. In front of it, on the right, behind the hedge, the valley plunged away towards unimaginable distances, swallowed now by the fading sunset and the coming night.

She wasn't interested in the view. As she gazed up at the house she could feel its attraction. She clenched her hands on the steering wheel and took a deep breath to control the surge of excitement which filled her. She had arrived.

Eventually she managed to pull herself together. With a shiver she engaged first gear and drove on up the lane.

It was only minutes later that Bryn appeared. He ran down the steps, his holdall over his shoulder, and climbed into his van. Reversing out he headed back down the hill unaware that somewhere above him Rhona Wilson had driven over the cattle grid onto the mountain and into the mist.

12

The dream of Catrin returned. Lying restlessly on her bed Andy had drifted into sleep, listening to the radio, slowly becoming aware that Dafydd and his daughter were home. Edmund had bedded down their horses, carried their luggage into the house and dumped it onto the flagstones in the hall, greeted his sister and vanished without a further word.

Catrin watched him go with relief, greeted Joan with a hug and ran upstairs to her bedroom. The room was ready for her, with a freshly shaken feather bed, and blankets. Her table was dusted, her books neatly stacked on the shelf near the window. Joan followed her upstairs, dragging Catrin's saddlebags after her, and proceeded to unpack, hanging up her gowns and her cloak from the pegs on the wall, folding clean linen into the coffers and throwing clothes that needed laundering onto a pile. 'So?' She glanced up at Catrin. 'Did the tour go well?'

Catrin shivered. 'We went to a great many places.' They had left home in the early summer. Now it was autumn and a gale was roaring up the valley, lifting the wall hangings and rattling the shutters. She reached for a shawl off the bed. 'I have missed being home, though.'

'Did you see any of the unrest?' Joan shook out her shifts before folding them. 'I hear there is war in the north.' She looked up and Catrin saw the gleam of fear in her eyes.

'We heard a lot about it,' she said, trying to keep her voice reassuring. 'We were up in the north as it started. We went to Ruthin, the first town to fall.'

'And the Lord Glyndŵr, the man they call the rightful Prince of Wales. Did you see him?' Joan's eyes were hard.

Catrin remembered the long nights when they had discussed their journey and the places they were likely to go. Joan knew they were planning to visit Sycharth. 'We were there just before the start of the rebellion. Prince Owain and the Lady Margaret sent us away to safety. We made the best speed we could all the way back.'

'I trust you did not swear allegiance to him,' Joan put in tartly. 'The man is a traitor. My father says he will be hung, drawn and quartered when King Henry lays hands on him, and the same goes for all his followers.'

Catrin was shocked to silence. 'And does everyone round here feel the same?' she asked eventually.

Joan shrugged her shoulders carelessly. 'Not everyone. There are always differences. Brother against brother, father against son. You know the way it is.'

'And you and your father are of a mind to support the king?'

'Of course. As will Edmund.' She narrowed her eyes. 'He was in a hurry to ride back to the farm.'

'My fault. We did not always see eye to eye.' Wearily Catrin rubbed her face. 'He is a strong character, your brother. He did not appreciate having to obey orders.'

'From you?' Joan stared at her fiercely. 'He wouldn't.'

Catrin gave a wry smile. 'Nor from my *tad* either. But he was a good guide. He got us there and he got us home without mishap. My father will pay him well, have no fear.'

Joan sighed. 'I don't understand why he didn't wait to be paid now.'

'He's been worrying about your father and the farm. I know he felt bad about leaving your father on his own.'

'He wasn't on his own,' Joan retorted sharply. 'Our brother Richard was in charge.'

'Then I don't know what it was, but something worried him. I am sure he will be back soon. As you say, he will want to pick up his money,' Catrin replied. 'And now, is there a meal ready, Joan? My father is ravenous. Between them, he and Edmund insisted we ride as fast as we could this morning. We left our camp at sun-up and the horses have been fed and stabled, but we are still famished.'

Joan gathered up an armful of clothes for the wash. 'It will be ready soon. I guessed you would be back today. You were seen approaching Painscastle by a king's messenger who passed on the news as he rode through Hay. One of the boys brought word up the hill.'

Catrin followed her downstairs. There was no sign of Dafydd and she guessed he was already in his study. His saddlebags lay open on the floor, his books and pens missing. Catrin bent to retrieve her harp and checked it carefully for damage after the long journey.

'Did they enjoy your music?' Joan enquired. She pushed aside the basket which held her spindle and carding combs and several hanks of raw wool and began to lay plates and spoons and knives on the trestle table.

Catrin nodded. 'I was well rewarded. Once or twice I played before the whole company, although mostly it was to the women in their quarters.'

'So, will you go again next year?'

'I hope so.' Catrin bent to throw a log on the fire as Joan disappeared into the kitchen. The rich smell of mutton stew was beginning to filter through the house.

Catrin and her father sat up late after their meal, close to the fire, alone in the house. Joan had asked permission to go to her father's for the night and Dafydd, with unaccustomed grace, had told her to take the mule now it had had a few hours' rest and stay two days if she wished. It meant Catrin would have to make do with the little servant Betsi to do all the housework, but she didn't resent the fact that he didn't give that side of his largesse a thought. He gave Joan a bag of coins, half of what was owed to Edmund, and bade her ride straight there.

'That was kind,' Catrin said. She pulled her cloak around her as the wind howled under the door. 'She was upset that Edmund rode off so fast.'

'Hmm.' Dafydd's comment was noncommittal.

'Have you spoken to the other servants?' She reached for her mug of warm ale and sipped it gratefully. Made by Joan and herself, it had a clear, full flavour, unlike many of the brews they had sampled on the hurried ride back. 'Betsi and Peter will have to look after things until she gets back.'

He nodded. 'There is much unrest round here, the same as everywhere else we've been,' Dafydd went on thoughtfully. 'People are divided. There are those who support the king, especially those who live across the Wye. Then there are those who say we have suffered too much under English laws which are so punitive towards those of Welsh birth. They say Owain is right. Enough is enough. We have to fight for our freedom.'

'It would be wise to keep our counsel though,' Catrin put in. 'This is where we live. In the past weeks we have been on the move and heard every degree of opinion. It is going to be very bitter if any fighting comes this way. It won't, will it?' she added. It was a plea.

Dafydd looked across at her. 'My dreams say it will. I fear it could engulf the whole of Wales,' he said softly. 'I am sorry, *cariad*, but my dreams say it will consume us all before it is done.' He paused. 'On the other hand, the news that flies around the country now is that Owain has retreated into the mountains and the rebellion is over.' He shook his head sadly. 'Time will tell all.'

Catrin went to bed later even than her father. She damped down the fire, checked the doors were barred and blew out all the candles but one. She picked it up and climbed wearily to her bedroom.

In her dream Catrin recognised Prince Owain at once though time had passed. He was there on the battlefield, at the head of his men, older than she remembered him and exhausted, but bravely leading the charge, his standard bearer at his side, his standard – red and gold now, no longer the black lion of Powys – rippling above them in the wind and rain. Then before her horrified eyes the standard had fallen, trampled in the mud, the man who carried it screaming in agony as an arrow pierced a vulnerable spot in his armour and tore through to his neck. Around the prince the men faltered, the charge losing its impetus, the enemy gaining ground.

The men-at-arms had closed round their prince and in minutes he had been spirited away to disappear into the wet fog that was closing round the battlefield. He lived. He always lived, but the battle was lost. The field was red with blood and scattered with dead men and the English Prince Hal was victorious. He was looking round, shading his eyes against the rain, gentling the great warhorse which was trembling beneath him, its nostrils dilated, its eyes huge with terror. She knew he was looking for Owain. He was always looking for Owain and she knew he would never find him.

Andy awoke suddenly, her hands clammy with fear. She could feel her heart pounding; the sound seemed to fill the room like the beat of a distant drum. She lay for a few minutes staring up towards the ceiling as the dream faded. It was of war, the smell of smoke, the shouts of men, the scream of horses, the enormous crash of cannon fire. That was what had woken her. The bang. She sat up abruptly. That bang had been real. Outside the house. Grabbing her dressing gown, she fled barefoot down the stairs, wishing she had a dog to let her know if there was someone in the garden. She paused behind the kitchen door, listening. Don't open it. The words rang in her head. Don't let them in. There are soldiers out there.

It took her a moment to realise that Pepper was there on his chair. He had been curled up asleep when she switched on the light. Now awake, he watched her calmly, clearly wondering what she was doing in his kitchen in the middle of the night. He might not be a dog, but he would have let her know if there was something dangerous outside. He would have fled.

With an exclamation of impatience she turned the key and pulled open the back door. The impenetrable darkness of the garden was full of noise, the rush of wind, the roar of water, the sound of rain on the flagstones. She stood on the doorstep, shivering in the cold night air, then she stepped back inside and closed the door, turning the key firmly in the lock.

Upstairs once more she sat down on the edge of her bed with a sigh, realising there was no way she would go back to sleep now. Reaching for her notebook, she began to write down everything she remembered about the dream. Half an hour later she was asleep, the notebook lying on her chest, the pen fallen on the floor. Outside in the garden the storm began to subside.

Waking slowly to the sound of a blackbird whistling mournfully outside her window, Andy lay still for several minutes in total confusion. She had dreamed again. After waiting so long, she had dreamed of Catrin's return home and she had dreamed of a battle. With a groan she turned over and jumped at the thump as her notebook fell off her bed and hit the floor. She reached over and picked it up. Had she written anything in it? There were several pages of scrawl. Once again part of it was illegible, but some was clear enough to read.

Andy read to the end of her notes and closed the book. She lay for a while staring up at the ceiling then wearily climbed out of bed. After her shower she felt marginally better; at least enough to pick up the phone to call Sian.

185

They met for lunch in the Blue Boar, choosing a table by the window in the corner near the fire.

'So have you dreamed about Glyndŵr again?' Sian had collected two menus and passed one to Andy.

Andy nodded. 'It was amazing. So real. I saw their home-coming, and then the scene switched to a battle. That was weird, because I think it was Catrin's dream. A dream within a dream. When I woke up I wrote it down, or as much as I could remember. It was pretty scrappy and incoherent. I don't remember waking up at all, but I must have. I obviously turned on the light, and I picked up the pencil and my notebook, but then I fell asleep again while I was doing it.'

'And you're still not afraid?'

'No. If the dreams get more warlike, I might be. There was a lot of screaming and blood and cannons and swords and flying arrows.' She paused. Without realising it, her eyes had filled with tears.

Sian pushed back her chair. 'I'm going to get us both a glass of wine.'

It was ten minutes before she came back after queuing at the bar and by then Andy had recovered. 'Sorry. Not like me to be such a wimp.'

'It was obviously very real.'

'It was real, I'm sure of it. I think it really happened.'

'And Catrin witnessed it?'

'I don't know. She was a kind of seer, like her father. A prophetess. Perhaps she saw it before it happened.'

'You know what they called Glyndŵr? *Mab Darogan.* That means the son of the prophets.'

Andy was sniffing into a tissue. 'Sounds a bit Islamic.'

Sian laughed. 'In the Middle Ages it meant his arrival was foretold by people who saw the future; seers. I think we're talking Celtic prophets rather than Old Testament, although I might be wrong. Like King Arthur, he was to be the saviour of the country. He stepped up to the plate when he was needed most. The Welsh were downtrodden and bullied by the English. The English didn't make good neighbours, did they. Look at the way the Scots feel to this day. There you go. Henry was fighting the Scots the whole time he wasn't fighting the Welsh. Or the French,' she added.

'You know your history.'

'I know my Shakespeare. Didn't you ever read *Henry IV Part 1* and *2*?'

Andy smiled. 'Alas. There you have the better of me. I'm not a literary scholar.'

'Never mind. You have other strengths.' Sian flapped the menu under her nose. 'But you won't have if you don't eat. You will fade away. Choose something and I'll go and order.'

Later, over coffee, they returned to the subject of Glyndŵr.

'Are you in danger of becoming obsessed by all this?' Sian was holding her cup in both hands, staring at Andy across the table.

'Probably.'

'And that's OK?'

'I think so. After all, I'm not really there, am I? I'm not going to get shot by an arrow or anything—'

She broke off, her gaze falling on her hand. It was still red and peeling from Rhona's fire.

Sian followed her gaze. 'Exactly.'

Andy bit her lip. 'What happened with Rhona is different from Catrin's story.'

In Catrin's past she was safe; an observer, a traveller from a distant land. Where did that quote come from? So, she had remembered something from her school English lessons.

'It is exciting, Sian. When I came up here I was a miserable, lonely wreck, unable to see any way forward. Now . . .' she looked out through the window, trying to arrange her thoughts. 'Graham was a bit of a Luddite really. And single-minded. I see it now. I abandoned my interests for him, but not any more. I've let myself get involved again. These dreams are reawakening the real me!'

'Wow.' Sian smiled. 'Then Meryn is the man for you. I do hope he returns soon.'

'And we won't mention any of this to anyone else,' Andy went on. 'The last thing I want is crowds of people coming and sitting on the lawn cross-legged, communing with the spirits of ancient Wales.'

Sian laughed. She drew an imaginary zip across her mouth. 'My lips are sealed. I promise.' She reached for her jacket. 'I must go. The dogs need walking. Keep me posted, won't you. And, Andy, take care. Don't get sucked in too far.'

When Rhona arrived downstairs for breakfast the next morning she found her fellow guests had already eaten and gone off to pursue their various projects. Blaming her late start on her long drive the day before, she ate breakfast quickly, grabbed her coat and camera and headed for her car.

She had had a sleepless night, much of it spent thinking about Sleeper's Castle. She had only caught a quick glimpse of the place, but it had gripped her imagination in a way she couldn't quite understand. She did not like country houses or cottages; she didn't like the countryside. She especially didn't like wild places with mountains, and yet here she was thinking obsessively about the place Miranda had chosen to hide herself away after nothing more than a brief glance in passing as the sun went down.

The night before when she had driven up past Sleeper's Castle onto the open hillside she had been swallowed in mist and darkness and managed to get herself thoroughly lost. The satnav refused to function and the place had had an eerie, lonely feel; all she had wanted to do was to obey the wretched machine and turn round and go back. It had been a relief when she had seen a signpost, crookedly standing alone at a crossroads, pointing back to Hay down another unfenced track in the sheep-cropped grass. It had been a long time before she had found her way back to the B & B.

She sat in the car trying to decide what to do. Part of her

desperately wanted to return to Sleeper's Castle but she knew she must resist. She knew it was the right place, she had seen Miranda's car, and she had the advantage. Miranda didn't know she was here and she meant to keep it that way. For now. It seemed obvious to drive down to Hay, but if she did that there was always the risk of running into Andy, something she had no intention of doing until she had fully formulated her plans.

In the end she drove to Brecon, sixteen or so miles away, found a large car park in the middle of town and headed into the tourist centre where she bought several guidebooks and carried them triumphantly to the nearest coffee shop so that she could sit in comfort and formulate her cover story.

Photography was a given. She loved it and had almost been a professional in her younger days. When she and Graham were first married she had taken the photos to illustrate his books, before he and his publisher had decided that watercolours were more sensitive and crowd-pleasing – another factor in her list of grudges against Miranda.

She skipped through her new guidebooks. This was obviously a very photogenic part of the world. She had never been to Wales before and in spite of all her preconceived notions about the place it was beginning to appeal to her. Quite apart from the weirdest foreign language she had ever come across in a lifetime of travel, blazoned unpronounceably across all the road signs, the town was charming, the views were spectacular and it had stunningly beautiful cloudscapes. To her surprise her fingers were itching for her camera before she had even finished her cinnamon Danish and coffee. Here the Brecon Beacons were the local mountains, but the mountains she was interested in because they cradled Sleeper's Castle, were the Black Mountains. The Beacons were pointed and wild and looked pretty threatening; the Black Mountains were rounded, many of them with flat plateaued tops that looked more gentle. Deceptively so, according to her books. Those were the ones she had to get to know.

She would avoid Sleeper's Castle today and instead use the

time to get her bearings and take a few photos so that, should anyone ask this evening or tomorrow at breakfast, she would have something to show them. So, she needed to find some yew trees.

Bryn was working near the house when Andy returned from lunch. He had pruned back a bed of herbs, piling the prunings into the wheelbarrow. She walked up to him before he had the chance to move away round the back somewhere and looked at the barrow, puzzled. 'Shouldn't you be drying all those herbs?'

He studied the contents of his barrow. 'Sue isn't here to use them. She told me to compost it all. It will make a fabulous rich mixture to go back into the soil for next year.'

She remembered what she had been going to ask him. 'Do you know anything about the history of this place, Bryn?'

'I'm not really one for history.'

'Aren't you a local man?'

'I suppose I am, yes.' He sounded doubtful.

She glanced up at his face. It was tanned and laced with fine wrinkles around the eyes beneath his thatch of wild brown hair and it was hard to guess how old he was. Early to mid forties perhaps. The tattoo on his arm, she could now see, was a small celtic knot.

'So, your family has lived round here for generations.' It was not a question and he didn't take it as such. He merely nodded. 'Up in the Golden Valley. Near enough.'

He was a good-looking man but when, as now, he was in surly mode he looked nothing but grim and discouraging. He turned back to the barrow. 'Was there anything else?'

She tried a smile. 'Am I asking too many questions?'

He looked taken aback. 'My life isn't really very interesting, Ms Dysart.'

'I don't believe that.' She was careful to keep innuendo out of her voice. She paused, then she went on: 'Please call me Andy.' She gave him what she hoped was a reassuring smile,

'I was hoping you would be a repository of ancient stories and legends about this valley and Sleeper's Castle. Everyone seems to have a different take on the place, and as you've been here a long time, I thought you might know more than they do. You have been here a long time?'

He gave a reluctant nod.

'Since before Sue bought it?'

He hesitated. 'I knew it before, but I didn't work here then.'

Wow! He had volunteered some information! She tried to keep the note of triumph out of her voice. 'So, you knew the old man who lived here before.'

'I didn't know him. No one really knew him.'

'He was something of a wizard I've been told.'

'Then you've been told wrong. He was a plantsman. A loner perhaps, but he was kind and very knowledgeable. I used to come here sometimes on my bike and he would tell me the names of the plants and what they were used for. He befriended a lonely small boy when I came to stay with my uncle in Hay.'

Andy went on eyeing him surreptitiously. She felt he had not intended to say so much.

She thought for a moment. 'Perhaps you can tell me something. We're so near the border here I'm finding it hard to work out who is English and who is Welsh. Some you can tell easily by their accents and their names, but others are more enigmatic about it.'

He gave a wry smile. 'Not enigmatic. Careful.'

'Careful? Not wanting to admit anything?'

'We have a long tradition of that round here. The March has been a place of conflict and mystery for centuries. Forever perhaps. We are Marcher people.'

'And the March is a liminal place,' she said almost to herself. 'A border, between one thing and the other. Like a river or the edge of the sea. A place where magic happens, where people disappear and wizards and prophets and poets feel at home.' She gave a small embarrassed smile. It was her turn to give too much away and he was going to think she was crackers.

191

But he didn't seem to think her words odd. After a moment he inclined his head gravely.

'Do you think that's why Hay became a town of books? It attracts people who like to live on the edge of things.'

He laughed out loud. 'It does that all right!'

'No, you know what I mean. People who are thinkers and dreamers; people who paint and write; musicians and poets and people who imagine things.'

'And which are you, Andy?' He held her gaze.

'I'm a painter.' She did not flinch at his direct stare.

'And a dreamer?' He took a firm grip on his shears and stepped away from her. 'If you live in this house, I think you have to be a dreamer.'

With that he turned away. She didn't try to stop him.

She walked back towards the kitchen. If she was a painter and a dreamer, what was he? A plantsman, obviously, and a thinker; an educated man, at a guess; and what else? Why had he chosen such an isolated way of life? Did he have a wife, a family? Did he live on his own? Perhaps he lived in the middle of Hay? Somehow she doubted it. It was more likely that he lived in a remote cottage somewhere. He had answered a few of her questions but then created more in their place. If anyone was an enigma it was her gardener, and he had not answered her first question about the history of Sleeper's Castle.

She didn't dream that night. Lying tossing and turning in her bed she tried to go to sleep, then she read a bit, from another volume, this time on the general history of Wales, then she climbed out of bed and walked around the room. She went downstairs and boiled the kettle to make herself a cup of tea, then she slipped on her coat and went outside to stand on the steps at the front of the house to look across the dark valley while she drank it. The night was still and silent apart from the sound of the brook falling over the rocks at the side of the house. There was a slight movement in the dark behind her and she heard a small chirrup. Pepper materialised out of the shadows and wound himself round her ankles. She bent and scratched him behind the ears. 'It's a beautiful night, fella,' she said softly, unconsciously adopting Bryn's name for him. She could see a light in the distance now. It was obviously a car, moving slowly on the far side of the valley, appearing and disappearing as the road wound across the faraway hills. It was strange how lonely the sight made her feel. She shivered, cupping her hands around her mug of tea. Pepper had vanished as quietly as he had come and once more she was alone with her thoughts.

Had Catrin stood here on this very doorstep all those years ago? The doorstep was made of local stone and it had been worn away into a smooth dip in the middle where countless men and women had walked over it through the centuries. Everywhere she went she could picture the place as it had been in Catrin's day. The new bits hadn't been there, of course, and the inside of the house had changed considerably, but the walls were the same, the window in her bedroom was more or less the same, the door to the side parlour – the room which had been Dafydd's study – was the same door. Their footsteps echoed through the building. Their voices were part of the house's fabric, theirs and generations of others after them.

The distant car had gone now. The lights had either been turned off or the road had disappeared down into the valley. The absence left her feeling bereft. Somewhere near at hand an owl hooted softly and a second owl further away answered with a quick double call which seemed to echo in the wood on the far side of the brook. She pulled her coat more tightly round her. A whisper of cold had crossed the garden. Soon winter would be here. As if in answer to the thought the patter of dead leaves blowing across the paving slabs made her shiver again.

Joan heard the news first. The king had arrived in Shrewsbury with a huge army. He then moved west to sack Bangor and headed on towards Harlech. Catrin was writing in her chamber upstairs when she heard Joan calling. She had returned from a visit to Efa via a farm at the edge of the mountain, and heard that the countryside alive with gossip. 'The English army won't be coming here,' Joan said as she sat down on Catrin's bed. 'They are all staying far in the north.' She gave a huge sigh. 'It's dreadful! To think of all that fighting! A whole army here in Wales! But Glyndŵr is defeated again. Once more he has fled.'

Catrin looked down at the page before her. Sitting at her little desk by the window she had been writing a poem about the autumn colours in the trees and the reflections of the sunlight on the brook as it flowed down over the rocks. It was her favourite subject. With a sigh she put down her pen. 'How did they get the news?'

'A pedlar who had been up north. He was in Welshpool when the king reached Shrewsbury. He had been planning to go there himself, but he changed his mind. He doesn't like soldiers. They are too quick to sample his wares and then forget to pay.' Joan bit her lip. 'Oh my, it's frightening.' Her eyes were huge and she kept clutching at her bosom.

Catrin managed a smile. 'As you say, I don't think they are likely to bother with us. We are far from the main roads. Even the drovers don't come down our valley. And it sounds as though it is all over.'

The charcoal in Catrin's brazier had gone out. Her eyes heavy with sleep she slid from her bed and, clutching a warm sheepskin round her shoulders, she crept down the stone stairway to the great hall where the fire in the hearth still glowed gently in its bed of ashes. Joan was asleep on her truckle bed close beside it. Without waking her, Catrin put a handful of twigs on the ashes and then a larger log and watched as the glow slowly stirred and one or two sparks flickered into flame. Shivering, she fetched a stool and put it as close as she could to the warmth.

Huddled in her sheepskin wrap she began to think about the dream that had woken her.

Owain, Prince of Wales was standing in the great hall of a castle. Swathed in a furred robe, with a sceptre in his hand and a coronet on his head, he raised his great sword to the cheers of his followers. There were hundreds of them packed into the hall and everywhere she could see his new standard: a quartet of lions, red on gold and gold on red. Beside him stood his lady, Margaret, and with them their sons and daughters. The cheers were still ringing in her ears as she stared down into the flames.

'Catrin?'

She jumped. Joan was sitting up, rubbing her eyes. 'What is it? Couldn't you sleep?'

Catrin held out her hands to the fire. 'No. I'm sorry. I had a dream.'

Joan frowned. 'Not like your father?' They both glanced across the hall and into the shadows towards Dafydd's study. 'Is he still there?' Catrin whispered. 'Didn't he go to bed?'

Joan pulled her cloak around her shoulders. 'He was still in there when I went to sleep.'

Catrin stood up wearily. 'I'll go and see.'

Quietly she pushed open the door to her father's study. He wasn't there. His fire had gone out. His candle had extinguished itself in a pool of wax. She closed the door again and went back to the fire. 'He must have gone up to bed.'

Her father's nightmares had continued almost without ceasing since they had returned from their travels. They were upsetting the whole house. He refused to describe them and he refused to explain the effect they were having on him, even to Catrin, but she knew what they were about. He was seeing war. He was seeing bloodshed. He was, like her, aware all too clearly of what would happen when their new prince set out to conquer his land, and yet he had encouraged him. He had told him he would succeed. He had told him as the other bards had told him that he was going to win and win gloriously. And he believed it, as Catrin believed it. How could Owain lose? His success was written in the stars.

Andy lay still, staring up at the ceiling. Her mind was seeking back and forth, frantically searching, but there was nothing there. No memory of a dream, no fleeting sounds, no voices echoing in the dark spaces between the beams. She closed her eyes in disappointment. Had she dreamt? How could she know? She tried to make her mind a blank, allow the details of the night to seep back. She remembered climbing the stairs at last, when she thought she was so tired she couldn't keep awake another moment. She had pulled the bedcovers round her, and snuggled her head down into the pillows, allowing the silence and the darkness to wrap themselves around her as she drifted deeper and deeper into sleep. But no dream.

She groaned with impatience. What was the point of anything if she couldn't remember the dream? Had something happened to Catrin in her dream and now she would never know because she couldn't recall the bloody thing! She sat up and thrust her feet out of bed, groping for her slippers. Outside it was raining she realised as a gust of wind spattered raindrops against the windowpanes. She could hear the thrashing of trees in the wind. No doubt more leaves would be torn off. In Catrin's world when she had last seen her it had been autumn too.

She doubted if any of the bookshops would be open before ten. That gave her time to shower and dress and eat breakfast. She sat at the kitchen table looking down the list of bookshops she had picked up last time she was down in Hay. What she wanted was a shop that specialised in local history. Not national history. Not Glyndŵr's history, but the history of the ancient houses scattered around in the hills: the old farmsteads, and fortified houses, even castles, which were hidden in the *cwms* and *bwlchs* that led off this part of the Wye Valley in the foothills of the mountains. She smiled. Was the word *bwlch*? She must also get a Welsh dictionary to find out the meaning of these names. Sleeper's Castle was uncompromisingly English. Why, when so many of the names far further east than this house, over the English border, had Welsh names? Dafydd had obviously been Welsh; he had been bilingual. She dropped the leaflet she was looking at and stared into space. What language did Dafydd and Catrin speak at home? Joan was English, and so, she assumed, was Edmund. Were they all bilingual? If they were speaking Welsh, how come she could understand them in her dreams? Where, for that matter, was the border? Was it a recorded place? Now there was a road sign on the way to Cusop from Hay saying *Welcome to England* in one direction. On the other side of the road, a little further up, there was one saying *Croeso y Gymru*. The border was obviously the brook, which ran under the road at that point and down to the River Wye. In the past, did the border constantly shift? One year a battle moved it, the next an army of men came by and moved it back again. That seemed too simplistic and in a way too arbitrary. Perhaps that was why they called it the March. Perhaps that implied an uncertainty, a blurring of lines which could broaden into several miles. It had been the same in Scotland; the border shifted up and down, and even the uncompromising Roman certainty of Hadrian's Wall had not fixed it. So perhaps borders were a result of the modern need to categorise and impose order; a political statement, which was absolute. On this side you obeyed English laws, on the other you didn't. On this side the satnav said you were in England. On the other it didn't. She frowned slowly. Of course. Wales's answer to Hadrian's Wall was Offa's Dyke. No question, she needed information. She reached for her laptop. The answer, it appeared, was easy. The border was fixed. The term the March was imprecise. She stared at the screen. What she needed was another book.

She felt better once she had a plan. After rinsing her few breakfast dishes she collected her purse and her jacket and headed for the door. The weather had worsened if anything. There was no sign of Bryn's van as she ran down the steps and dived into the Passat, pausing to listen to the rain hammering on the roof before she reached forward to put the key in the ignition.

She could think of a lot worse ways of spending a wet day. Shop after shop welcomed her into its warmth and she was directed up and down stairs, back between long lines of book-shelves, round corners, into attics and basements. More than once she was given website addresses to follow up later, and several times she found herself engaged in long conversations with local people. It was getting on for lunchtime when she walked into a shop on Church Street and found herself confronting Roy Pascoe.

'Roy!' At last she had found his shop.

Roy stood up from behind his desk near the door and kissed her on the cheek. 'How nice to see you!'

What he found for her was a Victorian map which showed Sleeper's Castle. *Castell Cysgwr.* The name was written under a tiny engraving of the house.

'Don't worry. You don't have to buy it.' He propped the framed engraving against the bookshelves and squatted down next to her so they could both look at it.

'It is a bit expensive.' She had noticed the price tag.

'There's a good market for these. They're collectors' pieces. Rare. Have you got a camera on you? You can take a pic if you like.'

She pulled out her phone and managed to get a fairly clear picture. 'I was wondering if the original name was in Welsh.'

'And indeed it was. A lot of places round here have bilingual names. It's all part of being on the border. There are pure Welsh names quite far into Herefordshire. They spoke Welsh round there well into the nineteenth century, I believe. But don't forget these castle towns were Norman bases, populated by Norman people who had morphed into English and were assimi-lated into the local population, which made things even more complicated than they were already.' He watched while she took another couple of pictures, then swung the frame back into its rack. 'Are you still enjoying living up there?'

She nodded. 'It's a wonderful old house. I'm fascinated by its history.'

'Ella told me she had run into you. I gather you've been having some amazing dreams. She said it sounded terribly exciting.'

Andy gave an uncomfortable smile. 'Indeed.' Tucking her phone back into her bag, she looked up at him. 'I do hope Ella won't tell anyone about that. It's the perfect place for me. I'm a solitary soul, by choice. I'm still working so I need time to myself and I value the chance to have a really quiet place to paint. Sue knew the pressure I was under sometimes when she offered the house to me while she was away. It's a godsend!'

Roy laughed. 'Point taken. I'll make sure Ella keeps quiet about anything you tell her.'

Andy blushed, mortified. She had obviously failed to be subtle. 'I'm sorry. I didn't mean that to sound the way it came out.'

Roy put his arm round her shoulders and gave her a quick hug. 'Don't be embarrassed. I know what a chatterbox Ella can be, bless her. I'll tip her the wink about keeping quiet, and I will do it tactfully, I promise.'

Andy gave him a grateful smile. 'Thank you.'

'Good luck with the research. And with your work.'

Andy's bag was heavy as she walked back to the car park and she swung it gratefully into the back of her car. As she did so she glanced up and found herself looking at a red sports car in the row in front. It had a black soft top, shabby and slightly torn like Rhona's. She stared at it hard; she couldn't remember the number of Rhona's car. Glancing round, her heart thudding apprehensively, she climbed into the Passat and pulled the door shut. Reversing out she swung left, to drive out on the far side of the car park and then up towards the exit, keeping her eyes skinned for any sign of Rhona. It couldn't be her car. Could it?

Cold with tension she headed back up the lane home, her

eyes constantly drifting to the rear-view mirror to check she hadn't been followed. Tucking the car into her usual parking place and retrieving her bag of books, her paranoia was so great that part of her almost expected to find the door forced open, but it was locked exactly as she had left it, as was the back door. The house was safe. She let herself in with a sigh of relief, threw the book bag down on the kitchen table and went to look at the phone. No messages.

The sight of what might have been Rhona's car had jolted her back to Graham and Kew. Had Rhona followed her as she had threatened? She went and pulled down the blind in the kitchen window so no one outside in the garden could see her and switched on the light with a shiver. Whatever the truth of the matter, she felt as though her perfect refuge had been violated.

Why hadn't she waited to see who owned the car? She could have ducked down in the driver's seat of her own if necessary. No one would have seen her.

'Stupid!' she berated herself. 'It wasn't her car. How could it have been?' She glanced at the chair where Pepper usually sat. There was no sign of him. Sitting down, she realised she was still wearing her waterproof jacket. She pushed her hands deep into the pockets and hunched her shoulders miserably.

Closing her eyes she found herself picturing the house in Kew, filling in every detail of the outside, the Virginia creeper on the front wall, now almost stripped of its glorious red leaves by the cold wind, the rain-soaked drive, empty of cars, the windows dark as the evening drew in, an unwanted flyer sticking out of the letter box, weeds beginning to grow in the front bed which bordered the roadside wall. She pictured herself walking to the front door and up the steps; she pictured herself raising her hand to the doorbell. She hesitated then she pressed her finger against the white enamelled button, hearing the peal of the bell inside the house. She already knew no one would come because that was the way she was picturing it. The hall was dark as it always was when it rained, the doors into the front rooms closed. Someone had left the door into the kitchen at the back open. If she pictured herself inside and walking towards it, she could see the kitchen table empty now of any books or guides or maps. It was scrubbed clean. The cups and mugs, which usually lived on the draining board beside the sink, had been put away. The kitchen was immaculate. And empty, as someone might leave it if they were going away for a few days.

She opened her eyes and sighed. She was no wiser, just more miserable.

Behind her the cat flap opened, making her jump. Pepper appeared and glared at her, wet and obviously cross, leaving a trail of neat paw prints across the floor. He shook himself and went to sit in front of the Aga, raising a paw to dry his face and ears. She smiled with relief. His company was reassuring. If Rhona was poking about in the garden intent on mischief, surely he would not have come in. Pepper was her watchdog and her guardian.

Her sketchbooks were her refuge. Carrying a mug of coffee she made her way through to the area of the living room she was beginning to think of as her studio, switched on the light and set the cup down on the table. The flowers she had been painting had wilted in their glass. Sadly she carried them back into the kitchen. She threw them into her compost bucket, then opened the back door and looked out into the garden. It took only minutes to gather some windblown roses, arrange them in a drinking glass, add a few papery honesty seeds, and carry the arrangement back to the desk. She dipped her brush in her water pot and began to sketch, almost at once lost in the drawing process, her mind concentrated in on itself, blank, receptive, open.

13

Yule came and went, snow engulfed the valley. The first signs of spring came, then more rain and yet more snow and it was after Easter when Catrin saw Edmund again. He had walked down the long road from home, wading through mud and slush and frozen mud, a huge bundle of supplies on his shoulder.

'You look like a pedlar,' Joan cried as she pulled him in through the door into the warmth of the kitchen. She hung his wet outer garments in front of the fire, scolded him for wearing his sodden boots indoors and treading mud all over the flagstones, and sat him on a stool to stick his feet out towards the warmth, letting his sopping hose steam gently while she made him a hot drink. Only then did she allow her curiosity about the contents of his bundle full rein.

'I have gifts for you all,' he said. 'I suspected none of you have been able to get to market for a while, the weather has been so bad.'

Their food and supplies and fuel had lasted through the worst of the weather but there was only enough to see them through a couple more weeks. Joan pounced on the cloth-wrapped parcels with glee.

'No, these are not for you.' Edmund took a bag out of her hand and pushed another couple aside. 'This is for Catrin and these two are for her father. And these are for you all, for the pantry.' He grinned at her, not missing the flash of anger on her face.

'"Catrin" is it?' she repeated the name, her voice heavy with innuendo.

He jerked his head back and surveyed her coldly. 'What else would I call her?'

'Mistress Catrin might be more respectful.'

He nodded soberly. 'It might. Where is she?'

'Probably writing.' Turning her back on the bag of gifts, Joan shook out her dishclout and chased one of the barn cats away from the fire. 'She'll be in the parlour, I dare say.'

He glanced at her in amusement, then stood up and walked towards the door, leaving a trail of wet footprints behind him on the flags.

Catrin was huddled beside a brazier, wrapped in her cloak, her hands swathed in mittens as she dipped her pen in the inkpot and bent closer to her page. The room was lit by several candles. There was no sign of her father. She glanced up as Edmund walked in, the draught that accompanied him flaring the candle flames and sending the shadows leaping wildly up the wall.

He gave a little bow. 'How are you? I thought I would come and make sure you are all safe and well after the snow.' She was much thinner than when he had seen her last. It had been a long winter and that and the privations of Lent had left her almost gaunt.

She stared at him her face blank, and he wondered if she even recognised him. Then her expression cleared and she smiled. 'Edmund, I'm sorry, I was miles away inside my head. There it was autumn and the skies were still blue and the trees were heavy with fruit.' It had been the strangest daydream. There had been a vase of flowers on the table in the great hall and a woman who wore men's hose and buskins instead of a long skirt had been painting them with work as delicate and intricate as a master in the scriptorium. To come back to reality and find herself scribbling verses huddled over the smoking fire was a shock. She shivered. 'Is your family well? Joan must be pleased to see you.'

'She is.' He looked away, abashed. His relationship with Catrin over the long months of their travels had been complicated. It had ended with a kiss. To see her again now after such a long enforced separation was unexpectedly uncomfortable.

'I bought you and your father some gifts.' Now he was here, it seemed wildly inappropriate to be so forward. 'I knew you wouldn't have been able to get to market after the storms and all the snow. I have left a bit of food with Joan, but I thought you might need pens and knives to trim them. Ingredients for your ink. I remembered you make it all yourself but once you told me how hard it was to find gum arabic and copperas.' He glanced up in time to see her face light up.

'Thank you, Edmund. I was nearly at my wits' end knowing I had enough only to make another jug. Joan collected baskets of oak galls while we were away, but the other things I have to buy. My father would have gone mad with fury and impatience without ink.'

'As would you, I would guess.' He looked across at the sheet of parchment on her table, weighted down by pretty stones to keep it flat. He hesitated then, bending to the fuel basket, he picked up a few lumps of charcoal, threw them on the fire and squatted in front of the brazier, holding out his hands to the warmth. The movement brought him close beside her. 'I doubted that you would get to church for the Easter celebrations or to market in all the snow, so I have brought sweetmeats and marchpane to celebrate.' He smiled as he pushed the little parcels towards her.

He saw her face light up as she pressed one to her nose and inhaled the scent of almonds and rosewater.

'Edmund, thank you!'

He nodded, brusquely embarrassed by her pleasure, then he looked at her again. 'I wondered if you had had news of Glyndŵr,' he murmured.

She didn't look up. 'Nothing for months now. We hear little of what goes on beyond the valley with all the snow.'

He looked shocked. 'Do they not send to enquire if you are all right?'

'We keep to ourselves and we look after ourselves.' Her voice dropped to a whisper. 'Like Joan, some of the people in the parish disapprove extremely of the rebels.'

'Nevertheless,' moving slightly closer to her he dropped his voice further, 'I hear sympathy for the Lord Owain is spreading all over Wales. People see him as a saviour. The hatred of the English and their laws is everywhere.'

'Except this valley.'

'Maybe you are too close to the border here. But you would not necessarily know who supports who. No one trusts anyone these days; people keep their views to themselves. Anger and unrest is spreading. More and more people are talking about the Lord Owain and what he stands for: the ancient royal families of Wales; freedom and pride in ourselves as a nation.'

She smiled. 'So you are Welsh now, Edmund?' she said, mocking.

He smiled ruefully. 'You are right to tease. But I have met him. I have seen him. I have heard him talk.'

'Where is he now, do you know?' Catrin's face was only two feet from his as she leaned forward, holding her hands out towards the glowing fire.

'No one seems to know. He vanished into the mountains, and pulled the mist and clouds round his shoulders and he disappeared from view.' He chuckled. It was a quote from one of Dafydd's poems from the previous autumn.

She ignored it. 'I know King Henry promised pardons for all who took part in the revolt provided they renounced all supposed allegiance to Glyndŵr,' she murmured. 'Most took that choice, even Crach.'

Edmund grimaced. 'And Owain's brother Tudur, and Gruffudd.'

She stared at him in horror. 'His own son?'

Edmund nodded. There was a long silence. 'It's not over, Catrin. There are more new laws against the Welsh and the Lord Owain is still free. No pardon was offered to him; the king confiscated his estates and gave them to one of his Beaufort brothers. But he is not defeated.'

'Lady Margaret? Catherine and Alys?' Catrin hardly dared ask the question, but Edmund didn't reply at first. 'All I know is that on the Welsh side of the border there is still much unrest,' he said at last. 'I hope they are all safe. I liked that man. Respected him.'

Catrin gave him a sideways glance. 'You would serve him if he called for support?'

'I would be sorely tempted. If there is a muster this spring I will be called to serve the king as an archer. But I could not fight against Lord Glyndŵr.'

They fell silent, both gazing down at the glowing coals, deep in thought, Catrin intensely aware of how close he was to her as he squatted, holding out his hands to the heat.

He was about to say something when the door burst open.

'Catrin!' Her father's voice, irritable as usual, rang round the room. 'What are you doing child? I need more ink!'

Catrin sighed. 'I will fetch it, *Tad*.'

'Who's that?' He had spied the figure in the shadows.

'It's Edmund, *Tad*. He has bought us supplies so that I can make your ink when we run out.'

Dafydd studied the young man as he straightened, towering above Catrin. She too stood up, hastily sweeping the pile of little gifts into the folds of her skirt.

'What are you doing in here alone with my daughter?' Dafydd glared at him belligerently. 'How dare you. Get out of here.'

'*Tad!*' Catrin's voice was sharp. 'It's Edmund. Don't you recognise him?'

'Of course I recognise him.' Dafydd took several steps forward, pulling his mantle more tightly around his thin shoulders. 'That does not mean I want him alone with you.'

'I'm sorry, sir,' Edmund bowed stiffly. 'I forgot my place. I will go.' He turned abruptly towards the door, his cheeks flaming.

'Edmund,' Catrin called, but he did not stop. In a moment he was gone and father and daughter were left glaring at each other in the swirling candlelight.

'Take no notice,' Joan said uncomfortably when her brother told her what had happened. He had refused her invitation to stay overnight and was putting on his boots. 'Come on, be sensible. You can't go back in the dark.'

'Why not?' he snapped. 'I've been walking these hills in the dark all my life.' He reached for his heavy courtepy, which was still soaking wet, and over it pulled the rough sheepskin jacket that had kept him warm on the road.

'Foolish boy!' She was all elder sister now.

He laughed grimly then abruptly he sobered. 'There is something I have always wondered. Why is she not married?'

Joan stared at him in shocked silence. Then she spoke. 'Edmund, you can't think—'

'No, I can't. I don't. But I would like to know.'

She was silent for a while, rubbing her hands up and down on her apron. 'No one has ever been good enough for her. One or two suitors came to ask for her hand when she reached marriageable age, but he chased them away. I heard her beg once, a couple of years ago now, but he said no, he needed her to look after him.' She sucked in her cheeks. 'It wasn't for a particular suitor she pleaded, but she told him she wanted babies like other women.'

There was a long pause.

Edmund put his hand on Joan's arm. 'Sis, I know.'

She shook him off crossly. 'I can marry any time I want if I want babies! I don't. It was my choice to leave home. The men Father selected for me were not to my taste!' she snapped. She glanced up at him. 'But you will marry again, Edmund,' she added more gently. 'Not Catrin, though. Don't even think about it. He's a selfish man. He will never let her go. He told her that her poems would be like children to her and that they would live for ever. I don't know if that comforted her. Maybe a bit, but in the long dark hours of the night how could it when she lies there alone.' She gave a deep sigh.

He reached into the bundle he had left on the floor. 'Here is an Easter gift for you. Did you really think I had forgotten you? Don't be sad.' He kissed her cheek.

'Get on with you!' She gave him a playful clip round the ear. 'And if you get lost in the cold and dark, don't you blame me!'

'I won't.' He was laughing as he let himself out into the cold wind.

Alone in her bedroom Catrin spread the little pile of parcels on her bed and looked at them. There were, as he had promised, sweetmeats. She opened the packet and picked one up and placed it on her tongue, savouring the taste as it flooded her mouth with sweetness. Another parcel held the ingredients for making ink: copperas crystals and gum arabic, and a small, exquisitely decorated penknife for trimming quill nibs and in the last was a tiny, exquisitely illuminated book. Catrin stared at it, mesmerised. How had Edmund been able to afford a book? She opened it, the thick vellum pages crackling slightly under her fingers. It was a copy of a poem by Iolo Goch, a poem describing Prince Owain's house at Sycharth. She began to read, her eyes filling with tears as his clever words evoked a picture of the beauties of the house and its surroundings. Tucked in the very back she found a note inscribed in a careful hand. *The Lady of Glyndŵr gave me this, her own copy, to give you as a present. E*

She sat holding the note for a long time. She had not even realised that Edmund could read and write. Carefully rewrapping the book she opened the coffer at the end of her bed and tucked all the presents away out of sight.

In the kitchen Joan glanced up from her dough. 'Your father was looking for you.' Her face was set in a heavy scowl.

'Was he?' Catrin watched the woman's hands as she twisted the dough back and forth, reaching for flour from the crock and sprinkling it onto the table before she slapped the lump down again. 'Has your brother gone?' she asked at last.

'Of course he's gone.' Joan punched the dough and folded it over. 'He's not good enough to talk to you any more, I hear.'

'I'm sorry,' Catrin sighed. 'I don't know what came over my father.'

'I do.' Joan looked up. 'He does not intend for you to be alone with any man ever, so you stay with him, the selfish old goat!' She looked up, mortified, and clapped a floury hand to her mouth, appalled at her temerity. 'I'm sorry. I spoke out of turn.'

'You did.' Catrin shook her head sadly. Joan had done no more than give utterance to her own thoughts. Not that she would ever consider Edmund as a suitable match, but that was not the point.

Miserably she turned and walked out of the kitchen, leaving Joan to stare after her.

Andy woke with a start. The paintbrush was still in her hand and the paint had dried on the tip. She shivered violently. The room seemed unnaturally cold. She reached out and touched her coffee mug. The china was icy. Daylight showed at the window. She had been sitting at the table all night. She pulled her sleeves down over her hands and hugged herself as she staggered to her feet. Iolo's poem. She had read it! It was included in at least two of the books she had bought. His description of the beauties of Owain's home at Sycharth was legendary.

She pushed back her chair and headed across the room. No wonder it was so cold. The fire had gone out. She stood looking down at the hearth. What fire? There was no fire. She had never lit one in this fireplace and yet she could remember it clearly, the molten logs glowing as they were consumed, collapsing, sending crimson sparks into the air as they turned to ash. And Catrin sitting, staring into its depths.

She turned away from the empty fireplace as something in the window caught her eye. The creeper on the front of the house was fluttering against the glass, half blocking the cold early light. She ought to ask Bryn to cut it back. The pretty tendrils normally framed the view of the distant hills, but there was something in the way.

It took a second to focus on the face staring in. With a little cry of surprise she launched herself towards the door. It was Rhona. Almost knocked off balance by the wave of shock and anger which swept over her she tore the door open.

There was no one there. Scanning the front garden she headed for the steps. She couldn't see anyone. Her car was on its own in the parking space. There was no sound of an engine in the lane, no smell of exhaust on the wind. She stood in the middle of the road looking up and down. Nothing. The high banks with their carpet of autumn flowers, the hedges, hung with old man's beard, the muddy strip down the centre of the tarmac, the loose scattering of gravel, all bore witness to a lack of passing traffic. No one had jumped into their car and raced away here. Sleeper's Castle was, as it always was, quiet and untroubled in its isolation.

She had imagined it.

From the open front door Catrin watched the woman who wore hose and boots and no skirt standing in the lane. She saw her turn round once, full circle, as though mystified by something, and then turn back towards the steps. She looked disturbed, anxious. Something was wrong.

Andy glanced up. A gust of wind sent the heavy door swinging shut. As she reached it, it banged in her face.

Andy stood, holding on to the Aga rail until she stopped shaking. The sight of Rhona's face, there on the far side of the glass, had shocked her to her core. It had to have been a trick of the light, a reflection thrown by the pale fluttering leaves, there for only a second before it vanished. Her brain had constructed the face. It could not have been Rhona. Could it? She pictured the small red car in the car park and bit her lip hard. It was inconceivable that the woman would track her down and follow her.

She spent the day painting and reading, but when the time came to sleep she was too stressed to consider going upstairs. Trying to put Rhona out of her head, she went back to thinking about her dreams, the dreams she felt she had dreamed but which she wasn't sure she remembered when she woke up. Sometimes she had written them down spontaneously but there had to be some more reliable method of total recall.

It took ten minutes to find the book she wanted. She remembered it from twenty years before when she had been studying paganism. Something Roy had said at that first supper party at Sian's had reminded her about it, the ancient Celtic practice of sacred dreaming, the art of foretelling the future through dreams, something Dafydd and Catrin both practised and which, in the hands of medieval seers and prophets, was presumably the direct descendant of the Druid art. Would it work for foretelling the past as well? Not foretelling; aftertelling. She pulled the book from the bottom of the pile and carried it back in triumph to the kitchen.

So many methods, but there was one she remembered particularly. And there it was, the place marked by a crumpled bus ticket. She frowned. The dreamer was sewn into a bull's hide. She didn't like the sound of that; knowing the Celts, did they mean a freshly slaughtered bull still dripping with blood? On the other hand, a treated hide, tanned and clean, would be no worse than having a leather sleeping bag. Being sewn in implied restraint – was that because one might want to run away from the dreams which visited the dreamer? She read down the page. The dreamer was often left near running water, which was of course the liminal place, between this world and the next, and often in a cave. The next morning the persons who had left him there would return to find out the answers to their questions. This was an Irish practice, it said, but also used in Scotland and other Celtic countries. Where more Celtic than Wales and by a running stream? The dreamer would be left in the sleeper's cave, it said. She looked up feeling a clutch of excitement in her throat. Supposing it was the cave, not the house, which held the secret of the seers? The cave at the bottom of her garden. All she had to do was go out there and sleep. She studied the page again. It couldn't be that simple. For instance, how important was the leather swaddling? She pushed back her chair and thought. Upstairs in the cupboard was her leather coat, normally kept for best, but what the hell. She could wrap herself in it to make sure she gave this her best shot. Then all she had to do was make sure that she had utter privacy. The only risk, the only person who could possibly disturb her was Bryn, but Bryn would not come here at night. He never came at night. She would wait until she had seen his car drive off down the lane then take her coat and make her way to the cave.

It took far more courage than she would have thought possible. Bryn was there from eight o'clock the next morning and stayed until just before four. Once he had left, she made her way to the cave with a sleeping bag and a couple of cushions and made herself a makeshift bed at the back against the rock face. Then she returned to the house and waited. She couldn't eat; she poured herself a glass of wine and looked at the salad she had prepared, figuring it would be harder to sleep on an empty stomach, but her appetite had gone. Pepper had had no such qualms, scoffing his own supper and disappearing out through the cat flap again with unaccustomed haste. It was only after he had vanished that she wondered if she should have kept him locked in. Supposing he followed her into the cave and kept her awake? But it was too late to worry about it now.

Fighting off the thought of Rhona lurking in the shadows outside, she reached for the heavy coat and put it on, dropped the torch in her pocket, turned out all the lights except the lamp on the dresser, took a deep breath and let herself out into the night. Locking the door behind her she pocketed the key. She walked up the garden slowly, without using the torch, letting her eyes grow used to the dark. Behind the clouds the moon threw a gentle diffused glow providing enough light to stop her walking into things.

The grass was wet and the silence was full of the sound of the brook cascading over its rocks. She stopped and looked behind her. Her senses were straining to hear and see, every instinct warning her to take care, but there was nothing untoward that she could see. As she looked round, the half-moon appeared from behind its cloud and flooded the lawn with soft silver light. The garden was empty. Taking a resolute breath she walked on, heading past the herb beds through the elder brake and on towards the darkness of the cliff. Outside the cave she paused. The entrance was in deep shadow, nothing but a blacker cleft in the blackness of the rock. Her mouth was dry and there was an uncomfortable tightness in her stomach. She gave one final look round and ducked into the cave entrance, stopping just inside in the absolute total darkness. Now was not the time to give in and reach for the torch. Holding her hands out in front of her she took one step and then another into the emptiness, aware of the change of atmosphere, the dry stillness, the slight musty smell, the rattle of a pebble under her foot as she made her way cautiously across the floor towards the back. It took longer than she had expected, as though the cave had grown larger. Her heart was thudding even harder now as she shuffled one step at a time, feeling for her sleeping bag with her feet as her outstretched fingers met the back wall.

In the event she almost missed it. In the dark she had begun to circle round without realising it. When she finally grappled against the cold rock she had to edge sideways for several steps before at last she kicked the soft pile of cushions. She knelt down and carefully began to wriggle into the sleeping bag – not easy in the heavy coat. When she finally managed it she found she was indeed swaddled so tightly that she could barely move. She straightened to lie on her back and lay for a while staring up into the dark. The cave was full of small rustlings and movements; surely the bats would be outside hunting in the dark? Best not to think of bats or rats or anything else that might live in there. The sleeping bag would keep her safe, only her head poking out.

Sleep wouldn't come. She found she was staring up towards the distant ceiling, afraid to close her eyes, conscious only of her own pulse beating in her ears. She screwed her eyes tight and counted to ten. Nothing. Sleep couldn't be further away. Perhaps if she forced her eyes to stay open the sheer stress of it would make her tired. She was tired. She was exhausted, but she was not sleepy. Not now. Her mind went back to Rhona. Supposing the face she thought she had seen really had been Rhona; supposing she was out there in the dark, watching.

Her eyes flew open again. She had forgotten the reason she was here. She had not asked herself the question. She had not told herself what to dream about.

'Catrin. I need to know about Catrin,' she murmured out loud. 'Does she see Glyndŵr again? I need to dream of the past.'

She could picture the house, she could picture Catrin walking to the back door and pulling it open, stepping outside, looking up at the stars and beginning to walk down the garden between the shrubs towards the brook, an empty bucket in her hand.

But the garden had changed. It had elaborate beds. There was a table and chairs on a veranda and Andy could hear traffic in the distance as she watched the figure of a woman climbing the steps, walking through the door and locking it behind her.

Rhona.

She was closing the shutters, walking through the hall to the front door and out, locking that too. She was climbing into the red Roadster. On the seat beside her was a road map. She was smiling. Andy looked down at the map. It was open to show the Welsh borders. As Rhona pulled up at the crossroads and looked from right to left and right again, the map fell off the seat into the footwell and lay splayed open. Hidden in its pages was an ornate dagger and the dagger was covered in blood.

14

Ella cornered Sian in the deli. 'I'm a bit worried about Andy. Have you seen her lately?' She was clutching a pack of organic pasta.

'Yes. We had lunch.'

'You know she's having dreams.' Ella lowered her voice, glancing around to make sure no one was within earshot.

'Everyone dreams there.' Sian tried to sound dismissive.

'But she's not used to living on her own.'

'True.'

'She's interested in the house.'

'Which is fine.' Sian kept her voice firm. 'Nothing to worry about.'

'You don't think she's in danger of becoming obsessed?'

Sian's heart sank. 'What on earth makes you think that?'

'Roy told me she's buying books on local history.'

Silently Sian cursed Roy, someone else who didn't know the meaning of the word discretion. Not that that was fair. She was his wife, for goodness' sake! 'She likes it here, Ella. She's making herself at home.'

Ella took a deep breath. 'Do you remember Joe, the guy who

lived with Sue for a while? Tall chap. Grey hair. She thought he looked like Richard Gere.' She paused as she headed for the till to make sure Sian had nodded assent. 'He was driven away by his nightmares.'

'He was driven away by Sue. They didn't get on when it came down to the basics.'

'No.' Ella shook her head. 'He had nightmares. He thought the house was haunted. He was convinced that he would be killed if he stayed there.'

'Killed!' Sian almost shouted the word. She put her hand to her mouth as she realised everyone in the shop was looking at her.

Ella looked round, embarrassed. 'Let me pay for these things and we can go somewhere. I'll tell you all about it. I thought you would have known. I thought Sue confided in you.'

Sian had thought so too. She followed Ella out of the shop and up to the market square. They headed towards a small table in the corner at the back of Shepherds.

'He told me he dreamt about battles,' Ella said, stirring her coffee energetically. 'Bloody battles. They became more and more real until he felt he was part of the action. He was terrified to go to sleep and even more terrified that if he did he would never wake up. He thought he was going to be killed.'

Sian was staring at her open-mouthed. 'Did you say anything to Andy about this?'

'No. Joe swore me to secrecy. I met him the day before he decided to go. He was at a pretty low ebb. He came into the shop looking for Roy, but he was away on a buying trip so I gave Joe some tea and suddenly he came out with all this stuff. Of course I didn't say anything to Andy. I didn't want to frighten her. But I've been thinking and I don't know if that was the right decision.' She looked at Sian miserably.

'Sue never said a word to me about this,' Sian said.

'Sue thought it was a load of baloney. Crap was her chosen

word,' Ella said. 'She thought he was making it up. But I don't think he was. I think he was really scared.'

'She would have told me.'

'What did she say when he left so suddenly?'

'Just that it hadn't worked out.'

'No. He ran away. Literally. Packed up one day, loaded his car and drove off without looking back.'

Sian sat back in her chair. 'And you didn't tell anyone?'

'I can keep secrets, you know.' Ella coloured. 'But I asked Sue. I was in an awful state. I didn't know what to do when I heard he'd actually gone. Sue was actually pretty rattled. She thought he had found someone else and she told me this whole spiel about his excuses and his play-acting and his behaving like a complete asshole – was I believe the term she used at that point – rather than just being honest with her. I told her about the legends and the history of the house that Roy goes on about, and the old guy who used to live there, but she didn't believe me. Not a word I said convinced her.' She sighed. 'Poor Sue. He was a nice guy.'

'He was,' Sian agreed. She picked up her mug of coffee and took a sip. 'Sue told me once that she had had some bad dreams up there,' she said after a moment. 'And she made me promise not to tell anyone. She reckoned she could ignore them and then they would go away. I assumed they had.'

Ella leaned forward. 'Joe thought he had been stabbed in one of his dreams. He showed me the scar. That was why he panicked. He thought he would actually be killed if he stayed.' She gulped down a mouthful of coffee.

'Joe actually showed you the scar?' Sian hung onto that one phrase.

She nodded. 'It was quite small. Deep. Obviously done by a sharp knife. I wondered if he had done it himself; not on purpose, nothing like that. Perhaps he did it in his sleep, but a medieval battle? I didn't know what to think. When Andy told me she'd started having dreams too, I was terrified for her. That poor woman is up there all alone, actually excited by everything that's happening to her.' She sighed. 'Wherever these dreams come from, they are real, in her head, and she admitted to me that they're addictive. Somehow we have to help her.'

After Ella had left, Sian sat for a while over her half-drunk mug of coffee. She remembered Joe clearly. He had been a nice man. All Sue's friends had had high hopes of him. Then abruptly he had left. She had never pressed Sue any further about what had actually happened, assuming Sue would tell her when the time was right, but Sue never did, displaying unusual reticence on the whole subject. All she had volunteered was a succinct and pithy dismissal of the entire male gender, the only exception being Pepper. 'I'll stick with cats,' she'd declared. 'You know they're not dependable, so they won't ever let you down.'

As for Andy: she remembered the red mark on Andy's hand and she felt her stomach turn over at the thought. 'Wherever these dreams come from they are real . . .' Ella's voice echoed in her head. Real.

Reaching into her pocket for her phone, she called Andy. There was no reply.

'I need to see you urgently,' she said softly into her phone. 'Ring me back as soon as you pick this up.'

Andy awoke from her dream in the cave in a complete panic, covered in sweat, fighting to be free of the constricting clutches of her coat inside the sleeping bag. When she was eventually on her feet she found the torch in her pocket and flashed it around the cave, seeing the beam of light wildly running up the walls and over the distant roof. Somehow she found the entrance and staggered out into the cold night and ran back towards the kitchen door. It took her several terrifying seconds to find the key and only when she was once more indoors and the door safely bolted behind her did she begin to calm down.

Her thoughts were all over the place. Tearing off her coat

219

she dropped it on the floor by the door. She sat down in Pepper's chair beside the Aga and put her head in her hands. She had dreamt. Of that there was no doubt. She had dreamt about Rhona, not Catrin, but then on the floor of the car she had seen a dagger, a medieval dagger. She took a deep breath and sat back, staring blankly in front of her. Had her dreams collided then, past and present, past and future? She realised that she was shivering violently. Somehow she made herself stand up, she filled the kettle and put it on the hob then she stood watching it, gazing into the cloud of steam long after it had started to boil.

Eventually she went upstairs and lay down on her bed without getting undressed. She lay there for a long time, looking at the window, her mind playing over and over that scene in the car. The T-junction, Rhona slamming on the brakes, the road atlas sliding inexorably towards the edge of the seat, falling to the floor, the pages splayed open and the dagger lying there, dripping with blood.

She did not sleep again that night.

It was only just light when she went downstairs, and groping for her car keys on the dresser she let herself out into the ice-cold dawn. Somehow instinctively she knew she had to find help, and the only person she could think of was Meryn.

She climbed out of her car and stood looking round. The attractive stone cottage, painted white and smothered in ivy and roses still felt deserted, the windows staring blindly out across the garden towards the distant hills. She looked up quickly as she heard the echoing cry of a buzzard and saw the bird in the distance, wheeling low in huge lazy circuits over the hill.

When she had come up to his house with Sian she had felt intrigued and excited at the prospect of, if not meeting Meryn in person, then at least of seeing his home, but now she realised it was quite different. Perhaps she shouldn't have come. This was a private place, a lonely place, with a strange otherworldly atmosphere, a place where shadows raced across the hills, thrown by the fleeting light of the rising sun, where *cwmau* and gulleys captured the darkness even in the bright light of day, where secret water threaded through peat moss hags and rocks, bilberry and heather.

Taking a deep breath she walked up to the front door and knocked. There was no reply, as she had known, she realised, that there wouldn't be. He wasn't here, so she should go. Now.

She hesitated. She needed him. She needed help and advice from someone who knew what they were talking about. Part of her wanted to climb back into her car and go home. Another part wanted very badly to go to the shed, as Sian had done, pick up the key and let herself in.

The door of the shed stuck a little as she pushed it. Inside on a shelf, which had been empty when they'd left, she found a bundle of post. So the postman at least had been here since she and Sian had paid their visit. She reached for the keys and took them off the hook. She weighed them in her hand, two silver keys on a ring with a small metal tag. She looked at it carefully. It was shaped like an oak leaf.

Slowly she turned round, wrestling with her conscience. As she reached the door, the keys still in her hand, an icy gust of wind blew into the shed and, for the second time in twenty-four hours, a door slammed in her face.

'Oh God!' she said out loud as she found herself in darkness. The only window, north-facing and smeared with green algae, was hung with dusty spiders' webs that effectively blocked the light.

She took a deep breath and hung the keys back where they had been on the hook.

'Sorry!' she whispered. She groped her way back to the door and pushed, terrified it might have locked itself. It opened easily. Outside the sun was higher now; the clouds still sent shadows racing across the ground. The buzzard had gone.

She opened the car door and slid into her seat. For several long minutes she sat there, her eyes closed, her heart thudding with fright. When at last it steadied she leant forward and reaching for the key turned it in the ignition.

Bumping down the drive and onto the track she glanced into the rear-view mirror. Was that a figure standing by the gate looking after her? She heard herself give a small whimper of fright and accelerated out onto the mountain road.

Bryn's van was there when she turned into the parking space. She sat without moving for a while after turning off the engine then she pushed open the door and climbed out. She was pleased there was no sign of him. She wasn't sure how she felt yet. Frightened. Embarrassed. Ashamed that she was still upset by the terrifying dream she had brought on herself in the cave. She had given way to the urge to seek help from a man she didn't even know. Slowly she climbed the steps and let herself into the house. There was no sign of Pepper in the kitchen and she was almost glad. He would have seen through her at once.

She noticed the light flashing on the phone and pressed the button to play the message. Sian's anxious voice made her frown. Her initial thought was that somehow Sian knew where she'd been. Whatever it was Sian needed to say, she didn't feel up to dealing with it at the moment. She went to the Aga and slammed the kettle on the hotplate. Perhaps a cup of strong coffee would stop her hands shaking.

The tap on the door made her jump. Bryn pushed it open. 'I thought I heard you come back. There was a woman up here asking for you.'

Andy stared at him. 'A woman?' She put her mug down.

'Red spiky hair. Wouldn't leave her name. Said you would know who she was.'

'Oh no.' Andy sat down at the table with a wail of despair.

'Not a close friend then?' he commented wryly. 'Anything I can do?'

She was incapable of rational thought. 'Have some.' She reached for the coffee pot.

He stepped inside the door, closed it and came towards the table. As he passed the sink he reached for the upturned mug, which was sitting on the draining board. She poured him coffee and he sat down facing her.

'I don't think I have actually seen someone turn as white as a sheet before in front of me. I thought it was one of those clichés you find in women's novels.' He took a cautious sip of the black coffee. 'So, you had better tell me about it. I have to say, I didn't like the look of her. She didn't go out of her way to lay on the charm. She appeared to think I was your toy boy. She didn't think much of your morals.'

Andy sighed. She took a gulp from her mug. 'That's because I lived with her ex for ten years. He was the love of my life.' She drank another mouthful.

'Ah.'

'She'd already left him,' she went on. 'She didn't want him, but when he died she changed her mind. She decided she had adored him.' Why was she telling him this? 'As his widow, she felt entitled. She destroyed his will and claimed the inheritance. Hence my present state of homelessness.' She did not try to hide her bitterness.

'And she's followed you here because . . . ?'

'I'm not entirely sure. She hates me with a vengeance.'

The dagger. She could see it so clearly, the blood still dripping from the blade. She took a deep breath and looked up at him helplessly. 'I sometimes think she might be certifiably mad. I'm terrified she's actually planning to try to kill me. I know that sounds ridiculous,' she added. Ridiculous or not, the dream had been a warning. She had sought the advice of ancient gods and they had responded.

'So you came here to hide from her?'

Andy nodded. She was afraid she was going to cry.

'If it's any comfort, I didn't tell her you were here. She

brought out the bolshie bastard side of my character. But I think she knew. She seemed pretty sure of herself.'

'I think I saw her looking through the window yesterday. I managed to convince myself it was a hallucination.'

'This is the house for bad dreams.' He watched her as she took another gulp of coffee.

'Isn't it.' She put the mug down abruptly. 'You know about the dreams?'

'I've worked here for ten years.'

'Of course. You told me.' She gave a weary smile. 'So, sometimes you sleep on the job?' The smile turned into a suppressed gurgle of unhappy laughter.

He picked up the coffee pot and refilled her mug. Ignoring her question, he asked, 'What are you going to do about this woman?'

'Rhona.' She sighed. 'I don't want to move on. She's already chased me out of my home, I am not going to let her chase me out of Sleeper's Castle as well.'

'I'm glad to hear it. So, what are we going to do about her?'

She smiled. 'You have no idea how good it is to think I have an ally. I don't know what to do. Up till now I've just been trying to avoid her. I thought, I hoped, seeing her was a dream.' She knew she sounded pathetic but at the moment she couldn't help it.

'I take it there's no point in us asking nicely for her to go away?'

'I doubt it. I think she's seriously unstable. Graham always thought so.'

'Graham being the gentleman in question.'

'Yes.'

Bryn put his elbows on the table and rested his chin on his folded hands. 'I don't suppose you want to call in the constabulary?'

Andy laughed. 'Too late. She's already thought of that one. She told them I was stalking her and they came up here to check on my whereabouts. Luckily I could prove I was here in Hay, and she was in Kew at that point so her case didn't stack up.'

She wasn't about to tell him she had started it with her sleepwalking, or dream-stalking or whatever her activities might be described as. She shuddered. And now she had dreamed again and this time it was a proper dream and it contained a warning.

'Even so, now she's followed you here it might be useful to tell the local police,' Bryn persisted. He rubbed his face with his hands, leaving a streak of earth across his cheek. 'You're not serious, I take it, about her wanting to kill you?'

Of course Rhona wanted to kill her. What was a dagger if not a warning? A warning her subconscious thought she would understand.

Andy sighed. She wasn't about to tell Bryn that she had wrapped herself in the hide of a bull and slept in the sleeper's cave and been rewarded by a dream of bloody daggers. She took a deep breath. 'No. People scream threats like that at each other all the time and don't mean it. It's that I'm not sure why she's gone to all the trouble of following me here. It makes no sense. She should be sitting back and enjoying her trophy house in Kew.'

She was being disingenuous, she knew.

'Think about the police option. It might be a useful backup,' Bryn persisted. He studied her face. 'You really are scared.'

'I'll be better after a bit. It's been a stressful few days. This was the last straw.'

'Do you know where she's staying?'

'No.'

'I'll make tactful enquiries. She would be fairly noticeable, I'd have thought – she's obviously not the retiring type. It would be useful to be able to keep tabs on her.'

Andy sighed. 'Maybe. I'm probably making a great fuss about nothing. She's a silly woman who is grieving in her own way.

She'll get over it. But thank you, Bryn. It might be reassuring to know where she was, you're right. Let's just hope she gets bored and leaves on her own. This isn't exactly her kind of country. She's a city girl. With a bit of luck, she'll go back to the States or somewhere one of these days.'

'She's American?' Bryn asked in surprise.

'No. But she's spent time there. I remember Graham saying she was happiest there and he wished she'd go back. To be honest I don't care where she goes as long as she doesn't stay here.'

'Well, for what it's worth, boredom is a fairly rational state; it's what one does to alleviate the boredom that's important,' Bryn said after a few moments' thought. 'She doesn't sound very rational to me, and I would worry about what she decided to do to keep herself occupied. After all, very few violent crimes make sense in the cold light of day. If she's suffering some kind of mental disorder, then maybe you ought to be worried.'

'You sound like an expert on the subject.'

He looked uncomfortable. 'I just want you to take care.'

'I will, don't worry.'

'Promise me you will lock your doors at night at least.'

She was about to say, 'I always lock my doors at night; I've lived in London, of course I do!', when she realised how feeble that sounded. Sue probably never locked her doors in her entire life. But then Sue wasn't a townie, always on the watch for potential burglars, and Sue wasn't being pursued by a homicidal woman in a bright-red sports car. 'I will be careful, I promise.'

'OK.' He stood up. 'I'll leave you to it. Thanks for the coffee. And remember, I'm around if you need me.' The words were comforting. It was only when he had gone out and shut the door behind him that she realised she didn't even know his phone number. She didn't get up and follow him. She could ask him next time she saw him.

Rhona spent an hour photographing the yews in Cusop churchyard. She was completely absorbed, enjoying the technical challenges posed by the light and the position of the trees, surrounded as they were by so many others in the ancient churchyard. The tiny church seemed almost to cower between them, overwhelmed by their size and venerability. Only when the light began to fade completely did she stop and put her camera away. She walked slowly back to her car and climbed in. She had carefully avoided thinking about her visit to Sleeper's Castle and her conversation with the gardener. If indeed that's what he was. He was a good-looking man. Obviously Miranda had picked yet another stunning, dependable male to keep an eye on her.

She was a fool to have gone there, but the sight of the van parked there on its own had made her careless. Miranda was obviously out and she had wanted to find out what was going on, see who was living there with Andy, look through the windows of the house, spy out the land. Only the sighting of the tall stranger with a spade watching her as she climbed the steps to the front door had shocked her into realising that she had better think up a story fast. The first thing that came into her head was the truth. More or less. He had been cagey. Was he naturally taciturn, she wondered, or deliberately obtuse? Or was he just a dim yokel who hadn't the wit to be either? In any event he hadn't denied that it was Sue Macarthur's house or that Miranda was staying there. Not that there'd have been any point denying it after she told him she'd seen her car there the day before. She gave a small satisfied smile. Whichever category he fell into, he was not someone she need worry about, that was for sure, and she had had the chance to get closer to the house.

Sian was standing on the back step when Andy opened the door that evening. 'I saw Bryn in town and he told me you were home,' she said as Andy let her in. 'Did you get my message?' It was growing dark. Andy glanced out into the garden behind her then shut the door and turned the key.

227

'I did. I am sorry, I should have rung you back. I got distracted. Did Bryn tell you what happened this morning?'

Sian shook her head. If she had noticed the door being locked, she made no comment.

'I had an unexpected visitor while I was out. Rhona – Graham's wife.'

'Oh my goodness!' For a minute Sian seemed to be completely thrown. She walked across to the table, took off her jacket and slung it over the back of one of the chairs. 'She must be the last person you want to see up here. But I haven't come about anything Bryn did or said. Can we talk, Andy?'

Andy fetched two glasses from the cupboard and poured them both a glass of wine. 'Go ahead.' She indicated the chair opposite hers and threw herself down in her own with an exhausted sigh.

'I had a long chat with Ella Pascoe, and what she told me rather scared me. I thought you ought to know about it.' Sian stared down into her glass without touching it. While she launched into her account of Ella's revelations about Sue and Joe, Andy sat silently, her eyes fixed on Sian's face. When she stopped, neither woman spoke for a while.

'Sue never mentioned someone called Joe to me,' Andy said eventually. 'Not a word.'

'I think she wrote him off as one of life's disappointments. From what Ella said, she didn't believe a word he said about his dreams.'

'No, she wouldn't.'

'Andy,' Sian said after another short silence. 'You remember you showed me where you had burned your hand . . .'

Andy stretched out her fingers and flexed them. 'That was not the result of a dream. I told you.'

'Are you sure?'

'Yes.' Andy sighed. 'No, perhaps a daydream is a better way of describing it, but it wasn't the result of a medieval battle. Far from it.' She stopped dead, thinking about the dagger.

228

Sian was studying her face. 'You said Rhona was here? Really here, or was it another dream?'

'If it was a dream, it was Bryn's dream. He spoke to her while I was out.'

'Why has she come?'

'I don't know, but I doubt if she's just being sociable.'

'Then why don't you come and stay with me? It makes perfect sense. That way the wretched woman won't be able to find you.'

'That's very sweet of you, but I can't.'

'Why not?'

Why indeed?

Because of Catrin. Because Andy had to know what was happening to her.

'Well, for a start there's Pepper.'

'We can come up here every day to feed him. And Bryn would be here.'

'No.' Andy sighed. 'I have to sort this out. I am not going to be chased out of yet another home.' She stood up and walked slowly round the table, then sat down again. 'No. I'm not going to go anywhere.'

All the dreams, all the history, were centred on this building.

Sian seemed to be reading her mind. 'Are you sure it's safe to stay here, Andy? Not only because of Rhona, but because of the dreams. If what happened to Joe is anywhere near real – you've got to think about it. Joe was not the hysterical type. He was a good, solid, down-to-earth bloke and he thought he was in danger here. Not from some psychotic former wife, like you, but from the past. He was so scared he left.'

'We don't know that for sure. Ella might have got hold of the wrong end of the stick.'

Sian opened her mouth to protest then closed it again help-lessly. 'You have to make your own decision.'

'And I will. I'm not looking for trouble, Sian. I really appreciate your warning me. But I know what I'm doing. And I won't do anything dangerous, I promise.'

'What about Rhona?'

'I'm keeping my doors locked. And I will do all I can to avoid her.'

Sian nodded. She pushed her glass away and stood up. 'Fair enough. I'll ask around and see if anyone I know has seen her. She must be staying locally somewhere.'

'Thanks. Bryn is doing the same.' Andy hesitated. 'Sian, please, stay and have some supper.'

'I can't, love.' Sian shook her head regretfully. 'I have to get back to the dogs. I've been out most of the day. But take care, please. And if you change your mind, remember you can come to me any time.'

Andy watched from the window as Sian disappeared down the steps, climbed into her car and pulled out into the lane. The sight of the red tail lights disappearing round the corner left her feeling desperately bleak. Glancing round the empty room, she drew the curtains. She checked the locks on the front door, then went into the kitchen and did the same for the back door. Pepper was sitting on the dresser, his paws tucked neatly into his chest. She had never been so pleased to see him.

It was spring. There was a vase of daffodils on the table.

'Edmund has gone!' Joan pushed open Catrin's door and stood on the threshold. Tears were coursing down her face. 'He's gone to fight for the rebel cause.'

Catrin looked up, startled. 'How did you hear? Are you sure?'

'Of course I'm sure!' Joan brought her apron up to her eyes and wiped them. 'The news is all over Hay. Allies of Glyndŵr captured Conwy Castle while the garrison were at prayer on Good Friday. The rebels are cock-a-hoop about it and men from all over the country are leaving their work to go and follow him. It's all your fault Edmund has gone, you and your father. If you hadn't taken him with you, he would never have seen him.' Her voice rose into a wail. 'Now Edmund will be killed and we'll all be arrested and hanged for treason.'

Catrin looked round desperately. 'Hush, Joan, you mustn't be so upset. He was going to be summoned for the muster anyway. As an archer and an able-bodied young man it was bound to happen. Fighting for Lord Glyndŵr would be no more dangerous than fighting for the king. In fact, it might be safer. Owain's army has the reputation of being the better fighting force.'

'Oh, so you know that, do you?' Joan cried. 'Well, if they are it is only because they pounce on the king's army from the hills and then turn and run away before our men have the chance to fight back and win.' Her voice was heavy with scorn. 'We could have proved Edmund was needed on the farm. We could have done something. Your father could have pleaded for him.' Her voice echoed hysterically round the room.

The study door opened and Dafydd looked out. His face was peevish. 'What is all this noise?'

'Nothing, *Tad*.' Catrin seized Joan's arm and squeezed it warningly. 'Don't say anything,' she whispered. 'He mustn't be upset. He is finishing a poem which has taken months to compose.'

Joan sniffed. She directed a look of pure dislike at Catrin's father then turned and flounced back to the kitchen.

'What was the matter with her?' Dafydd peered short-sightedly after Joan.

Catrin ran across the room, caught his hand and drew him back into his study. She closed the door carefully. 'Edmund has gone to join Prince Owain,' she said softly. 'Joan is distraught.'

'Edmund has gone already?' Dafydd queried crossly. 'No. He said he would wait for me.'

'What do you mean?' She froze.

'I am going to Prince Owain. I have to recite my poem and tell him my forecast for the future. He is destined for such great glory—'

'You knew Edmund was going?' she interrupted him.

'Of course I knew. I asked him to come with me. I can't go alone.'

'And what about me?' Catrin's eyes were blazing.

'You can't come. It was nothing but trouble when you were there. Never again. It is too dangerous for a woman. That's why the Lord Owain sent you away. You have to stay here and run the house.'

'I am not staying here. I am going with you!'

'No.' He tightened his lips in fury. 'I forbid it.' He walked across the room and picked up his staff, which had been leaning in the corner. 'And now I am going to find out what the truth of this is. I will have to go to see Edmund's father.'

'You can't.' She stared at him, aghast. 'Edmund's father is loyal to the King of England. He is an Englishman!'

'He allowed Edmund to come last year.' She recognised the stubborn note that had crept into her father's voice.

'Yes, when the country was at peace. Now Gwynedd and the border March is awash with blood, there are armies roving the hills. Your gentle patron has proclaimed himself Prince of Wales, and apparently he has captured Conwy Castle!'

Dafydd's face broke into a smile. 'Has he now! I foresaw a great victory. I saw stone walls with the standard flying. I saw men on their knees—'

'It was on Good Friday,' she said. 'He took the garrison by surprise when they were at prayer.'

He looked at her uncertainly. 'I have to go to him, Catrin.'

She gave up.

'I know.' She turned away helplessly.

The next morning Peter, the stable boy, knocked on the back door. He refused to be intimidated by Joan, demanding to see Mistress Catrin and when Catrin came to the door he handed her a folded piece of parchment. 'From Master Dafydd, mistress,' he whispered. He glanced at Joan. 'I was told it was a secret.'

Catrin closed her eyes in despair. 'Thank you, Peter. You may go back to the stable.'

She took the note and turned away, well aware of Joan's

eyes following her curiously as she walked into the great hall. She stood by the fire and opened the folded parchment.

Edmund waited for me after all. He called for me this morning. Do not try and follow us, we will be safer and go more swiftly on our own. Do not fear for us, dear daughter, we will be under God's protection. Your loving father, D

Catrin stared at it, not sure whether to be furious or afraid. Turning, she walked towards her father's study. It was empty, the fire out. His writing materials and his scrip were gone. Slowly she made her way outside. Walking round the back of the house she went to the stable. The cob's stall was empty. She saw Peter peering at her from the grain store. 'What time did they leave?' she asked bleakly.

'Before dawn. They told me not to tell you until after you had broken your fast.' He looked very scared.

'Was it just the two of them?'

The boy nodded.

'And did they tell you where they were going?'

'No. Hereford market, I thought.'

She smiled. 'Of course. Why didn't I think of that. Thank you, Peter.'

When Catrin returned to the kitchen, Joan was sitting at the table, staring into space. 'They've gone,' she said slowly. 'Betsi saw them leave this morning before cockcrow.'

'I know.'

'They've gone to join the rebels,' Joan said slowly.

'No one must know, Joan.' Catrin sat down opposite her. 'I know you don't approve, but for your family's sake as much as mine you must tell no one.'

Joan pursed her lips. 'That's treason.'

'It's common sense. If anyone asks we can always claim ignorance. They did not tell us where they were going. Peter thinks they have made an early start for the market. In Hereford.'

'And when they don't come back?'

'We will think of something.' Catrin groped in her pocket and pulled out the scrap of parchment. She walked over to the fire and dropped it into the heart of the flames, watching as it blackened and curled and finally turned to ash. 'We will say my father decided to go on his usual tour early this year. No one will question that Edmund went with him as he came with us before.'

'They will when Edmund is summoned to serve in the army.'

'Then again we will have to say that he accompanied my father on his travels. If I ask your father, what will he say?'

Joan was rubbing her eyes. 'I don't know. He will be so angry.' Again she dissolved into tears.

With a sigh Catrin stood up. She climbed the stairs to her bedroom and closed the door behind her.

Her father had forbidden her to work in trance. It was too dangerous, he had said, without the years of training that he had been given by his father as he was growing up. Now was not the time to worry about what her father had told her. He had lied to her. Her apprenticeship to him was over. She was now the poet in residence at Sleeper's Castle, and it was her job to act as seer and bard and keeper of the stories of the past and of the secrets of the future.

In her dream Catrin watched Glyndŵr.

She saw him in an encampment with his followers, studying a map, which was spread on a folding table under his rippling standard. She saw the campfires of the cooks who fed his army, smelling the roasting venison and mutton as it turned on the spits, hovering in the shadows watching the men carefully oiling their yew-wood bows, rubbing the hemp strings with lumps of beeswax against the rain and checking the ever-growing piles of arrows. These were the bowmen of Wales, the best in the world, and daily more and more came to answer the call to fight for their country.

Catrin stood behind Owain, watching him trace a valley on the map with his finger. She saw him shiver slightly as her shadow fell across him. He looked up, puzzled, failed to see anyone near him and went back to scrutinising the map.

He was an experienced soldier. He knew his men could not face a large English army. He was contenting himself with raids; his lethal archers would pick off the enemy at river crossings and in narrow valleys. This war of attrition wore down the English, but still he needed the morale boost of capturing castles.

When Conwy Castle had been taken, Owain Glyndŵr himself was far away. Two of his followers – his kinsmen, Gwilym ap Tudor and Rhys ap Tudor, brothers from the Isle of Anglesey – had planned and carried out the daring raid. In spite of searching high and low across the mountains and hidden valleys, Harry Percy, who men called Hotspur, appointed Justiciar of Chester and North Wales by King Henry, had failed to find any trace of Glyndŵr. Furious and humiliated by the way the lowly Welsh rebel had managed to evade him, Hotspur contented himself with besieging Conwy with a force of five hundred men equipped with siege engines.

The Welsh held out and Glyndŵr stayed elusive.

Catrin looked back across the mountains to Conwy as the sun sank into the river mouth and now in her dream she looked forward to midsummer. The gates of the castle were opening. She watched fascinated as the garrison began to troop out, led by the Tudor brothers and their closest friends. Recognising the impasse of the siege a deal had been struck; a treaty drawn up between the Tudors on one side and with Hotspur and fifteen-year-old Prince Hal, the king's son, on the other. The garrison of the castle would all go free with full pardons. All except nine men, chosen as scapegoats to set an example to the people of Wales as to what would happen if they rose again in revolt.

Catrin watched with increasing horror as the chosen men were paraded to the allotted place. She saw their faces as they realised their fate. The king had decreed that they be drawn, disembowelled and hanged, finally beheaded and their bodies quartered before the true Prince of Wales, his son, Prince Hal, and the silent crowds. Catrin tried to close her eyes. She did not want to see. She fought to wake up as the scene progressed, but she was held there as unwilling a witness as the men and women and, God forbid, children, who surrounded them. She could hear the screams of the men as they went to their lingering and agonising deaths, the gasps of horror from the watching townspeople and the garrison who only hours before had been their friends and allies. Men and women turned away to vomit as they watched, and only then did Catrin realise they were unable to move away as the surrounding soldiers of the king forced them to witness the end all traitors could expect. Only when the quartered hunks of meat which had once been men were loaded onto carts to be taken away and displayed in the places decreed were the onlookers at last allowed to disperse.

Later local men appeared and cautiously, as if not sure if they were permitted to do it, they began to shovel sawdust onto the bloody ground, worse than any battlefield, looking up at the circling buzzards and kites and crows. The birds, always the witnesses of death, would feed well on the offal that had escaped the carts.

As Catrin fought free of the dream she found herself sobbing hysterically. Someone was knocking at the door of the room. 'What is it? What is wrong?' Joan beat on the oak planks with her fists. 'Let me in.'

Catrin staggered to the door and lifted the latch before pushing past Joan and running downstairs. She only just managed to get outside before she was violently sick into a bed of wild daffodils.

'What is it? What happened? Is it something you have eaten?' Joan followed her more slowly. Catrin couldn't reply.

'Oh God! Oh God!' Andy woke with a start. She was going to be sick. In the distance she could hear Joan's voice calling anxiously. 'Would you like a mint infusion? It will calm your stomach,' and then the voice faded away to nothing. The room was empty, the only sound the brook outside, the constant ripple of water coming in through the open window. Andy stood up and ran towards the bathroom, her legs wobbly as another wave of nausea left her shivering. She had seen men being torn apart; men being systematically viciously tortured to death in front of her. No, not her. Catrin. It had been a dream, a dream they had somehow shared. As she reached the bathroom she let out a moan of grief and horror and stared at herself in the mirror, terrified by the sound she had made. It had been dragged up from somewhere deep inside her, somewhere so primitive, it terrified her. She ran the cold tap and splashed her face with water. The wave of sickness was retreating but the scene she had witnessed wasn't. It was still clear in her mind. She had been there. She had seen it through Catrin's eyes and it was beyond horrific.

Drying her face on a towel she staggered downstairs to the kitchen. Pepper was sitting on his chair by the Aga gazing contemplatively into space. He looked at her. She saw his eyes widen, the pupils sudden slits of terror. He leapt off the chair and was out of the cat flap before she could call out. She stood staring after him. What had he seen? Or sensed? She didn't like to think.

She walked over to the sink and filled the kettle, somehow comforted by the mundane action. Her hands as she turned off the tap were shaking. This was the most vivid dream she had ever had, as vivid as the waking dreams that had taken her into the garden of her old house in Kew to see Rhona and her depredations.

Leaning on the Aga she tried to think rationally about what had happened. On waking she had appeared to move from one reality to another. She had heard Joan's voice clearly as the echoes of Catrin's world had faded; it had been like a door closing on the life she had been a part of only moments before.

This was fascinating, she reminded herself sternly. She could not afford to block out the memories, however dreadful they were. She doubted if she could do it anyway, but to exorcise them at least partially, or perhaps to deprive them of their power, she should write them down, reduce them to notes, put them into a filing box labelled research.

Not so easily done. How could any human being do that to another? She could still see the faces of the men who had so efficiently eviscerated their fellow human beings. They were impassive, cold, just doing their job, trained killers, killing. She felt her stomach turn over again at the memory.

Mint. Joan had suggested mint tea. That seemed like a good idea. She walked over to the door and opened it. It was growing dark now and a damp chill was settling over the garden as she made her way slowly towards the herb beds beside the brook. There were all the moisture-loving herbs, marshmallow, meadow-sweet, comfrey and several kinds of mint, lovingly tended by Sue she was sure, yet allowed to run riot through the bed. She broke some stalks of mint and carried them back towards the house, sniffing them as she walked, feeling them soothing her almost at once.

Halfway across the grass she heard from somewhere behind her a loud snap as if someone had stepped on a fallen branch and it had cracked under their weight, the sound echoing across the garden, clearly audible above the sound of the water. She stopped. She had forgotten Rhona. The executions at Conwy had driven everything else from her mind. She looked round, her heart thudding with fright, aware that the garden was quickly descending from dusk to darkness. Impenetrable shadows stretched across the herb beds, and the water in the brook was black, tinged only here and there with a silver runnel catching the last of the light.

'Who's there?' she called. 'Rhona, is that you? Stop playing silly buggers. We need to talk.' She waited, listening. The noise of the water blocked out all other sounds with its deceptively cheery babble. She wanted to scream at it to be quiet, to let her hear whatever else there was to hear. She took two steps along the path towards the house and stopped again. 'Rhona?' The mint was wilting in her grasp. The scent of it surrounded her, blocking her senses. She was holding it too tightly and her hands were wet with sap. She took another half-dozen steps, her fear threatening to overwhelm her. The solid black shape of the house in the distance wasn't far. All she had to do was run. She turned again, hesitating, looking towards the sound she had heard. There was nothing there. The darkness was empty and still. If anyone was out there, they too were holding their breath, listening. She heard herself give a small whimper like an animal in distress; a few more steps. Whoever it was hadn't noticed she was moving.

Her nerve broke. She began to run, reached the back porch, dived inside the open door, and slammed it shut behind her. She turned the key in the lock and leant against it panting.

The door had been open. Wide open. Anyone could have walked in while she was on the other side of the garden. She stared round the kitchen. Dear God, perhaps Rhona was in here with her. Paralysed with fright, she found she couldn't move.

The kettle had begun to boil. Steam was pouring from the spout, condensation running down the window. She gave a little sob. 'Pull yourself together,' she muttered. 'For goodness' sake!'

The rattle of the cat flap made her jump, then she smiled. 'Pepper?' He walked across the room, stopped, gave her a look of withering contempt and jumped on his chair. Whatever aura of horror had clung to her before must have gone. That was a comfort. As was the thought that he would not have come in so calmly if there had been anyone else in the house. Pepper, her watchdog.

She pushed herself away from the door and went to lift the kettle off the hob. In her panic she had dropped the mint leaves somewhere out in the garden. She saw the green stain on her hands and smelt the sweet minty odour.

239

One way of guaranteeing that Pepper stayed indoors with her would be to feed him. Putting down his plate she stood and watched as he ate, admiring his concentration as, single-mindedly, he chewed his way through each biscuit and then licked the plate for every last crumb. He finished with a drink of water then retired to his chair again to wash his whiskers. She smiled. She envied him his centeredness and his appetite. She had lost all desire for food. Abandoning the idea of going out again and repeating the mint-picking episode, she sipped a cup of camomile tea and tried to read a book, choosing one of Sue's to distract her. It was Beth Chatto's *Garden Notebook*, pulled from a shelf of gardening books in the living room. She couldn't face one of her own, they were too spooky. At ten she turned on the TV to watch the news. She dozed off and woke with a start. It was nearly midnight. Pepper was curled up on the chair, his tail wrapped round his nose, fast asleep.

She didn't want to go to bed. She didn't want to go back to Catrin's story. She didn't want to relive any of that scene. Nor did she want to go upstairs alone. 'I don't suppose you would come up with me?' she whispered to the cat. He opened one eye. Greatly daring, she stooped and picked him up. Cradling him in her arms like a baby she headed for the stairs, leaving the lights on and the TV quietly talking to itself in the corner. Pepper tensed and she waited for him to wriggle free, but he relaxed and let her carry him up to her room. She put him down carefully on her bed and, kicking off her shoes, lay down beside him, not attempting to get undressed, leaving the bedside lamp switched on, merely pulling the blanket over her as she lay, keeping as still as possible so as not to disturb him. He snuggled up into the pillow, yawned and went instantly to sleep. She smiled. 'Sweet dreams,' she whispered.

By the window Catrin stared at her thoughtfully. She knew the woman had shared her nightmares and for that she was sorry. She knew she was afraid of falling asleep and knew exactly how that felt. She tiptoed closer, seeing that almost as soon as she had lain down sleep had overwhelmed her in spite of all her efforts to fight it. Did she know how to stop the dreams, she wondered? Perhaps not. She didn't seem to know how to regulate them at all. Her attempts at dreaming true had been unplanned and wildly uncontrolled. Surely she had not intended to draw the red-haired virago to her.

She stepped closer, examining Andy's clothes, noting the stitching on her jeans and her heavy knitted sweater with almost professional curiosity. Such clothes would be warm and practical. She took another step closer and Pepper woke with a start. He sat up, his ears flat against his head, leapt off the bed and fled out of the door. Andy gave a small moan and turned over, reaching out for the comfort of the warm, solid little body. In her sleep she did not notice that he had gone.

In the bedroom at the B & B Rhona woke and lay staring up at the ceiling, wondering where she was. The room was eerily quiet as the country always was. No cars; a darkness outside the window which was total. She wondered idly where the nearest street lamp was and smiled uncomfortably. She couldn't imagine why Andy should want to live in such a godforsaken part of the world. But of course she had to. She was running away. Hiding. Rhona smiled again. Knowing someone was that frightened of you was extraordinarily exhilarating.

She remembered when the psychiatrist had spent a stupidly large amount of time questioning her about her enjoyment of watching other people's pain, going right back to the children at school whom she had taken so much pleasure in hurting. Chinese burns. Her speciality. In the end her mother had been asked to take her away from the school, which had suited her fine. She reckoned the shrink got as much of a kick out of hearing her talking about it as she did recalling her actions.

She raised herself on her elbow and thumped the pillow. The action, however much it relieved her frustrated impatience, did

241

not make the bed any more comfortable and after a few minutes she reached out and turned on the bedside light. It was time she did some serious planning. Her fellow guests were all leaving the next day and her hostess had asked her how long she would be staying. Fair enough. The woman had a right to know. She ought to move on and maybe that would be sensible. It would be easier to disappear if she kept moving. These hills seemed to be full of extraordinarily lonely houses, the perfect place to keep a low profile. She was pleased now that she had had the good sense to book in under an assumed name.

She cursed herself again for her stupidity in going to look for Miranda yesterday.

Easing herself into a more comfortable position, she wondered whether Graham had ever told Miranda about her. She imagined he had, at great length, going into detail about her supposed misdemeanours. After all, during some of their worst quarrels, he had referred to her as a witch; and worse. Little did he know. She smiled grimly.

The people she had picked on had always asked for it. If they'd left her alone and minded their own business she would not have had to punish them. She should have punished Graham. She might have got round to it in the end if she hadn't been distracted by that nice man from America. They had spent a long time together on a wonderful trip across the States, she and Abner, and then it had all gone wrong. He had begun to irritate her. She sighed. Dealing with him had been less enjoyable than she had hoped; she'd been forced into the rapid change of plan when a local cop had begun to take an interest in her. She had had to cut her losses and come back to England before it got out of hand and by then Miranda was there gloating over her conquest of someone else's husband.

Outside it was beginning to get light. She could see the pale outline of the window behind the curtains now. She wriggled down under the duvet. Another couple of hours' sleep and then it would be time to go down for breakfast. Later she would go to the bank and collect some cash and after that she would go back to Sleeper's Castle. The thought sent a shot of adrenaline through her body. It was the perfect place to confront Miranda. She had never set foot inside the building but some strange instinct told her it was a house that was accustomed to creating its own history; a house used to violence. And if she didn't find Miranda there alone there were hundreds of miles of wild mountainous country around it where, if fate played into her hand, their confrontation would happen.

15

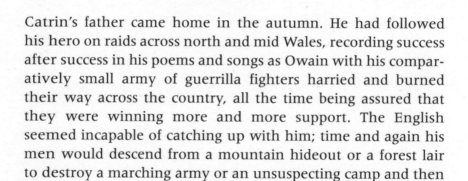

Catrin's father came home in the autumn. He had followed his hero on raids across north and mid Wales, recording success after success in his poems and songs as Owain with his comparatively small army of guerrilla fighters harried and burned their way across the country, all the time being assured that they were winning more and more support. The English seemed incapable of catching up with him; time and again his men would descend from a mountain hideout or a forest lair to destroy a marching army or an unsuspecting camp and then he would be gone again, leaving his victims to lick their wounds.

Catrin had watched in her dreams as manors and castles were taken and destroyed; she saw the horror of men and women turned out into the night as their homes burned behind them. She witnessed Owain's rage when he heard the monks of Abbey Cwm Hir had betrayed him to the English and watched the destruction in August of the abbey. Then came the horror of the capture of New Radnor Castle. 'No!' she murmured in her dream. 'No, please, no.' The surviving men of the garrison had been rounded up by Owain's army, sixty or seventy captives in all, and beheaded in revenge for the treachery at Conwy. Their bodies were hung from the castle walls.

'Were you there?' Catrin asked Dafydd. Her face was pale. 'Was Edmund part of it?'

Dafydd looked away, unable to meet her eye. 'I was with Owain until he despoiled the abbey. It was in the patronage of the Mortimers, his vowed foes. You do see, don't you? There was no choice. And then we took Montgomery. He failed to capture the castle at Welshpool but the area around it was burned. To punish the enemy.' He paused, clearly uncomfortable. 'It had to be done. This is war. We went on to Powys Castle and there we failed.' He gave an anguished sigh. 'Its constable, John Charlton, was too strong. We withdrew to the hills.' He glanced at her. 'The Lord Owain told me to come home.'

'Why? If you were supporting him, lauding his victories.' Catrin didn't know what else to say. The detail of the scenes she had witnessed was terrible and she had been forced to watch, unable to wake up, just as her father was forced to watch in reality from hillsides or distant vantage points.

'Because,' he cleared his throat and laboured on, his voice hoarse. 'Because the fight is possibly coming this way. I don't know what he plans, he would never tell me, but he studies his maps and he listens to his spies and he follows the valleys and rivers with his finger and he smiles as he has warning of the movement of the king's army or news of a castle or a manor or an abbey which is badly garrisoned and rumoured to support Henry of Lancaster. No one knows where he will appear. No one knows what he will do next.'

'But you are his seer!' Catrin cried out. 'You must know.' She was terrified.

He didn't reply. 'He would not attack us,' he said doggedly after a moment. 'He spares the homes of his supporters.'

'He sent you home because he knows he will come to Hay?' Catrin grabbed his sleeves and forced him to look at her. 'Tell me, *Tad*. What have you seen?'

He glanced round warningly. 'Where is Joan? She must not hear this.'

'You know very well she has gone to visit the farm. *Tad*, our friends, our neighbours!'

He clenched his teeth stubbornly.

'We have to warn them.'

'No! We can say nothing.' He seized her wrist. 'We know nothing, Catrin. That is the way he works. No one knows. No one is warned. He may not come. He may turn and ride back to the west coast tomorrow. He may have already gone.'

'Yet he sent you home to protect me,' she whispered.

'He knows the way of soldiers in war,' he said dryly. 'He would not want you harmed. And people like me slow him down. He has his own seer who rides with him into battle. I am a hindrance so it is better if I am not with him. I can serve him as well from here with poems and stories.' She could hear the bitter hurt and rejection in his voice.

'Did you tell him of your bad dreams?' she asked in a whisper. 'Where he is destroyed?'

He shook his head. 'I dream of success and glory as much as I dream of blood,' he said slowly. 'He does not always win, that is the way of war. I do not speak of the bad times, it is bad for morale. It undermines confidence.' It was almost as if he were repeating someone else's words.

Catrin walked across to the fire, her back to her father. She shivered, pulling her thick woollen shawl around her more closely. 'I have dreamt too. I have seen battles and victory and defeat. I have seen great areas of the country laid waste and people starving, their livelihood destroyed by one side or the other. Is it worth it, *Tad*?'

'Of course it is worth it. It is for freedom! It is for our true prince!' Her father gave her a scathing look and turned towards his study. 'Something women cannot be expected to understand.'

She stood looking down into the embers for a long time after he had slammed his door behind him, wondering what the woman in men's hose, the woman who seemed to be called Andy, would say to that last comment. She had tried to shield her from the worst of the dreams but it had not been easy; she was too open, too receptive. It had not surprised Catrin to see this new shadow in the house. The ghosts from the past and from the future were as much a part of the fabric of the building as she was herself. Some reacted to her, some didn't.

Catrin thought back wearily to her own childhood when her father had begun training her to be a dreamer, to look into the future and to recall the past. She had had a natural facility for it and all too easily slipped into trance, led in by the flicker of flames or the shimmer of leaves against a summer sky. He had taught her to switch off, to erect barriers, to direct her attention to the question of the hour. She had never found that easy. Girls from the farms nearby would find their way to her door and give her a present or pay her a farthing to tell their fortune and sometimes she would comply, but other times she saw nothing but pain and travail for them and if she told them that they were angry and threatened her. Eventually her father forbade her to do it any more. When the pictures came unbidden she was silent. When she tried to avoid them, they came in dreams and again she was silent.

With a sigh she walked out of the room, out of the house and went to stand on the bank of the brook, listening to the babble of the water. Even that sound was capable of sending her away into a distant place over the hedges and the fields, down the mountain, across the great River Wye and out towards the north, the forest of Radnor, where even now a secret army was cautiously creeping through the heather towards Hay.

Andy was sitting in the coffee shop alone, sipping a double espresso, staring up through the window towards the castle walls. That ancient slab of keep and the huge old doors in the massive walls were part of the original building. The other end of the castle, the Jacobean mansion house, was out of place, incongruous now she had seen the original, intact, through Catrin's eyes. She took another sip of coffee, feeling it bite, shock her system awake. She had seen the brushwood piled up against the walls, the flames taking hold, the shouting men charging the gate with battering rams and watched them burst open as easily as a lanced boil. The garrison was not expecting trouble. They had been expecting it to be a market day like any other. Another hour and they would have opened the doors themselves. The banner of Glyndŵr was at the head of the shouting horde as they charged up the ramp that led to the gates and on into the inner courtyard. The garrison was small and ill trained and only half-hearted in the defence of the castle. They fled, as did the people of Hay. There were to be no bodies hanging from these walls. The Lord Owain had a soft spot for Hay – why, no one could imagine, unless he knew the towns-folk were secretly on his side – but the castle must be razed, great holes punched in its defences, its stores looted and its weapons stolen so it was of no further use to king or baron on the English side. A token number of houses were burned, cattle slaughtered and then the invaders were on their way, leaving the place undefendable, a jagged ruin rising skywards in the centre of the town, visible from far away across the river as a warning to any who stood in the way of the Lord of Glyndŵr. He moved three miles downstream to Clifford Castle, which like Hay was barely defended, and then he turned his attention to the cloud-topped barrier of the Black Mountains which stood between him and his goal of Abergavenny.

'Andy?' The voice broke into her daydream. 'Sorry I'm late.' Sian eased herself in between the spare chair and the table, slopping her coffee into its saucer as she put it down on the table. 'Have you been waiting long?'

'No. I was getting a fix in quickly to wake me up.' Andy gestured at her cup. She glanced out of the window. The small car park was full, the castle behind it sleeping peacefully against an intensely blue sky. In front of the war memorial a group of children were laughing and messing around as their teacher tried to call them to order. It all looked very ordinary.

'Shall I get you another coffee?'

She realised Sian was talking to her. 'Sorry. No. Thanks.'

'I take it you haven't been sleeping well,' Sian commented dryly.

'No. I haven't.' Andy gave a wry grimace. 'Actually my dreams have been a bit gory, better forgotten. What I wondered was have you had any information about Rhona? Bryn hasn't heard anything and I've a bad feeling about her.'

Sian's left eyebrow shot up. 'I don't like the sound of that. Your bad feelings are probably like other people's storm warnings. I'm afraid I haven't. I've phoned various people I know who do bed and breakfast and no one has seen a woman answering her description. And I don't think she's at any of the pubs in Hay. The trouble is there are so many people doing B & B now. She could be anywhere.'

'I thought it was a long shot, to be honest.' Andy sighed. 'I'm just so angry that she should follow me here. This is my haven. Somewhere that has nothing to do with her. Hasn't she done me enough damage!' Andy bit off the words. 'Sorry. I'm a bit frazzled.'

There was a short pause.

'Are you managing to get any painting done?' Sian thought it wise to change the subject.

'A bit. I'm going to try and arrange one of the bedrooms as a studio. There isn't enough light in the great hall where I'm doing it at the moment. As the days get shorter there's less and less daylight in that house. The walls are so thick and the windows small.'

'It wasn't built for light. It was built for warmth. To keep the wind out.'

Andy nodded. 'If I was staying here forever, I would be tempted to build a proper studio. A sort of wooden summer house with large windows, but that would be too hard to heat, and it wouldn't be easy to defend.'

'Defend?'

'She might torch it or something.'

'Oh Andy, this is awful. You're joking!'

'No. I'm not. She seems to have a really vicious streak.' Andy bit her thumbnail. 'Anyway, that's not going to happen obviously, and one or two of the upstairs windows in the more modern part let in a good north light. I am going to buy some decent lights as well and I will ask Bryn to help me move the furniture around to give me a bit of space.'

'Wow. You must have made a bit of headway with him then.'

Andy laughed. 'I think he has a kind streak buried deep in there somewhere.'

Bryn came up trumps. He helped her push the spare-room bed against the wall, out of the way, he distributed the superfluous chairs between her bedroom and Sue's and brought a table upstairs for her to work at. He even offered to take down the curtains to let in more light. They threw a rug over the bed which, without pillows and with a few scatter cushions, immediately became a divan. When it was finished he looked round critically. 'Not bad. You're right, you'll still need a decent light or two in here. I'm afraid you can't get round the fact that this is an old house.'

She nodded. 'It's perfect though. I needed a dedicated room for a studio.'

'Do you have an easel?'

'Not for the kind of thing I do. I use watercolours mostly.'

'Your paintings are good.'

'You've seen them?'

'In the living room. As you say, you have no privacy there.' He grinned.

She glanced at him uncomfortably. When had he been in the house looking at her paintings? Better not to ask.

He noticed her hesitation. 'I'll leave you to it now. You'll want to put everything in its right place. If you need anything else lifting, just call me.'

She stood listening to his footsteps as he ran down the stone staircase. Two minutes later the back door banged shut and she was alone.

It took an hour to bring all her painting things upstairs and arrange them round the room. By the time she had finished it was perfect, and to crown it all Pepper had taken up position on the divan sitting critically watching her as she put her jars of brushes in place and arranged some of her books on the shelves.

It was beginning to get dark when she heard Bryn's van start up. She stood listening to the sound of the engine as he turned in the lane and set off down the hill until it died away in the distance and she was alone. Almost at once she found herself wishing they had not taken down the curtains. She felt very exposed, standing in the brightly lit room as it grew darker outside. 'I think we might get a blind for that front window,' she said quietly to Pepper. 'It wouldn't block the light in the daytime and it would make me feel a whole lot safer at night if no one can spy on me.'

Later she turned off the light and went through into her own bedroom. It felt cosy and safer in there, with the curtains closed.

Joan had gone home for a few days. A message had come, begging her to go and see her mother, who had been taken ill. Catrin was standing in the kitchen surveying the pot of rabbit stew, which Joan had left for them, when there was a knock at the door. She opened it and a blast of cold wind and rain swept in. With it came two cloaked figures. One of them pushed the door shut and slotted the bar in place. Then he pulled off his hood.

'Edmund!' she cried. 'You've just missed Joan—' She broke off as the other figure began to take his own cloak off. Both men wore mail. 'My lord Owain,' she stammered.

Edmund took Glyndŵr's cloak and hung them both on the back of the door to drip on the floor. 'I sent the message to

Joan,' he said. 'We couldn't have her here when I brought Prince Owain up to see your father.'

Glyndŵr smiled at Catrin. He took her hand and raised it to his lips. 'It is good to see you look so well, Mistress Catrin. I trust your father is too. The ride he did in my wake round Wales wore him out, I fear.'

'He is well, thank you. He is in his study,' she said softly. She looked from one man to the other. 'Shall I show you?'

Edmund stayed in the kitchen as Catrin led the way to her father's study and opened the door. '*Tad*, there is someone here to see you.'

As the door closed behind their guest Catrin stood for a long moment staring at it. Then she turned back to the kitchen. One of the stew pots was now on the fire. 'We are hungry. You don't mind do you? It is not every day a lady gets to entertain the Prince of Wales.' He grinned at her. His hair was dripping over his hauberk. 'Shall we light a fire in your hall and entertain in style?'

'Why has he come?'

'To consult his seer, as he always does when he travels round the country.'

'But he sent *Tad* home.'

'To look after you. And to stop him proclaiming death and disaster in front of the whole army.' Edmund's face grew solemn. 'Your father has a habit of being too honest about his dreams and he is constantly contradicting himself.' He picked up a wooden spoon and began to stir the pot. 'If my sister made this it will be good. It is a shame you can't tell her it was eaten by the prince.' He looked up. 'Have you heard the news from Hay?'

Catrin looked at him anxiously. What she had seen, she had seen in her dreams. 'We have had no one by in the last few days.'

'We took the castle.'

'Took?' She stared at him.

'As in captured and dismantled.' He grinned. 'Don't worry.

No one was killed. He knew it was our home town and the natives seemed friendly.'

'How can you capture a castle without killing people?'

'By guile; clever tactics. And especially if it is manned by sympathisers.'

They walked into the great hall. He bent over the log basket and began to gather logs.

'Since when have you been the prince's special companion?' Catrin asked abruptly. 'You and he, here alone?'

'Since he needed to be guided up the hill to Sleeper's Castle. Who else would do it?' Edmund turned to the hearth.

'Why don't you light the fire next door in the parlour,' she whispered. 'It will warm more quickly and be more private.'

'Private?' Edmund shot a look at her suspiciously. 'Is there anyone else here?'

'Peter, the boy who minds the horses, and the girl, Betsi. They are both outside.'

As Catrin spoke they heard a loud knocking on the kitchen door, the rattle of pails and the creak of the door hinges.

'Get rid of them!' Edmund reached for his dagger.

'Betsi has been milking the cow. Don't worry. She won't recognise him.'

'But she will recognise me and she will tell Joan. Send her away!'

Catrin ran back into the kitchen. She unbarred the door and opened it, aware that Edmund was listening. 'Sorry, Betsi. Bring in the milk. I barred the door against the wind. It keeps rattling.'

The girl crossed to the cold slab in the pantry and began pouring milk from her wooden pail into one of the large earthenware jugs.

'Joan said I was to heat up her stew for you, mistress' – she glanced over her shoulder – 'but I see you have already started it.'

'Yes, thank you, Betsi,' Catrin tried to steady her voice. 'I started because my father has a quinsy. I thought it might tempt him.' She was thinking furiously. 'You may leave us and go on back to the cowshed, Betsi. It will be warm in there. Don't come back till morning.'

She didn't move until the girl had grabbed her shawl from the table where she had thrown it and made her way to the door. Betsi paused, looking at the two long wet cloaks hanging there, then she pulled the door open with a creak of hinges and went out, the handle of her pail rattling as she banged the door behind her. She didn't give the cloaks another thought.

Edmund appeared at once. 'Well done. We can't risk it. Word gets out so quickly.'

'I'll serve supper in the parlour to keep it private,' Catrin said. 'The windows are shuttered.' She hesitated. 'If you want supper. Won't he want to leave at once?'

Edmund looked over his shoulder towards the study door. All was silent in there. 'Go on heating the stew,' he said, 'and I will build the fire. We were hungry when we rode up here. I don't see that that will have changed. Especially when it smells so good.' He grinned.

'Won't Betsi see your horses?' Catrin blurted out. 'She will notice—' She had noticed the two cloaks on the door. Tomorrow Catrin would have to give her an explanation for their presence.

'No. Don't worry, we left them out of sight—' He broke off as the study door opened. Dafydd beckoned. 'Come here, Catrin. You, Edmund, find us some food.'

Catrin smothered a laugh as she saw the look of indignation which flashed across Edmund's face. 'It seems it will be your turn to stir the stew after all,' she teased.

Glyndŵr was sitting behind Dafydd's writing slope. 'Catrin, your father reminds me that you too are a seer.' He leant back against the wall, tipping the high stool on which he was perched onto its two back legs. 'I need to know what you see for Wales.'

Catrin was struck dumb. She saw her father's face darken, but he said nothing.

'I have dreams,' she said hesitantly. She took a deep breath and squared her shoulders. 'Sometimes I see battles. I don't know if they show the past or the future.' She lowered her gaze.

'I think you do.' Glyndŵr's voice was soft. 'Don't be afraid of me, Cat. Wherever I go I make a point of visiting local seers. I missed you this summer, but your father was right not to bring you. The battle lines are no place for you.' He smiled warmly and held out his hand. Mesmerised, she stepped closer. She was still wearing his silver ring. 'I want the truth.' He held her gaze. 'Even if it is not good. I want to know if you see the same things as your father.'

'In the battle I foresee, you are winning,' she said, suddenly shy. 'But the people suffer. Their towns are burned. Their fields are laid waste, their animals killed. There is no food. The armies take it all. I saw an abbey burning, the house of God. I watched flames pouring from its roof.' Her voice rose slightly and broke and she looked at him, agonised.

Dafydd moved towards her as if to stop her but Glyndŵr raised his hand. 'No, let her speak. You realise that much of that damage is done by the English armies, Cat,' he said gently. 'It is their way to punish the people for supporting me. And they do support me.'

'They do. They hate the English laws and taxes. But this is a terrible price to pay.' She took a deep breath. 'I suppose I have never seen men die before.'

'And even in your dreams it is a fearful sight.'

She nodded mutely.

'It will be worth it, Cat.' He smiled again. 'I will win. I will drive them out.' His quiet certainty made her feel strangely warm and safe.

Edmund had set up the trestle table in the parlour. He had built up a large fire and the room was warm and welcoming when they seated themselves on the two settles. Catrin had laid the table with their best silver spoons and her precious glass goblets from the aumbry, part of her mother's dower which had escaped her father's ire. The stew and the soft bread which Joan had baked just before she left that morning seemed to satisfy the three men but Catrin ate very little. She studied their guest as he sat opposite her. He was still a handsome man, tall and well built, his hair and his long forked beard greying now, his blue eyes compelling as he looked from one to the other in the room. He had a kind smile. She remembered that from the last time she had seen him when he had declared himself prince beneath his black lion banner. She felt his charm and his strength and his absolute certainty.

Dafydd seemed ill at ease. Catrin saw Glyndŵr reach out and touch her father's arm. 'I value your visions, Dafydd. There will be setbacks and I need to know about them,' he said. 'My other advisors and seers are too afraid to tell me what may go wrong. I need to know so I can take evasive action. Your vision is as valuable as anyone's. But I need your insights to be private. I do not want my men disheartened.'

Dafydd scowled. 'I am sorry. I spoke out of turn. I cannot always control my own horror at the sights I see.'

Glyndŵr sighed. 'I understand.' He stood up and stepped back from the bench. 'And now we must go. I thank you for your hospitality, Cat.' He smiled at her. 'I have a gift for you.' He felt in his purse and pulled out a small silk kerchief. It was wrapped around a bracelet of silver filigree. Gallantly he fastened it round her wrist, shaking his head at her stammered thanks. 'Now we must ride. My men await me and we head on through the mountains towards Abergavenny.' He tapped his nose. 'Not a word of our visit.'

Catrin struggled to waken but the dream had her now. The smell of smoke was torrid. A building had been torched. A large building. A church, its soaring arches and flying buttresses etched against the fury of the flames. She tried to murmur a prayer but no words came. She saw the brothers streaming out of the smoke, fleeing into the hills. The soldiers let them go, contenting themselves with watching the windows shatter and the lead melt. The stone would not burn, but the monks' dorter, the refectory, the prior's house, all were ruined.

Her own tears woke her and she lay there in her bed staring towards the window. The shutter had come unfastened and between the mullions she could see the cold moon shining down on a silvered countryside. The moon felt nothing; there was no mercy there, no answer to prayer. In the silence of the dawn she heard an owl's long lingering hoot, the cry of the harbinger of death.

16

Andy woke with a start as the echo of the owl's call died away. She sat up clutching her duvet under her chin, staring across her bedroom. It was only just growing light.

Glyndŵr had been in this house. He had stayed for supper and then vanished into the night. She could remember exactly how he had looked in the dream; he was thinner now than when she had first seen him, his face worn and tired. He was gentle and kind to Cat. She liked the way he called her Cat. But he was a strong personality. Of course he was. He would take no nonsense from anyone, that had been clear. She sat up and wrapped her arms around her knees. The room was cold. The radiators hadn't come on yet. She was trying to remember what he had said. He spoke English. But again, it was her dream, and in her dream everyone spoke English. But then again, didn't one of the books say he had been trained as a lawyer in London. Wasn't he an Oxford man and a man of the borders with an English wife?

There was so much to remember. She climbed out of bed. Dragging on her dressing gown she went downstairs in search of her notebook. She had to write all this down as soon as possible before his words slid from her memory. She turned on the kitchen lights and rummaged on the dresser for her pen and the notebook she had left on the table then she retreated back to bed. There she began to scribble, words, mannerisms, looks, their clothes – both visitors had been wearing chain mail under their wet cloaks. Edmund was taller than his prince and much younger. About the same age as Catrin, she guessed. She paused, pen in mid-air. He obviously still fancied her. Did she reciprocate the feeling? It was an awfully lonely life for her up in the mountains with her irascible father, Joan and the two other servants as her only companions. Did she have friends? After all, she hadn't witnessed every moment of Cat's life. There was Efa, of course. Maybe she had neighbours as well, girl friends, the wives of farmers up the valley. Somehow she doubted it. Her life as a poet and a seer was something so different; akin to being a religious recluse, like one of Rufus's heroines, Julian of Norwich. She lay back against the pillow. Was Cat a believer? She remembered Edmund mentioning the privations of Lent. Had Cat gone to church at Easter? Everyone did in medieval times, didn't they? But then, where was the church? She thought back to the small lonely stone-built church up in the next valley, the church that served the scattered parish which was home to Sleeper's Castle. She had visited it with Sue and Graham. It had been built in the twelfth century and was dedicated to someone called St Cewydd, the Welsh rain saint. She remembered that detail with a smile. That surely would have been Cat and Dafydd's church, as it would be hers if she decided to go. And if St Cewydd was a rain saint he too must have had an influence on the weather of this oh so rainy country. Had Cat invoked him in her magic spells, or was it Taranis, the Celtic god of thunder she called on? Andy didn't know.

She was glad Edmund had reappeared on the scene. She had been terribly afraid he would be killed in battle. She pictured him as she had seen him in her dream. He had toughened up.

Life as a follower of Glyndŵr's army was hard. He had good muscles in his arms, a broad muscular chest and a weather-beaten handsome face beneath the wild flax-coloured hair which burst irrepressibly from beneath his woollen cap. Men and women in those days seemed to have their hair covered all the time. Even little Betsi in the cowshed had a shabby linen head-scarf tied over her head. All the smart women Cat had met on her travels were exotically clothed in beautiful gowns and elaborate headdresses with exquisite jewellery. Well, Cat wasn't doing too badly in that department either. She didn't seem to wear jewellery, apart from the silver ring her prince had given her, but now she had at least two other lovely pieces.

Andy's mind strayed back to Edmund. He reminded her of someone. The set of his mouth, his eyes, even the wild hair. And then it dawned on her. It was Bryn. He bore a strong resemblance to Bryn.

She lay back against the pillow, chewing the end of her pen as she pondered the similarity. Both men came from somewhere in the next valley as far as she knew; was it so far beyond the realms of possibility that they were related, that Bryn was a descendant of the dashing Edmund? She grinned to herself. It was a beguiling thought.

Did Edmund hold a special place in Owain's trust now if he accompanied him to visit Catrin and Dafydd alone, or was it merely, as he had said, that he was a part of Glyndŵr's house-hold and a handy guide into the hills? More likely the latter surely? But she would love to know more.

To know more all she had to do was to dream.

But it was no use, however hard she tried, she could not go back to sleep. Perhaps if she went for a walk it would clear her head. Throwing on her clothes she went downstairs, grabbed some breakfast and let herself out into the cold morning.

As she headed up the lane, she realised she had not yet properly explored the mountain tracks on foot. The only times she had ventured any distance up here had been by car, on her way up to Meryn's house and it took her far longer to reach the cattle grid than she had expected and the lane was far steeper. Her heart was thumping uncomfortably as she neared the top and she had to stop to catch her breath. Edging her way through the gate beside the grid she found herself at last on the open hillside.

Behind her the narrow lane was lined by high banks and hedges heavy with vegetation, but here the grass was cropped close and she could see sheep everywhere she looked. The view opened up almost at once to panoramic views of the distant mountains to the west and north and further round towards the north-east to the deceptively gentler rolling hills of the Radnor Forest, which she remembered so vividly from when Catrin and her party had traversed them. She gasped at the beauty around her. When she had driven up here with Sian the view had been obscured by thick fog. Now, the faint trails of mist over the distant hollows and streams – known, Sian had told her, as dragon's breath – only added to the magic. On her right a mountain stream ran down through the ferns, cutting deeper and deeper into the hillside, making its own valley, thick with ash and alder. She turned full circle, taking in the high slopes of Hay Bluff and Twmpa, noting in the distance a small, scattered herd of wild ponies grazing amongst the bracken and bilberries. Here and there she could see an occasional thorn tree, twisted and tortured by the wind, cowering low in a sheltered clearing, obviously a favourite spot for the sheep to shelter from the elements; and everywhere the golden flowers of gorse.

She debated briefly whether to stay on the road, or to turn off and set out across country. It would be impossible to get lost here with the huge flank of the Bluff like a wall on the horizon. As she narrowed her eyes, staring up at it, she saw a brief finger of sunlight catch the windscreen of a car and she remembered that there was a road up there, traversing the side of the steep slope, heading south into the Gospel Pass. She walked towards the watery glimpses of the sun for a good half an hour, watching the sunbeams cut through the clouds to lie slanting across the distant countryside. From time to time she could see a faint rainbow arcing out across the landscape and watched the fierce rain showers racing across the ground towards her. She pulled up her collar and pushed her hands deep into her pockets, turning her shoulder to the rain as each shower struck. Overhead she heard the wild yelp of a buzzard and glancing up she saw it gliding above the Bluff, catching the thermals as it soared ever higher.

She was climbing now, quite steeply, exhilarated by the walk but feeling increasingly tired. Soon she would have to turn round and begin to loop back or she wouldn't have the energy to retrace her steps. She smiled to herself. If she had wondered whether this would tire her out she could wonder no more. She was beginning to ache all over from the effort of the walk. She was obviously not as fit as she had imagined. Turning, she scanned the horizon.

It should be easy to retrace her steps. If she kept the great massive of the Bluff to her left shoulder she couldn't go far wrong. She walked a few steps and stopped again. A deep gulley ran across the steep hillside in front of her. At its foot there were several thorn trees and she could see the rushes in the hollow growing round a small spring, the trickle of water winding off to lose itself in lush grasses. She didn't remember seeing that before. For the first time she felt a quiver of unease. Raising her hand to shade her eyes she surveyed the horizon slowly turning a full 360 degrees. Hay Bluff was still there to her left as she stopped again. She glanced up at the sun to check. Twmpa was ahead of her; to the north was the view of miles upon miles of rolling countryside and distant hills. She couldn't get lost. All she had to do was to keep the mountains in their allotted positions. She caught her breath as she saw something move on the near horizon, silhouetted against the sky in a dip between two low hills. Not a pony or a sheep but a human figure. Someone was standing there watching her. It was too far away to see which way they were facing, but even so she knew they were watching her. She could feel it. She walked on slowly. When she raised her head again and looked cautiously round the figure had gone. She took another bearing on the hills and set off again. Any moment now she would see the ribbon of roadway ahead of her, winding back down towards the cattle grid and the lane.

It was several minutes later that she saw the car, the sun glinting on the windscreen. It was pulled up on the close-cropped grass at the edge of the road about half a mile below her. She stopped dead. Far away though it was she could see the colour clearly. Red. The roof down. A sports car. Rhona's car? Please God, no. She looked round nervously then back at the car. The sun had disappeared behind a cloud and it had gone. There was no sign of it. She was alone in the vast landscape. Far away to her right she could see a group of ponies grazing near one of the thorn trees. Their heads were down, their tails swishing gently against the flies. If there was anyone there, they would know. Even as the thought crossed her mind she saw them raise their heads, all concentrating on the same spot some distance from them, their ears pricked. First one, then another, then all of them lowered their heads once more. Whatever had caught their attention had gone. She gave a quick glance round again and resumed walking, heading this time further to the right, away from the place she thought she had seen the car. Her feeling of tranquillity had gone. She could feel her anxiety mounting. It couldn't be Rhona; of course it couldn't. How would she know where Andy was? Unless she had come to the house, seen her leave and followed her at a distance.

Andy stopped. She was once again on the edge of a steep gulley. It cut across the hillside in front of her, if anything more precipitous than the first she had seen. She surveyed the bottom of the rocky declivity. It was carpeted with sedge and bog cotton.

It ran from east to west in front of her and the only way to pass it was to climb down and then up the other side. She took a few steps to her right trying to see a way round it, then stopped dead as a voice spoke behind her.

'How strange to see you here, Miranda. Always you seem to be in my way.'

Andy turned slowly. Rhona must have made her way up the narrow track behind her, hidden by the steep contours of the hillside. She was standing only a few metres from her. Dressed in a short-waisted jacket and jeans with knee-high leather boots, her red hair blowing in the wind, her eyes were hidden by dark glasses.

Andy managed to hide her shock. 'I'm only in your way, Rhona if you persist in following me,' she said. 'What on earth possessed you to come all the way up here?'

Far above, a buzzard was wheeling below the clouds. Its wild yelping cry rang across the empty hillside, almost carried away on the wind.

Rhona took a couple of paces closer. 'Can't you guess why I came?' She was out of breath.

'No. You're hardly dressed for the occasion.' Andy could feel herself beginning to shiver. Cold and exhaustion, combined with a real fear of this woman were creeping over her. She was terribly aware of the gaping ravine behind her, the miles of empty hillside in front. 'Those boots are better suited to Knightsbridge, not the mountains.' She managed to put a sneer into her voice. The wind was getting stronger. 'Presumably you followed me from the house?' In a landscape void of human life they were totally alone.

Rhona took another step closer to her and in spite of herself Andy moved back. The gulley was only steps away.

'Tell me why you've come, then we can both go our separate ways.'

'You're right. We need to talk.' Rhona pushed the hair out of her eyes. 'About Graham. My husband.'

'What is there left to say?' Andy edged a couple of steps sideways. She had to get past Rhona, away from the drop.

Rhona moved closer. 'There is a great deal to say I would think.'

There was barely a metre between them now. Andy glanced round wildly, trying to see a way out. She could feel herself beginning to panic. She tried another step sideways. Rhona matched it.

'Please move, Rhona. Let me come past.' Andy's boots were losing their grip on the slippery ground. She lunged frantically to one side, trying to dodge around the woman, but it was no use. She was off balance.

Andy heard herself scream as she felt herself slipping and the grass disappeared from beneath her feet. For several seconds she fell backwards, then she hit the steep rocky slope. She grappled desperately with clumps of bracken and grass to halt her fall and felt it being torn from her hands as her weight carried her on down until she tumbled awkwardly with a splash into the moss at the bottom. With a cry of pain she felt her ankle double up under her.

When at last she managed to look up Rhona was standing above her on the edge of the defile, looking down with interest. 'Oh dear,' she said at last. 'That was silly of you. I hope you can still walk. It would be awful to be marooned out here with a broken leg.' She smiled.

'Why?' Andy cried. She tried to sit up and fell back with a groan. 'For goodness' sake, help me. Give me a hand.'

Rhona appeared to consider the suggestion. 'No, my dear. I don't think you can expect that. Not after everything you have done to me. After all, you started all this by insisting on coming back to Kew. Creeping around in the garden, spying on me in the house. Mocking me. Trying to terrorise me.'

'I didn't!' Andy cried. 'How could I have? You're imagining it!'

But it was true, she knew it was true.

'I don't know how you did it.' Rhona was thoughtful. 'It doesn't really matter. This is payback time, you must see that. Serendipity. Kismet.'

'I never came to Kew,' Andy protested again.

Rhona took another step forward as if to see better. 'It must be very cold down there,' she went on conversationally. 'You're right out of the sun. I wonder, did you tell anyone where you were going? That delicious gardener, for instance?'

When Andy said nothing she smiled. 'I thought not. He wasn't there when you left, was he. You know, it's strange. I hadn't even begun to think of the right way to dispose of you. So many options. And here you are, throwing yourself at my feet as if you had chosen to help me with my decision.' She looked round critically and then gave a sigh. 'I don't really want to get my feet wet, but I think I must. To be sure.'

Slowly she began to make her way down the side of the gully, slipping here and there as she went. Andy watched, mesmerised, as she came closer. At the bottom she stopped, steadied herself and then examined her boots critically. 'Damnation. You are right. They're going to be quite spoiled.'

Even now Andy thought she might hold out her hand to help her. It was only at the last minute she saw, incredulously, Rhona take careful aim with a vicious kick at her head as she lay on the ground. Somehow Andy threw herself sideways and managed to dodge the full force of the blow. It glanced off her shoulder, but it was enough to throw her sideways into the ice-cold wet moss again. She lay still, unable to get her breath, a vicious pain slicing through her shoulder as she tried to raise her face out of the water and gasp for air.

Behind her she heard Rhona laugh. 'That was so satisfying.' She seemed to be talking to herself. She stepped closer and bent over Andy. 'I do hope you haven't got a mobile on you, dear. I suppose I'd better check.' She began to search with almost professional dexterity through Andy's pockets and almost at once she found it in her jacket. Rhona slapped away her feeble protests and pulled it out triumphantly. Without hesitation she threw it over her shoulder. It fell with a splash into the cold black water of the spring.

She turned away without giving Andy another look.

It took her several minutes to climb out of the gully. Andy could feel tears of rage and despair burning on her cheeks as she lay in the icy water, pain knifing up through her ankle and round her shoulder, but instinct told her to lie still. If Rhona thought she had any fight left in her, she might come back.

It wasn't until she reached the top that Rhona turned and looked round. 'I imagine it will get very cold up here later,' she said conversationally. 'It's very easy to die of exposure in this sort of place. I am so sorry, dear. But you do see, I have to leave you here. Out of the way. For Graham's sake.' She raised her hand in a languid wave and stepped back out of sight.

Taking a deep breath, Andy tried to move. Only one thing mattered. To get out of the ravine before her body closed down completely from shock. She was soaked through and shivering violently, waves of pain travelling up her leg into her hip. Cautiously moving her arms, she reached out, trying to get a grip on bunches of bog cotton to pull herself free of the engulfing water. It was hard to lift her head; at least the water wasn't deep enough to drown her. She managed to raise herself on her elbows and looked round to see if she could spot her phone. There was no sign of it and anyway she had heard the splash as it fell into the spring. It wasn't worth looking for it. What was important was to get herself down to the road.

It took her an inordinate amount of time to drag herself out of the ravine. Every inch was agonising as she pulled herself up the steep side, dragging her useless ankle over rocks and clumps of heather, unable to take any weight on it and feeling the bruise in her shoulder as a searing pain every time she moved. When at last she pulled herself over the edge of the last of the rocks and lay on the soft grass on the level ground she was spent. She couldn't even lift her head. Her teeth were

267

chattering and she was overwhelmed by icy rigors, shuddering helplessly.

For while she must have lost consciousness. When she woke she was aware of the strange sensation of being bathed in sweat at the same time as shivering violently. Andy was still lying on her face but she was aware of a shadow falling over her. 'So, you came back to gloat,' she whispered. If Rhona chose to stick the dagger in her back she wouldn't even have the strength to protest. Somehow she managed to roll over and look around. There was no one there. She couldn't move any more than that so she lay staring up at the sky. She could see the buzzard now, circling lower than she had ever seen it. She could see the outline of the feathers in its wings, the spade-shape of its tail. It soared up and away and round and then came back, angling its wings to make the turn. The sun had moved a long way towards the west. It was casting long shadows across the ground and she could feel the whisper of cold in the wind. She must have been there for hours. Without her phone she had no idea of the time. If she wanted to live she knew she had to drag herself to her feet and start moving down towards the road; at least then she would have the chance of getting a lift back to civilisation. She tried to move her leg and let out a small cry of pain.

She felt ridiculously weak and shaky. She tried to manoeuvre her arms behind her to push on the ground to get the leverage she needed to sit up. Her fingernails were split and torn and her hands were lacerated from the effort of climbing up the sides of the gully. It was as she tried to take the weight on her injured shoulder that the pain took her in a black wave and she fell back. Her last thought was of Catrin and the visit of the prince.

Joan had returned from her visit mid morning, the mule loaded with supplies from her father's farm. She was full of the excitement of her trip home and news of her mother who had made a strangely swift recovery from her mysterious illness. As she unloaded bottles and jars and dried vegetables and fruit, and stored them in the pantry she talked on, never pausing to ask how Catrin and her father fared.

She never guessed that Edmund had visited the house; never had the slightest suspicion that the prince had been with him. Catrin had washed the dishes herself. There was no sign of their night-time visitor; she had hidden her gift behind a hollow stone in her bedroom wall. The other things, the writing materials for her father, Joan would never question, nor the extra food. They could be explained away if she ever asked by the visit of a travelling pedlar.

There had been no sign of a passing troop of horsemen; the hillsides were empty. It wasn't until a sennight later that news came of the devastation of Llanthony Abbey, so close across the mountain and along the pass, the monks turned out into the night, the sacred looted and scattered and made profane. The prince's army had then marched on to take Abergavenny Castle before turning towards Usk.

Catrin bit her lips in misery. To destroy the house of God. Was that not sacrilege?

Time passed. There was no more news of the rebellion. Autumn turned to winter and winter into spring. Dafydd had developed a cough and had taken to his bed for several days at a time, but now he was stronger and growing restless.

'Are you going with him this year?' Joan asked. She hefted a skillet onto the table and pushed up her sleeves.

'No,' Catrin sighed. 'If he goes, he will go with Peter.'

Joan raised an eyebrow. 'I won't ask where he is going.'

'His usual progress, from house to house.' Catrin glanced up. 'You haven't heard from Edmund?' It was many months since he and Owain had walked out of the house and into the night.

'No word.'

The two women looked at each other for a scant second and

looked away. If Joan pretended she didn't know where Edmund was, it was better left that way.

Catrin woke with a start. Someone was shouting. Her heart hammering, she climbed out of bed and reached for her heavy mantle. The house was freezing cold. Opening the door of her bedroom she peered into the solar next door where her father slept. In the glow of the dying embers in his brazier she could see his bed was empty. The shout came again, from downstairs. She ran down the cold stone steps in her bare feet and looked round the hall where Joan slept near the fire. The woman was sitting up, her eyes wide, clutching her blankets round her.

'It's my *tad*,' Catrin whispered. 'Go back to sleep. I'll see to him.'

She knew what had happened. It had happened so often before. He had fallen asleep propped against the wall on the stool beside the fire in his workroom and his dreams had woken him. She lifted the latch on the heavy door and pushed it open. Her father was standing looking down at the fire. She could see the stool on its side, the cushion lying on the floor where he had knocked it as he climbed to his feet.

'*Tad?*'

'Go away. I'm sorry if I woke you.'

He stooped wearily, reached for a log in the basket nearby and threw it on the fire. They both watched the sparks fly upwards. The candles had long ago burned down.

'What is it? What made you cry out?' She closed the door behind her and moved closer to him. 'Please tell me.'

He shook his head. 'I told you, girl. Go away. Go back to bed.'

'Not until you tell me. Let me fetch you some wine.'

'No!' His shout echoed round the house. 'I told you to leave me. Now.' He straightened his shoulders and strode towards the door. Opening it, he gestured at her to leave. 'Now!'

There was nothing she could do. With a sigh she walked past him out into the hall. He slammed the door behind her.

Joan had lit a candle from the embers and set it on the table. She too had thrown logs on the fire and the hall was full of leaping shadows. 'Nightmares again?' she said. She yawned.

'He won't talk about them. He gets no rest.'

Joan shuddered ostentatiously. 'They must be bad.'

Catrin said nothing. Joan could not read or by now she would have looked at the documents on Dafydd's desk and seen the words he could not help writing again and again before he scratched them out because he did not want to believe them.

Blood. Fire. Death.

Catrin pulled her mantle round her more closely. 'I am going back to bed. Put out the candles, Joan, and try to get some sleep. It will be dawn soon. I feel it by the chill in the air.'

As the weeks passed news came via the same routes as always. They listened to gossip in the market, they welcomed visitors to the kitchen and heard from them news from every direction. The numbers of Owain's followers grew daily; his army was now known as *Plant Owain*: the children of Owain. Most Welshmen supported him quietly, cautious as to where their neighbours' loyalties lay, but the men still flocked in their dozens to his standard. Meanwhile Dafydd paced up and down the great hall of the house, smacking his fists together in frustration.

'You could have gone to the prince. You didn't have to stay here with me!' Catrin reminded him yet again as she followed her father into his study and watched as he sat down at his desk.

'Do I look as though I want to be riding across the hills in the vanguard of an army!' he exploded. 'I am too old. I am no soldier. You know that better than I. I ache in every joint of my being, there are times I couldn't climb on my horse without someone there to give me a boost up my backside.'

271

He did not see her wry smile at the words. She knew better than anyone the pain he was in, his hands knotted from holding his pen, his back an agony of spasms from leaning forward over his desk.

'And besides,' he went on, more quietly now, 'I still have no good news to give him. I hear he captured Welshpool at last and seized Prince Hal's baggage train; I hear of other bards and soothsayers foretelling victory for Wales, and I wonder where I have gone wrong. I see victory, oh, I see victory at first, but then . . .' he paused. 'Then I see disaster. My nightmares are of disaster.'

As were Catrin's now. The night before she too had dreamed of death and destruction, and again it was of a house of God, but this time the blazons on the knights were English. She saw the silhouette of soaring arches against the flames, heard the screams of the monks and then the most awful thing of all, the crying of children. She had watched in frozen terror as she saw men-at-arms rounding up a procession of small children; they were dragged from their mothers, screaming and crying and chained together like little animals as the rain began to fall. As she watched, the bedraggled convoy was led away into the hills and out of sight. 'There are hundreds of them,' she heard herself murmur as she woke, her pillow soaked with tears. Little Welsh children, taken away to England by order of the king.

'Little Welsh children,' Andy echoed. She was burning up with fever, racked by dreams. Again a shadow flitted overhead. Somehow she forced her eyes open. The sky was darker now. Another shadow swept over her, a black shape in the air. She looked up and saw the circling birds, two buzzards now, no, three and other birds, larger, with the great forked tail of the red kite. She heard herself give a whimper. They had gathered to look at her. Great hunting birds, their amazing eyesight scanning the slopes below, they had seen her easily, so why had no one else? 'Help!' Her cry was so feeble it was barely audible.

She saw the birds veer away slightly, then they returned, circling ever lower. She could see them in such detail now, every feather of their wings and tails, as they circled ever downward, closer and closer. They were huge.

'Dear God, they're planning to eat me!' The thought hit her all at once. She had seen carrion birds circling the corpses on the battlefield in her dream. That was their job. Cleaning up corpses. Tearing at the bloody meat, stripping the bones. They had seen her fall and their instinct had kicked in. They saw her as a meal. Somehow she summoned the strength to shout louder and wave her good arm. They veered away sharply once more, but then, seeing she was still on the ground, they closed in again. She could see the great gleaming eyes as they looked down at her, feel the wind under their wings. One of them let out a wild yelping call, triumphant, echoing over the empty moors and hills.

She looked round frantically. She needed a stick to wave at them, to help her stand and try to walk. There were no sticks. No trees near her. She took a deep breath and dragged herself up to her hands and knees. Which way? She had lost all sense of direction. Look for the Bluff. That would guide her. Her head was swimming; her eyes wouldn't focus. With a single last little cry she collapsed back onto the ground.

While Joan was fetching more water from the brook a shadow appeared in the doorway. Catrin knew Pepper well. She was amused by her ghost cat, fond of him even. She knew he could see her too. She saw his eyes widen, the pupils narrowing into a vertical slit as he watched her. He sat down to keep an eye on her as she made her way across the kitchen to throw more logs on the fire beneath the cooking pot. Joan came in, a pail of water from the brook in each hand. Pepper jumped up and vanished through the door.

Catrin followed him into the garden and stopped abruptly, staring out across the valley. Something was wrong. Out there on the hillside someone was calling. She pictured that other woman, Andy, the woman she saw sometimes in her house, the woman she thought of as the ghost in men's clothes. She sighed. It couldn't be her. The garden was silent again now. The cat had gone.

17

The shadow had stopped moving at last. The birds must have overcome their caution and landed on the ground. Andy screwed her eyes tight shut, waiting for the cruel beaks to start tearing at her flesh. She felt a hand on her face, touching her forehead. Fingers pressing gently under her jaw, feeling for her pulse.

Rhona!

Her eyes flew open and she let out a cry of fear.

'Hush, you're safe.' It was a man's voice. His hand touched her forehead again, then he ran his fingers down her shoulder, gently pressing her collarbone. She let out another whimper, her eyes everywhere, scanning the darkening sky, the surrounding hills, the man bending over her. He was no more than a silhouette. She couldn't make out his face clearly. 'The buzzards,' she whispered. Her mouth was dry, her voice no more than a murmur.

'They've gone,' he said. 'It was the birds who showed me where you were. Lie still now. Let me see how badly hurt you are.'

She felt him run his hands down her legs as he crouched beside her. The touch was impersonal, professional. He reached her ankle and she couldn't stop herself letting out another cry of pain.

'Twisted rather than broken, I think,' he said. 'You've taken quite a tumble.'

He stood up and she saw him grope in his pocket. He pulled out his phone then slipped off his jacket and tucked it round her gently. Her eyes followed him as he took a couple of steps away from her and punched in a number. 'Gareth, I've found a young woman up here on the moor near the spring at the head of Nant Rhyd-goch. She's had a bit of a fall and I need your help to get her to the house.'

Switching off the phone, he turned back to her.

'Are you a doctor?' she asked. And then she thanked him. Or she thought she did, though no sound came. She drifted off to sleep, opened her eyes and saw the sky growing crimson in the west. It was very beautiful. She tried to smile and must have slept again. When she woke it had grown dark but for the small streak of red on the western horizon. There was another man there now and a pony. Was it Catrin's? She couldn't tell. She felt the soft touch of its nose as it lowered its head to examine her. The second man had brought blankets and a flask of something hot, and the two men hoisted her onto the saddle, sitting sideways, wrapped up warm. When the pony started to walk she found the motion restful. Her ankle and shoulder hurt, but not so much now. She dozed. It was dark, but they seemed to know where they were going. 'Where's Rhona?' She remembered saying that out loud. They stopped and asked her who Rhona was and should they go back. 'No,' she whispered. 'No, she tried to kill me.'

The first snows drifted up the valley in mid November and with the cold came conflicting news from every side. Owain Glyndŵr was besieging the great castle at Caernarfon. He had raised the gold and white standard of Uther Pendragon on Twt Hill and six hundred men had died; then they heard that he had lost as many men as had the king. Glyndŵr withdrew from the castle realising he could not capture it, garrisoned as it was, and then the rumours said that he was asking the King of England for pardon and restitution of his lands.

'No!' Dafydd exploded with rage. 'He would not do that. His allies have won battle after battle. He has supporters all over the land.'

Catrin stared at him. 'Three hundred of his men have died, *Tad*. Is that not enough? Would peace not be an honourable end to all this?'

'Peace? You really believe that the king would grant him a pardon, pat him on the head and send him home?' Dafydd shouted. 'The king would have him executed!'

'No! King Henry is said to be an honourable man, *Tad*, surely. If he has promised—'

Dafydd didn't deem the remark worthy of an answer. He turned and stalked back into his study, banging the door behind him.

Joan stepped forward out of the shadows. 'Did you say three hundred men had died on each side?' she whispered.

'So I was told.' Catrin bowed her head in despair.

'There is no word from Edmund,' Joan said quietly. 'My father has tried to find news of him. Do you know where he is?'

Catrin sat down on the bench and leant wearily against the wall. 'I have heard nothing from him, Joan. If I had I would have told you,' she sighed.

'Now the weather has turned, won't they disband the armies? Isn't that what usually happens in winter?' Joan asked, her voice harsh with anxiety. 'So they can come home and be fed at the expense of their families and have their wounds tended and their terrors comforted so that they can go back and fight again in the spring.'

Both women looked towards the window where they could see snowflakes drifting down out of the leaden sky.

'That is what usually happens, yes.'

'And have you not dreamed that that would happen this time?'

'Joan, I don't know. My dreams are muddled.' Catrin dropped her head into her hands with a groan. 'I just don't know.'

Catrin must have dozed off. It seemed a long time later that she heard a tapping at the window. Her eyes opened and she stared across at the shutters. Perhaps she had imagined it. The sound came again, this time louder. She dragged herself to her feet and went to the front door. Pulling up the heavy beam that barred it shut she opened it a crack and peered outside.

'Catrin?' It was a whisper in the darkness.

'Edmund?' Her heart thumped unsteadily at the sound of his voice. Surely she was imagining it? 'Where are you?' In the deep shadows there was no sign of him.

'Here, behind the bushes. I didn't want Joan to see me.'

With a glance over her shoulder at the closed door to the kitchen, Catrin stepped outside onto the snow-covered grass. He was crouching behind the bushes, a sack over his shoulders.

'What are you doing? When did you come back? Why don't you come in?' Catrin held out her hands and he seized them.

'I don't want Joan to hear. You know only too well how indiscreet my sister can be. She'll shriek out something and rouse your father. I had to see you before I go.'

'Go? Go where? I don't understand.'

He pulled her closer. 'I came back to see my father.' He was whispering in her ear now. The snow was drifting more heavily down from the heavens. 'I only went home for a few hours. I came on a mission with messages for supporters in the mid March. Better you don't know who or why. Now I am on my way back to the prince's side. There will be no peace this winter, Cat.' He was looking anxiously into her eyes. 'I'm sorry.'

'And your father?'

'Has disowned me.' He tightened his lips. 'He threatened to

hand me in. I may not come this way again for a long time. That is why I had to come to say goodbye.'

Catrin's fingers tightened over his. He pulled her closer and held her to him. 'I am sorry it had to be like this. I want you so much.' He was silent for a while as she clung to him. There was no argument now. She had missed him like a physical pain. She loved this man and knew that he loved her. 'If I had been a rich man, if I thought one day I would inherit the farm, things might have been different,' he murmured. 'As it is, I should not be here. I have nothing to offer any woman. Your father is right. I have no place at your side.'

'My father? You spoke to my father about me?' She pushed him away and stared up into his face.

'Last time I was here, with Prince Owain. Your father guessed how I feel about you. He made it clear I would never be accept-able to him as your suitor.'

'And me? Did you not think to ask me?' she cried furiously.

'Sssh.' He glanced behind her into the house. 'How could I ask you? I have nothing. Nothing, Cat.' He had adopted the Lord Owain's nickname for her.

'I shouldn't have come,' he continued. 'It was probably madness, but I wanted you to know how I felt.'

She had snowflakes lying on her hood. There were more catching in her eyelashes. He reached up and gently pushed the linen coif back from her hair. Then he leant forward and placed a kiss on her forehead. 'Be safe, my Catrin. Write wonderful poetry and make me proud.'

She gave a small inarticulate cry and clung to him. 'I will come with you!'

'You can't.'

'I can. All I need is my thick cloak—'

'No. It was unfair of me to come.' He hugged her close, his eyes closed.

'Edmund—'

He dropped a quick kiss on her lips, then he pushed her away. 'Go back in. Shut the door. I will do all I can to keep you and your father safe.'

'What do you mean, safe?'

He shook his head. 'I'm a good archer. I will earn money. I am trusted by the prince. Who knows, perhaps I will be knighted on the field of battle and I will come back Sir Edmund, and then your father will have to stop despising me and allow us to wed.' He tightened his arms round her.

Behind them the kitchen door swung open and the pale lantern light spilt out across the paving slabs into the garden. 'Catrin?' Joan's voice echoed towards them. 'Catrin? Are you all right?' Her tone grew shrill.

'I'll have to go,' Catrin whispered. 'If she looks for me she'll see you and make enough noise to bring my father down, you're right.' She caught his hand and held it tight. 'Stay here, I'll come back in a moment.'

'No time. There are men waiting for me on the track. We're going together. God be with you, my darling. I will return for you one day. I swear it.' Releasing her, he faded into the shadows. She heard his footsteps crunch on the snow, then he was gone.

'Catrin?' Joan's voice was growing panicky. She had run into the hall and was staring towards the open door.

'I'm coming.' Catrin took a deep breath and turned towards the house. She had no time even to savour the feel of his arms.

It wasn't until later, as she climbed to her bedchamber and began to remove her coif and her veil and let down her hair, that she allowed herself to close her eyes and dream a little of the handsome man in the garden, the man who had told her he loved her.

She lay still, shivering, her head on the pillows, the bedcovers pulled up round her ears, lulled by the sound of the brook outside the window. Her room was ice-cold. The shutters barely kept the wind out. Her father had promised her curtains for her bed and even glass for the window, but it hadn't happened. As so often when he suggested improvements for the house, he forgot them again almost as soon as he had mentioned them, so immersed was he in his work. And when the spring came, he too would be gone again. He would ride to the prince's court wherever it was, take his poems and his stories and his assurances that all would be well with the campaign to make Wales a country in her own right, independent of the English king, and the prince would listen and nod and smile at the confirmation that his plans would succeed and that Dafydd ap Hywell, like his other soothsayers, was sure of victory.

As slowly her eyelids drooped and she lay still waiting for sleep to sweep her into another world she was afraid that her father would wake and come storming upstairs to castigate her for waking him, or that Joan would arrive carrying a mug of camomile infusion. But no one came. The house was silent. Out on the lonely hillside she heard a vixen scream.

'That sounds like the woman who was staying with me for the last few days.'

Megan Jones was standing in front of Sian in the queue at the Co-op. They had met in the grocery aisle. 'She was a bit of an oddball. Not like my usual guests at all. Very English, red hair, like you said, cut all spiky and modern – which looked odd on an older face. But her name wasn't Wilson.' She began to stack her purchases on the conveyor belt. 'She called herself Jenkins. Myra Jenkins.' She reached for a quart of milk and heaved it onto the conveyor belt. 'I've got a week without guests, thank goodness. I sometimes think I'm getting too old for this caper. We've had all our rooms full since the Festival.'

'In what way was she unusual?' Sian tried to sound casual. 'Apart from the hair.'

'She said she was a photographer. Well, maybe she was. She made a great show of letting me see her camera, but somehow she didn't handle it like a professional. I can't quite explain. It

281

was more a hunch.' She stacked butter and cheese behind the milk. 'You know how you get a feeling about people? The other couples were very nice. Quiet. Normal. But she had something about her that made me feel uncomfortable. Sixth sense, you know.' She moved up to the till and smiled at the young man as she reached for her carrier bags.

They resumed the conversation in the car park.

'She left first thing this morning. As I said, she paid in cash, but then I don't take cards any more.' They stopped behind Megan's car, their laden trolleys in line abreast.

'She didn't ask about Sleeper's Castle?' Sian asked.

'No.' Megan was a short dumpy woman, with an open friendly face which had begun to look anxious. 'Why?'

'Sue Macarthur rented it out to a woman called Andy. Nice lady. We've got to know each other a bit and she told me about this problem she's been having with her former chap's ex. It seems the woman's something of a psycho: she's followed Andy up to Hay and has been threatening her. I said I would try to find out where she's been staying, but if she's gone, then maybe the panic is over.'

'She said she was going towards Stratford,' Megan said. 'But I think she was lying.'

Sian stared at her. 'Why would you think that?'

'Instinct. I've been running a B & B for thirty years. One gets these feelings about people. Like if someone isn't going to pay. Or if they've come away for a dirty weekend.' She gave a little snort of laughter. 'Of course there's no such thing any more, is there. No one cares who spends the weekend with who, except perhaps the poor old husband or wife who's being cheated on.' She sighed. 'I'd better get back, Sian. I still have to feed Cedrych and the boys.'

'If you think of anything else, will you ring me? I know it's a long shot, but did this woman leave an address with you?'

'She did.' Megan bent to open the tailgate of her car. 'But I'll wager it doesn't exist. Or if it does, it won't be hers.'

'And if it is hers, Andy knows it anyway because it is, or was, her address.' Sian sighed. 'I'm not quite sure how or why Andy let the woman chase her out of the house. It happened when she was still in shock after her fella died.' She hauled her trolley round and pointed it in the direction of her own car. 'I know none of it's really my business, but I can't help worrying about her after the things she told me about this woman, and I sort of feel she needs a friend.'

Megan stood watching as Sian headed towards her car. Her two dogs had been asleep in the back and she saw them leap up, tails wagging as Sian approached. Megan sighed. It was late and she still had a lot to do before she could put her feet up this evening and watch a bit of mindless telly.

As she reached her car Sian's phone rang. She fumbled for it and glanced at the screen. 'Meryn? Where are you? We've missed you!'

When next she woke Andy was in a bed, wrapped in a dressing gown, her shoes and her jacket gone. Her ankle had been neatly bandaged and apart from a dull ache it had ceased to pain her. She was warm and safe.

'Andy?' A voice she knew. 'Andy, are you awake?' It was Sian.

Andy forced her eyes open. She was in a small bedroom, whitewashed, pretty. 'Where am I?'

'You're in Meryn's cottage. He found you on the hill.' Sian was sitting down on a chair beside the bed. 'Gareth Vaughan brought his pony to carry you back here and he recognised you. Meryn rang me.'

'Everyone knows everyone.' She could barely get her tongue round the words. 'Meryn found me? He was the doctor?'

'He came home yesterday.' She looked over her shoulder as the door opened. 'She's awake.'

'How are you?' Meryn appeared behind her. He was tall, Andy saw now, with dark hair greying at the temples. He smiled down at her. His eyes were a vivid blue.

'Better.' She smiled back. 'How did you know I was there?'

'My friend the buzzard told me.' He smiled. 'I saw the birds were taking quite an interest in something down there on the hillside and thought perhaps I would go and see what it was.'

'They were going to eat me.'

He threw back his head and laughed. 'Luckily for you they only like carrion and you were far from that.'

She found she was smiling too. His laughter was infectious. His face sobered almost at once. 'I can see though how scared you must have been. They are large birds. A kite can have a six-foot wingspan.'

'And enormous claws.'

'Talons,' he corrected. 'But you're right, they are vicious-looking, as is that huge beak. Now,' he leaned back against the wall near the bed, looking down at her, his face stern. 'Who is Rhona?'

Andy gave an involuntary shiver. 'Why? How do you know?'

'Because out there, while we were getting you onto the back of the pony, you told us that she had tried to kill you.'

Andy saw Sian bite her lip. She leaned forward and took Andy's hand. 'What happened?'

'She followed me. I'd gone for a walk. It was stupid, but I didn't see her. Then she was there. I slipped down a cliff into a little valley and I landed badly. I thought my ankle was broken. She came down after me and I thought she was going to help me, but . . .' Her voice faded.

'But?' Meryn was looking at her sternly.

'She kicked me. I think she intended to kick me in the face, but I ducked and she caught my shoulder.'

'Oh, Andy!' Sian squeezed her hand again.

'She threw my mobile in the spring. I couldn't find it.' Tears trickled down Andy's face. She closed her eyes, exhausted.

'We should call the police,' Meryn said.

'No.' Andy's eyes flew open. 'I don't want the police. It would be my word against hers and they wouldn't believe me. They would say I imagined it. Perhaps I did imagine it. Perhaps I dreamed it all.' The room was beginning to swim round her again.

'I don't think you dreamed it,' Sian said grimly. She was looking at the bruises spreading up Andy's neck to her jaw. 'I don't think you dreamed it at all.' She gave Meryn a quick glance.

'I think we need to discuss all this when Andy is feeling a little stronger,' Meryn said quietly.

Sian bit her lip. 'And perhaps we needn't worry for now. Rhona's gone, at least for the time being.' Sian told them about her encounter with Megan at the supermarket.

'If you hadn't found me, it might have been days before anyone reported me missing,' Andy murmured. 'I remember now. I wanted to go for a walk. My car is still at home. No one would have missed me.' She tried to sit up. 'Except Pepper! I've been out all day – I didn't even give him any breakfast.'

Meryn smiled. 'That cat!' He said softly. 'Probably the most pampered animal in Wales! I'm sure he's more than capable of looking after himself for a few hours. Although I have to say, I'm amazed Sue didn't take him with her.'

'To Australia?' Sian said. 'I don't think Pepper would have agreed to that.'

They both laughed. It was a quiet, friendly sound and Andy lay back and looked from one to the other, overwhelmed with unexpected happiness.

'Back to the important issue,' Meryn went on. 'You're safe, Andy, you're not too badly hurt. It's a miracle that you aren't suffering from hypothermia, but luckily it's not too cold a night and we caught you in time. You will have appalling bruising to your shoulder tomorrow, I'm afraid, and to your ankle, but neither is broken. I've poulticed your ankle with Sue's wonderful comfrey ointment from your own garden at Sleeper's Castle, and I've put some in a pot for you to take home to rub into your shoulder and neck. Sian and I have decided that she will

285

drive you back there now so you can make your peace with the cat, then she'll take you home with her and look after you. You and I will talk again when you're recovered.' He smiled, gave a little bow and left the room.

'Does he know you and I came up here?' Andy whispered as he closed the door behind him.

'He must do. I left him a note, remember?' Sian stood up. 'I think we should try and get you into the car before you get sleepy again. He gave you a fairly hefty potion to drink which he said was part sedative and part painkiller.'

In the event Andy fell asleep in the car. She didn't wake until they reached Sian's house. 'We stopped off at Sleeper's Castle but I didn't have the heart to wake you,' Sian said firmly when Andy protested. 'I went in and checked everything was OK. I left a meal in Pepper's bowl but he didn't appear. I turned the lights out and locked up after me, so you needn't worry until tomorrow. Then we can discuss our options. Police and doctor – not necessarily in that order.'

Andy was too tired to argue. She hobbled into Sian's house with the help of a couple of thumb sticks from the umbrella stand in the hall, then fell into bed. She didn't even wake up when Sian removed her shoes and tucked her under the duvet.

Andy woke abruptly, half sat up in the bed and fell back as the pain in her shoulder hit her. She lay still, disorientated, trying to work out why she was in Sian's spare room. Her nails were torn and broken, her palms grazed and raw, her wrist lacerated. Someone had cleaned her wounds; she could see traces of something sticky round her fingernails. She sniffed at it. Herbal. Slowly it was coming back to her. Her feet were bare. She waggled them and nearly fainted with the rocket of pain that shot up her left leg. Not so lucky then.

The door opened and Sian's head appeared. 'Ah, you're awake. How are you feeling?'

It was over an hour before she was able to sit down at Sian's breakfast table, showered, hair washed free of grass and leaves, wearing borrowed clothes. By then she had remembered most of what had happened.

Sian put down a glass beside her plate. 'Painkiller.' She smiled. 'One of Sue's tinctures. Meryn has prescribed it four times a day. Willow and comfrey and St John's Wort and lots of other mysterious ingredients which will have you cured and back to robust health in no time at all. He gave you a pretty hefty dose of it last night. You slept like a log.'

By midday Sian was driving her back to Sleeper's Castle. It was only as they were parking that Andy remembered Pepper again.

Sian laughed. 'Don't you worry. He's been attended to. I'm sure he will complain, but as I told you I fed him myself last night.'

It took a lot of effort for Andy to haul herself up the steep steps to the front door, and through to the kitchen. There she collapsed on a chair. Pepper, as predicted, had a lot to say about people who stayed out all night. Even when he was finally mollified by a few extra special treats in his bowl he sat on the corner of the dresser and glared at the two women.

'He's not going to let me forget my betrayal.' Andy stretched her ankle out in front of her with a groan.

'Spoiled brat of a cat.' Sian ruffled his ears. 'I rang Meryn before we left and told him you refused to rest and that you wanted to come home. He'll be over soon.' She glanced at her wristwatch. 'He wants to check your ankle.'

'I hope he doesn't expect me to go to a doctor.' Andy bent and rubbed it ruefully.

'No, he won't expect that. Unless he thinks you've broken something.'

'I haven't. It's a bad sprain, that's all.'

A diagnosis which Meryn confirmed half an hour later as he was re-wrapping the bandage round her ankle. Andy studied him carefully as he worked. He had sensitive, artistic hands, like Graham, with long strong fingers, and he conveyed an air of calm confidence. She found she was smiling. 'I've heard your reputation. I think even if it was broken the bones would knit immediately if you told them to,' she commented in amusement.

He laughed. 'It has been known.'

'Really?'

'No, not really. The healing comes from within you. I just add a bit of ointment and a bit of confidence.'

'And some pizzazz!' Sian added.

'If you like.' He glanced up at her. 'So, Andy. Have you worked out any more about what happened?'

Andy shook her head. 'It's all a bit blurry. I don't really remember Rhona being there. If I said she was, I suppose she was, but I might have imagined it.' She screwed up her eyes, trying to picture the woman out there on the hillside.

'If she's a tall rangy woman with bright red hair and a cream jacket, she was seen by others,' he said. He was packing his pots of ointment and spare bandages back into the canvas bag that he had brought with him.

'Really?' Andy paled. 'Did they see her push me? Where did she go?'

'She was a figure on the horizon. I'm sorry. But she was there.'

'She threw my phone into the spring,' Andy said. 'That would prove that there was someone else there. But I suppose it has gone for good now.'

'I'm afraid it will have.' Sian stood up. 'Was it insured? We'll have to get you fixed up with a new one. I'm sorry. I'm going to have to leave. There's somewhere I have to be. Would you like me to come and collect you this evening, Andy? I don't think you should be on your own until you're feeling better. And until we know what that woman is up to. Whatever she did or didn't do, she's not someone I like to think of wandering around here. I know Megan said she was leaving but I don't think I believe it.'

Andy sat back in the chair and stretched out her foot, waggling it experimentally. 'Thank you, but don't worry. I'll be fine. I would rather be here. I'll lock myself in, I promise.'

Sian didn't stay to argue the point, but Andy saw the look of worried concern she threw Meryn on her way out.

Meryn didn't move. They listened to Sian's footsteps as she walked through the hall to the front door and they heard it bang behind her. Minutes later the sound of her car engine faded away as she drove off down the lane.

'You and I need to discuss a few things, I think,' Meryn said. He leaned back in his chair.

Andy nodded, feeling inexplicably nervous. 'Sian told you she brought me up to your house to see if we could find you.'

'And then you came again on your own.'

She felt her cheeks colour with embarrassment. 'How did you know?'

'I set wards when I leave the house for any length of time. You know what that means?'

She nodded again slowly. 'Magic guardians? I've read about them.'

'They alerted me to your presence. I think they chased you away, for which I apologise. You have no need to be embarrassed about coming. You needed my help. I'm sorry I wasn't there to give it.'

'I needed your help because of my dreams. I've been dreaming since I came to live here.'

'And you want to stop?'

'No!' she almost shouted the word. 'No, I don't want to stop,' she repeated more calmly. 'I want to know what happens. I want to be a part of Catrin's life – Catrin is the woman I keep dreaming about.' She broke off, realising what she had said. 'I'm not sure if it's safe,' she added. She felt instinctively that this was a man she could trust. 'It isn't only Catrin I dream about. There's something else. It's the reason Rhona wants to harm me. It's my fault: I started it.'

289

He listened without interruption as she told him of her daydreams about Kew. Once she had started talking, she found she couldn't stop.

'You see, I think she was telling the truth when she accused me of stalking her. I didn't intend to do it. I only wanted to go back to where I had been so happy with Graham.'

'And have you been back to Kew in your dreams since Rhona came here?'

'Once. The house was empty.'

He stood up and walked towards the window, gazing out for a while, deep in thought.

Andy watched him in silence.

'Who taught you to do this?' he asked at last.

'My dad, I suppose.'

'And he never taught you any safeguards?'

'I don't think so. I'm not sure he did it deliberately. We just loved all the same things. History. Old buildings. Spooky stories. I found it easy to travel inside my head. I thought all children did it.'

'A lot of children do,' he said. 'They don't have the restraints that adults feel. They don't need things to be logical. The sad part is that the ability is destroyed so easily, so to keep it into adulthood is rare. That's why people who can see ghosts or travel as you have done in the present, or experience the past or the future, are so often feared or ridiculed. They can't be taken seriously because to do so would mean admitting that such things exist, so they learn to keep quiet.'

He turned and leant with his back against the sink, arms folded. 'Some of the most intelligent scientists in the world are believers, you know, and they're on the way to finding out how all this works. I sometimes think it's only when they have succeeded in manufacturing computers and robots with extra-sensory powers that they will acknowledge that humans have had that facility as long as humans have existed. And not only humans, of course. It's common in the animal world because animals aren't tortured by existential philosophies. They can't describe what they see and feel in words, but they can convey to us something of what is going on. We're the ones who are slow to understand.'

As if on cue, the cat flap rattled and Pepper appeared. He walked across to Meryn without hesitation and rubbed against his legs. Meryn squatted down and picked him up. Pepper seemed delighted.

'By the time I came to live here, I'd convinced myself that all this stuff was rubbish,' Andy went on. 'That I'd imagined it to please my dad.'

'And now you know it isn't rubbish at all. Well, now that we've established that you have a very powerful, if somewhat unpredictable, talent, what do we do about it?' Meryn held the cat up against his shoulder and rubbed his back like a baby. Andy could hear Pepper purring from where she was sitting. 'I will rephrase that. What do you want to do about it?'

'I want to control it. Somehow I was burned on Rhona's bonfire when she was destroying my letters from Graham.' She held out her hand. 'I tried to snatch one out of the flames. I don't think I want things to get that real.'

Meryn scratched Pepper behind the ear. 'It's interesting that Rhona can apparently see you as clearly as you see her,' he said.

Andy nodded. She said nothing.

'So we must assume she has a certain facility herself.'

She thought about it. 'I suppose it's possible.' She looked doubtful. 'If she has, I don't think she would have told Graham. He hated anything to do with the supernatural. That was why I never told him about the things I felt and saw. I tried to stop it happening. I pretended it was my imagination. I left all my books with my mother, so he never saw them.'

'You put great value on your books, but you don't need books to tell you anything about all this,' Meryn said gently. 'So, while you were with your partner you tried to stop it happening. Did that work?'

'I found I could ignore things.'

'But they went on happening.'

'Sometimes.'

'Dreams?'

'Occasionally.'

'What you call daydreams?'

She nodded.

'Visions. In trance.'

She stared at him, horrified. 'No. No, nothing like that. That sounds creepy. They're just daydreams.'

'All right. Daydreams. And you induce these deliberately?'

'Yes, I suppose I do.' She thought for a minute, trying to find the right words. In the event they were simple. 'I shut my eyes and picture myself there.'

'And when you are asleep?'

'Ah, that's completely different. That's the problem. I don't seem to be able to go there because I want to. I know what I want to see; to hear. I know where we were in the story, but sometimes it doesn't work. Sometimes it skips huge bits of information – as if years have gone by. At first I thought events followed on logically, but they don't. And the dream bleeds through into when I'm awake, but not in the same way as the daydreams. I sometimes think Catrin is here in the house. She's left the dream and walked in through the door. Sometimes she's there, over there,' she waved her hand at the kitchen door. 'Watching me. Our eyes meet. She's as real as you or me. And Pepper can see her.'

He smiled, running his hand up and down the cat's back. Pepper squirmed with pleasure. 'Pepper is very psychic. More so even than the average cat, and the average cat is always psychic.'

'So does that confirm whether Catrin is real or not?'

'She is real to you both.'

Andy shook her head. 'No. Those are weasel words. I need to know. Is she a ghost?'

'You and Pepper can see Catrin. And Catrin can see you. That's enough. That is all you need to know.'

'How do I find out if she really existed?'

'You want to read about her in books?' He smiled tolerantly. 'Andy, that may not happen. She may not be an important person in history. She may not even be a footnote. But for you, here, she really existed. Her story is her story.'

She exhaled crossly. 'I want to know if she was a historical character. Did her father really live in this house? Was Edmund real?'

'Edmund?'

'One of the sons of a farmer in the next village. Catrin has fallen in love with him.'

'Ah.'

'No, not ah!' She was becoming cross, but then she realised that he was laughing.

'Period? Do you know when she lived?'

'Glyndŵr.'

'And have you read the history of the period? Do you know if the things that happened to her and her father really happened? That surely is easy to check.'

'I bought some books about him,' she admitted.

'And have you read them?'

'Yes.'

'But there is no mention of Catrin?'

'No.'

'The history fits though?'

'I think so.'

'But you're not happy?'

She shook her head. 'I wanted some sort of proof that Catrin existed.' She held his gaze defiantly. 'I couldn't bear it if she wasn't real.'

18

It was still winter when the comet came, a streak of red fire, low in the north, trailing its tail across the sky. Dafydd spotted it first, standing in the garden, staring out across the Wye Valley towards the bare hills of the Radnor Forest. His eyes were wild with excitement. 'Catrin, come here!' he shouted.

Grabbing her cloak, Catrin ran out into the dark. Snowdrops were everywhere and in the dingle and the valleys snow still lay thick on the ground, but here in the garden the winds had scoured the herb beds bare. 'What is it, *Tad*? What's happened?' Joan ran out after her, followed by Betsi and the new scullery maid and Peter.

'Look!' He pointed exultantly.

It was a dragon, the symbol of Glyndŵr.

They all stood staring up at the sky. It seemed to hang there above the hills then, as they watched, the snow clouds came and enveloped it and it was gone.

Dafydd turned to Catrin, triumphantly. 'It is a sign!'

Behind them Joan snorted derisively and turned to go back to the house. She had been devastated when her mother sent a message with a scullery maid that Edmund had been to see them. He had told their parents of his allegiance to Glyndŵr, thinking to reassure them that he was alive. His father had told him he would rather he were dead!

The maid had delivered the note to Catrin. There was a postscript at the end, for Joan, telling her to keep the girl who brought the note to work in the kitchen at Sleeper's Castle as they could no longer afford to pay her the penny a week that she had cost them. Catrin agreed to take her; anything to mollify Joan a little as she stamped around the house.

In her lonely bedroom that night, Catrin had scribbled a love poem for the first time in her life.

Then she'd thrown it on the fire.

'There are signs and portents everywhere!' Dafydd crowed triumphantly. 'And now in the heavens themselves!' He led the way back inside the house and the new girl, Megan, barred the door behind them. She stared at him apprehensively. She was terrified of her new master, though Catrin doubted if he had noticed the girl's existence. He walked over to the fire and held out his hands to the flames. Catrin wondered briefly what he had been doing outside staring up at the sky. Had he known the great dragon would appear? She sighed. Of course he had. He was a seer. She pulled her cloak around her miserably. Could Edmund see it, wherever he was? The very thought of Edmund made her heart ache. She had received her first declaration of love and he had gone before she had had a chance to tell him how she felt. She wasn't sure how she felt, except that she had an aching void somewhere in her middle and at night now, instead of dreaming of the future of Glyndŵr, she sometimes dreamt of Edmund.

It was morning. Andy lay for a while, aware that in her total exhaustion she had slept right through the remainder of yesterday and then through the night without waking. Eventually she sat up and somehow dragged herself to her feet, staggering into the bathroom.

Meryn had left her something he described as a sleeping draught, she remembered that. 'In case the pain is bad at night. It will help,' he had said as he left, 'but it may stop you dreaming.'

She had poured it down the sink.

She had been too tired to go on talking and he had suggested she rest. Much to Pepper's chagrin, Meryn had pushed him off his lap and, promising that they would talk again soon, he had let himself out, reminding her to lock the door behind him.

Before she went upstairs Andy phoned about her mobile. It turned out to be easier than she'd expected to arrange a replacement. It could even be delivered by courier. She smiled. Somehow that felt like a small triumph. Something that would thwart Rhona's plans.

It had taken a long time to haul herself up to her bedroom. She wasn't going to wait until night-time to try and sleep. Besides, she was so tired she couldn't keep her eyes open however much pain she was in. She collapsed into bed and lay for a moment, trying to get into a comfortable position. It was impossible. Her ankle was throbbing and her shoulder ached so much she began to wish she hadn't been so hasty in disposing of Meryn's potion. In the end she lay flat on her back, her foot propped on a pillow, and closed her eyes. Her last thought as she drifted into sleep was about the back door. Had she locked it after Meryn left? Almost certainly. She couldn't remember.

Stripping off her bandages she ran a hot bath and climbed in to lie back staring up at the ceiling as the warmth soaked through her bones. It had been so cold out there in the garden watching the comet. And snowing. And then in her bedroom it had been cold as well, as cold as ice, the wind inserting icy fingers through the mullions and shutters as though neither were there. As though there was no glass there.

Which there wasn't. In Catrin's time.

In spite of the warmth of the water she shivered. She remembered the comet from reading Glyndŵr's biography.

Somehow she managed to lever herself out of the bath, dress in warm clothes and go downstairs to lift the kettle onto the hob. There was no sign of Pepper.

It was as she sat sipping the tea that she heard a loud knock on the door. She put down the mug. The clock on the wall said it was after nine. Andy staggered to her feet and managed to hop towards the door. She put her hand on the key. 'Who is it?'

'Bryn.'

With a sigh of relief, she turned the key and pulled open the door. 'Come in.'

Bryn walked in and closed the door behind him. He stood watching as Andy staggered back to the table. 'What on earth have you done to yourself?' he asked abruptly.

'I had a fall,' she replied. She managed a smile. There it was again, just for a second, the resemblance to Edmund. It made her feel cross and uncomfortable.

'Where?'

'I was out walking.' She resented the almost accusatory tone of his question.

'On the Bluff?'

'Yes. Somewhere up there. I don't know where I was exactly.' She sighed. 'If you must know, I met up with Rhona and we had a bit of an altercation.'

'Which resulted in your ankle being damaged?'

She hesitated. 'It was an accident, I slipped down the cliff—'

'My God, Andy!'

'I know. I was stupid to let her get near me.'

'But she brought you home?'

'No.' She bit her lip. 'No, she left me there.'

He stared at her.

'Meryn found me.'

'You have contacted the police, I take it.'

'No.'

'Why on earth not? That woman is obviously dangerous.'

'I will be more careful in future. I don't want the police involved.' She glared at him. 'That's my decision and it's none of your business. Understand? Did you want something, Bryn?'

He looked taken aback. 'I just wondered if you wanted me to go on with my autumn planting as usual?'

She gazed at him askance. 'You're asking me about the garden? Surely Sue gave you instructions before she left?'

'She did, but you seemed to be showing an interest.'

'And what do you think would happen if I told you to alter the whole place? "Change the herb beds, Bryn. I want some garden flowers here. Oh, yes, and while we're at it, perhaps you could root up those dreary shrubs." I don't think so!'

He folded his arms. 'OK. I get the message. Your experience has obviously made you a bit cranky,' he said conversationally. 'I can see why.'

'Cranky!' She almost exploded with fury. 'I'll say I'm cranky. She nearly broke my ankle out there, she wrecked my shoulder. I feel like hell and you come in and ask me stupid questions which, if I answered them, you would ignore anyway!'

He took a deep breath. 'OK. Sorry I asked. Business as usual then.'

And with that he turned, walked back to the door and let himself out, closing it with exaggerated care behind him.

She hardly noticed he had gone.

Pepper was sitting on the floor beside her, she realised, looking up pleadingly. 'I suppose you want feeding again,' she snapped. 'I'll bet you're his familiar. You're here to spy on me and then report back!'

Pepper ignored the comment and settled down to wait. In his experience humans always gave you what you wanted in the end.

Rhona was waiting at the bottom of the hill when Bryn left work that evening. He didn't notice the car tucked into the lay-by, or the fact that it pulled out behind him, only moving ahead when he pulled into the pub. By the time he had ordered his drink she had turned and followed him into the car park.

There was no one else by the bar. She walked up to him and smiled. 'Hello there. Do you remember me? I'm a friend of Miranda's.'

He was sipping from his pint of local-brewed lager. 'I remember.' He kept his face carefully schooled. If this was the woman who was supposed to have attacked Andy he wasn't going to betray the fact that he knew what had happened. Not yet. She ordered herself a gin and tonic and they stood in silence as it was poured. The barman glanced at them both in turn and kept his cheery remarks to himself. He took her money and retreated to the far end of the bar.

'Did you tell her I had dropped by?'

He shrugged. 'I told her some woman had come over.'

She smiled coldly. 'Some woman?'

'You didn't tell me your name.'

She inclined her head slightly in acknowledgement. 'How is she?'

Bryn didn't look up. 'Fine as far as I know.'

'Have you seen her today?'

He nodded.

'Are you sure?' He could see her body tensing. 'I heard she'd had an accident.'

So, she hadn't been back to check what had happened after she pushed Andy. He put down his tankard and studied her. 'Where did you hear that?' He wiped the back of his hand across his lips, deliberately boorish. She had an interesting face. Handsome, but very hard. Her eyes were darting round the room, avoiding his as he studied her.

She looked flustered at his question. 'I was talking to a friend of hers.'

'Oh?'

'I'm not sure of her name. She said she had heard that Miranda had been hurt in a fall.' Rhona took a sip of her drink.

She gave him a quick glance. 'But if you say she's all right, she must have got it wrong.'

Bryn could see her thinking fast. Had she planned to leave Andy on the hill all night? He took another gulp from his glass. 'She was fine when I left her just now,' he said. He kept his voice flat. Bored.

Rhona took another sip from her G & T and he saw the flash of irritation cross her face. Was that because her plan had failed; he hadn't given her the news she wanted?

'I'm glad she's OK.' It had finally dawned on her that she should make some kind of response. 'Did you pass on my message to her?'

'Did you leave a message?' He narrowed his eyes.

She looked flustered for the first time. She obviously couldn't remember what she had told him.

He reached into his pocket and produced an old receipt. He turned it over so he could write on the back. 'Remind me of your name,' he said. He produced a pencil. 'And where you are staying. I'll let Andy know so she can get in touch.'

She drained her glass and banged it down on the counter. 'Forget it,' she said hastily. 'It's too late now. I'm on my way back to London. I'm sorry not to have seen her, but maybe next time I'm down this way I'll ring her.' She turned towards the door.

Bryn did not do more than give her a curt nod as she walked outside.

'Freaky woman.' The barman moved back up the bar. He had interpreted Bryn's indifference correctly.

'And some,' was Bryn's succinct reply.

He wandered over to the window and looked out. Her car was not exactly discreet. Red, like her hair. He noted the number down on the back of his scrap of paper and watched as she drove away. She was heading in the opposite direction to London.

19

It was high summer and there had been a battle. A big one. A stranger was sitting at the kitchen table, a young man, his arm swathed in bloody bandages. He had fled the field and travelled south over the hills by night, fighting off nausea and fever, looked after in lonely farmhouses and by shepherds on the moors. Somehow he had kept going. He had crossed the Wye Valley and was heading into the Black Mountains, back home to his parents' house. Somehow he had found his way up the *cwm* to Sleeper's Castle.

Joan was heating mutton broth for him while Catrin peeled off the blood-soaked bandages to reveal a deep arrow wound. His name was Jac. 'I was fighting next to Edmund,' he told them. 'We drew bows together and we won.'

Catrin glanced up in time to see Joan's face set in a tight white mask. 'Where is he now?' she asked sharply. She turned back to her pot.

Jac didn't seem to hear her question. 'It was a glorious victory,' he said. His voice was growing weaker. 'The day before John's Eve. The Lord Owain had stopped at the church of Our Lady at Pilleth to pray at the holy well when we were told the English army under Sir Edmund Mortimer was approaching far away along the river valley. We took position on the hill at Bryn Glas.' He rocked forward, his head on the table. 'Our men burned the church,' he whispered. 'God forgive us, we burned the church. But it was a glorious victory,' he murmured again.

It had been a spring of glorious victories. Heartened by the appearance of the comet foretelling success and triumph for his cause, Glyndŵr had gone from strength to strength. With more and more followers behind his banner he had ridden to the attack and concentrated his attentions on the northern lands of his enemy Sir Reginald Grey, finally capturing him in April and demanding a huge ransom from the king. And now it seemed his successes continued.

Catrin looked sadly down at the young man who lay before them. He looked so vulnerable and so young. Victory, but at what cost?

'Help me with him, Joan,' Catrin commanded. 'We'll lay him on a mattress next door. I can dress his arm while he sleeps.'

Joan stared down at the young man. 'He said he served next to Edmund,' she whispered.

'And Edmund told him to find us,' Catrin replied. 'Help me, Joan.'

'Why didn't he come himself?' Joan hadn't moved from the fire. 'Is he dead?'

'No, of course he's not dead.' Catrin felt a clutch in her throat. 'He would have said. Help me!' She managed to force her hands under the boy's armpits and drag him upright. Joan reluctantly put down her spoon, bending to pick up the young man's feet. Between them they half carried, half dragged him through into the great hall and settled him down on a mattress by the wall. Catrin pulled a blanket over him and looked down at him. Her hands were sticky with fresh blood. 'He is badly wounded. We have reopened the worst of the injuries. Fetch me water and cloths.'

It took them a long time to clean him up and bind his wounds, and somehow Catrin forced a little warm water containing a healing tincture down his throat. As he fell back asleep, she looked up at last. 'We will let him sleep then when he wakes he will be ready for your broth. That will do him more good than anything.' Her hair had come loose, hanging from beneath her coif and she brushed it back off her face with the back of her hand. 'He'll tell us more once he is rested.' She had left a streak of blood across her temple.

Joan looked at her miserably. 'Edmund must be alive, mustn't he,' she said bleakly.

'Of course he is,' Catrin replied.

Joan walked away towards the kitchen. Catrin didn't follow her. She went outside and made her way to the edge of the brook. She washed her hands and face in the icy mountain water and refastened her hair under her hood before she went back indoors.

Joan was chopping cabbage. 'I'll throw this in with the mutton,' she said. 'Do you suppose your father was there?'

Catrin bit her lip. 'I don't know. I have heard nothing from him since he left.'

He had gone while the dragon sign was still there in the northern skies. It had been visible for several weeks before fading into the distance. In Hereford market the word was that it foretold disaster for the Welsh; for the Lord Owain and his followers it was a sign of triumph, a portent of a destiny written in the stars.

It was late evening when Jac awoke, much restored and ready to eat a huge bowl of Joan's mutton broth. His fever had gone and with it his reluctance to talk. He described the battle, the enormous numbers of men and horses involved, the curtains of arrows that rained down onto the enemy, the forests of spears, the thunder of the horses' hooves as they charged.

'So why did you flee?' Joan asked sharply.

'I got lost.' Jac's eyes flooded with tears. The women had realised a while ago that he was a great deal younger than they had first assumed. 'Terrible things were happening. I didn't know where to go or what to do. I couldn't find the prince's archers. Edmund had told me that if anything happened to him I was to go home, and if I came this way I was to look for you.' His bravura at describing the battle had melted away and he was a little boy again, lost and alone.

'If anything happened to him?' Joan's voice was harsh. 'What happened to him?'

'I don't know.' He looked up at her pleadingly. 'I couldn't find anyone I knew. Everywhere there were strangers, they were shouting, and this man came up with a halberd and there was a horse that was screaming and screaming with a spear in its neck and he lifted the halberd and he killed it and it rolled over and it was so quiet.'

'All right, Jac.' Catrin leaned forward and put her hand over his on the table. 'I think you have told us enough.'

He was sobbing hard. 'It was the women.' He gulped back the tears and reached with a shaking hand for his mug of ale. 'The local women and the camp followers climbed the hill and they were attacking the bodies of the English.' He looked up at them miserably. 'I keep seeing what they were doing. It was . . .' He stopped, groping for a word that wouldn't come. 'It was awful.'

Catrin and Joan glanced at each other. 'Let's not think about that,' Catrin said at last. 'I want you to have some more ale and then sleep. When you are strong enough, you can continue on your way to your parents.'

'It was because of the children,' Jac went on, as if she hadn't spoken. 'One of them told me it was because of what the English army had done to the little children at Ystrad Fflur.' Tears spilled over and ran down his cheeks. 'They raped the women; then they dragged the little children away and hurt them – so they had to pay. Even in death, they had to pay. You do see, don't you? They had to pay.'

Catrin found she couldn't speak. It was Joan who reached

for the jug of ale and topped up the boy's mug, and Joan who led him back to his mattress and covered him with the blanket again, tucking him in and pushing his hair back from his hot face with a gentle hand as if he too was a child.

Catrin walked outside and stood staring up at the luminous night sky. It was July now; the battle had happened weeks ago. Was Edmund still alive? Had he been involved in the horrors the boy described? What had happened to the Lord Owain's army? Was it still together, or had it disbanded and retreated into the hills to celebrate its victory?

Slowly she walked down the path, her soft leather shoes silent on the stones, through the vegetable beds towards the cliff. The cave was a blacker blackness under the stars. She crept in and stood listening. In that cave was all the wisdom of the earth; in there was the answer to her every question. Sometimes it answered her; sometimes it was cold and unresponsive.

Huddling in the corner she waited, listening to the sound of the brook in the distance, lulled by the inner silence of the cave. As her eyes closed she did something she had never done before. She reached out to her father.

He was sitting in front of a campfire, staring into the flames. She saw him start a little as he felt her questing and she saw his increasing anger as he realised what she had done, but he did not push her away. He was exhausted. Not afraid, but not at ease with what was happening around him either. Gently she probed further.

He had been there, seen the battle and now she could see it too, the columns of marching men spreading out below them, trying to avoid the boggy ground where the River Lugg wound through the flat valley bottom, heading for the steep hill where the Welsh lay in wait. Mortimer's army was splitting, heading up towards the church, some following the trackway, others trying to climb the hill. Did they not know the enemy was there? She could see the knights on their horses, harnesses bright, pennants flying jauntily, the archers following and then the foot soldiers. They were confident, invincible. None were expecting the attack.

She winced miserably as she saw the first block of Welsh archers rise to their feet, take their stand and loose a storm of arrows down into the faces of the men and horses below them. She could see the boy, Jac, and next to him, grim and focused, she could see Edmund reaching into the bag at his waist to pull out another arrow. She heard, as she had heard so often in her dreams, the screams, the thunder of hooves, the shouts and yells, the clash of swords, the splintering of lances, and over it all again and again the whistling howl of the flights of arrows before they thudded into shields and mail and flesh.

The end was swift. Blocks of archers in the valley bottom changed sides and turned their weapons on their own. From the hillside on Bryn Glas, behind the lines, her father had watched the glorious triumph, the scattering of Mortimer's army, the limping wounded, the dead and dying horses. He had seen men out of control, pursuing their enemy, and he had seen the women of the Welsh breaking out from the camp around him and setting off down the hill. They were holding knives.

Catrin shuddered with horror. 'Where next?' she asked. 'What is going to happen next?'

Dafydd heard her question. 'We are marching south. We are heading back towards Hay.' And she felt his fear and his denial.

Then she saw the prisoners. The Lord Owain was standing, exhausted, beneath his standard as his men at last regrouped. And there, a man on each side holding his arms, another holding a sword to his back, was Sir Edmund Mortimer himself, pushed to his knees on the grass. For a long time the two men looked at one another, then Owain gestured at the soldiers to release the younger man. He stepped forward and offered him his hand so that he could rise. 'A fair battle, Sir Edmund,' he said, 'and a vicious one.'

Sir Edmund was too overwhelmed with exhaustion to reply.

They both knew what would follow. Sir Edmund would be taken into captivity far behind the lines and a ransom would be asked from the King of England. Neither knew if it would be paid.

Owain turned to address someone behind him and there, for a brief second, Catrin saw Edmund, her Edmund, standing in the shadows. The firelight was playing on his face; she saw it drawn and tired and smeared with blood, but he seemed uninjured. He moved slightly and looked aside into the darkness beyond the firelight, and she wondered if he knew she was watching.

When Andy woke next morning she was on the sofa, covered by the rug. She remembered Bryn coming in. He had asked about the planting. Then she had read her history books for a while, checking out the horrors of the Battle of Bryn Glas and done a bit of sketching before she lay down on the sofa, exhausted. Then Bryn had come into the house again. He had knocked on the door of the great hall and said something about a parcel.

Fighting the twinge in her ankle she dragged herself to her feet and made her way into the kitchen. There it was on the table. The courier had delivered her new mobile and Bryn must have signed for it. She remembered it all now and felt a flush of embarrassment for her earlier rudeness. In spite of it he had asked if she was all right, and he had pulled the rug over her before he left.

It was as she was heating a pan of soup on the Aga that she heard a knock at the door.

'Andy? It's Meryn.'

She let him in, casting a quick glance over his shoulder into the garden, then bolted the door again behind him.

'You still think Rhona is going to come and try to finish the job?' He sat down opposite her at the table and accepted a small bowl of soup.

'I don't know what to think.' She was disorientated, she realised, her head still partly in the past. She was conscious of him studying her face. 'I was asleep; dreaming,' she explained. 'Then I realised I was hungry.'

'That seems a healthy sign.' He smiled. 'This is good soup. Did you make it?'

'Do I look like a soup maker?' She laughed, then stopped. 'No, that's wrong. I used to love cooking and I will cook again, but in the meantime, this is not bad. I found it at the deli. As I did this very passable bread.' She pushed the loaf towards him. 'The dream was about Catrin,' she went on. 'And the battle at Pilleth. Does that mean anything to you?' Her eyes clouded as the memory came back to her. She put down her spoon.

'Oh yes, that means something. The Battle of Bryn Glas. It was a major victory for Glyndŵr, wasn't it. A great many men were killed. The Herefordshire levy was all but wiped out, if I remember rightly.'

'And the awful women?' she whispered.

'Ah, the women. Yes, the camp followers are reputed to have descended onto the battlefield after it was over and mutilated the bodies of the English dead, something vociferously denied by Welsh historians, who say it was a vicious piece of propaganda by the English to discredit a great victory by the Welsh.' He pushed aside his empty bowl.

'I didn't see them doing it,' she whispered. 'Catrin told me, and I looked it up just now.' She sighed. 'Perhaps I shouldn't have done that.'

'I think you should. Doing so will help to give you perspective. Distance you a little, perhaps. You seem to have no choice but to hear this story, unless you opt to move out of the house and go far away. Catrin wants you to know what happened. But you need the tools to deal with this.'

'And if I had them, you think I could cope?'

'I think you can cope. And I'll be here to help you if you need me.' He smiled encouragingly.

'Why does she want me to know?'

'Perhaps she can't help it. It may be that she has to go on repeating the story to anyone who will listen. A form of post-traumatic stress disorder as we would call it nowadays.'

'Which is still going on, even though she's dead?' Andy could feel her throat constricting as she said the words. 'Do you know what happened to her?'

'No.'

She looked up. 'Are you sure?'

'Yes. I admit I have heard parts of the story from people who've lived here, but I have never heard how it concluded. If it concluded.'

'Joe?'

He looked startled. 'You know about Joe?'

'Only what Sian's friend Ella told me.'

Meryn gave a sigh. 'I don't know what happened to him. I wish he had confided in me. I begged him to, but he decided he didn't want to put himself through it. It needs a very strong stomach to experience something like this night after night, Andy. I don't know what happens in the end, but I have the feeling that whatever it is builds to a climax and it is at that point that people feel they can't go on.'

'And Sue?'

'Sue has always refused to talk about anything to do with what she chooses to call hocus pocus.' He smiled fondly. 'A very strong lady, Sue.'

'She promised me once that there were no ghosts here.'

'Really?' Meryn smiled.

'Do you think she set me up?'

'Surely she wouldn't do that. She knew you needed help.'

Andy grimaced. 'That might be her idea of help. To distract me. Take my mind off Graham and Rhona.'

'Which it would have done, if Rhona hadn't followed you?'

'Maybe.'

'And now you're saddled with a fearsome lady stalker in the present day and another in the past.'

She grimaced. 'I don't think Catrin is a stalker. And she's not fearsome.'

'No. But don't let her become too intrusive. We must make sure you're in control of the situation.'

'She must have been – must bc – a very unhappy lady.'

'Certainly a restless spirit.' He pushed back his chair and collected her soup bowl with his own. Putting them in the sink, he filled the kettle, put it on the hob then turned back to her. 'Can you manage to make your own coffee? I need to go, I'm afraid. I've promised someone I will be with them this evening on the far side of the moon.' He winked. 'Can I suggest you take the mixture I left you and have a good night's sleep tonight, without dreams. Then think about how much you want to be there for Catrin.'

She hadn't told Meryn that she had thrown away his sleeping draught. She sat for a long time over her coffee after he had gone. Meryn had told her to stay in control, but he hadn't told her how. Perhaps he imagined that Rufus had given her instructions, her own Dafydd, passing on his knowledge and his wisdom. The longing to talk to her father was overwhelming. Climbing stiffly to her feet, she went over to the dresser and picked up the landline. 'Dad? I need to talk to you about something.'

Even as she heard herself saying the word 'dad' she could hear the echo in the room: '*Tad*. Come back. I need you. *Tad* . . .'

20

Looking down at the parchment notes lying in a basket on the table in her father's study, Catrin found herself swallowing hard. The theme was still consistent. War. Defeat. Bloodshed. Disaster. Warning after warning, in spite of Glyndŵr's continuing success.

Dafydd had returned to the house in the autumn last year as the weather deteriorated. The storms had been so consistently bad that the English army had retreated in disorder, once again convinced that the weather was on the side of the Welsh rebels, many of their archers deserting to offer their services to Glyndŵr, the man with magic on his side.

Dafydd had brought news with him of the ransoming of Sir Reginald Grey – the Lord Owain's coffers were richer by ten thousand marks! When the ransom demand for his other captive was firmly refused – hardly surprising, given that the hostage had a better claim to the throne than King Henry himself – Sir Edmund Mortimer pragmatically changed sides. The two men formed an alliance, sealed by the marriage in November of Mortimer to Owain's daughter and Catrin's friend, Catherine.

This spring Dafydd had postponed his tour; he had been ill for several months now, coughing through the night as he lay awake tormented by his dreams. News filtered through that Prince Hal had burned Owain's homes at Sycharth and Glyndyfrdwy, and now it was June and Dafydd had not yet left and it seemed the war was coming to him. The English were reinforcing the Marcher castles in the expectation of a Welsh attack, and Owain's armies had moved south in a massive offensive. By the Feast of St John they were laying siege to Brecon, only sixteen miles away.

Catrin glanced up at the ceiling. Her father was upstairs asleep, exhausted after hours of bending over his desk, scribbling with a succession of goose feather quills, hurling each one into the corner of the room as it split and defied his efforts to trim it further. 'I have to go to him,' he had whispered to her at last, before he staggered towards the stairs. 'I have to go. I cannot ignore the signs.'

'I too have dreamt, *Tad*,' she had replied.

He looked across at her from the doorway, his face a combination of anger and anxiety. 'You dream of defeat?' He had never quite forgiven her for her intrusion into his dreams at Pilleth, and he would never forget the moment that she had proved herself to be as good a seer as he.

'Yes.' Her mouth was dry.

'Is it this house?' he asked desperately. 'His other seers tell him he will triumph and he does. I see triumph, but always I see defeat too.'

She shook her head in confusion. 'Maybe it is that if these stones speak at all, they speak true,' she said softly. 'They speak what will be, not what we want to hear.' It sounded like a plea.

Once he'd left the room she turned back to his desk. The candle flames quivered throwing the dull light shivering across the walls. She could hear the shuffle of his shoes on the flags and then the faint sound of his footsteps as he climbed the stairs. Normally he would have locked the pages away in a coffer; none of the servants could read, so it was to stop her seeing what he had written. Today, however, he was too weary and too dispirited. The pages betrayed his usual dismay; his confusion and his horror. She glanced at them, then turned away.

Catrin and Joan had planned to go to the market as soon as it was full light. Catrin lay for a while in her bed, dozing restlessly in the warmth of the summer dark, afraid to sleep in case she dreamed. It was already dawn when Joan woke her.

They took her grey pony, sitting one behind the other on its broad back. For the homeward journey they would fill the saddle-bags and throw panniers across her withers to carry their purchases. Sunrise was spreading a warm pink glow across the eastern sky as the pony picked its way down the steep track towards Hay. The transition from the quiet of the foothills to the bustle and noise of the town was abrupt; on entering the Lion Gate they left the pony at the Black Lion Inn and headed towards the market place, their baskets over their arms. Threading their way through the throng beneath the castle walls they were swept up in the excitement of the morning, listening to the shouts of the vendors, the music from a hurdy-gurdy, the bellowing of cattle being driven towards the shambles, the ringing of a bell in the distance. Instinctively Catrin put her hand over her purse; there were pickpockets and thieves and cutpurses mingling with the crowds, ever-alert for the unwary shopper. She and Joan exchanged happy smiles. They both enjoyed market day and for Catrin it was a relief to be free of her father's exhausting presence, if only for the inside of a day.

Above them stood the great castle, its walls patched and recently strengthened – castles up and down the border March had been repaired in readiness for the Welsh as they moved south and east across the country – but its great doors were unbarred. No one looked for an attack today and the town walls were manned with lookouts.

The women separated. Joan, her purse stocked by Catrin before they left home and now hidden beneath her cloak, went in search of various items for her larder, her basket filling rapidly as she moved from stall to stall, striking bargains wherever she went. Catrin made her way towards a stall selling silken threads and needles, dyes and powdered pigments wrapped in small parchment packets and little linen pouches. When she asked for copperas she was greeted with a shake of the head. Turning to another stall she eyed the shoes and stockings longingly before moving on towards a glover, then another who sold parchment. Beyond she could smell the pie stalls and the bakers. The rich aroma on the air reminded her she was hungry.

She felt a tug at her sleeve and turned. A tall man stood beside her, dressed in a long dark robe, a scrip at his belt. She looked at him, startled. He beckoned her away from the crowds, glancing round to make sure they weren't being watched. 'I have a message for your father,' he murmured.

Catrin frowned. Hefting her basket higher on her crooked elbow she followed him into the shadows between two buildings. The overhanging upper storeys meant it was cold there out of the sunlight. It smelt of urine. Obviously someone had taken the opportunity of its relative privacy to relieve himself in the mud. She gathered up her skirt fastidiously and waited to see what the man had to say.

'Does your father plan to join the rebel army?' he asked abruptly. She recognised him now. He was reeve to John Bedell, whose family owned houses in the town and farmed estates in the Wye Valley between Hay and Brecon.

She tensed. In these days it was impossible to know friend from foe.

The stranger held her gaze, then slowly, almost regretfully, he sighed. 'This is just a friendly warning, mistress, and I mean you no harm by it. Tell him not to go. The king is asking for the names of supporters of the traitor, Glyndŵr. Any who are reported will be taken up. If they deny it and swear allegiance to our good King Henry, they will be offered a pardon. If not, they will be arraigned.'

Catrin felt herself grow cold. 'My father was ill all winter,' she said firmly. 'He plans to go nowhere. And what makes you think my father would support the rebel cause anyway?' she demanded.

He put his head on one side. 'A word to the wise. I make no accusations, but remember: people watch, people talk. However quietly you think you live, however privately, there is always someone who sees.' And with that he was gone, slipping further down the alley and out of sight round the corner.

Catrin stood still, looking after him, her heart thudding with fright, then she turned and walked briskly back into the sunlit market square. She looked for Joan in the throng but there was no sign of her. A boy jostled close to her, sneakily reaching for her purse, and she slapped him away. Another man pushed past and a woman she knew from a farm in the hills waved and called a greeting, her own basket overflowing. Everywhere there were people she knew; no strangers; faces she had recognised since she was a child. Overwhelmed by the noise and the bustle, she turned back, trying to spot the man who had spoken to her, but there was no sign of him.

The shadow of the castle lay over the ground, cold and implacable as, slowly, she retraced her steps towards the inn. There were no watchers on the battlements, no panic-stricken rush to bring in more weapons. Below in the square, the crowds had thinned, the stallholders were packing up, the hurdy-gurdy man shouldered his instrument and set off between the shops, taking the lane down towards the river and the ford.

Joan caught up with her as they neared the inn at the sign of the Black Lion to retrieve the pony. With a grunt of relief, Joan tied her baskets onto the saddle, did the same for Catrin's and filled the panniers with foodstuffs she had carried strung over her shoulder. She threw a glance at Catrin. 'You can ride if you want to. You haven't bought much. He can take the weight.' Catrin nodded gratefully. She was tired and worried. Not wanting Joan to notice, she grimaced and rubbed her foot.

'I've blisters on my toes. I should have bought new shoes.' She managed a smile as she climbed into the saddle from the mounting block in the stable yard. 'We'll take turns though. It's only fair. It's a long way.'

'And all uphill,' Joan responded ruefully. Nevertheless she walked alongside the pony's head cheerfully enough and before long was telling Catrin the latest gossip, embellished with much colourful language, as they left the town and headed out between the fields towards the narrow trackway that led up into the hills.

Catrin listened with only half an ear, still preoccupied with what the reeve had told her. He had guessed her father was sympathetic to the Lord Owain, that much was clear, even though they had tried to keep their loyalties secret. How had he found out? Who had betrayed them?

'They are bringing arms and cannon into the castle, did you hear? And strengthening the walls.' At last Joan's monologue penetrated her preoccupation. 'John Bedell is moving in to supervise, with the king's commission to hold town and castle for him against the rebels.'

Catrin stared down at her. 'Where did you hear that?'

'Everyone was talking about it. They are bringing in stores and food.'

'So they are expecting another attack?' Catrin asked.

'Must be.' Joan shuddered as she plodded on. 'The rebel army is already outside Brecon, so everyone is saying. It is terrifying. If they come, I will have to go back to my parents. They will need me.' She glanced up and Catrin thought she saw something like guilt in her eyes before she looked away again. They were both thinking of Edmund.

Someone was knocking on the door. Andy dragged herself awake and looked at the clock beside her bed. It was six in the morning. There it was again, downstairs. The front door. Someone was banging on it with their fists.

With a groan she dragged herself out of bed and pulled on her dressing gown. It took several minutes to make her way downstairs.

'I was beginning to think there was no one here.' When at last she cautiously pulled open the door she stood staring at the figure on the doorstep in disbelief. It was her father.

'I left home in the early hours and drove overnight. No traffic, so I made it in remarkably good time.'

'But what are you doing here? Why have you come?'

His face clouded. 'You rang and asked me, darling, don't you remember?'

He hadn't changed since she saw him last. He was a stocky man, with hazel eyes and faded red hair showing traces of grey. His face was rugged but kind and as always there was a humorous twist to his mouth even when, as now, he was clearly concerned.

She looked at him in confusion. 'I don't remember much at this moment, I'm afraid. I was asleep. Why didn't you ring me?'

'I did. Your phone was switched off.'

'My phone?' She froze. 'I lost it. The new one has only just come.' And she hadn't even opened the parcel.

As she let him in, he glanced round the kitchen. 'I'm sorry. It is early.' He smiled. 'Why don't you go and get dressed while I bring my bag in from the car, then we can have breakfast and catch up.'

When she came back downstairs he was cooking eggs and bacon on the Aga, coffee was already made and the table was laid. 'I brought breakfast with me,' he said as she appeared. 'I called your mother before I left and she reminded me you wouldn't have any decent grub in the house. I take it this cat is expecting to be fed? I couldn't find any food for it.'

Pepper was sitting on the corner of the table, his tail swishing gently in irritation.

Andy smiled. She was feeling happier than she had for days. It was just as if she was a child again; now she could relax and put all her problems and all her fears into someone else's hands. Her daddy was there, so now everything would be all right. She filled Pepper's bowl and sat down opposite her father, aware for the first time that he was studying her carefully.

'You've lost a lot of weight, girl,' he said critically. 'And you're as pale as death. What has been happening? From the beginning.'

By the time she had told him the whole story she found she had eaten everything he put in front of her. She sat back with the second cup of coffee he had poured and fell silent. For a while he said nothing, processing everything she had said, then, pushing back his own cup, he stood and headed for the doorway. He walked out of sight into the hall. She could hear his footsteps on the flags growing fainter as he moved deeper into the house. After a while they died away. She waited quietly, sipping her coffee.

Eventually he returned and sat down again. 'Interesting.'

'Can you feel it?'

'I can feel a lot of things. Cold. The age of the place. But there does seem to be a sense of anger and resentment, which feels as though it is directed at me.'

'I don't understand.'

'I've come with the express purpose of sticking my nose in where it is obviously not wanted.' He reached for the coffee pot. 'This is cold. I'll make some more. Dafydd . . .' He raised his eyebrows and peered at her over his glasses. 'Very protective of his patch, I'd say. Very suspicious. Very angry.'

Andy stared at him, astonished. 'I've never sensed him here. Only Catrin.'

'I suspect he's responding to the arrival of another man on his patch. Perhaps another father.'

His expression changed from one of concern to glee. 'I haven't done this in years! Sandy doesn't like this sort of stuff any more than your mother did, so I'm out of practice. Oh, Andy, I've missed you, girl.'

When he returned to the table with the brimming coffee pot he sat down and reached for her cup. 'What did your friend Meryn say about Dafydd?'

'Nothing. He never mentioned him. Meryn hasn't done any "stuff" here,' – she hooked her fingers into inverted commas – 'All he's done is talk technique and ask questions. Mostly he was concentrating on my ankle.'

Rufus glanced down at her feet, now swathed in socks and slippers. 'Perhaps we should discuss Rhona before we move on to discuss Dafydd and Catrin. She seems to me to be a more immediate physical threat. I take it you have called the police.'

'No. Everyone keeps saying that! There isn't any point, Daddy! There are no witnesses and the policeman who came up here before would say it's my imagination. He has us down as a pair of jealous women squabbling over the bones of their lover.' Her voice broke slightly. She looked up at him and saw the twinkle in his eyes.

'A vivid description, if I may say so.'

She found herself smiling back. 'It's not funny.'

'No, it's not. I've always suspected that woman had sociopathic tendencies. I couldn't understand why Graham married her in the first place. He seemed too sensible to make a mistake like that.'

'He regretted it bitterly.'

Rufus took a sip of coffee. 'Why on earth didn't he divorce her?'

'I think he felt guilty in some way. And responsible.'

'But she had other men?'

'Oh yes. Several, I gather. But they all dumped her.'

He grinned. 'It is a great shame you went and accosted her. That must have frightened the life out of her. And it obviously made her angry.'

'I didn't do it on purpose. When I thought about Kew it was because I was feeling so lonely and miserable here, but I was only daydreaming, I never expected her to see me.'

319

He thought for a minute. 'We have to do something. If the woman seriously tried to kill you—'

'I don't know that she did,' Andy interrupted. 'That's the point. I was very confused when I came round.'

'Whatever she intended, she left you there to die,' he reminded her sternly.

'And I won't give her the chance again. She'll get bored, Daddy, I'm sure of it. Graham used to say Rhona was some kind of nymphomaniac, always needing to find herself another man. As soon as she does, she'll forget about me. After all, she has what she wants, which is the house and everything in it. Leave it, please.' Andy gave him a rueful smile. 'Let's talk about Sleeper's Castle.'

'Which is fascinating.' He sat forward, his elbows on the table. 'This place obviously has a very strong anchor into the earth. I'm not surprised. These old Welsh houses are built of local stone. They've never really been separated from the bedrock they came from. You can probably see the old quarry from here. It's the same in the Highlands and parts of upland England. You get a strong sense of rootedness, which you don't get with wooden or modern houses. Then if you have a powerful crystalline structure in the stone, it gives you a ready-made sounding box. You can get it in old brick houses too; the sand and clay from which the bricks were made has the same effect, though more diffused. Here you have an immensely strong instrument, which if you know how to use it has wonderful capabilities. Clearly, generations of occupants of this house have known how, probably going back hundreds if not thousands of years.' He rubbed his hands together. 'What a fabulous place!'

Andy laughed. 'So speaks a psychic architect! Daddy, you are incorrigible.'

'It's part of my charm. But it's also useful. Such places are wonderful, but I suppose they're potentially dangerous too – as you've been finding out. But, my darling, sweet Andy, before we do anything else, somehow we have to neutralise this Rhona woman – and I've only got two days.' He caught at her look of dismay. 'I'm sorry, girl, but I have meetings scheduled next week that I can't get out of. I can always come back though.' He reached for the coffee pot again. She had forgotten how addicted to coffee her father was.

'So what do we do?' she asked meekly.

'I don't know yet. If you absolutely refuse to call the police we are rather stymied.'

'Leave Rhona to me, Daddy. I will be careful, I promise. I wanted to talk to you about the ghosts. There are so many things you know about and I've forgotten. And I wanted you to meet Meryn, but he's away until next week. You men and your meetings.' Somehow she made herself smile.

He looked at her anxiously. 'Oh, girl, I'm not sure I am going to be much help. It's such a long time since we did any of this stuff together. I can't remember what I used to say.' He stared round the room. 'It sounds to me as if this Meryn chap is the expert. But don't worry. We'll have a plan before I go. What you need is an on–off switch. You have to learn to control what's going on.'

'That's what Meryn said.' She smiled again. 'And he asked me if you had taught me how to do it.'

He looked taken aback. 'I'm not sure that's ever been one of my talents, but we can always try.' He stood up and stretched. 'I'm not sure even how to begin, to be honest, but I'll try and think of something. Now, let me go out into the garden and walk about a bit. That was a long car journey and I'm stiff. No' – he held up his hand as she made to get up – 'I suspect you should be resting that ankle. Let me go on my own. I want to get the feel of things round here, outside as well as in.'

She sat quite still after he left, feeling the emptiness of the kitchen. She had always been very close to her father as a child and had felt her parents' split very deeply, however civilised and careful they had been to make their divorce as pain-free as possible for their only child. The realisation that he was only going to stay for two days had come as a hammer blow.

With a sigh she climbed to her feet and hobbled next door into the living room. He had sensed Dafydd in here at once. She tried to empty her mind, allow herself to become receptive. Nothing happened. Walking across the room, she stopped in front of Sue's bookcase. The low morning sun had thrown a beam of light across the floor, striking the book jackets. Like the books in the study they were mostly about plants and herbs and gardening, but one book stood out. She frowned. Broad, with a shiny red jacket, squat, next to the larger format plant books, it sat there, beckoning. The Oxford Shakespeare. The *Complete Works*. She could see the bookmark projecting from the top about a third of the way in. Reaching out almost against her will, she pulled it off the shelf. She almost knew at which play the book was going to open. She could hear Sian's voice in her head: 'Didn't you ever read *Henry IV Part 1*?' Sian, yes – she could see her reading Shakespeare – but Sue? What reason did Sue have for reading these plays, other than a specific personal interest?

The words leapt off the page at her. Someone called West. Her eye went automatically to the *Dramatis Personae* at the top. The Earl of Westmorland was reporting news to his king.

> *. . . there came*
> *A post from Wales, laden with heavy news;*
> *Whose worst was, that the noble Mortimer,*
> *Leading the men of Herefordshire to fight*
> *Against the irregular and wild Glendower,*
> *Was by the rude hands of that Welshman taken,*
> *And a thousand of his people butchered,*
> *Upon whose dead corpse there was such misuse,*
> *Such beastly shameless transformation,*
> *By those Welshwomen done, as may not be,*
> *Without much shame, re-told and spoken of.*

Andy dropped the book on her knee and sat staring into space. Shakespeare was talking about the battle at Bryn Glas, the battle described to Catrin in such awful detail.

When Rufus came back inside twenty minutes later he found Andy engrossed, sitting on the sofa reading the play. He stared at her in astonishment. 'There is a sight I never thought I would see: my daughter, deep in the works of the Bard. So, what's brought this on?'

She looked up. 'I am such an illiterate! I had no idea Shakespeare had written a play about Glyndŵr. Everybody in the country probably knows all this stuff, and here am I, totally ignorant.'

Rufus came and sat down beside her. He picked up the book and flipped it open. 'I remember doing this for O level.'

'Oh, not you as well!' she exclaimed crossly.

He laughed. 'This event was obviously pretty shocking. But remember, this may not be accurate history. Old Shakespeare was writing for a Tudor audience. Lots of propaganda.'

'But the Tudors were Welsh, weren't they?' She sat back and closed her eyes with a sigh. 'Oh, Daddy. This battle, with Welshwomen mutilating the English dead: Catrin wasn't there, but Dafydd was and she seems to have seen it through his eyes. It was terrifyingly vicious.'

They both looked up. The sunbeam had vanished and deep shadow had seeped into the corner by the bookcase. A gust of wind in the chimney stirred the ashes and Andy groped for her father's hand. 'Did you hear that?' she whispered. 'It sounded like a sigh.'

He glanced round, a frown on his face. 'I think we might go back into the kitchen,' he said quietly. He pulled her to her feet.

Once there, he pushed her gently into a chair and went to make more coffee. She swallowed. 'That was Dafydd, wasn't it.'

He shrugged his shoulders. He was measuring coffee into the

cafetiere. 'From what you say, he was obviously a deeply troubled man.'

'As anyone would be who had witnessed all that. But I've never sensed him here before.'

'Maybe because you've made a connection to his daughter. I don't suppose he's happy with me being around.'

'Really?'

He sat down opposite her and grinned. 'Do you realise that you are still clutching a volume of William Shakespeare?'

She slid the book onto the table.

'King Henry IV seems to have been a fairly pugnacious man,' Rufus said. 'I will confess, I can't quite remember how the story goes, but wasn't there a guy called Fluellen? The stereotypical Welshman? Maybe that was another play. I read them such a long time ago. But of course Glendower himself is there.' He reached forward to push down the plunger on the coffee pot. As he did so, the kitchen lights began to flicker. He abandoned the cafetiere and sat back, staring at the light hanging over the table. It swung gently back and forth.

Andy watched it nervously. She could feel herself growing cold. 'Is it Dafydd?' she whispered.

Rufus was watching the lamp, frowning. 'I'm not sure. This is where I often wish I could in all honesty cross myself and tell any marauding spirits to go in the name of the Lord, but alas I cannot invoke someone I don't believe in. I have to fall back on a thoroughly British sense of fair play.'

'And the fact that you are Scots and definitely not English?' she managed a smile. The lamp had drifted to a standstill. It was shining steadily now.

'There's no reason to think he's not friendly, is there?' Rufus went on. 'As far as you can make out, Catrin wants to tell you her story, that's all?'

'That's all.' Andy began to pour their coffee. Her hand was shaking. Her father was stirring things up. 'I wanted to know how to turn off the dreaming if I need to, not stop it altogether.

This is Catrin's house, after all.' She was trying to sound positive and she knew it sounded silly. 'It's all very well being scientific and questioning and enthusiastic about ghosts, but when one is in the great hall, as Sue calls it, alone and the lights are flickering and the wind whistles in the chimney and one is aware that there are people here who do not rest in peace, it's a bit hard.' The flickering lights had added a whole new element to the situation; she was not happy, she realised, with the idea of sharing a house with Dafydd.

'I wonder why they're not at peace,' Rufus went on. He rubbed his chin as he often did when he was thinking.

'That is the story Catrin is trying to tell me.' Andy staggered to her feet and limped over to the dresser. 'Here's my record of the dreams. There's a definite progression of the story.'

The light flickered again and she broke off nervously as she dropped her notebook on the table in front of him.

'And this is a full account of what you have dreamed?'

'Yes.'

'Catrin's version.'

'I suppose so, yes.'

She wasn't sure what happened. Perhaps she had put the coffee pot down too near the edge of the table. As it fell onto the flags and shattered with a terrible crash of breaking glass, the light finally went out.

21

'Who wrote this?'

Dafydd was standing in her bedroom, the manuscript of one of her poems in his hand.

Catrin stood in the doorway, white with anger. 'I did.'

'You copied it. Where did you find it?'

'I composed it myself.' She darted across the room and tried to snatch it from his hand. 'Why are you in here?'

'I wanted to know what you did for hours in here on your own.' His face was thunderous as he dangled the parchment out of her reach. 'You have no business to try to write poetry like this!'

'What do you mean? I don't understand. You taught me.'

'I taught you so you could versify, so you could make up songs to sing to your harp in the bowers of ladies, not write proper poetry.'

She stared at him, confused. 'I don't understand. It is a poem about the garden. Is it no good?'

He clenched his fists, crumpling the page as he did so. 'Yes, it is good.'

'And you aren't pleased?' She looked at him anxiously. His

face was drawn and tired, his hair awry. 'You haven't written about the Lord Owain?' he asked. He gestured towards the small coffer where she kept her poems. She saw now that the lid was open.

'No, of course I haven't written about him,' she whispered. 'My poems are about flowers and trees and birds. They are about peaceful things. I don't write about my dreams.'

'And your dreams,' he said, his voice dripping acid, 'enable you to follow me where you have no business to go; they talk of war and destruction and are anathema to the Lord Owain. You have to stop.'

He threw her poem on the floor with an expression of disgust and stamped out of her room. For several heartbeats she was too stunned by his resentment and venom to move, then she ran forward and bent to pick up the piece of parchment, dusting it gently and smoothing the creases as she rerolled it and reached for the ribbon to tie it closed. One day she would have her poems bound into a book. Until then they would live in the coffer. The notes and verses she had scribbled about her dreams were hidden safely under her mattress. She glanced across at her bed. Her father had not thought to look there. The bedcover was smooth and unruffled.

He left the house three days later with Peter at his side. He was riding to join the Lord Owain, she knew that, though when she challenged him he denied it. A glance at Joan – tight-lipped on the doorstep beside her as they waved goodbye – confirmed that she too had guessed where he was going.

The two women went back into the house. 'Well, that is all we will see of him for the next few months,' Joan said grimly. 'Please God and the Blessed Virgin the men of war stay away from this house.'

'Amen,' Catrin said softly.

Later she went up to her bedroom. When she opened her coffer, the poems had all gone.

She found the remains of the pages of parchment smouldering

on a bonfire at the bottom of the vegetable garden. Sadly she raked out the surviving scraps. Most of the poems were safe inside her head, but it broke her heart to think her father would do such a thing.

'Oh, *Tad*,' she cried as she looked down at the dirty mess at her feet. 'Why?'

Joan had followed her. She looked down at the remains of Catrin's poems. 'Because he is jealous of you, that's why. I have heard him recite and I have heard you. You are better than him by far. Had you not realised?' She turned and stamped back towards the kitchen, leaving Catrin to collect the remnants of parchment into her apron.

The King of England came to Hay in September. He had marched with his army from Hereford, executing suspected traitors and giving their lands to his supporters wherever he went. From Hay he marched on to Talgarth and then to Brecon, where he offered peace to the people of Breconshire. At Sleeper's Castle they waited and prayed the king's soldiers would pass them by. Catrin and Joan did not go down to Hay. They worked in the garden harvesting vegetables and herbs, they sewed and they brewed cider and ale. Joan spun and knitted with her bone needle, and Catrin wrote down her poems.

God answered their prayers. The king's soldiers did not ride up the lane towards the scattered mountain parishes. At the end of September the king returned to England. Tempers cooled and Joan rode again down to Hay on market day. Catrin stayed at home. There had been no word from Edmund all summer. Both women prayed for him, separately, quietly, and both secretly wondered if, should anything happen to him, they would ever get to hear of it.

Andy stood back and allowed her father to enter the cave alone. She turned her back, feeling the warmth of the sunshine on her shoulders as she listened to his footsteps. He took several paces and stopped. Then there was silence.

'Hi, Andy. How's the foot?' Bryn walked up behind her. 'I met your bête noire last night. Rhona followed me to the pub.'

Andy stared at him in horror. 'What did she want?'

'Mainly to ask how you were. I suspect she wanted to know if she had managed to finish you off. I told her you were fine. I assume that was what you would have wanted me to do?'

Her mouth had gone dry. 'Yes. Thank you.'

'Don't thank me, Andy. Go to the police. She's dangerous.'

'I've told you, I am not going to do that.' She turned away from him.

He watched her walk away. 'I see you've brought in a cave expert,' he called after her.

She stopped and looked back. 'The man in the cave? He's my father.'

'Really? He looked like an expert, the way he walked in.'

'He's an expert on ghosts not caves.' She met Bryn's eye almost defiantly.

'He should be at home round here then,' he replied. He followed her. 'Has he reached a verdict yet?'

Andy gave a wry smile. 'Too soon. So, which ghosts have you seen?' Somehow out here in this context, in the sunlight, it was all right to ask. She kept her voice light-hearted.

He gave the question some thought. 'I see figures in the distance sometimes; in the garden.'

She waited for him to be more specific, but he said no more. He turned away again and strolled off back to his flowerbed. She did not pursue him.

She walked slowly down to the brook and sat down on her favourite outcrop of rock, staring into the water. The sunshine had managed to find its way through the overhanging trees and sparkled on the surface as it gurgled and splashed over the steep incline towards the road. She watched it, half mesmerised, for several minutes.

'What you need is an on–off switch!' her father had said. Something to control that strangely fuzzy feeling, that concertinaing of time and space; that feeling she was experiencing now, as she stared down at the water.

She could see the garden in Kew, see the house, the blinds drawn at the back to keep the sun out of the lower rooms. 'No!' she said it out loud. The picture faded. If the blinds were drawn, Rhona was still away. Still here. Still planning to pay her back for whatever she imagined Andy had done to wreck her marriage.

A shadow fell across the path. She looked up. 'Have you seen all you want to see?'

But it wasn't her father.

It was a tall man wearing doublet and hose, a hat with a rolled brim, a short cloak, his face tanned and weather-beaten, his shoes dusty and worn although they had once been smart. He was carrying a battered leather bag, a kind of briefcase, she realised. Their eyes locked for a brief second, then he was gone.

She leapt to her feet, her heart thudding uncomfortably. It was the man from the market; the man who had spoken so quietly and confidentially to Catrin, the man who had warned her to be careful. What did he want? What was he doing here, at Sleeper's Castle? Did Catrin know he was here?

She realised how stupid that thought was as soon as she had stepped forward out of the shade into the patch of sunlight where, just for a moment, the man had stood looking at her. Was he spying or had he come to warn Catrin again?

'Andy?' She heard the voice but was too stunned to react. 'Andy?'

Rufus had made his way out of the cave, walked along the path and come to a halt beside her. He followed her gaze, peering at the paving stones a few feet in front of her. 'What is it? What happened?'

'I saw a ghost,' she murmured. 'I saw a real, definite ghost.' She looked up at him. To her surprise she wasn't afraid. 'I recognised him and I know he saw me. He was someone Catrin knew. The man who warned her off when she went to the market.'

'Go indoors now and write it down while it's fresh in your mind.' Her father gave her a little push. 'I'll be in in a minute.'

He stared after her as she walked back towards the house, concerned. As soon as she had disappeared inside he turned away and headed to the flowerbed where Bryn was standing watching them, leaning on his spade. Rufus put out his hand. 'Rufus Dysart, I'm Andy's father.'

'She told me.' Bryn shook his hand with seeming reluctance then stood back and waited.

Rufus said nothing, scanning Bryn's face, then finally he smiled. 'Sorry. I have to know if I can trust you.'

'And can you?' Bryn raised his chin slightly, holding the other man's gaze.

'I think so. Andy has bitten off more than she can chew here, I fear. She needs allies. I hope you're one of them.'

Bryn held his gaze. A faint trace of humour showed behind his eyes. 'She doesn't always welcome help.'

'I think she will now. I hate to think of her here alone. This place is quite isolated isn't it.' Rufus paused. He saw the other man give the briefest of nods and echoed the movement. 'My daughter is a brave woman and she's intrigued by all this and she thinks I can tell her how to cope.' He paused. 'I blame myself for inspiring her interest in ghosts when she was a child. I moved away and left her and her mother and I haven't been there for her since, not properly and she has this vision of me arriving like some guardian angel.' He gave a self-deprecating smile. 'Graham put her off ghosts, but now she is fascinated again and just when she needs my help, I can't be here for her. I have to leave in a day or so; please, tell me what you think goes on here.'

'As I understand it, this house has been called Sleeper's Castle for centuries, perhaps millennia,' Bryn said gravely. 'People have always known its power, but Andy seems to have woken things up somewhat.'

'Is there danger?' Rufus tossed back the question sharply.

Bryn considered the question. 'Usually people leave.'

331

'We both know that Andy isn't going to do that.'

Bryn pursed his lips. 'She will if it gets bad enough.'

'Meaning?'

'Just that. Things can escalate. The history of this place is still very much with us. This house. Wales. And the March. Whoever said that the past is a foreign country was wrong.' He paused.

Rufus acknowledged the remark with a nod. 'And now we have this lunatic woman running amok round here as well. Andy mustn't get hurt. She doesn't seem to take it seriously. She refuses to call the police.'

'I will try and persuade her. Unfortunately, they came up here when Rhona called them, and I think Andy's right. They won't follow this up without anything more concrete to go on. She refuses to confirm that the woman attacked her. Perhaps she genuinely doesn't know,' Bryn said grimly. 'But I will try and keep an eye on things. I can make no promises. As for the ghosts . . .' He gave a small shrug. 'Has Andy introduced you to Meryn? He is the man to sort that out.'

'She mentioned his name. Can he be trusted?'

'Absolutely.'

'Unfortunately, I gather he's away at the moment.'

Bryn sighed. 'I wish sometimes he would stay put for a while. He's always rushing off to sort out other people's problems. This is a place of enormous strength. I think the whole mountain is, to be honest. His cottage which is up on the mountain is another source of power. Meryn uses it to charge his batteries. Other people do too round here, often without realising it, but that can be too much for them; it can burn one out. It can stir one up. It can destroy people.'

'Should I make Andy come away with me?'

'With all due respect, I think you would find that hard.'

'You seem to know her very well.'

'In fact she and I have barely talked.'

Rufus stared at him in astonishment. 'Then perhaps you should.'

Bryn nodded slowly, then seemingly deciding that the

conversation was over, he turned and walked thoughtfully back to his flowerbed.

Rufus joined Andy in the kitchen. 'I was speaking to your gardener. He said you and he had hardly ever talked.'

She looked up, pen in hand, and to his astonishment she blushed a little. 'I find him a bit intimidating. I think he resents me being here instead of Sue. But we get along all right when we have to. He's there for me.'

Rufus studied her face and grinned. 'I think you should make a friend of him, Andy. He knows a lot about this place and its potential.'

'And he spoke to Rhona.'

He stared at her. 'He didn't mention that. What did he think?'

'I'm not sure. He was wary. He seems to be quite shrewd about people. He knows she's dangerous.'

'She's that all right.' He sounded impatient. 'You have enough to cope with here without a mad harridan chasing after you.'

'Dad, you've never met her!'

'Oh, but I have. Don't you remember? You and Graham gave a party when you moved in with him. Somehow Rhona found out about it and gatecrashed. She was hell-bent on spoiling it for you. It was me that gave her a lift back to central London. I had plenty of opportunity to get to know Mrs Wilson on that drive, and my views have not changed. She is a loose cannon and to be avoided. The thought that she's up here somewhere does not fill me with reassurance.'

'I wish you could stay longer, Daddy.' She said it very quietly.

'So do I. And I will come back, as soon as I can.' He stood up. 'Now, forget everything else for a few minutes while you finish bringing your notes up to date, then you and I are going to have a cup of tea. I wish you would come away with me, girl.' He reached out across the table and squeezed her hand as it lay there on her notebook, pen clutched between her fingers.

*   *   *

333

By the time Dafydd returned, Catrin had copied out all her poems again. She had found another coffer, this one with a lock and key, and she had rearranged her bedchamber. There was no sign now that this was the study of a woman who wrote; her writing table had been pushed back against the wall and merely held her combs and boxes of trinkets. Her books were on a high shelf and looked as if they were seldom touched. She had found a workman in Hay, one of the men who had helped to rebuild the town, who agreed to come up to Sleeper's Castle and put the long-promised glass in her window, and she had bought a new tapestry for her wall. She had a feeling her father would raise no objections after what he had done and she was right. He went into her room almost as soon as he returned.

She followed him up the stairs and waited at the turn of the step on the landing, watching as he paused by her door, pushed it and entered, standing on the threshold for several heartbeats as he studied the room. She heard him give a grunt, but whether of satisfaction or of disgust she couldn't tell, then he turned away and went back to his own chamber. Neither of them mentioned the burning of her papers. She did not speak about her poetry to him again, nor ask him about his trip. The bond between them had been broken. She knew he must have been at Machynlleth when Owain was crowned Prince of Wales, and at Harlech where the now-named Prince Owain IV, flush with successes all across Wales, had set up his court. She longed to ask about her friends, Catherine and Alys, and their mother, Margaret, so kind and so warm to her when she had last seen them four years before, but she kept her counsel.

She visited her father's study less than she had before; she allowed Joan to wait on him more. If he missed her constant attendance on him he gave no sign. She guessed that he knew their relationship had been ruptured beyond repair and sadly she acknowledged to herself that perhaps he didn't care. When she was working on a poem in her head she made sure he would never guess what she was thinking about; if she scribbled on her wax note-tablets, she hid them up on the cross-beams of her room where he would never see them at first glance. She wrote at night, by the light of her candle, a stool pushed against the door so she would have warning of anyone creeping down the landing to come in and catch her in the act. Quietly she burned with resentment and looked forward to the day he left again.

Joan accosted her one day as they were picking the last of the sloes from the blackthorn hedges. A cold wind had blown through the garden tearing leaves off the trees. 'You can't go on like this, you know. You will have to speak to him in the end.'

'I do speak to him.' Catrin didn't have to ask who she was talking about.

'He is very unhappy about you.'

'The feeling is mutual.'

'He knows he did something terrible.'

Catrin stared at her. She put her hands on her hips. 'He told you so?'

'No. Of course he didn't. He would never admit it.'

'And I will never forgive him. So we will not talk about it again.'

'He saw Edmund when he was with the Lord Owain.' Joan glanced at her slyly.

'Did he? He never mentioned that.' Catrin could feel the colour rising in her cheeks.

'He feels that Prince Owain,' Joan could not resist a slight sarcastic emphasis on the title, 'trusts my brother. He told me. He keeps him near his side. He is more than a mere archer in the army.'

'Why are you telling me this?' Catrin asked.

'I thought you would like to know. He is not out skirmishing with his fellow archers, he is there in the castle, playing at kings and queens with the family; with the Lord Owain's wife and his sons while they plan sedition and revolt.' She glanced sideways at Catrin, who sighed deeply. 'Don't bother, Joan. It doesn't interest me. Edmund doesn't interest me. The Lord Owain doesn't interest me. I am not permitted to accompany my father wherever he goes; I am a lonely stupid woman, left to rot in the country. I am not permitted to marry and have my own home. I am not permitted to travel beyond the local market, and my destiny is to wait upon my father hand and foot.' She let out an angry cry as a blackthorn caught her hand.

Joan shook her head. 'My, we are in a state! That is not like you. Why don't you tell him how you feel?'

'He knows how I feel.' Catrin put her bowl down on the grass and sucked her bleeding finger. 'Here, you finish picking these.' She turned away and stumbled over the herb beds towards the brook, where she stood for a while, feeling the spray on her face, breathing in the cold wet smells of autumn. The recent storms had turned it into a torrent of swirling leaves and thundering brown water. She couldn't hear herself think over the roar as it poured down over the rocks towards the track below, and that was the way she liked it.

Behind her, Joan watched her for a while before going back to her berry picking.

At an upstairs window Dafydd was looking out. He could see her clearly down there by the brook and he scowled.

Andy watched, her attention focused on him as he turned away from the window. He was in Catrin's bedroom. He walked slowly back across the floor and stood looking down at the coffer in the corner, the coffer where she kept her manuscripts. He already knew it was locked, he had rattled the lid earlier. He glanced round the room sourly then he turned and headed towards the door.

'Catrin!' Andy leaned forward towards her. 'Be careful. He is eaten up with malice.' She could see it so clearly. And so could Joan.

* * *

'Andy!' Rufus squeezed Andy's hand gently. 'Andy, come back!'

She sat up with a start. She had been leaning forward across the kitchen table, her head in her arms. Rufus slid into the chair opposite her and looked at her, noting her confused expression. Her eyes were unfocused and for a few seconds she stared at him without recognition. He held onto her hand. 'Come back, girl. Look at me.'

She withdrew her hand and sat back in the chair, pushing her hair away from her face. 'I'm sorry. Did I fall asleep?'

'You did.' He waited.

'I was dreaming, wasn't I?'

'I think so.'

'Did I talk in my sleep?'

He shook his head. 'Tell me what you were dreaming about.'

'I can't remember.'

'You can. Think back. Don't try and force it.'

They sat in silence, facing each other and wearily she closed her eyes. 'Dafydd was in Cat's bedroom,' she said at last. 'He was spying on her. He was so angry that she had had expensive glass put in her window. He went and examined it. It was set in a lead frame. A workman from Hay had done it for her in the summer while her father was away.' Her eyes were open but she was staring into the distance. 'I don't think she realises even now how jealous Dafydd is of her.'

She pushed back her chair and stood up. Limping over to the sink she picked up a glass, filled it with water and drank it, staring out of the window into the garden. 'You were talking to Bryn earlier?' Her voice was normal again.

'I was. He seems a nice man. Dependable, I should say.' Rufus left it at that and Andy was silent. She put the glass down on the draining board and turned back. 'I suppose I had better write it down.'

'Do you think you will forget it if you don't?'

'No.' She lowered herself into her chair. 'No, I think I'm afraid I might lose the detail. The small things. Or alter it in my head later as I think about it. There's so much happening and it drifts away into the shadows as I wake, just like any dream.'

'That shouldn't be a problem. You can train yourself to remember more and more. And you can train yourself to ask questions of the dream.' Rufus's eyes were alight with interest. 'I envy you this so much, Andy. What an experience!'

She gave a wan smile. 'You don't think it's dangerous then?'

'Dangerous?' He frowned. 'I don't see how it could be if you're careful.'

'That's what Meryn said,' she sighed.

'I think you need to listen to this Meryn chap and get him to give you some lessons, girl.' He reached out for her hand again. 'I sense from what you say that he hasn't done it yet out of respect for me, but I'm not the expert round here. All I can say is that you mustn't do it if it worries you.'

'It doesn't worry me, but it makes me tired.' She looked up at him again. 'I don't think it's the kind of sleep that exactly refreshes one.'

He pushed back his chair. 'Go and take a shower to wake you up properly. Later I'll drive us out somewhere for a nice meal. How does that sound? Forget all this for a while.'

She smiled back at him. 'That sounds good. I would like that.'

In the corner of the room Dafydd ap Hywell ap Gruffydd, poet and seer, scowled blackly. His daughter had somehow brought these ghosts into his house. The evil dreams that beset him of death and defeat were linked to these apparitions. His daughter had been playing with magic and witchcraft in his absence and she had allowed the house to be overrun with demons.

Rhona had found a spot in the lane higher up, near the cattle grid, where she could pull off into a passing place and see clearly over a gate down across a field which sloped out of sight towards a forested hillside. It had taken her a while to realise that the lane had doubled back on itself as it climbed so that she could see the grey, lichened roofs of Sleeper's Castle nestling into the wooded hillside immediately below her. It was the perfect lookout point from which to survey the place. She left the car, hauled herself over the gate and set out across the field, scattering sheep before her as she walked. As she reached the top of the slope she moved more cautiously, aware that she might be silhouetted against the skyline.

She could feel the power of the house, even from here. It was like a magnet and the more she looked the angrier she felt. It was as though some ancient force was feeding her rage.

The front door was open. She narrowed her eyes then reached into the pocket of her raincoat and pulled out a small pair of binoculars. There was a figure standing in the doorway. A man. He was leaning against the doorframe, staring out towards her. She gave a smug smile. There was no way he could see her so far away. She trained the glasses on him and studied his face. She remembered him. It was Andy's father. She pocketed the glasses again and stood still, thinking. He had divorced Andy's mother and gone off to live in Northumberland or somewhere with a new wife and had masses of new children over the intervening years, so the chances were he was only here for a fleeting visit.

Rhona smiled as she turned away from her viewpoint and headed back up the field. She was beginning to enjoy this whole enterprise. She had always thought of deer-stalking as a stupid and mindless occupation, something her own father had enjoyed which had taken him away from her and her mother for long swathes of the summer holidays, but now she was beginning to understand why he had found it so intriguing. It was the fascination of pitting your wits against another living creature, albeit one who didn't know it was being hunted. She could almost feel her trigger finger itching as she thought about it. She had no gun, that was the problem. She stopped in her tracks, unaware of the sheep bunching near her, nervously eyeing her as she stood, her boots wet with rain in the middle of the field. A gun. But then she knew nothing about shooting, so maybe that was not an option. Part of the enjoyment of stalking your prey was waiting to see what opportunities fate would present.

22

Catrin was on the hillside picking mushrooms. Her basket was almost full and she straightened, her hand to her back, as her shadow lengthened across the grass to stand and look out towards the distant peaks of the Brecknock Mountains. Something was moving in the heather below her. She refocused her eyes trying to see what it was; a sheep or a wild pony or perhaps one of the sturdy small cows that grazed up here on the commons. She stared round looking for a cowherd and as she scanned the view, her hand shading her eyes against the reddening sunlight as it sank further into the west, she could make out a figure walking towards her. She watched incredulously, not wanting to believe her eyes. 'Edmund?'

He ran the last few paces and swung her into his arms. Abruptly he put her down. 'I am sorry. I was so pleased to see you. How are you, Catrin?' He held her at arm's length and studied her face.

'You followed me up here?' She felt the old mix of longing and indignation. She took several steps backwards, looking at him closely. 'How did you know I was here?'

'Joan told me you were mushrooming and I remembered you told me you used to come up here to the common below Pen-y-Beacon.'

'I did?' She was shocked.

'You did.' He tried to look solemn. 'I can tell you the exact moment. We were sitting at the bottom of the lowest table waiting for your father to recite when we were in the castle at Chirk and you mentioned that you hoped we would be home in time for the mushrooms on the hill. A moment later the ladies whisked you away to sing to them in their solar.'

'That was years ago!'

'And so much has happened since then.' He sighed.

For the first time she began to look at him properly. His face was tired and lined.

'Why are you here?'

'Always to the point. I have errands to run. I thought I would drop in on my sister.'

She was taken aback. 'And me?'

'Oh, yes, Cat. And you.' He held her gaze so intently she dropped her eyes, embarrassed.

'The Lord Owain has become very great now. He has triumphed all over Wales,' she said slowly. 'We hear he is based at Harlech and he holds parliaments.'

'And he negotiates with the kings of France and Scotland.' He smiled at her. 'He is truly Prince Owain now. Prince of all Wales.'

'The king will never stop fighting him.'

'I remembered how much gossip you hear, in your eyrie where only the buzzards and eagles fly.' He moved away from her and sat down on a tussock of dried grasses. He patted the ground beside him. 'You can be my ears and eyes. What do they say in Hay?'

Catrin hesitated only a moment before coming to sit beside him. She tucked her long skirts round her knees and told him about the reeve's warning. So much had happened since then.

The Welsh army had broached Hay town walls a second time and burned many of the houses, then they had surrounded the castle and battered holes in its defences, but already all was being rebuilt and an experienced knight from England, Richard Arundel, had been brought in as the new castellan.

'We did not fare so badly as some other places,' she said, glancing at him. 'I've heard it said that it's because the Lord Owain has friends in Hay. But Hay is like everywhere else, no one knows who supports who. Men try to farm their fields and watch in despair as armies pass by leaving nothing but devastation. Up in the hills we do hear things. We hear of battles far away up the border and we hear of treaties and we hear of the king in London ranting on about us thieving Welsh and forbidding the encouragement of bards.' She gave a bitter little smile. 'And I wonder,' she went on sadly, 'what has happened to Catherine and Alys.'

'They are well.' Edmund smiled. 'As you know, Catherine is married to Edmund Mortimer and now she has a baby boy.'

'And Alys?'

He smiled. 'Alys is happy. I think she is in love.'

She gave him a shrewd glance. 'How do you know?'

'I know.'

'Who with?'

'Ah, that I can't tell you.'

'Can't or won't?'

He didn't reply. They sat silent for a long time, then she turned back to him. 'Are you a spy, Edmund?'

He laughed. 'Me? No. I'm a lowly archer.'

'An archer who travels the country and never seems to be part of the fighting army, who, I hear, follows his prince and talks to him daily, who is close to his family and knows their innermost secrets; who is allowed to leave alone and travel the countryside asking questions?'

It hadn't occured to her up until now that Edmund had started on his current path while accompanying her and her

343

father on their annual progress through the border country. It was then, after all, that he had first visited the households of the Marcher lords, mixed with their servants, encountered members of the *uchelwyr*, those Welsh landowners who were almost to a man now supporting Glyndŵr. And it was while in the service of her father that he had come to the notice of the Lord Owain, who had obviously recognised his potential. He was brave, he had contacts, he had initiative and charm; so when he had offered his services as an archer, Glyndŵr had found a better use for his talents. And now Edmund was more mature, more educated, more serious and probably more useful to his prince than Catrin could ever imagine.

She was waiting for an answer. He put his head on one side then he tapped the side of his nose. 'It seems to me that it is you who are the spy! You are well informed, Cat. As for me, I come and I go. The prince knows you all; he has been to your house; he knows I want to make sure you are all safe. As does he. He values your father's prophecies. And yours.' He leaned back and stared up at the sky, the sunlight on his face. 'I miss you, Cat. I think about you all the time.' He was still staring up, squinting at a small cloud. He didn't look at her.

She said nothing for a while. Then, 'I think about you too.'

'Annoying, isn't it.' He gave a wry smile.

She laughed. 'Infuriating.'

'What do we do?'

'There is nothing we can do. Our lives run on separate paths.'

He sat up and reached for her hand. She was still wearing the prince's silver ring. 'Supposing we could do something. Supposing I spoke to your father again?'

'It would still do no good. He does not intend that I should ever marry.' She looked at the ground glumly, then turned startled eyes on him. 'If that is what you meant?'

'Yes, that's what I meant.' He brought her hand to his lips and brushed it gently with a little kiss.

She let out a sob, snatching her hand away from him. 'Please don't. He will not countenance it! He wants me to be his servant and there is nothing I can do.'

'Why not?' He reached over and caught her hand again. 'Cat, your father is a selfish bully. I have watched him order you about; I have seen him steal your ideas and suppress your talent whenever he could, I have seen him destroy your confidence. You have only to say the word and we can go away together.' He paused for a short moment then went on: 'I want to take you back to Harlech and we can be married there. The Lord Owain would give you to me, I know he would, and if he didn't I would take you. We will marry somehow. Unless,' he paused, 'unless you think I am not good enough for you. If that is the case, then there is no more to be said.' He was studying her hand, counting her fingers.

She tried to pull away. 'No!'

'No, I am not good enough for you?'

'No, I do not think that. But I cannot leave my *tad*.'

'I thought you had more courage than that, Cat.' He was reproachful.

'I have enough courage for anyone!' she shot back at him. 'But I owe him everything. My mam died when I was born. I took her from him. It is my duty to stay with him.'

'At the cost of your own happiness?'

'If needs be, yes.' She scrambled to her feet. Then she turned and reached down for his hand again. 'You must go. You were going anyway, weren't you? You are on a mission for the Lord Owain. You only stopped here to give yourself a pretext for coming to Brycheiniog if anyone should see you. You came to see Joan. Well, you have seen her. Now go.' She turned away and began to run blindly away from him.

He watched her, running over the rough ground. Her basket of mushrooms lay overturned at his feet.

'Cat!' he called. 'Cat, wait.'

He overtook her easily. Grabbing her arms, he spun her to face him and pulled her close. For a while they stood there in silence, Edmund holding her against his chest, then he raised her chin so he could look into her eyes. She didn't struggle as he brought his lips down on hers.

When at last they drew apart he found she was crying. 'Cat—'

She shook her head numbly. 'Please, go.'

'But—'

'But nothing! It can never be, Edmund. Never!' She moved away from him and retraced her steps to where her basket lay on the ground. Stooping, she scooped the mushrooms back inside, then picked up the basket and put it on her arm.

He stood still, watching until she was out of sight, walking quickly back towards the track which led down into the valley. Never once did she look back. Only when she was out of sight did he move. He glanced up at the steep hillside above them and turned in the opposite direction to the one she had taken. He would walk over the shoulder of the mountain towards the next valley and home to visit his mother. Tomorrow he would head on to Hereford and the real reason he was here.

'Andy?' Bryn was watching her as she stood gazing into the brook. She hadn't moved for a long time. She looked up at him, confused.

'Edmund? You've come back!'

His eyebrows shot up towards his hairline. 'Nope. Try again.'

She rubbed her eyes.

'It's Bryn,' he reminded her.

Embarrassed, she stepped away from the bank. 'Oh God, I'm sorry, Bryn. I came out for a few minutes' fresh air. I must have been daydreaming. What did I say?'

'You called me Edmund.' He smiled. 'I'm flattered.'

'Flattered?' She pushed her hair out of her eyes. 'Why? Do you know who Edmund is?'

'I do, yes.'

She stared at him anxiously. She could feel herself blushing. 'You know the whole story then?'

'Only some of it.' He gave her a sympathetic smile. 'Don't worry, I won't tell anyone.' He stepped away from her, turning towards the garden, giving her a moment to compose herself. 'Your father was asking if I'd seen you. I think he wants to take you out somewhere,' he said as he walked away. 'He's round the front.'

She stood still, staring after him, then she retraced her steps towards the house.

He glanced over his shoulder once. He was laughing.

Rufus was sitting on the bench at the front of the house, staring out across the valley.

He glanced up at her. 'Were you dreaming? I saw you down by the brook. I thought I would leave you to it, but it'll be getting cold and damp before too long.'

'I was dreaming about Cat.' She couldn't bring herself to mention Edmund. 'She was picking mushrooms.'

'Magic ones?'

She laughed. 'I don't think so, though she was in the right place if I recall. No,' she took a deep breath. 'She was talking to Edmund. I'm beginning to suspect – no, *she* is beginning to suspect – that he was acting as a spy for the rebels.'

Rufus gave her a sidelong look. 'And do you agree with her?'

'I don't know. I wish I knew more about it all.' She caught her father's eye and laughed. 'I do realise that Cat is almost certainly not a huge figure on the historical stage. She's not important.'

'That's a bit harsh.'

'I know. But she isn't, is she, in the great scheme of things. And she's not a strong enough personality. She's dominated by her father. Unless she breaks free of him, she won't achieve anything.'

'And how do you know she won't?'

Andy drew breath to reply, then fell silent. 'I don't.'

'Well then—' Rufus rose to his feet, his hand shading his eyes. 'Did you see that?'

'What?'

'A bright flash on the hillside up there. My guess is that someone is watching us through binoculars.'

'Rhona!'

'Could be. She's not a crack shot, is she?' He smiled.

'That's not funny, Daddy. I have no idea what she is. I only wish she would go away.' She stood up too. 'Let's go round the back. She can't see us there.'

'And miss watching the sun go down? I don't think so.' Rufus sat down again. 'I'm tempted to make a rude sign so that she can see we've clocked her presence.'

'She can see that by the way you're studying the hill. Besides, she'll have gone by now.'

'Good. Even more reason not to move. I like it here.' He stuck his legs out in front of him and crossed his ankles.

A sound on the path made them both look up. It was Bryn, his jacket slung over one shoulder, his canvas bag on the other. 'Goodnight, folks,' he called.

'Goodnight!' Rufus replied. Andy raised her hand.

Rufus looked at her quickly. She was blushing. He said nothing. It was a long time after Bryn had driven away and the sound of his engine had died in the distance that Rufus turned to her. 'Go and get your glad rags on. Your father is taking you out to supper, remember?'

'I'm looking forward to it.'

'You'll have to tell me where though.'

They went to the Old Black Lion. It was the place Catrin and Joan had left their pony on that market day six hundred or so years ago, when a town wall had surrounded Hay. They chose a table in the corner near the fire in the heavily beamed bar and had a leisurely meal, then sat for a long time over their coffee. It was as Rufus was beginning to think about calling for the bill that Andy turned to him. 'Do you remember when I was a child we used to travel together.'

He was patting his pockets, looking for his wallet. 'Travel, you mean to France—' He broke off. 'You mean into the past?'

'We did, didn't we? I'm not making it up?'

He whistled through his teeth. 'No, you're not making it up. But, Andy, I'm not sure it actually worked, to be honest.'

'It worked, Daddy, I know it did.'

'Girl, I pretended it was real.' For the first time that she could ever remember, he looked flustered. 'It was like a bedtime story. Sometimes when you were little you were frightened to go to sleep. Your dreams scared you.' He paused with a frown and looked up at her. 'Even when you were very small you dreamed, Andy. You didn't need a special house to do it in. I would try to reassure you. I would tell you to go to sleep and dream and your daddy would be there too, to look after you.'

'But you were there?' It sounded like a plea.

'I wanted to be there. I would watch you as the fear went away and you began to relax; I would close my eyes as you did and I would try so hard to be with you wherever it was you were going. Sometimes, most of the time, you slept quietly – at least, to start with. But sometimes . . .' He looked down at the tabletop, his face a picture of anguish. 'I could see your little face begin to move, to change, and your eyes would open even though I knew you were still asleep – and I could see the terror in them. I wanted to be there for you, Andy, so badly, but I didn't know how. When you started to cry and scream, your mother would come and she would wake you and hold you tight until you calmed down. She used to blame me for frightening you.' An expression of acute sadness crossed his face.

Andy stared at him mutely. 'But, Daddy, you were there for me. I can remember in my dreams. You would come; if I looked and looked, I knew you would be there like a knight in shining armour. You would always come . . .' Her voice died.

'I'm so sorry, darling.' He sighed. 'To be honest, I've never been that much of an expert on all this stuff. You've remembered it wrong. It was such fun doing all those things with you. I wanted to believe in ghosts. I loved our visits to haunted houses and old castles. I loved the idea of ghosts, but whether I actually saw any . . .' His voice drifted into silence.

'Excuse me, sir,' an apologetic voice broke in. 'We're closing soon.' They looked up and realised that the room was empty. The waiter had been turning off the lights one by one behind the bar. Rufus glanced at his watch. It was almost midnight. 'Oh my goodness, I'm sorry.' He stood up. 'I had no idea it was so late.'

In the car park behind the pub he groped for her hand. 'We remember things differently, Andy. Everyone does. It's part of the mystery of time. I want to be there for you, I really do, and I will try, but I can't promise. From what I've heard of him it is Meryn you must go to now; he will know what you should do.'

They climbed into the car in silence.

When they reached the house Andy directed Rufus on up the lane. It was a clear night and the mountains were stark silhouettes against a starry sky. He pulled off on the flat grass and turned off the engine. They walked a little way up one of the sheep tracks. The air was cold and still, the stars glittering in an obsidian-black sky. A sheep bleated in the silence and far away it was answered by the high-pitched call of a bird. Andy shivered. 'It's beautiful, isn't it.'

Rufus reached out for her hand. 'You don't have to go on with any of this, Andy. You could come home with me. Forget about Sleeper's Castle. Bryn could look after the cat. The house would be safe in his hands.'

'It would, wouldn't it.' She was looking up. 'There's Cassiopeia.'

'Called by the ancient Celts, Llys Dôn,' Rufus said. 'You are in Wales now, Andy, I think that's the better name for it.'

'Is that what Catrin would have called it? I'll ask Bryn what it means.'

She didn't notice the glance he gave her.

'Shall we go back?'

She was still looking up. '*Tad* – look, a shooting star!' The silver streak in the sky flashed over their heads and was gone. Neither of them noticed what she had called him.

Joan was stirring a pan of pottage on the fire when Catrin opened the kitchen door and stepped inside. Joan dropped the spoon. 'So, did Edmund find you?'

'Yes.' Catrin took off her cloak and hung it on the back of the door. 'He remembered where the mushrooms grew. I had told him about them apparently.'

Putting her basket down on the table she did not notice Joan's expression. Joan pursed her lips. 'Your father has been calling for you.'

It was Catrin's turn to let her face betray her. She considered turning round and going outside again but she overrode the urge and with a sigh headed towards the inner door. Joan turned back to her pottage.

Dafydd was standing staring down into the fire in the great hall. 'Where have you been?' he asked testily as Catrin appeared.

'Collecting mushrooms.' Automatically she went over to the log basket. She threw a lump of oak onto the flames. 'Why did you want me?'

'I need you to be within call, Catrin!' he said. He was wearing his fur-lined houppelande and had pulled a short cloak round his shoulders, practical but expensive items he had brought back with him from his last travels, but still he was shivering.

'Well, I'm here now.' She stood beside him, gazing into the flames.

'I need you to go down to Hay,' he said at last. 'I have to know what is happening.'

'We would have heard if anything was happening,' she said patiently. 'You know how fast word travels.'

'No, I need you to go. I dreamt that the king's army was close by.'

351

'And you no longer trust your dreams?'

He looked up at her. 'How can I, when they are so often wrong?'

She felt a wave of compassion as she saw the misery and uncertainty in his eyes. With a sigh he pulled his cloak even more tightly round his shoulders and turned to walk back into his study. He closed the door behind him. Catrin stood for a while where she was then slowly she made up her mind. She let herself out of the front door and made her way round to the back of the house. She crossed the garden and, looking round to make sure she was not observed, she took the path towards the cave.

The darkness closed round her with its usual stillness. The acrid smell of bat droppings and the dusty bitter-sweet scent of dried fern surrounded her. She had left a coarse *brychan* spread over a pile of fern and she sat down on it. At the entrance of the cave there was a sliver of faint light; the last of the evening was draining into night. She could hear the bats beginning to rustle and stir overhead. Soon they would fly one by one out of the entrance and she would be alone.

Edmund was riding up an avenue of elms towards a large house. She didn't recognise it, nor the men he spoke with, quietly, in the shadows. She saw him pass letters to one of them, she saw them direct him to the kitchens where he would find food, she saw him flirt with the kitchen maids, she saw with an aching heart one of the ladies of the house, a daughter presumably, petite and slim and pretty in a rich kirtle and surcoat, who just happened to be there, who smiled at him and flirted with her eyes and laughed at his jokes. He was at ease with her; he went on eating, he enjoyed the audience of cooks and maids and servant girls.

Then he was gone, back on his horse, and it was a fine horse, not a mountain pony, and he was wearing good clothes, not ostentatious but well made, cantering back down the long avenue and out onto the open road, heading north now towards the next manor house or castle or farmstead, with the next letter. She watched as he journeyed on, wondering if he were aware of her longing eyes, trained on his back. Once or twice she saw him look round, saw him frown and give a little shiver as if he knew someone was watching him. She looked down at her own worn gown and mantle, her scuffed working shoes and even in her dream, she sighed. Somehow Edmund, the farmer's son, had transformed himself into a trusted messenger, working for Prince Owain and his court.

The dream changed. She could see the prince now with his royal household. He had secretaries to write his letters, he had advisors to stand beside him as he wrote to the kings of Scotland and France, to the pope himself, to the disaffected nobles of England who, like him, were enemies of his neighbour, the man he called Henry of Lancaster, who called himself the King of England. Her father was right. All his warnings, his fears, his nightmares of blood and slaughter had been wrong. Blood and slaughter there had been, but Owain had won, he had triumphed and the new Prince of Wales was a true-born Welshman, descendant of ancient lineage, foretold by Merlin and Taliesin and yes, by her father too, and all of Wales had risen to support him against their overbearing, vindictive English neighbours.

But . . .

In her dream she shivered. She could see the shadows closing in once more. She was no longer in a royal castle. She heard shouts and smelled smoke. She saw men marching, banners held high and then she saw the banners lying trampled in the bloody mud of the battlefield. She could see no faces, recognise no escutcheons on the breastplates of the knights. She heard a horse scream and saw the lance snap as it pierced its chest. The destrier fell and with it its rider, pinned under it, his leg twisted and snapped in three places. The man who thrust a sword through his ribs did no more than a farrier would, killing man and horse to put them out of their pain. Where were they, the men who led this battle, Prince Owain and Prince Hal? They

353

had given orders to their followers, but it was impossible to see through the rancid smoke. And then they were fleeing. Men-at-arms and archers, their arrows spent, turned and ran for the shelter of the woods, their morale gone, their courage failed at last. But who had won? She couldn't tell. These were the men of her country, the neighbours and friends she knew, brother fighting against brother, cousin against cousin. Their houses were burned, their churches desecrated, their fields destroyed. She could feel herself there, on the edge of the battle, watching as the armies faded away into the mist, into the silence which was engulfing the scene – the silence of death.

'Andy, wake up.' The voice was quiet but persistent. 'Come on. Don't go there now. We must go home.'

Andy was reaching back into the dream, fighting the voice; she didn't want to come back.

'Andy. Now.' The voice was stronger, louder.

'*Tad?*' She felt a hand gripping hers and she clutched at it. Opening her eyes, she looked round, startled. She and her father were standing on the hillside in the dark. It was bitterly cold.

'Cat was in the cave,' she said in confusion. 'She was trying to see the future.'

'I want us to go home, Andy.' Rufus pulled her after him. 'We can talk about Catrin later. It's very cold up here and very late. Come on. Back to the car.'

The kitchen was warm and cosy when they let themselves back in. Pepper was curled up on his chair asleep. He glanced up briefly and closed his eyes again.

Andy shut the door and drew the curtains, then she turned to her father. 'We were going to try and travel together,' she said.

'I think I told you, Andy, it isn't possible,' Rufus replied gently. 'Do you realise how late it is? You must go to bed and tell yourself firmly that you don't want to dream any more tonight. You're exhausted.'

Andy shook her head sadly. 'If only it was that easy. I've told you. I can't switch it on; I can't switch it off.'

'And yet you can if you travel in the present. To Kew.'

She sighed. 'I'm not even sure about that any more. Please. Let's try. If it doesn't work, we can forget it and go to bed. Remember how you used to do it with me? We would sit on the sofa together and hold hands and you used to say, "Close your eyes, Andy, and wish you were somewhere else," and I used to say, "Where shall we go tonight?" and you used to choose somewhere, and then you would count us down.'

'And then you would fall asleep, Andy, and when you were little I would carry you up to your bed and when you grew too big to carry I would put a blanket over you and leave you on the sofa to sleep.'

'Until Mummy found out what was happening and told you off.' She smiled at the memory.

'She thought I was frightening you.'

'Only because the dreams could be a bit frightening and sometimes, when I looked for you in my sleep, you weren't there.' She bit her lip.

'I was never there, Andy,' he said gently.

'Let's try. Just to make me happy.' She reached for his hand. 'Come and sit beside me on the sofa.'

'You're a persistent child, aren't you!' he said.

She nodded. 'Always was. If it doesn't work I'll never mention it again, I promise.'

They sat down by the light of a single table lamp in the corner of the room. Andy reached for the throw, which lay over the back of the sofa, and pulled it over their knees. 'Ready?'

'You're scaring me, girl,' he said with a smile. 'What if it works?'

'Then we will watch together and you will be with me to keep me safe.'

He gave her a sharp look. 'Oh, Andy! I've explained—'

'I know. Don't worry. I'm only observing, hearing her story.'

355

He took a deep breath. 'Well, I'm tired enough to sleep! Racing around on the mountains after midnight is a bit retro for an old chap like me. So, come on, girl, let's be quiet and close our eyes. See you in the morning.'

'You have to hold my hand, *Tad*.' Andy groped for his hand under the rug and held it tightly.

Rufus found his mouth had gone dry. He lay back and closed his eyes. Suddenly he felt afraid.

They were both asleep within minutes. For Andy it was like opening a door. She stepped through, staring round eagerly. Where was she? Where was Catrin? Then she heard it, the thunder of hooves, the jingle of harness and spears, carried on the wind up the valley. There were shouts and in the distance a shrill, terrified scream. Frightened, she drew back. '*Tad*—'

She felt his hand warm and reassuring in hers, then he was pulling away. She grabbed at him desperately, she lost her grip and flailed about, trying to find him in the dark, but it was no use, he was gone.

23

'Catrin! For the love of the Blessed Virgin come away; come and hide!' Joan had caught her hand. 'Quickly. We'll go to the cave.'

Andy stirred restlessly. It was a different season, a different year. Both women looked older and more careworn.

'*Tad?*' Catrin was frantic, looking behind her.

'He's not there, I looked.'

'Who are they?' Catrin could feel herself beginning to tremble as she followed Joan towards the door into the garden.

'It doesn't matter who they are,' Joan retorted. 'They are armed men and if they find women alone in a remote place like this they all act the same. Come *on*!'

They ran down the garden path through the rain, fighting their way through the brambles and nettles that had grown across the path over the summer. Someone had piled brushwood in front of the cave entrance. Joan pulled it aside and pushed Catrin through then she turned and, her breath coming in short quick gasps, she pulled it back across behind them. She put her finger to her lips and whispered, 'They may not even come up the track. With luck they are heading west and will ride on together.' They crouched side by side in the dark, waiting. 'Where are Betsi and Megan?' Catrin breathed.

'Long gone into the hills. It was Betsi who told me they were coming. She had been down to the next farm; it is a large army. They are handing out pardons to people who throw themselves at the king's feet and beg for mercy for taking part in the revolt. You can't say he doesn't keep trying to win people back!'

Catrin stared at her unseeing in the dark. 'You seem to know an awful lot about the king's plans!'

'So does everyone. He has made it his business to inform the whole country. If you took your nose out of your books once in a while, you would know too.' Joan broke off. She clutched at Catrin's sleeve. 'Listen!'

The two women strained their ears through the sound of the rain on the trees and bushes outside the cave entrance. They could hear nothing. Catrin tiptoed away towards the back of the cave. She had had no time to grab a cloak or a shawl and she was shivering. She hugged her arms around herself and leaned against the ice-cold wall, closing her eyes against her terror. 'Where is *Tad*?' she asked. 'I didn't hear him go out.'

Joan was still by the entrance, peering through the brush-wood. 'I don't know. He wasn't in his study or upstairs.'

'They wouldn't hurt him, would they? An old man on his own?'

Joan glanced back over her shoulder. 'Your father is not old, Catrin.'

'He is by most people's standards!' Catrin retorted. To her he seemed as old as time itself. His obsession with the past, with people's ancestry, with legends and myths and the Wales of yesteryear had rooted him in the past he seemed to live in.

'Well, however old he is the soldiery is not renowned for its respect of anyone,' Joan said succinctly. She turned back to her spyhole.

'Surely they won't bother to come up the track?' Catrin went on quietly. Her teeth were chattering. 'They must look forward to getting to their next billet and a campfire in this weather. I've heard they hate the Welsh weather. They think the Lord Owain has magical powers to call down the clouds and storms over them.'

'And doesn't he?' Joan's voice was harsh.

Catrin hesitated. 'The weather certainly seems to be on his side,' she said cautiously.

'Unlike a lot of people round here,' Joan put in sourly. 'Especially the burgesses in Hay and the farmers. Like the Bedells. They are tired of having their fields and their businesses destroyed. They have mended and refortified the castle; once more it is held for the king and this time it will be secure.'

Catrin froze, the memory of her encounter with John Bedell's reeve two years before coming back to her. 'So I had heard.' He had come up to the house once, looking for her again. Joan had told him Catrin was visiting neighbours up the valley. Had he come to warn her again? She didn't know and he had left without leaving a message.

The women fell silent.

'How will we know when they've gone,' Joan whispered after a while. 'One of us will have to go and look.'

From outside in the garden they both heard the alarm call of a blackbird, shockingly loud in the silence. Joan tiptoed back from the entrance and flattened herself against the back wall next to Catrin. In the distance someone was knocking loudly at the front door. They waited, heart in mouth, and then they heard the sound of men's voices. Somewhere close to them a horse whinnied. Joan reached for Catrin's hand in the dark. Catrin held her breath. They could hear the jingle of harness. The men had ridden around the side of the house and into the garden. They heard shouts now and the sound of cracking timber and swishing leaves. They were using their swords to slash at the plants in the garden as they rode up and down the vegetable beds.

'There is no one here!' They heard another voice in the

distance. 'Search the place, men.' There was a sound of splintering wood as the back door caved in under someone's boot. There was a long, long silence. The two women waited hardly breathing as they strained their ears, then at last they heard the sound of voices again, the neigh of a horse. 'Shall we fire the place?' A shout echoed round the garden.

'It would never catch in this accursed rain!' someone replied. 'And anyway, we've no more time. We have to move on. They were clearly warned we were coming.' The voices were close to the cave. The women could hear the snort of the horses, the stamp of hooves and the creak and squeak of leather from the men's saddles. One of them raised his voice. 'Ride on!'

They were so close to the cave the swinging haunch of a horse struck the brushwood over the entrance and it sagged inwards towards them. Joan stuffed her fist into her mouth to stop herself screaming. Catrin pulled her close. She could feel herself shaking. She prayed to the Blessed Virgin and all the saints: wherever her father was, let him keep quiet. If he stormed out now he would be lost and so would they. She felt Joan bury her face in her shoulder as they clung together.

'It is a poor enough place,' sneered one.

'Peasants!' cried another, the disdain plain in his voice. 'Not worth looting.'

'But the poet! There were orders to take the poet!'

'Can't take him if he's not here,' the first responded. 'Come on, let's away. I want to get out of this accursed rain.'

They heard the horses moving off, the shouts of the men growing more distant until the garden was silent again.

It was a long time before the two women dared creep to the cave entrance, which was half exposed now, the brushwood scattered across the floor. 'They didn't see,' Catrin whispered. 'They didn't see what was in front of them.' Her voice was cracked, her mouth dry with fear.

Joan tiptoed past her into the garden. The beds were a mess of hoof prints and broken plants. Their crops had been deliberately destroyed, the precious vegetables trodden into the mud. Cautiously they crept back towards the house. The back door was hanging open. They stood in the doorway and surveyed the kitchen. The pot had been pulled off the fire and thrown on the floor. Joan's mutton stew was spattered greasily across the flags, filling the air with its rich smell. Everything had been upturned and broken.

Catrin let out a whimper of distress. She ran to the inner door and out into the great hall. The doors on the aumbry were hanging open, her beautiful glasses smashed on the flagstones, the silver spoons gone. She did not give herself time to think, heading towards her father's study. His treasured books had been pulled to the floor and stamped on judging by the muddy footmarks all over them, his writing materials scattered and ink thrown on his manuscripts. Someone had tried to tear some of the pages, given up and a pile of his writings had been thrown onto the fire, almost extinguishing it. Catrin bent and pulled them off the glowing logs; the sheer weight of parchment had served to damp it down. She whirled round with a sob and headed back across the hall towards the staircase. 'Did they go upstairs?'

They had ripped the bedding and mattresses with their swords; someone had pissed on her father's bed. She wrinkled her nose in disgust then turned, heart in mouth, towards her own room. Her bedding had suffered the same fate; her combs and little pots of hand salve had been swept off the table and scattered, her gowns and her best cloak had been pulled from the hooks on the wall and torn into pieces, her few books pulled from the shelf on the beam, her precious glass window shattered, but the lock on her coffer seemed to have defeated them. Perhaps they assumed it contained nothing more than a woman's clothing, or perhaps it had been at that moment that the officer had called them back downstairs. For whatever reason, it seemed to have been left untouched.

Joan puffed up the stairs behind her and peered over her shoulder. 'Holy Mother of God,' she breathed. 'What a mess.'

Catrin stared round. She was in a state of shock. So much destruction and wanton hatred displayed in her own little sanctuary; such a mess in the whole house, such damage to her father's study. They had known who lived here, the man in the garden had said as much.

Joan put her arms around her. 'At least they didn't fire the house,' she whispered. 'Good solid stone; it wasn't worth them bothering.'

'Only because they didn't have time and because it was raining.' Catrin felt her eyes fill with tears.

'So, where is your father?' Joan said at last.

They looked at each other bleakly.

'Come on.' Joan held out her hand. 'We had better start to look. Then we have to clear up the house.' It was time to become practical. She glanced up at Catrin's little window and sighed; she knew how much that small triumph had meant to Catrin and how expensive it had been. She glanced round the room again. 'Did they find your necklace?'

Catrin frowned. She had never mentioned it, never worn it – what chance had she to show off such finery – afraid that Joan would ask where it had come from. Obviously Joan had been poking about and found it. She walked across to the angle of the wall where two roof beams met. There, behind the pegs which held them in place, was a knothole in the oak. The necklace and the silver bracelet were still there, in their small leather bag. 'They didn't find it,' she whispered.

'Good. Then you can sell it and raise money to pay for repairs and food now our stores have gone.' Joan was still doggedly practical. She turned and made her way back to the staircase. 'The first thing I have to do,' she called over her shoulder, 'is clean up the kitchen. At least they couldn't destroy good iron cooking pots. Then we will burn the bedding. You go and look for your father. I imagine he is cowering somewhere up on the mountain. When he hears the army has moved on through the valley he will come home. It's a pity he didn't think to warn his daughter there was danger on the way when he ran off to save his own skin!'

She clattered down the stairs leaving Catrin to survey the wreckage of her chamber. Only then did the tears begin to fall.

'Andy! Andy, it's morning. Wake up.' The hand on her shoulder shook her gently. 'Come on, sweetheart. Wake up. I've brought you some tea.'

Andy opened her eyes. She was lying on the sofa in the great hall covered by a rug; her father was standing beside her, a teacup in his hand. Outside, it was daylight. Her face was wet with tears. He put the cup on the little table beside her and produced a tissue. 'Here, wipe your face. I had to wake you. I couldn't bear the sound of your sobbing any longer. What happened?'

Andy sat up slowly and looked round in confusion. The room was shadowy, different. Modern. 'The English army came through the valley. They were looking for Dafydd. They trashed the house,' she stammered. She wrinkled her nose. She could still remember the cold rich smell of greasy mutton and the acrid fumes of urine on Catrin's bed. She hugged herself, shivering. 'You weren't there. You didn't come with me.'

'I tried, girl.' He sat down on the sofa beside her. 'I'm sorry.' He studied her face with a frown. 'I've been thinking about this, Andy. I don't think it's such a good idea doing all this dreaming. Look at you. You were crying your heart out. Your mother would be furious if she knew I had encouraged it or even condoned it. She was really worried about you being here, all alone in this house. It's not a good place to be. Why don't you come back to Northumberland with me. Please. Let us look after you for a bit. Give the dreams, and Rhona, a chance to calm down.'

She lay back against the cushions. It was a tempting suggestion in so many ways. He passed her the cup without a word and watched as she took a tentative sip. She smiled at him. 'In many ways I would love to, but you know I can't. I have to find out what happened.' She brushed her face with the back of her hand; it came away damp from the tears on her cheeks. 'I'm sorry if I upset you by crying. It was only because I was so involved in the story. I wasn't in danger.'

He frowned. 'Are you sure?'

'Of course I'm sure. It was a dream. I wasn't there.' She gave a wry smile. 'I'm sorry you weren't either. I was so sure you could come with me.'

'Front row of the cinema,' he commented wryly.

She gave a nostalgic little smile. 'I used to love going to films with you. I could sit beside you in the dark in the cinema and know that you were there to look after me if the story got too frightening. But I'm grown up now. I know how frightening real life can be and you can't always be there, Daddy, to make it all right, any more than you can comfort me after a bad dream.' She sighed. 'For good or ill, I have arrived in this house, I have stumbled upon a slice of its history and I want to see the story through to the end. Who knows, perhaps I'm going to write Catrin's life history for her. You do understand, don't you.'

He never had been able to resist that pleading voice. 'And how are you going to deal with Rhona?' he asked softly. He knew the change of subject was a sign of defeat.

'I shall keep my doors locked and I won't engage the woman in conversation on the edge of any more precipices.' She smiled. 'I promise.' She handed him her empty cup. 'What about one of your stunning breakfasts while I've got you here? Could you go and make it while I head upstairs for a shower?'

She watched as he walked across the room and disappeared towards the kitchen. She wished she felt as confident as she hoped she had sounded.

Bryn shut his laptop and pushed it away with a sigh. He had spent an hour scouring the Net to no avail, unable to find anything of interest about a woman called Rhona Wilson, or at least not one who matched the description of the woman he was looking for. He stood up and went over to his coffee pot, shaking it experimentally. Just enough to squeeze out another cup. Cradling it in his hands, he wandered over to the window and stood looking out at the little courtyard at the back of his cottage which stood at the bottom of a narrow alleyway below the castle in Hay. Small, stone-built, ancient, it suited him fine.

His ex had forced the sale of their modern house and taken most of the contents. He hoped she would never realise what a relief it had been. He had disliked the house intensely and most of the stuff in it. That should have warned him they would never make it past the first year of marriage. It had been a disaster. Their lust had carried them through for several months, then as it waned they discovered they had almost nothing in common. But at least they had managed to agree the fact fairly amicably and the split had been pretty painless once he had given her everything she wanted. He gave a wry smile at the memory. Luckily she had not wanted anything to do with the belongings he regarded as treasures, and thank all the gods they had not had a child.

This little terraced house was perfect, furnished with what he had salvaged from his parents' old farmhouse after they died. It had upset them enough when he had chosen to go to university, sailed into Oxford and chosen a subject that had nothing even remotely agricultural about it. It would have broken his father's heart to know he had sold the farm, but there was nothing else for it. Hill farms were hard work and made little money; you had to have a passion in your soul for the work, and his passion was for people, not sheep.

It had come as a terrible shock when his father had died so comparatively young, and even more so when his mother had followed him only two years later. After that there was nothing to keep him in the old place. It was sad that Sally had waltzed off with so much of the profit from the sale, but in a way it was a good thing. It kept him grounded and it had in the end brought him back to the soil he loved so much. Nowadays he was happy to pour his love into other people's gardens; his own little yard was perfect when he returned home too tired to lift a finger. He had collected some old terracotta pots and olive jars and nurtured a few highly coloured tumbling plants to brighten the wooden seat which was placed in the sunny corner. That was all he needed.

He turned and surveyed his bookshelves in search of a volume on local history that he wanted to lend to Andy. He scanned the titles ruefully. He should have sorted them out by now, but he loved them like that, all jumbled together. It meant when he was looking for something he could be distracted by something else.

As had happened a couple of hours ago when he had pulled out a book on dysfunctional psychology. It secretly pleased him that his clients had no idea their gardener had been a practising psychologist. None of them had ever thought to ask – and why should they? He smiled to himself. Psychology was a deep and enduring interest, but not, he had discovered, one he wanted to spend his life pursuing. Obviously when push came to shove you couldn't take the land out of the boy, however hard you tried. With his marriage over, so was his career. He only had to support himself now, and he had decided it was time to please himself and go back to gardens.

Opening the door he walked outside and sat down in the sheltered patch of sunshine with his mug. There were already four books stacked on the small round table out there, together with the Sunday papers. Normally that would have kept him happy for several hours, but today he was restless. The way Rhona Wilson had attacked Andy and later brazenly accosted him in the pub had filled him with foreboding. She had obviously followed him from Sleeper's Castle; thank goodness he had not come straight home or she would know where he lived.

He glanced at the top book on his pile. It was a survey of socio-pathic behaviour in women. Rhona's behaviour had rung warning bells with him from day one. Such calculated actions, to the extent of tracking Andy to Wales and following her, possibly with the intention of harming her, would almost certainly be part of a pattern, a pathology, maybe even dating back to childhood. His years of experience had not deserted him and he trusted his instincts. He reached for the book, took a sip from his cup and settled down to read.

Rufus took his daughter out to lunch at the River Café. He was still worrying about leaving her alone.

'I told you, Daddy, I'm fine.' She sounded irritated. 'I have friends if I need anyone; I am in control of the situation; I have work to do, proper painting work, and I'm looking forward to a lovely stay here.'

'And Rhona?'

'I keep telling you: Rhona will get bored. She'll get another bee in her bonnet. The moment we get a few days of really bad weather she'll be off, if she hasn't gone already. Why on earth should she waste precious time stalking me?'

Rufus didn't answer. To him the answer was obvious: the woman was a jealous obsessive. Andy was being disingenuous at best, blind at worst, about what was going on. He sighed. 'I'm so sorry I have to go this afternoon. If there was any way I could cancel those meetings next week I would. It's only that—'

'I know!' She leaned forward and tapped him on the arm. 'Don't worry. I know I have a famous architect for a father and buildings would fall down all over the north of England if he wasn't there to monitor things.'

He laughed. 'I wouldn't put it quite like that.'

'I would. And you have another family waiting for you up there. They need you. I'm grown up, Daddy. I'm supposed to be able to cope on my own. But' – she held up her hand as he

367

opened his mouth to protest – 'I also know I can ring you. And if I need you, I will, I promise.'

They had not mentioned the night before. She had travelled into the past alone while he had slept untroubled on the sofa. When she awoke much later she found he had covered her with a rug and gone up to bed. She didn't know how anguished he had been as he stood looking down at her, knowing she was far away, unable to follow her.

She held it together until he left at teatime, then she locked all the doors and cried.

Instead of making her feel secure, locking herself in gave her a sense of claustrophobia. She walked backwards and forwards round the ground floor, then opened the back door again and called into the garden for Pepper. He had obviously not approved of her father and had made himself scarce most of the time Rufus was staying there, but now, as if knowing that the coast was clear, he appeared almost at once.

Half an hour later she rang Sian, who arrived at seven with an Indian takeaway. 'So, how are your various wounds?' Sian doled out the assorted cartons on the table, poured some wine and produced a bag containing two poppadums.

'I'm better. Much better.' Andy reached for a glass and raised it in a toast. 'You are an angel. I can get around now; but I've been relying on my dad to drive me everywhere for the last two days and it gave me the chance to heal. I'm missing him already.'

'I thought you might be.' Sian broke her poppadum in half with a loud snap. 'So I have a bit of news for you. Meryn is back. He rang me yesterday to see how you were and find out when your dad was leaving. I don't think he wanted to tread on his toes. So, I wondered if you would like me to drive you up to Meryn's tomorrow. I can drop you off and he will bring you home.'

'That would be marvellous. There's so much I want to discuss with him.' Andy heard herself give a contented sigh.

Behind them the cat flap clicked. Pepper jumped through and stopped dead, glaring at Sian.

Andy watched Pepper stalk across to his empty bowl, inspect it, then turn and head towards his chair. 'He didn't like my dad being here. We saw almost nothing of him.'

'Another male on his territory, I expect.' Sian put down her fork. 'This is gorgeous, but maybe I chose something a bit too hot! How are you doing?'

'I love it.' Andy leaned forward. 'Graham and I had a lot of curries in Kew. It was a bit of a fetish of ours.' She paused, lost in her memories. Pushing them away firmly she stood up. 'If you clear the plates and dig in the freezer for some ice cream I will get my laptop. I have lots of books on Glyndŵr now, but I have to confess I hadn't thought of looking up Sleeper's Castle on the Internet.'

She found it in a catalogue of listed buildings.

There was a short paragraph:

Medieval fortified farmhouse with possible 14th–15th-century origins. Added 18th-century service wing, possibly on earlier foundations. Stone-tiled roof; two storey. Some window apertures original with heavy oak or stone mullions. Front door original with heavy chamfered oak frame, stone label, cambered inner arch, old oak door. Stone floors and part of roof original with stout purlins. Chamfered ceiling beams to inner rooms. Remnants of larger building footprint, possibly destroyed as early as 15th century.

'That's all.' Andy pushed the laptop across the table towards Sian.

'It doesn't say who lived here or if it belonged to a particular family. I don't suppose anyone knew what happened up here. It's pretty remote,' Sian said after scanning the screen.

'But so are lots of houses round here. I get the impression . . .' Andy hesitated. 'From my dreams, I get the impression that news travelled pretty fast. It's hard to imagine life without radio, phones and the Internet. Already we're forgetting what it was like even ten years ago! But the people were still interested, still curious, still afraid of what might happen next, they still loved gossip and people travelled a lot from house to house and even if it was only at the market once a week, they still kept pretty much up with the news. People would have known.'

'Much like today,' Sian put in. 'Have you heard the chat that goes on down at the market on Thursdays? That market has been there for hundreds of years. Well, presumably it is in essence the same market that Catrin would have known. It makes me smile sometimes when I'm wandering round it. I can picture the women in long dresses and poke bonnets with baskets on their arms with the farmers leaning on the stalls, smoking clay pipes, with their dogs at their feet – and everyone talking nineteen to the dozen, all in the shadow of that great castle.' She glanced up. 'You're tired, Andy. I should go.'

'No . . . sorry. I was thinking about Catrin in the market.' Andy stood up. 'Would you like a cup of coffee? It's my turn to do something. I can hobble round perfectly serviceably. In fact, it's scarcely a hobble any more, thanks to Meryn's magic mixture.'

Sian shook her head. 'No, thanks, I must go. The dogs have been on their own a lot today and they deserve a quick walk before bed. And for the record, I think you will find it's Sue's magic mixture, not Meryn's. He's not into herbal medicine, apart from using it, of course. What time would you like me to collect you tomorrow . . . ?'

It was a cold clear night. As Andy stood at the top of the steps, waving after Sian's car as it disappeared down the lane, she shivered. One of these days she was going to wake up to find the countryside covered in frost. She glanced up at the sky. Cassiopeia was still shining as brightly, a huge W in the sky overhead. The silence round her was intense. She had already learned to fade out the sound of the brook tumbling down its rocks as she listened for the call of an owl. Almost on cue she heard it, far away in the valley, a long quavering hoot, the reply coming from far closer, the sharp, echoing 'quick, quick' of its mate somewhere in the field across the lane.

And then in the distance she heard the sound of a woman's voice, crying.

'*Tad, Tad*, where are you?'

The only answer was the rustle of leaves as an icy breeze swept up the valley from the north.

24

The horses and the mule had gone. The stable door was open and there was no sign of them. 'How could they!' Joan was white with rage. 'What use would little horses like that be to those great soldiers?'

She had chivvied Catrin into giving up her futile search in the dark for her father, to help her find enough dry hay in the barn to make new mattresses. 'He'll turn up, you know he will. He's a wily old bird. He won't have got caught.'

But that was what they both feared. Had the men run into Dafydd as they left the house?

Joan had piled the soiled bedding in a heap on the ruined vegetable beds and set fire to it, even to Catrin's embroidered bedcovers. They stood and watched as the flames soared into the night sky. 'Perhaps the sight of that will bring him home,' Joan commented tartly. She glanced at Catrin, who was standing there numbly, watching the pall of bitter smoke rising from the stinking bed linen. 'And Betsi and Megan and Peter. I hope they're all right.'

'Do you think they'll come back?' Catrin murmured at last.

'Of course they will.'

'Betsi and Peter have always been loyal to us,' she said doubtfully.

'And I'm sure they're still loyal,' Joan replied stoutly. 'They'll be back soon, you'll see.'

They surveyed the fire in silence.

'At least the mattresses burn well,' Catrin said with a sigh.

'And it will take us no time at all to run up something makeshift out of rugs to replace them,' Joan said. 'Thank our Blessed Lady they didn't fire the barn, because that has enough dry hay to stuff them with ten times over. We will get through this, Catrin. And they didn't fire the hayricks either so be thankful for what they did not do.'

As they watched the flames die down, Catrin shuddered. 'Why? Why did they do that? We have never harmed anyone. We are a peaceful family.'

Joan turned to her, her eyes wide. 'Catrin! Your father is a poet, a bard, a seer. They are banned! He supports the rebels. Everyone knows that. He may not pick up a sword himself, but he exhorts others to follow his precious prince!' Her voice was heavy with sarcasm. 'Come on, can you really be so simple?'

'Then if we are so dangerous, why do you work for us?'

'I don't know,' Joan replied tartly. 'Maybe because I need the money.'

Catrin didn't reply. She stood watching the bonfire until it was no more than smoking ash, then she turned away without a word. It was then that she saw the figure standing by the paddock gate watching them. Her father was holding one of the horses by its reins.

'*Tad!*' she gasped.

Dafydd began to walk forward, dragging the unwilling pony with him.

'How much damage did they do?' he asked, barely looking at her.

'They smashed everything!' Catrin found the tears running down her face again as she ran towards him. 'It was awful. We hid in the cave, but they destroyed everything. They wrecked your study.' She was expecting him to hold out his arms for her to rush into, but he stood rigid, looking straight past her. 'My study?' he repeated the words, his voice cracked with emotion. He dropped the reins and walked stiffly towards the house, ignoring Catrin completely.

Joan was watching. She ran to catch the pony. 'I will put her in the paddock. You go with your father,' she said.

Catrin followed Dafydd inside, watching as he picked his way across the devastation of the kitchen without seeming to notice and walked slowly across the hall. There was less damage there as there was less to be damaged. The ashes of the fire were scattered around, a stool smashed against the wall, the cushions and smaller wall hangings torn and trampled by muddy boots, the doors of the aumbry hanging open with the scatter of the broken glass, but the benches and the high-backed settle against the wall and the table were undamaged. In the doorway to his study he stopped and looked round slowly at the broken desk, the scattered, damaged books, the charred pages littering the floor, the feathers from his cushions scattered all over the room, ink spilled and spattered everywhere. His face was white. Catrin could feel the hard knot of grief like a lump in her chest. 'I am so sorry. There was nothing we could do. We hid,' she whispered.

He turned away and walked back towards the hearth in the hall. 'Were you hurt?' he asked at last. His voice was flat and unemotional.

'No. I told you. We hid. Where were you, *Tad*?'

'When I heard them coming I took the pony and rode up into the hills.' He was rubbing his hands together slowly as if to try and warm them.

'Why did you not warn us?' she asked softly.

'I knew you would be all right.' Still he did not look at her. He seemed to be studying the cold ash which was all that remained of the fire. 'Why don't you get Joan to light this? The house is cold!'

'Of course, *Tad*. I will ask her.' Catrin moved away towards the kitchen. Had he even given them a thought, she wondered as she went through into the kitchen. There was no fire left alight save out in the garden. She scrabbled through the cooking implements, looking for flint and tinder, but when she found them her hands were shaking too much to strike them. Joan took them from her and lit the fire in the kitchen hearth. She had swilled out the pot and filled it with water from the brook. Hanging it on the trivet she pushed Catrin towards one of the stools, which she had set upright by the table. 'I'll brew some camomile to soothe you.'

'My *tad* wants the fire lit next door,' Catrin said slowly. Her teeth had begun to chatter.

'Let him wait.' Joan went to the pantry and pulled open the door and murmured a prayer of gratitude. In their rush to destroy the kitchen, they seemed to have missed it. The crocks of flour and oatmeal were still there, undamaged. The slabs of cheese and butter, the jugs of oil, the boxes of dried fruits and the barrel of salt fish. Even her loaves of bread from her last baking were still there.

She moved to the buttery. That had fared worse. All the ale and cider had gone, and the wine, but the herbs were still there, hanging in their linen bags from the high beam. She brought out one of them and crumbled a handful of brittle orange heads into a pewter jug. She bent to pick up some smashed shards of pottery from the floor, studying them sadly. They had once formed part of a pretty fruit bowl.

'You should go home, Joan. To your father. You cannot want to stay here with us,' Catrin murmured.

'And why not? I doubt you two are capable of sorting all this mess out by yourselves,' Joan retorted.

'Catrin?' Dafydd's voice echoed through the doorway.

'You stay here.' Joan put her hand on Catrin's shoulder as she made to stand up. 'I will see to it.' The jar of tapers on a high shelf near the window had escaped their attentions as well, Taking one she lit it and walked out through the door.

Catrin slumped across the table and put her head in her arms. She was too weary and miserable to move. Only when Joan returned did she raise her head.

Joan was smiling. 'One piece of good news. They did not find your harp,' she said. 'You had left it in the corner of the great hall and they failed to see it in the shadows.' She pushed back her sleeves. 'Your father is by the fire through there. There were enough logs to build it up. I will go out to the store by and by and fetch more. He had his cloak with him so he's warm enough.' She grimaced. 'He even had time to grab that before he fled.'

'Is the pony all right?' Catrin asked wearily. Even the news about her harp didn't cheer her.

Joan nodded. 'The other two are there too. He left the gate open when he rode out and they strayed. That saved them. They're all back together now.' She poured boiling water into the jug, then set it to steep. 'I will fetch some hay in a while and we can stitch up a couple of mattresses. Luckily there is plenty of sacking in the barn. They did not touch your drying herbs either.' She glanced up. The bunches of lavender and lovage, meadowsweet and pennyroyal were still hanging from the kitchen ceiling. She smiled. 'You'll not mind sharing a rug or two from the barn? Whatever they smell of, it would be better than what your own smelt of before we burned them. You rest now and I will make a start on cleaning up all this mess.' She looked round and wrinkled her nose.

'Catrin!' Again the voice from next door, irritated and impatient; Joan put out her hand. 'Stay where you are. I will go.' She stood up with a sigh.

The fire was burning quietly with only the occasional crack and snap of logs when the back door slowly creaked open. Catrin sat up abruptly, frightened. 'Who is it?' she cried.

One of the farm cats put its head round the door and surveyed the room. It crept in, keeping an eye on her as it headed towards a splash of spilled stew on the floor. It seized a piece of cold mutton and turning ran outside again with its prize.

Catrin gave an exhausted smile. At least someone had benefitted from the afternoon's work.

Sian picked Andy up the next morning shortly after ten. It was a glorious sunny day, the air cold and fresh, the visibility as she climbed out of Sian's car and stood outside Meryn's cottage seeming to go on forever as she surveyed the view across the foothills, the Wye Valley and on towards the Radnor Forest. Elfael.

Sian didn't come in with her. As she turned the car and drove off, Meryn opened the door. 'You look much recovered,' he said as he pointed her towards an armchair near the fire. It was obviously newly lit and the room was full of the sweet spicy smell of burning apple. Andy leaned back in the chair and relaxed. She had woken after her dream, unable to shrug it off, convinced she would find the house trashed, expecting to smell burnt parchment and soldiers' piss as she walked slowly from room to room. The bright clean bedrooms and the tidy ground floor, the cold early sunlight finding its way through the windows seemed unreal; it was the dream that had been authentic. She had been disorientated and upset and Pepper had refused to come near her, viewing her through huge, suspicious eyes and fleeing out of the cat flap when she bent to pick him up.

She told Meryn everything. He listened without comment, sitting opposite her, leaning forward in his chair, his eyes fixed on her face.

'Glyndŵr was a fascinating man. And you have had the enormous privilege of meeting him and witnessing his world,' he said when she had finished. 'To travel into the past like this is an experience dreamed of by historians. But we have to consider the risks.'

Reaching out towards her he took her hands. He turned them palm up and studied them.

'Did you touch anything in your dream?'

'Touch anything?' she echoed, confused.

'Did you follow Catrin round the room? Did you try to help her? Did you run your fingers over any surfaces, reach out to touch her, to comfort her? Did you sit down with them to eat the food?'

Andy shook her head slowly. 'No. I was only watching them.'

'You can smell what they smell.'

'Yes.' She made a wry face.

'Can you feel the heat of the fire?'

'Yes.'

'Can you taste anything while you are watching? The bitterness of ash or the acidity of urine in the air, for instance?'

She hesitated. 'Taste and smell are so close.' She shuddered. 'Indeed.'

'This is important, isn't it?'

'It helps me work out what is happening to you.'

'So they aren't just dreams? What I am seeing is real?'

'I believe so, yes.' He thought briefly. 'I remember being told something of that house's fascinating history. As you know, its reputation goes back centuries. From what you seem to be saying, it was Catrin's house, or the house of her ancestors and yet it is her father who is the bard.

'Bards in Wales had a special place,' he continued. 'They were genealogists and historians to the people. People's ancestors mattered. They linked them together from the highest to the lowest. They were kin. I think you said Dafydd toured the houses of his patrons each summer?'

She gave a quick nod.

'That was the way it worked, the way they earned their living. They told the past, they foretold the future. Glyndŵr had a favourite bard, a man called Iolo Goch, I looked it up. Owain was a famously superstitious man and consulted bards and seers wherever he went. He had magic crystals and at one point a stone which could, so the story goes, make him disappear.'

'Superstitious?'

'Ah, you are right to query my use of the word. An anachronism. Most people were what our age would call superstitious in medieval times. I believe one of the kings – it may even have been Henry IV – had a man put to death because his claim to be a seer was reckoned to be false; his predictions did not come true. One had to have a certain success rate to be credible!'

'I wonder why Catrin's mother fell for Dafydd.'

'Who knows? Her father can't have been enchanted with the idea of a penniless bard as a son-in-law. Perhaps he wasn't penniless though. Perhaps he was a successful poet, like Iolo. After all, they lived off the rewards of their trade: gifts from their patrons. So, perhaps Catrin's father really was enchanted. These guys weren't above a bit of magic here and there.'

'Weather magic too,' Andy murmured.

'Of which Glyndŵr was said to be a master,' Meryn smiled gravely. 'Or so the English said. They didn't seem to be able to believe that Welsh weather could be that bad all on its own. They were convinced the weather was colluding with the rebels.'

'Whereas I know, or suspect, that it was Catrin who taught Owain's daughters, and they in turn taught him. Does that make her his weather consultant? You know more about all this than I do,' Andy said. 'I'm beginning to feel very ignorant, in spite of reading the books.'

'You'll get there.' He leant forward and threw a log from the basket on to the fire. 'Weather witching is a fascinating topic. It veers from local folklore to the invocation of ancient gods and elementals and nature spirits, a practice involving what we might call high magic. A serious subject, to be studied and learned in every period of history and in every nation of the world. Now we rely on the Met Office. Far less glamorous, but probably no more accurate.' He smiled.

He sat back in his chair again. 'So, your father has been here. How did his visit go?'

'It was lovely to see him again. He was intrigued by my

dreams about Catrin, but he couldn't tell me how to switch off.' She glanced up and pulled a wry face. 'He didn't know how. He could feel the atmosphere at Sleeper's, but I think he's forgotten much of what we used to do together. It was when I was a child after all. He's had other children since then.'

'Do you get on with your half-brothers and half-sisters?' Meryn leaned back in his chair. He looked at her over steepled fingers.

'Half-brothers.' She smiled. 'Oh yes, we get on quite well. But they're much younger than me, and we don't see each other very often. And we don't have much in common, to be honest, beyond sharing a father.'

'That is quite an important link.'

'I suppose so.'

'Was he worried by your activities at Sleeper's Castle?'

She nodded. 'Although he was more worried by Rhona, if I'm honest. We talked a lot about the dreams and the ghosts, but,' she hesitated. 'He said it was something he enjoyed sharing with me when I was a child. He said he made a lot of it up.' She looked up and he saw the bleakness of betrayal in her eyes. 'I believed him. What I thought we used to do together, the dreaming, the travelling into the dreams, the ghost-hunting, it was all pretend. He's obviously very sensitive to atmosphere and he knows a lot about old houses,' she added almost hopefully, 'but he said to ask you about the rest. Apparently Bryn told him you were trustworthy.' She gave a sheepish grin. 'What he really wanted was for me to go home with him. He thought I'd be safer there.'

Meryn chuckled. 'Remind me to thank Bryn for the reference.' He cleared his throat. 'Your father's probably right on that last point.'

She glanced at him ruefully. 'Well, I told him I was staying. I want to know what happens. And besides, I didn't want him to feel he had to cancel his meetings to entertain his loopy daughter.'

Meryn smiled sympathetically. 'As a matter of interest, do you think you are loopy?'

'No!' She was indignant. 'Well,' she added as an afterthought, 'I wouldn't necessarily tell anyone else about what is happening. Just you and Sian.'

'If it helps, I don't think you are loopy. But I do think you need to learn some basic rules fairly urgently. So, what I am going to say next is something you must take on board. You must not, Andy, in future, touch anything or anyone when you are dreaming. You are an observer. A voyeur, if you will, you are not a participant. I am concerned that if you physically touch something, you could ground yourself in the dream space. You haven't, as yet, but as you become more involved with Catrin's story, the temptation might arise. I've been thinking about your experiences and your response to the situation, and I want you to be able to continue as long as you want to, but safely. You must not risk this becoming an obsession, and you must not, ever, risk getting pulled into the past.'

'You mean I could get stuck there?'

'That is exactly what I mean. I think it unlikely—'

'But I could interfere with . . .' she paused, grappling for the right word.

'What they call the "space-time continuum" in science fiction movies? Exactly.' He smiled. 'I don't think you would get stuck. I think you would in the end revert to normal sleep patterns and "surface" slowly the next morning, but we don't want you to lose control of the situation. So, that is my first lesson. Don't touch.' He stood up. 'I take it a coffee wouldn't come amiss? I think we've covered all we need to for now.'

She looked at him, askance. 'That's it?'

'That's it.'

She opened her mouth to argue, but he was already on his way out of the room.

She sat back, feeling obscurely cheated, surveying the room, noting the table, the books and papers, the laptop, closed but plugged into its charger. There was an umbrella stand by the door, with its quota of thumb sticks, walking sticks and even a huge umbrella. Was his Druid staff hidden amongst them? She smiled at the thought. Through the window she could see a small gnarled rowan tree, the branches heavy with scarlet berries. There was a vase of wild flowers on the table, and a couch with a pile of old tapestry-covered cushions in the corner. She focused on the cushions, a feminine touch in the very masculine room, and wondered idly if he had ever been married.

He returned with a tray. The plate of home-made biscuits suggested that he was either a cook or he had been down to Hay that morning. 'The answer is no, no one would have me,' he said, amused, as he put down the tray.

She blushed. 'How did you know what I was thinking?'

'Ah, haven't you heard of my reputation as a wizard? And I'm a mind-reader as well!' He handed her a mug of coffee. 'Don't be embarrassed. Women often look round my house and ask themselves that question. I can't think why.' He sat down again, pushing the plates towards her.

'If you can't think why, you can't be completely all-seeing and all-knowing.'

'Touché.' He laughed.

'Which is a tiny bit comforting.'

'Sorry. Was I lecturing before? I am so used to doing it.'

'And you're good at it. It's reassuring to talk to someone who knows their stuff and believes in a life beyond the mundane. I have for so long lived with a man who rubbished anything even slightly out of the ordinary.' She hesitated. 'I know the lesson is over, but can I ask one more thing? I've noticed: these dream experiences are becoming more and more intense; more real. Is that because I'm getting used to it? Practice makes perfect.'

'Maybe.'

'They are not just dreams, are they? We're calling them dreams, but somehow they're more than that.'

'We could call it time travel.'

'Does that mean it's all still happening?'

'In a way, yes.'

'But it can't be changed.'

He looked quizzical for a moment. 'For the purposes of this discussion, probably not.'

Getting to his feet he bent to pick another log out of the basket and throw it on the fire. There was a loud crack and a roar of flame. A shower of sparks flew up the chimney.

He picked up the poker and pushed the logs back. 'Have you seen any more of the fearsome Rhona?' he asked without turning round.

'No, but Bryn has. She accosted him in a pub. She's still in the area.'

'I am sorry. You don't need the extra worry of that woman on your heels all the time.' He went back to his chair.

Andy was staring into the fire. 'You couldn't turn her into a toad or something, could you? Or even better, make her disappear in a puff of smoke.'

He laughed quietly. 'I think you're muddling me up with a witch.'

'Didn't you just say you were a wizard? I thought that was a male witch.'

'My mistake.' He sighed. 'I'm afraid making people disappear is against the moral code expected of wizards these days. Doesn't it explain that somewhere in *Harry Potter*?'

'You didn't go to Hogwarts?'

He laughed. 'I would hate to tell you where I went to school.'

'Why?'

'I prefer to give the impression that I leapt fully formed from my mother's womb.'

She laughed with him. 'OK. I'll have to guess.' She put her head on one side. 'Someone told me you were Scots.'

'No. I'm Welsh born and bred.'

She wouldn't let it go. 'So, there is a mystery here. Let me guess. I bet you went to Eton.'

'No, but you're not far off.' He gave a chuckle. 'Winchester, if you must know. And yes, Oxford. I'm sorry. I put my hand up to being a posh boy. Once, a long time ago. It does my street cred no good at all. I would prefer it if a rumour went round that I attended Hogwarts.'

'OK. Your secret is safe with me.' She sighed. 'Meryn, Sian said you wouldn't mind driving me home.'

'Are you worried it will be on the back of my broomstick?' He stood up.

'If it is, I'm sure you won't let me fall off.'

In the event he drove a battered Fourtrak which had been parked round the back of the cottage. Andy surveyed it critically as he opened the door for her. 'This looks old enough to have been around in the days of Glyndŵr.'

'Ouch!' He laughed out loud. 'Is that a gentle hint that I should upgrade?'

She was laughing quietly to herself as she climbed in.

Meryn followed her indoors and went with her as far as the kitchen, pushing her gently into a chair with an admonition to rest her foot, but declining her offer of food.

'I need to work.' He hesitated. 'Take care, Andy, and please, please, please watch out for Rhona. I have a bad feeling about that woman. Alas, one cannot dismiss her as a dream. She is all too real, I fear.'

Having bolted the door behind him, Andy turned to find Pepper watching her expectantly from his perch on the edge of the table. 'I'm afraid he couldn't stay,' she said, hearing the disappointment in her own voice as she spoke. 'You trust him too, don't you.'

Rhona had spotted the old Fourtrak up at the top of the hill near the cattle grid. Miranda was the passenger. Neither she nor the man driving had noticed her and she had set off after them with interest. She slowed to a standstill in the lane round the corner from Sleeper's Castle, cut the engine and allowed her car to creep forward on the brake. He had pulled into the parking place beside the Passat and she watched as he walked round and opened the door for Miranda. He helped her out and she saw Miranda leaning heavily on his arm as he helped her up the steps to the front door. Rhona smiled in satisfaction. Miranda's ankle was obviously still giving her trouble.

The man reappeared a few minutes later and climbed back into the car. Not Miranda's father, who had left the day before; someone else. A stranger. So, the bitch had betrayed Graham's memory with another man beside the gardener.

Ignoring the temptation to follow him she pulled into a farm gate a quarter of a mile up the road from Sleeper's Castle, tucking the car in to the hedge well out of sight, then she retraced her steps down the lane. It was hard to approach the house without being seen. It stood up over the road and the front garden and it was impossible to guess whether someone was looking out of the windows, but she risked it, running up the steps and ducking round the side where she crouched close to the wall, her heart thudding with exertion and excitement.

The garden was alive with movement. The bushes and trees were swaying and rustling in the wind and she could hear the roar of water from the brook that ran under the road outside the house. It was an elemental place, full of energy. Slowly she stood up and peered in at the window beside her. The room was empty, small, seemingly unused. She felt a prickling in her fingers and she glanced down at her hands, which were clutching the windowsill. It was almost as if the stone was giving off small electric shocks. She let go hastily and rubbed her hands on the front of her jacket, then she tiptoed on, turning the corner to look along the back of the house. There were lights on here. She felt another rush of excitement and crept on.

The first window she came to looked into an enormous shadowy room, lit by several lamps. Although it was almost midday the garden was dull. It was beginning to spot with rain. The room had a heavily beamed ceiling. Judging by the positioning of the furniture the fireplace was on the wall near her and now she studied the layout of this back elevation of the

house she saw the huge stone chimney beside her. There was no one in the room but the lamps gave the impression that it was in use and at any moment someone – Miranda – might walk in. She peered round the chimney stack and began to make her way onward towards the next set of windows. Above her the clouds were thickening and the rain was growing heavier. She smiled to herself. She could feel the tension rising. Miranda was very close.

25

Andy was sitting at the kitchen table staring at her emails. She couldn't believe what she had just read. It was from her agent, Krista.

Sit down, Andy. And take a deep breath. I've been trying to ring you – don't you ever turn on your mobile? Listen to this. A friend of Graham's called Donald O'Sullivan has contacted me, looking for you. He's been in the States for the past year and didn't know that Graham had died. He was devastated to hear the news and couldn't understand why you hadn't been in touch and weren't in Kew any more. I explained the situation and – guess what? You are not going to believe this! – He was one of the people who witnessed Graham's will! <u>And he has a copy</u>!!! Why are you not answering your phone? <u>Call me!</u>

Andy stared at the screen. Don O'Sullivan. Why hadn't she told Don that Graham had died? She hadn't told all kinds of people because their addresses had been hidden away in Graham's study and presumably destroyed on Rhona's bonfire. Don had been a good friend, one of their best friends. But friends sometimes get put on hold if they go away; they always pick up where they left off later, when they come back; that's what friends do. Don! She took a deep breath and picked up the phone.

Her new mobile was sitting there on the side. She had changed her number, for obvious reasons, and hadn't told more than a handful of people yet. She should have told her agent, for goodness' sake. What was she thinking? And how many other people had been trying to get in touch with her?

'Krista? I'm sorry. I lost my mobile. Let me give you my new number and then you can tell me how I can contact Don.'

When she had finished talking to Krista, and to Don and to her new solicitor as recommended by Krista, Andy sat for a long time staring into space, exhausted by the enormity of what had happened. It had been so unexpected; so potentially life changing. She hadn't realised how lost she had been when she had first arrived at Sleeper's Castle, or how much she had invested emotionally in this place since. Now suddenly she was in danger of being dragged back to Kew again. Her home had been there, on the other side of the country, all her memories, everything she loved. Rhona would be evicted and Andy would be the owner of a two-million-pound house. But was that what she wanted?

Pepper had jumped on the table and was sitting, watching her intently. He disliked it when she was on the telephone. It meant her attention was elsewhere. It sometimes meant she had not even noticed him. She reached out and scratched his ears. 'Now what do I do?' she said quietly. There was nothing she could do. It was in the hands of the solicitors now. She sighed. Rhona had no idea of the tsunami that was about to hit her. She was away. That was all Andy could tell them: that she had good reason to suspect the woman was touring in the Welsh borders. She didn't know Rhona's mobile number, she had never thought to make a note of it.

The house was very quiet. She got up and glanced out of

the kitchen window. The garden seemed very empty. There had been no sign of Bryn today and she found herself wishing she could see him out there amongst the herbs. He would be a good person to talk to, she realised, and she needed to talk to someone. Her father would be tied up in meetings until the evening, she could phone him then. Her mother always taught in the afternoons, so her phone would be switched off until after six. Meryn had made it clear he was busy. Sian had gone into Hereford for the day. There was no one she could confide in.

She turned away from the window impatiently. 'So, Pepper my friend. What do you think I should do?' She frowned. He had gone. She hadn't heard the cat flap so he must have gone upstairs to make himself comfortable on one of the beds. She wandered through into the hall and stopped abruptly. She could smell smoke.

The hearth was empty. The room was very cold. 'Catrin?' she called softly. 'Are you there?'

Catrin was standing in the doorway, watching her, a perplexed expression on her face. She was holding on to a heavy curtain, which was half drawn across the doorway. Andy frowned. Where had that curtain come from?

She stepped closer. Catrin smiled at her and put her finger to her lips as a voice rang out behind her. 'Catrin? Where are you? I need you!'

It was the voice of Dafydd and it was very close.

Andy froze.

'Catrin!' he called again. 'I need ink and parchment. I need a new wax tablet for notes. I need new candles. Where are you?'

Catrin had tied an apron over her skirt; she had been working since daybreak, cleaning her father's study, sweeping the ashes, scrubbing the flags, collecting any scraps of parchment which could be rescued from the fire and reused, and taking the others outside to burn later. She was exhausted but still he stood there giving orders, making no effort to help her. Joan was upstairs, cleaning the bedrooms. Betsi and Megan had returned with Peter, nervously creeping back from their hiding place in the hills as dawn broke the morning after the raid. The girls were helping Joan; Peter was working in the ruins of the garden.

Catrin bent to drag a coffer away from the wall to sweep behind it. 'Stop!' Dafydd cried. 'Don't touch that.'

'There is dust and ash behind it, *Tad*,' she retorted wearily.

'I told you not to touch it!' he repeated, his voice harsh. She ignored him, edging it away from the wall. A loose flagstone was catching beneath one of the feet. It rattled out of place and revealed a hollow beneath it. 'Don't you dare touch that!' Dafydd cried. 'Leave it, Catrin, it is none of your business.'

She gave him a piercing look and dropping to her knees she dragged aside the flagstone. A small box had been hidden there. She was past listening to him. She lifted it out, astonished at its weight and opened the lid. It was full of coins.

Dafydd was apoplectic with rage. His face went crimson as he lunged towards her. She scrambled to her feet and staggered with the box over to the table; it was so heavy she could barely carry it. 'How much is in here?' she asked, her voice dangerously low. 'You make us live like paupers; you tell me I have to sell my necklace to pay for repairs, you forbid me to have new glass in my window and all the while you have money hidden here!'

He scrabbled the coins she had spilled back into the box and slammed the lid shut. 'That is for when I can no longer work. You know Henry of Lancaster has passed a law in his parliament forbidding payment to minstrels and poets in Wales. He means to punish us for the rebellion, which he blames on us. Soon I will have nothing,' he whined, picking up the box and clutching it to his chest.

Catrin looked at him in despair. 'How much is in there? I saw old florins, nobles. *Tad*, it is a fortune!'

He knelt and replaced the box in the hole. Then he dragged

the coffer back across it and pushed it hard against the wall. Catrin noticed he had no difficulty with its weight, though she had struggled to move it.

'Where is that stupid woman who works in the kitchen?' he asked brusquely.

'You mean Joan?' Catrin asked coldly. 'She is upstairs.'

'Good. I don't want her knowing about this. If she finds out, she will blab to the world and we will be murdered in our beds by thieves.'

'We were nearly murdered in our beds yesterday,' Catrin retorted. Her fury was making her tremble as she stood before him.

'Rubbish. All they did was mess the place up a bit.' He sat down on his high stool in front of the desk, nailed back together by Peter, as if to prove that everything was back to normal. 'Go and find me some parchment, Catrin.'

She stared at him. 'And where am I supposed to find parchment? You think I have reams of it stashed away in my bedroom?' She broke off, appalled. Did he know about her own new writings? She had one or two precious pieces of blank parchment saved, but she was not inclined now to give them to him. Her need was as great as his. She had begun, she realised, to despise him.

She dusted down her apron and stood looking at him for a few moments. He ignored her. 'I will go and help Joan upstairs,' she said quietly. 'On the next market day I will go down to Hay and see if there is parchment to be had. You will have to give me the money for it. I have none.' She turned and walked out of the room.

She found Joan in the garden, surveying the wreckage of their vegetable beds. 'At least the ponies are safe,' she called to Catrin over her shoulder. 'And the sheep in the top field and the pig. They didn't find them. And most of the hens are here. No eggs though. All this has upset them. I still thank the Blessed Virgin they did not fire the ricks.'

'What are we going to do for food?' said Catrin, coming to stand beside her.

'You will have to buy something in.'

Catrin glanced at her. Joan seemed to assume they would have the money. 'Did you know my father can no longer be paid for his songs and his poetry? King Henry has forbidden it. He thinks poets and minstrels spread sedition.'

Joan gave a hollow laugh. 'And don't they?' When no answer was forthcoming she went on: 'You know men will still pay him. People will ignore what parliament says as they always have. There is no rule of law in Wales any more.' She sniffed. 'He must have money hidden away,' she went on. 'It's not as though he spends anything on the house.'

Catrin tensed. What had she seen? Then she relaxed. Joan was an intelligent woman. She used her eyes. She must have realised her employer was a miserly skinflint. He would hardly travel the length and breadth of Wales every year unless he was well paid by his patrons. She sighed. 'I will see if I can get him to find a few coins,' she said meekly. 'But everyone is in the same boat. The armies have laid waste to crops and driven off livestock all over the country. The pedlar who came selling ribbons last week said as much.' She paused sadly, thinking of the futility of buying a few ribbons and how happy she had been with her lovely pieces of red silk.

'He said there would be famine this winter,' Joan pointed out gloomily. 'The Welsh forces burn the fields to punish the English farmers, and the English soldiers burn the fields to starve out the rebels. It doesn't matter which side does it, the result is the same. The people starve. It is always the people who suffer. King Henry's lords and knights can ride back to London. Everyone is rich in London. Everyone eats well there.' Her voice was bitter.

Catrin had never been to London, but somehow she doubted that what Joan said was entirely true. Speculation would do nothing to solve their present problem though. She walked over to the paddock. Her pony was leaning over the gate, watching them. She rubbed the little mare's face gently. 'I hope we don't have to sell you, *cariad*,' she murmured. 'That would break my heart.'

Slowly they were replenishing the pantry. Between them they had managed to harvest a few vegetables from the ruins of the garden beds; they gathered hazelnuts, blackberries and sloes from the hedgerows as they did every year, there were apples and pears and Peter as usual brought fish from the brook for Joan to salt down. In the end Dafydd reluctantly produced a handful of silver coin and the next market day Catrin and Joan took the pony and the mule down to Hay with empty panniers, hoping to buy at least a few basic supplies. It was pouring with rain and the tracks were slick with mud. They were soaked before they were halfway there. The market was less full than usual. People were scanning the half-empty stalls anxiously, without their usual banter and laughter. The army marching through the town towards Brecon had frightened everyone. Catrin was uncomfortable. She felt eyes watching her. Stallholders served her but there were no cheery greetings as she shook off the rain and stepped round the puddles, trying vainly to shelter under the canopies that kept goods dry. She and Joan bought leeks and parsnips; they bought several ells of sturdy cloth and a couple of small barrels of cider to replace the precious stocks which had been spilled or drunk by their unwelcome visitors. To her relief, Catrin found the stallholder who brought a small selection of rolls of blank parchment from the bookshops and parchmenters who plied their trade round the cathedral in Hereford. There were always clerks and reeves who needed more, so he often came to country markets, even in the rain. When all her silver was spent, Catrin called Joan and suggested they set off home. 'I don't like it here,' she whispered as yet another farming neighbour cut her dead. 'They blame us in some way.'

'Well of course they do! I told you: your father is known to support Glyndŵr, who is to blame for the ruin of this town, the burnt houses, and bare fields. He is to blame for everything that has happened. It doesn't matter where these men come from. We had peace before, and good weather. And then Glyndŵr has even called down the rain – everybody says so!' She pulled her cloak more closely round her shoulders and glared at Catrin.

Catrin did not reply.

Dafydd was waiting when they got home and held out his hand for the parchment almost as soon as they dragged the panniers inside. Catrin pulled the parcel out and gave it to him. Without more money, she told him bluntly, there would be no more to write on. When she asked to keep some of the parchment for herself, he refused, demanding to know what she would want it for and she cursed herself for betraying her need and again for letting him see how upset she was.

It was on the first day of true autumnal gales that she caught him in her bedroom, rattling the lid of her coffer.

'What do you keep in here that it needs to be locked?' he demanded when she walked in.

She glanced round the room angrily. 'What are you doing in here?'

'I am waiting for you to unlock this chest.'

'No. I won't!' She folded her arms, her cheeks flushed with anger. 'It is none of your business what I put in my own coffers. How dare you come poking around in my room?'

'Open it!' he shouted at her.

'I told you, no!'

'If you don't do as I say, you will no longer live under my roof!' he bellowed. 'Do it now!'

Catrin heard the sound of footsteps on the stairs. Joan appeared, panting. 'What is going on here?' she demanded.

'It is none of your business, woman. Get out of here!' Dafydd shouted. 'Open it.' He turned back to Catrin.

'I have lost the key,' she said defiantly. 'Please, get out of my bedchamber. I have nothing of interest to you in here.'

'Then you can leave my house.'

She stared him in the eye. 'I think you will find it is my house!' she said softly.

She wasn't sure if that was true, legally, but the house had come from her mother's family, that much she knew.

His face turned deep crimson. 'How dare you!'

'I dare.' Never in her life had she stood up to him like this. Ever since she was a child she had obeyed him and given in to his bullying, but this was the last time she was going to let him browbeat her. As the wind battered the house, roaring down the chimneys and rattling the shutters, she stood her ground.

Abruptly he turned round and walked out of the room, elbowing his way past Joan as she stood in the doorway.

The women stood in silence as they listened to the sound of his footsteps walking slowly down the stairs. Seconds later they heard the slam of his study door.

Joan heaved a huge sigh. 'Oh my!'

'He'll calm down.' Catrin bit her lip.

'I hope so.'

'He will have to. He needs me too much to throw me out.' Catrin didn't feel as certain as she sounded.

Joan looked at the coffer. 'Are those your poems?'

She nodded. 'I am not going to show them to him.'

'He's so jealous of you, but you know that, don't you.'

Below they heard the door of the study reopen, Dafydd's footsteps across the flagstones and then his tread on the stairs again. Slowly he climbed towards them.

'Go, Joan,' Catrin whispered. 'You don't need to be here. This is between him and me.'

Joan slipped away. Catrin waited for him, her heart thudding uncomfortably in her chest. Dafydd appeared in the doorway. Ignoring her, he strode across to the coffer. She realised he had a hammer and chisel in his hands. He bent to the lock.

'No!' Catrin flew at him. 'How dare you. Leave it alone.' She tried to push her father away. He elbowed her aside as though she wasn't there and inserted the blade of the chisel under the lock.

Rhona caught her breath. She had watched Miranda, sitting at the kitchen table, closing her laptop and leaning back in her chair then she had got to her feet and wandered over to the window. Rhona ducked down out of sight, waiting. She felt ridiculously excited, her mouth dry with nerves like a child, playing hide and seek. Would Miranda find her?

Nothing happened and after a while she stood up cautiously, peering back inside. Miranda was sitting at the table again. She had closed her eyes. She was falling asleep. Rhona grimaced. Boring. Then she snapped to attention. Miranda was standing up again and there was someone else there. Rhona felt a shock-wave course through her body. There were two women in the room with her. Why hadn't she realised that Miranda wasn't alone in the house? They were dressed in strange clothes, with long skirts. One carried a broom in her hand. Good grief! What was going on? Talking, the women walked out of the door and Miranda followed them.

Rhona ducked away from the window and ran back to look into the living room and, sure enough, the three women were in there now. Miranda was standing by the door, watching the other two. They seemed to be talking animatedly as they ran across the room and through a large doorway in the far corner. Miranda followed and stood on the threshold watching them. She was somehow detached, watching but not taking part. There was a man in there and there seemed to be an argument going on between the three of them. Miranda wasn't involved; she was spying on them, lurking in the shadows. One of the women turned away, her face red with anger, and walked swiftly into the kitchen. Rhona dodged back to see where she was going and found she was heading for the door. She was coming outside. Rhona shrank against the wall. It was too late to move.

She heard the rattle of the latch, she heard the door open. She heard footsteps run past her, but she saw nothing. There was no one there. She could feel an electric tingling in her hands, just as she had at the side of the house and she realised she was clutching at the stones of the wall beside her. She let go as if it had burned her.

What was happening? The door was still closed. It had never opened. She looked into the kitchen. It was empty.

She took a deep breath. Who were they? What was happening? Was the house haunted? What other explanation was there for what she had seen? She had heard the door open, heard the woman run past her.

She felt a shiver run down her spine.

Tiptoeing to the living room window she peered in again. There was no one there either. She glanced round. She must have been watching for longer than she had realised. What meagre light there was was leaching from the sky. Under the rain-filled sky it was growing dark.

Where was Miranda?

Cautiously she approached the back door and tried the handle. The door was locked. No one had come out. Behind her, upstairs, a light came on in one of the bedrooms and a narrow strip of light flooded across the lawn. She tiptoed away from the wall, looking up in time to see Miranda appear in the window. She pushed it open and stood looking out. Rhona froze but Miranda didn't see her and as Rhona watched she turned away, facing into the room. Rhona craned her neck up to see in but it was impossible. She looked round. The garden behind the house rose quite steeply. It might be possible to gain enough height to look in. She moved off a few paces, then a few more until she could just catch a glimpse into the lighted room and see what was happening.

'Leave her things alone!'

Andy could contain herself no longer. They were in her

bedroom, the echo of their angry voices ricocheting off the walls. 'Stop it, you horrible man. Leave her alone!'

She saw Catrin and Dafydd freeze in mid-action, and turn towards her, their faces white. Neither one of them moved, as if uncertain what they had seen or heard, then they faced each other again. She saw Dafydd swing back towards his daughter, the chisel in his hand. He raised his arm and lunged at her. Catrin screamed, her shoulder pouring with blood. Andy threw herself between them, trying to knock the chisel out of his hand. She heard Dafydd howl with anger and fear, she felt a searing pain in her arm, then everything went black.

Rhona stood rooted to the spot, her eyes fixed on the window. They had vanished. Suddenly. Just like that. Between one moment and the next the man and the young woman had gone. She had watched the whole thing through the narrow mullioned window. There had been a fight. She had seen the flash of a blade and then she heard the scream. There was blood everywhere. She had been able to see it all, floodlit as if on a small stage and she could smell it too, the hot, angry exhilarating smell of violence. She waited, her eyes straining towards the window. Nothing. There was no sign of anyone, no sound from inside. She was alone in the garden with the howl of the wind and the roar of water from the brook. All she could smell now was wet earth and leaves and the clean cold mountain air.

Andy woke to find herself lying on her bedroom floor. Confused and very stiff and cold, she made no attempt to move. She could see a last few pink streaks in the sky through the window as the clouds blew away. All she could hear was the moan of the wind in the chimneys. The wind. She had been listening to the wind in Catrin's bedroom. Slowly she remembered. Catrin and her father. The quarrel.

With a groan she tried to sit up. An agonising pain shot

through her forearm and she clutched at it. Her hand came away sticky with blood.

'Oh no!' She heard her own tremulous voice as she staggered to her feet. She made her way towards the door and groped for the light switch. Her arm was a mess; her sleeve was stained, her hand now wet with blood. She had left bloody fingermarks on the wall around the switch. She was trying to work out what had happened. She must have hit her arm against something or caught it on the corner of the chest of drawers. Still dazed, she went into the bathroom and held her arm under the cold tap. The wound was about an inch across, straight, narrow and deep. It could only have been made by something very sharp.

'Like a chisel.' She heard herself say the words out loud. Trembling slightly, she pulled off her sweater and shirt and threw them into the bath then she scrabbled in the cupboard for the small first aid box she had seen there. The bleeding wouldn't stop. This couldn't be happening. She couldn't have been stabbed in her dream and woken up with blood pouring down her arm. It had to be some kind of psychosomatic response. She stood there shivering for several more minutes, pressing tissues against the wound, trying to staunch the flow. Glancing in the mirror she saw herself, naked above the waist apart from her bra, her face white as a sheet and tear-streaked, blood oozing through the wet tissue as she pressed wad after wad against the gash. It wouldn't stop bleeding. He must have nicked an artery. 'Oh God!' she heard herself whimper pathetically.

If he had done that to her, what had he done to Catrin? He had stabbed her in the shoulder, she remembered now. She remembered the blood, Catrin's agonised scream, her own inter-vention. She threw another handful of paper into the lavatory and reached for a towel. She had hurled herself into the fray in Catrin's defence without a thought. She remembered how Catrin and Dafydd had turned to look at her when she had spoken. She had shouted something and they had heard her. Both of them had heard her.

Joan. Where was Joan? She would know what to do, she would know how to stop the bleeding. Catrin's bleeding, not hers. Andy sniffed hard and mopped at her eyes, trying to clear her head, trying to get a grip on herself.

Still unsteady on her feet, she returned to her bedroom and pulled open a drawer, looking for a sweater. Somehow she pulled it on without getting too much blood on it, then she turned to the door. There was a proper first aid box in the kitchen, in the dresser cupboard. She had never opened it, but knowing how efficient Sue was, she probably kept it stocked. Even a herbalist must have decent-sized plasters.

When she finally managed to stem the bleeding she examined the wound. It needed a couple of stitches, that was obvious. She ransacked Sue's box and found dressings and tape to hold them in place. Shock was setting in. Her hands were shaking so much she could barely cut the lengths of tape. How had this happened? How was it possible? And now, far too late, she remembered Meryn's warning: *Don't touch anything. Don't let anything touch you.*

What should she take for shock? Hot sweet tea, wasn't that what they usually said? Her eyes travelled across the kitchen. The kettle seemed an insurmountable distance away. Pepper was sitting on the windowsill outside, watching her through the glass. She tried to steady her breathing. His eyes were huge. Frightened. Her gaze travelled to his food bowl. She vaguely remembered feeding him a long time ago, but he had hardly touched the food. His biscuits lay there, most unsampled, with a scatter across the floor leading towards the cat flap as though he had bolted with his mouth full. 'Pepper?' she called. It would comfort her to have him near her. He ignored her. He was gazing past her towards the door into the hall and she saw his eyes grow if possible even larger, his fur on end, staring in panic before he stood up and with a yowl of fear leapt into the darkness.

Andy swallowed. She looked round at the door. Whatever

he had seen, it had scared him so badly she wondered if she would ever see him again.

A figure was standing in the doorway. She heard herself give a little cry of terror as she pushed back her chair and stood up. It wasn't Catrin. She stood, riveted to the spot as she saw Dafydd take a step into the kitchen. In his hand he was carrying the chisel. The blade was still red with blood, her blood. He was dressed as he had been when he had entered Catrin's room in his long woollen gown, gathered at the waist with a leather belt from which hung a leather purse. He had shoulder-length grey hair and a short sparse beard. His eyes were the colour of flint and they sought hers. 'In the name of Jesus Christ and all the saints, begone from this house!' he cried. He raised his hand and made the sign of the cross. 'Demon, witch, *bwgan*!' He took another step forward.

Andy didn't wait. Whirling round she snatched the car keys off the hook by the back door, wrestled it open and fled. Forgetting her ankle, forgetting the injury to her arm, she hurtled down the steps three at a time, desperately pointing the key to unlock it. She dived into her car, slamming the door on the night and with shaking hands tried to fit the key into the ignition. The car stalled and she tried again, increasingly desperate. She backed out and, wheels spinning, turned up the hill, the accelerator flat to the floor, seeing the headlight beams arcing into the sky as she burst out across the cattle grid. She had to find Meryn.

Instinctively she had pulled the back door shut behind her, but she hadn't locked it. With a slight click it slowly creaked open in the draught from the wind and light from the kitchen spilt out across the garden. The figure of Dafydd ap Hywell appeared, standing in the doorway, looking out.

He didn't cast a shadow.

26

Rhona was sitting in her car in the dark. She had locked the doors. What had really happened back there? What had she witnessed from the garden as she looked into the house? She wasn't sure. The car headlights behind her in the lane and the straining roar of its engine took her by surprise. As Miranda's car flashed past her she almost didn't react but as soon as she registered whose car it was she fired the engine and, wheels spinning, lurched out of the gateway and onto the lane to follow her.

Her car rattled over the cattle grid and out into the short-cropped grass of the lower slopes of the hillside. She could see sheep grazing as the lights illuminated the view, and then two ponies, their heads down chomping steadily. Did these animals never stop eating? Didn't they sleep? She scanned the road ahead. She could see Miranda's tail lights in the distance.

Each steep turn of the tarmacked road seemed identical. Every now and then a gorse bush or a small twisted tree loomed out of the dark and then vanished again as her headlight beams moved on. She reached a double bend and almost lost control, skidding into a patch of rushes. The headlights illuminated the

gleam of water, then it was gone; somehow she swung the car
back onto the road. Miranda's lights had disappeared. She swore
and pressed the accelerator to the floor. She wasn't even sure
why she was following her; it had been an instinct, obeyed
without a second's thought, but now that instinct was in
complete control. She had to find out where it was that Miranda
was going in such a hurry.

There was nowhere she could have turned off the road.
And then she saw the car again. She had gained on her. She
saw the red tail lights, the twin beams of the undipped headlights, sweeping across the hillside. Miranda was slowing.
Rhona stamped on her brakes. The Passat had turned off the
road. She could see it now, driving straight up the mountainside, or so it seemed. Cautiously she approached the place
where it had turned and she saw a gate, partially hidden by
a clump of thorn trees. Miranda was driving up what looked
like a farm track. Rhona let her car drift to a stop, turned off
her engine and waited in the dark. She could see Miranda's
lights swinging all over the place as she negotiated the steep,
bumpy track, then abruptly they stopped and almost immediately went out. Rhona strained her eyes through the windscreen; was that a house up there? She could see it now.
White-painted and totally isolated it showed up faintly against
the dark of the hillside. Turning on the engine and engaging
first gear, she drove carefully through the gate and parked
behind the clump of trees.

Before she climbed out she leaned across and pulled open
the glove compartment. In it she kept, amongst other things,
her sunglasses, a torch, a pack of tissues and a large clasp knife.
She took the torch, and after a moment's thought, the knife as
well, and slipped them into her pockets, then she pushed the
car door open, surprised at the strength of the wind up here
as it threatened to snatch it out of her grasp. She regained
control of the door and closed it softly, pushing it firmly shut
and then locking it. It looked as if it would be quite a hike on

foot up the steep gradient of the stony track, but she didn't care. She was fizzing with energy.

'What on earth have you been up to?' Meryn had pulled open the front door almost before she had knocked. He drew her inside and looked her up and down compassionately. 'You have been in the wars, you poor thing, and you have what my friends the Pascoes would call bad vibes. You have picked up a few nasty shadowy entities.' He walked towards his desk. He must have been working, she saw. The lamp was on and there were papers and books scattered around his laptop.

'I'm sorry. I've interrupted you,' she stammered through chattering teeth.

'It doesn't matter.' He stooped and opened a drawer. 'First things first.' He brought out a tightly woven bunch of dried herbs and a box of matches. 'Come and stand here, where I can see you, and let me smudge you. You know what that means, I'm sure.'

'Cleansing my aura.' She smiled bravely. 'Very New Age.'

'And effective. We have to start somewhere.'

He lit the dried herbs and let them flare. As soon as they had caught properly he blew them out gently, leaving a stream of strongly scented blue smoke, which he proceeded to waft around her. 'The original American peoples use sage for this, but I prefer to use local plants; local remedies for local entities,' he said softly. 'So, are you going to tell me what happened?'

'It was Dafydd,' she whispered.

'I am assuming you ignored my warning and touched something?'

'I didn't have any choice. He was trying to kill Catrin.'

'And he attacked you as well?' At last he acknowledged the bandages where a smear of blood had soaked through. He walked slowly round her, waving the smouldering herbs, the smoke growing more dense and pungent with each passing moment. Andy started coughing. 'Stand still,' he commanded.

'I'm sorry, but I need to do this. I will look at your arm when I've done.'

He went on slowly circling until the bunch of herbs was reduced to a pile of simmering ash, which he caught in a small bowl. 'That is purely cleansing. Like washing your hands. Right, the next priority is your arm. Can you slip off your jumper?'

To her surprise she found she was unembarrassed standing before him in her bra as he cleaned the wound. He was calmly professional. 'Not joking, but you have no idea where that chisel had been before he stabbed you with it. And however much you like and care for Catrin, you don't know where she's been either, so I think we need a bit of prophylactic infection control here. Calendula,' he explained as he dabbed a piece of cotton wool in a small bowl of warm water.

He rebandaged the arm and helped Andy put on her sweater again, then he loaned her another to go on top of it. 'From a local black sheep,' he said, smiling as he pulled the soft thick wool over her head. He steered her to a chair by the fire. 'Now you're ready to tell me everything. From the beginning.'

When she had finished he eyed her calmly. 'Well, the good news is that you didn't bring Dafydd away with you. The bad news is that he's probably prowling round Sleeper's Castle looking for you.'

She blanched. 'Please, can you get rid of him for me?' she said pathetically. 'I'm way out of my league here.'

He laughed. 'Not that much out of your league. You know your stuff but you're untrained and you have made the worst possible mistake in that you have got yourself involved. We have to extricate you from your entanglements before we can sort all this out.' He sat down opposite her. 'I suggest you stay the night here. Let the house calm down a bit. Then we can go back in daylight.'

She hugged the black sweater round her. It was knitted in thick heavy oiled wool and was very warm. 'I think I might have left the door open,' she said in a small voice. 'I mean wide open. I ought to go back.'

The track swept round behind the house and, leaving the comparative shelter of the hedge, Rhona ran, bent double, towards the outbuildings at the back.

She walked on the grass, though she doubted her footsteps would be heard above the wind. It had risen steadily, and was whipping the clouds across the sky as the sun set in a fiery blaze behind the mountains. She paused to look at it and thought wistfully of her camera in the bedroom of the pub in Brecon. It didn't matter. This was much more exciting than photography.

The garden of the house was surrounded by hedges; there was a gate, but it was standing open. She could see his old four-wheel drive now, parked under the rowan tree outside the front door next to Andy's car. This was the lair of Andy's new man.

She could see there were lights on in the house. It wasn't a big establishment. It was a typical Welsh stone cottage, white-painted, symmetrical. The place could be a year old or five hundred years old, it was hard to tell. Rhona found herself imagining how exposed and lonely it must feel in the winter, with the snows and gales sweeping across the mountains. She smiled, exhilarated. The wind was stronger now, tearing at her hair, making her eyes water.

She stopped in the shelter of a wall and paused to get her breath back. It was bitterly cold up here, her light jacket almost comically ineffective against the weather as it closed in. Behind her the sky was black save for that splash of vivid colour on the far horizon which was settling into duller shades of salmon and terracotta. Shoving her hands in her pockets she crept back towards the corner of the building and peered round. It was dark here and hard to see. She looked left and right and ran, stooping, to the wall of the house. Flattening herself against it, she edged towards the window. The curtains were carelessly drawn and one corner at the bottom had caught on something, leaving a small gap through which light streamed into the garden. She approached it cautiously and looked in. It was the kitchen. There was no sign of anyone in there. It was old-fashioned in a style which nowadays would probably be highly desirable and classed as retro. A small oak table, four bentwood chairs, a butler's sink – probably original – a stove, a dresser. Herbs. There were plates and mugs on the draining board, and papers on the table. An old square Roberts radio sat on the windowsill only inches from her head as she peered in. She craned her neck to see through the open door into the rest of the house, but the corridor outside the door was in darkness.

Rhona smiled exultantly.

Her face was almost touching the glass when an arm appeared, pulled the curtain down and her view was cut off abruptly. She jerked back, her heart thumping with fright. Had he seen her? She didn't think so. Nevertheless she didn't want to take any chances. She crept back towards the sheltering outbuildings and stood there waiting for her breathing to return to its natural rhythm. The last of the sunset had faded to a single narrow streak across the sky. In minutes it would be completely dark. Somewhere close by an owl hooted.

Cautiously she began to retrace her steps towards the front of the house. All the downstairs windows were lit now, all the curtains firmly closed. Her glance skimmed across the cars, sitting outside the front door. Her fist tightened on the knife in her pocket and she smiled. Pulling it out, she opened it and stepped towards the Fourtrak. Behind her the owl hooted again.

Meryn stood up, an anxious look crossing his face. He held up his hand for silence, listening intently. 'Did you hear that?' he whispered.

Andy shook her head. She shivered. And then they heard it again. An owl. Meryn hurried to the door and stood behind it, listening.

Andy rose to her feet and tiptoed after him. 'What is it?' she murmured.

'There's someone out there.'

'Rhona?' She mouthed the word.

'Quite possibly.' He reached for the light switch and unlocked the door. Pulling it open he peered out into the dark. The outside light had come on, illuminating the gravelled parking space with the two cars. It was deserted.

He stepped outside and looked round. 'She's gone,' he said.

'Are you sure?'

He looked up as the shadowy outline of a bird flew silently across the lighted space and disappeared into the dark. 'I'm sure.'

She laughed. 'Another watchdog?'

'Part of the crew.' She saw the look of anxiety that crossed his face. 'I hate to say this, but is there any reason to think Rhona might go home via Sleeper's Castle?'

Andy shuddered. 'It's the sort of thing she would do.'

'I fear you're right.' He stood staring down the track into the dark. 'Would you like me to go there to check on my own? You could lock yourself in here safely and let me deal with it.'

'No. I want to come.'

He sighed. 'You do realise you can't do anything to help Catrin?'

'Are you sure?' She met his gaze steadily. 'Catrin and her father can see me. They have both in some way crossed over into the present day now, maybe as ghosts, maybe as dreams, I don't know, but Dafydd's chisel was real enough, so why can't I take bandages and antiseptic, if that's what is needed.'

He gave a thoughtful nod. 'An interesting speculation. All right. Let's go. Would you like me to drive your car or shall I take mine?'

The answer was made for them. As Meryn closed the front door and they approached the cars they saw all four tyres of his old Fourtrak down on their rims.

'The vindictive bitch!' Andy said succinctly. 'I'm so sorry.'

'People seem to be making rather free use of their knives tonight,' Meryn said dryly. He put his keys in his pocket. 'Luckily we must have scared her off before she got round to your car as well. I could sense she'd gone. She has an extraordinarily powerful forcefield, that woman. Interesting.'

Andy managed a smile. 'Will your owls still be on watch here?'

He smiled. 'Oh yes. The night shift is on duty until dawn.'

Rhona pulled up outside Sleeper's Castle and sat, gazing up the steps towards the house. She felt the prickle of intense excitement as she opened her car door, the visceral power that the place exuded. She took a deep breath and climbed out, her hand closed round the knife again.

She pushed the front door gently. It was obviously locked. She walked along the front of the house, tiptoeing towards the first ground-floor window. It was hard to get close enough to look through it, it was so framed by twisted stems of wisteria but, careful not to make a sound or agitate the remaining leaves too much, she managed to peer in at last. The room was dark and she could see nothing. She eased herself away from the wall and resumed her circumnavigation of the house. There were no lights round the front at all. It felt abandoned and uncared for even after so short a time. She crept on round the corner. There was a faint light coming from the kitchen. The back door was not just unlocked, it was wide open. She gave a triumphant smile. Tightening her grip on the knife in her pocket she tiptoed towards it, keeping her head down below the level of the windowsill. She straightened as she reached the door and looked in.

The room was lit by several flickering candles. It looked derelict, unfurnished, save for a large table and a few stools. The ceiling was hung with pans and baskets. She gasped as she looked round. A man was standing in the middle of the

409

floor, looking straight at her. She knew instantly who he was although she had only seen him through the window in the distance before. He was quite elderly, she could see now, with long straggly grey hair, hidden beneath a black coif which seemed to fasten under his chin. He was wearing something which looked a little like a black dressing gown, and in his hand he held a large chisel. The blade was dripping with blood.

Rhona stared at him for two or three seconds, then he was gone.

She felt a scream rising in her throat. She recoiled, staggered back a few steps away from the door then turned and ran.

She returned the way she had come to the head of the front steps, throwing herself down them, slipping down the last two and falling on her knees on the rough gravelled surface of the parking area. Somehow she scrabbled to her feet and managed to open her car door. She threw herself in, slammed the door after her and sat with her head resting on the steering wheel. She was shaking violently.

Managing to get a grip on herself at last she raised her head to look out of the windscreen and up towards the house. She half expected to see the man standing looking down at her, but there was no one there. It was as it had been when she arrived: deserted and as quiet as the grave.

She backed the car out and turned down the lane and all at once found she was laughing hysterically.

Sleeper's Castle looked deserted when Meryn pulled in. He turned to Andy. 'Now, I want you to stay here until I tell you to come up, OK? No arguments. You've been badly hurt and you're in no fit state to run or jump or wrestle man, woman or ghostly demon at the moment. Do I have your promise you will do as I ask?'

Andy nodded meekly.

'Good. Now lock yourself in.'

As soon as he had disappeared out of sight round the back of the house she could feel her fear coming back. She stared up at the house, holding her breath. It was several minutes before the lights started to come on. She saw the downstairs windows light up one by one, then a few seconds later the upstairs, until every window in the house was lit. Finally the front door opened and Meryn appeared. He ran down the steps and came round to her side of the car, opening her door as she unlocked it. 'OK. Everything seems to be all right. You're right, you'd left the back door wide open so the place is freezing cold, but apart from that I can't see anything amiss. There's no one there that I can see.' He helped her out.

He led the way back to the kitchen and came to a halt near the door. Opening it again he paused on the doorstep. 'I do sense there was something of a confrontation here,' he said. 'My guess is that Rhona came here, and was about to walk in but she stopped.'

'You think she saw something?'

'Why else would she change her mind? That lady is very susceptible. The atmosphere round here has been fractured. I'm sure you can feel it.'

She could, now she came to think about it. There was an almost indefinable tension in the air, something which set her teeth on edge. It would explain something else.

'Pepper hasn't come back.' His bowl was still sitting untouched amidst its scatter of biscuits.

'Pepper wouldn't have come back if Dafydd was still in this dimension.' Meryn opened the doors to the pantry and scullery and peered inside. 'No one here.'

She followed him painfully up the stairs, glancing into one room after the other. In the spare room, which she now thought of as her studio, he paused. She watched as he glanced at her paintings and sketches. After a few moments he moved on without comment. There was blood in her bedroom and in the bathroom basin. She stood in the doorway surveying it. 'That's

411

mine, I'm afraid. I was rather hoping that we would find it had all disappeared,' she said wryly. 'What a mess.'

'Nothing that can't be washed out.' He walked on through into the other bedrooms. 'No, I think all is as it should be.'

'And Dafydd?'

He thought briefly. 'Let us adjourn to the kitchen. With the back door shut, the range will have had a chance to warm it up by now, and we can have a think.'

They broached Sue's emergency whisky then sat down opposite each other. Andy took a sip from her glass and sighed. 'The doors have closed again, haven't they?'

He didn't ask her what she meant. 'I think you're right. For the time being, and as long as you stay awake, we're safe.' He gave her a teasing smile.

'As long as I—?' she repeated. 'You mean I can't go to sleep here?'

'I'm thinking about it.' He rested his chin on his clasped hands. Eventually he looked up to find her watching him acutely. 'You like it here, don't you? This house, I mean. This hasn't put you off? You would like to stay here?'

She looked puzzled. 'Of course.'

'Because the quickest and easiest way of sorting out the problem would be for you to move out. I think others have solved the problem that is Sleeper's Castle by doing just that.'

She stared at him, aghast at the idea. 'But some have stayed.' It sounded like a plea.

'Some have stayed,' he agreed.

'You don't think this is why Sue's gone, do you?' she asked after a moment. 'The real reason?'

'I don't know. But I suspect if she'd encountered Dafydd in all his murderous fury she might have thought it a good time to leave.'

There was a long silence. Andy was aware that he was watching her, not anxiously, not impatiently, just waiting for her to think it through.

'I haven't been here very long, but I've grown to love this house. I want to get to know all its secrets and its strengths and its weaknesses,' she said slowly. 'I want to live here in every season. I want to paint it. I've painted nothing but flowers for so long, it would be a liberation to paint buildings again and scenery.' She sighed. 'But Dafydd changes things.' There was another long silence. 'I am very afraid of Dafydd.' She reached for her glass and took a small sip. 'Something else happened today,' she said. 'I heard that I may get my house in Kew back. A copy of Graham's will has been found. I might after all be a comparatively rich lady.' She gave a grimace. 'With a home in Surrey.'

Meryn went on watching her without comment. He'd grown very fond of this complicated, stubborn young woman and, he realised, he felt a genuine paternal protectiveness towards her.

'Strangely my reaction was not one of relief, it was one of utter disappointment. Until,' she went on, 'until I thought, "If I sell the house in Kew, I could buy Sleeper's Castle."'

'If Sue wants to sell.'

'If Sue wants to sell.'

'But only if you can sort out Dafydd.'

'I couldn't. But you could.'

He nodded slowly. 'We could try together. It would rather depend on Dafydd and Catrin. And the house.' Meryn pushed his chair back and stood up. He wandered across to the Aga and leant against it.

'Then I must try and make my peace with them.' Andy looked down at her arm ruefully. 'If I have enough courage.' She shivered. 'I'm not sure I do now.'

'You have masses of courage, Andy,' he said. 'The fact that you're still here demonstrates that clearly. But there are obviously problems we have to tackle before you can feel comfortable here. The first thing we have to do is to see if you have done irreparable damage by allowing that door to open between Catrin and Dafydd's world and ours. If we can deal with that then the

413

second is to teach you how to control the dreams. You would have to learn to guide them into, shall we say, less dangerous pathways; and to wake up immediately you felt things getting out of hand. If you could do that, would you have the courage to stay, do you think?'

'I hope so. If you're there to help me.'

'You're sure?' He studied her face closely. 'Right. Perhaps we should start now.'

She hesitated and he saw the flash of fear that crossed her face. 'An easy lesson to begin with. To put you in control. Waking up.'

'That sounds good.'

They both turned as the cat flap clattered and Pepper appeared. He paused inside the door and looked round, then he walked suspiciously over towards his bowl.

'All clear, I think,' Andy said quietly.

Meryn glanced at her. 'But you knew that. You felt it yourself.'

'I think I did, yes.'

'All right. First lesson. As you fall asleep, think about waking up the moment you want to. Think about snapping your fingers like this' – he clicked his thumb and second finger – 'and being awake. Immediately.'

'It can't be that easy.'

'It can.'

'And if it doesn't work?'

'It will.' He looked at her sympathetically. 'End of first lesson. You know, Andy, you look exhausted. Why don't we leave it there for now? Go to bed and to sleep with the knowledge that you can wake up at any point if you need to. I'll stay here if you will let me. Downstairs. If I can borrow a pillow and a rug I'll be fine on the sofa next door, and I can keep an eye on things.'

He was right. She was so tired she could hardly think straight. She stood up. 'Are you sure I will be safe?' In spite of herself, her voice quavered.

'I'm sure.' He saw her swallow nervously and he groped in his pocket. He produced a small leather bag on a thong. 'I guessed you might be nervous and I have something here which will ward off bad dreams,' he said. 'Vervain, the Enchanter's Herb. It will keep you safe and allow you to sleep soundly.'

She took it from him. 'Are you serious?'

He nodded.

'And it really works?'

'It really works if the intention is there.'

'Yours or mine?'

'Both is best.'

She gave a small, sceptical nod as she slipped the thong over her head. 'Good night then.'

'Goodnight, Andy.'

He stooped and picked up Pepper, who purred and rubbed his face against Meryn's cheek.

The knock on the kitchen door was soft and hesitant. Joan looked up nervously. Any visitor these days was a matter of concern. She walked over and listened intently. There was a long silence, then another knock even softer than the first. She put her hand to the latch. 'Who is it?'

'It's Edmund.'

She gave a little cry of joy. Dragging open the door she looked outside. He was standing in the shelter of the wall trying to get out of the rain. 'Edmund?' Her greeting died on her lips. 'What is wrong? What is it? What's the matter?' She caught his arm and pulled him inside.

He drew back. 'Are you alone?' His voice was hoarse.

She nodded. 'Master Dafydd has gone away.'

'And Catrin?'

She looked at him quizzically. 'She has gone to visit a neighbour. The old witch up on the mountain.' Joan wrinkled her nose.

'So you are alone here?' He breathed a sigh of relief. 'Thank

God. I need your help.' He staggered in and threw himself down on a stool beside the table. She gasped. As he walked into the pool of candlelight she saw the red and brown stains on his tunic and she smelt the stink of infected flesh. His face was a pasty white. 'I caught an arrow in the chest. It went clean through my mail. We had a surgeon with us and he dug out the barb and dressed the wound. I thought I would mend, but it's gone bad.' His voice faded and he began to sway.

She caught his shoulders. 'Where did you come from? How did you get here? You can't have ridden.'

He smiled. 'I did. I rode with two other men. They were going home too. Everyone scattered. We had to save ourselves. They were going to beg for the king's pardon. There have been some terrible battles, Joan. Everything is going wrong. Prince Owain was in South Wales. He sent us on a foray under his brother, Tudur, to secure Grosmont Castle. We burned the town, but the king had sent reinforcements. So many men! We weren't expecting them. We were defeated utterly.' He paused, his strength waning. 'We went on to besiege Usk Castle. We were certain to take that. Tudur had been told there would be no more than a hundred men against us, but again there were thousands.' His voice broke. 'They poured out of the walls; they slaughtered us. Those they did not kill in battle, they beheaded. Tudur was killed. Owain's son Gruffudd has been captured and hauled away to London.' His voice broke. He was shivering violently. 'All is lost.'

'A pardon?' Joan narrowed her lips, seizing on the one word as he fell silent. 'You said the men with you were seeking a pardon. Will you get a pardon too?'

He tried to shrug his shoulders. 'I have no money to pay the fine. You can be sure Father won't pay it for me.' He winced as another wave of pain swept over him. 'Can you slap some ointment on this, Sis, please and let me sleep a bit. It would be so good to be out of the rain for a while.'

'Catrin will be back later,' Joan said.

'She won't betray me.'

'No, she won't.' Joan pursed her lips again. 'No more than I. We need her to dress your wound. She knows more about medicine than I do.' She pulled his padded doublet open and looked at his wound. 'This is bad, Ed.'

'I know. Sorry.' He was swaying on the stool.

She grabbed his arm. 'Come on. Come and lie down. There is a pallet in the hall. I will pull it near the fire. Then I will send Betsi to fetch Catrin.'

He was asleep almost before his head hit the pillow. She pulled rugs over him and went back to the kitchen. She refilled the water pot and put it on the fire. Catrin would have to clean that wound and they would have to cut away the putrid flesh.

She stood staring into the fire. Edmund was dying. She had seen wounds like that before. People seldom recovered from flesh that had gone bad like that.

It was nearly dark when Betsi came back with Catrin. Joan had several candles lit on the kitchen table. 'I thought maybe we could lay him on here,' she said quietly. Catrin walked past her into the great hall and went to kneel beside Edmund. She pulled back the blanket and studied his wound. He didn't open his eyes. He was sleeping restlessly, muttering feverishly as he tossed and turned. She put a cool hand on his forehead. He was burning.

'Can we lift him on the table between us?' Catrin didn't look round. 'He is a heavy man.'

The three women looked down at him doubtfully. She shook her head. 'In that case I think it is better to do it here, then he can sleep again.' She glanced up at Joan. 'If you and Betsi put the candles round and light the sconces, then bring in hot water and tear up some rags for bandages, I will go and see what I have in the stillroom.'

She kept two or three small sharp knives in there, and her pots of ointment. She looked over the jars and bottles of lovingly made remedies. It had taken her a whole summer to replace

417

her stocks after the raiders had smashed everything in here. Thank the Blessed Virgin they had not found her knives, carefully wrapped in a piece of linen at the back of the top shelf. She reached for them now and studied them. She had seen deep wounds like this before. They festered from the inside; the arrow would have taken dirt deep into his body, as would the knife of the man who had removed it, so it made sense to dip her own knife into a remedy to take it to the source of the poison. She had no need now to consult her mother's notes on remedies. She had known them all by heart for many years.

She wiped the blades in a tincture of calendula and pressed them into her pot of beeswax melted with honey and rye meal and powdered centaury, then she turned back to the great hall. She felt an icy calm. Lying there, Edmund was not the man she loved, he was an injured animal, like the pony who had staked herself on a sharp pole last spring. She had saved her with dressings and by stitching shut the wound. She knelt beside Edmund with her basket of tools and pots and potions. Joan was sobbing quietly. Catrin looked up. 'Take this thread and my needles and put them in the boiling water. It softens the gut so I can stitch the wound easily when I have finished. Please, Joan, go.' The woman's weeping was making her nervous. 'Betsi, I want you to hold the candle close like this so I can see. I have to get every bit of this bad flesh away.' She picked up the largest knife and took a deep breath. 'He won't feel anything, he is far away now, in his dreams.' She closed her eyes briefly and whispered a prayer to St Bride then she brought the blade of the knife towards the wound.

He moaned and flinched and once or twice his eyes fluttered open, but she was able to make a good job of cleaning away the rotten flesh, cutting it back to healthy pink tissue. Instinctively she let fresh blood swab the wound before she sprinkled it with the powdered centaury and covered it with a cabbage leaf, one of the blessed healers, washed of earth in the thundering waters of the brook and packed over it with clean linen dressings. She and Joan bandaged him tightly, then she pulled the blankets over him. 'If he lives until morning I think he will be all right.' She smiled at Joan in exhaustion. 'Let's clear all this mess away. Betsi, will you go and boil more water. We could all do with something hot to drink.'

When she had gone, Catrin put her hand on Edmund's head gently. 'I have done my best,' she murmured. 'Oh, Joan, how did he have the strength to get here?'

Joan was weeping, her face wet with tears. 'He's a fool,' she said bitterly. 'He always has been, but maybe he did the right thing in coming to you.' She looked up at Catrin. 'You know he loves you, don't you.'

Catrin nodded.

'I blamed you for everything – meeting the Lord Owain, letting him be seduced away to the rebels, letting him go so far away, putting his life at risk,' Joan said miserably.

'I know you did.' Catrin put out her hand and patted Joan's arm. 'I blamed myself too. But Edmund is an archer. He loves his bow and his skill. He was always going to serve someone. He wasn't born to be a farmer like your father.' It was no more than he had said himself a dozen times when she had begged him over the years not to go back.

Joan scrubbed at her eyes sadly. She climbed heavily to her feet. 'We'll let him sleep now.' She sniffed. 'I am going to go and make us all a posset. Betsi has no more idea how to make that than she does how to stitch a silken tapestry, so best I go and supervise!'

Edmund slept for hours. When he woke his fever had gone and his eyes were bright. It was several days before he could sit up and more again before he could walk a few steps across the floor.

Catrin and Joan took turns at nursing him and keeping a lookout for visitors. What they would have done if a stranger had been seen climbing up the track from the road they weren't sure, but Catrin had lit a candle to St Winefride and prayed that they would be hidden from visitors, then secretly, away from Joan's gaze, she recited the incantation to Llŷr, the ancient god of the sea to call down the Druid's mist across the mountains to shroud them from prying eyes.

It was as Catrin was stirring more tincture into melted butter to make a new pot of ointment that Andy saw her wince and put her hand to her shoulder in pain. 'Is it still bad?' she asked.

Catrin dropped the spoon. She turned round slowly. Andy saw her eyes widen. She made the sign of the cross.

'Sorry. I didn't mean to frighten you,' Andy whispered. She took a step backwards, then pulled up her own sleeve and exposed the bandage still neatly bound across her forearm. 'Mine is sore too. Where is your father now?'

As she spoke, she realised her question made no sense. Time had passed in Catrin's world. Her shoulder, though clearly still painful, was mended. She had been making medicines, tending Edmund. The seasons had moved on and Dafydd was away, she had said as much. Catrin had seen her but she had not responded. Maybe it was time to leave. She took a deep breath, raised her hand and snapped her fingers together.

Meryn was dozing on the sofa with Pepper sprawled across his chest when Andy crept downstairs in the cold early morning light. Before she slept the night before she had taken off the Enchanter's pouch and tucked it in the far corner of the room.

She stood for a second looking down at them, man and cat, and Meryn's eyes opened at once. 'So, you dreamt? Did it go well?'

'How do you know I dreamt?'

He sat up slowly and pushed the reluctant cat onto the floor. 'I guessed you would take off the pouch. Did you stay in charge of the dream?'

'I did as you told me. I clicked my fingers.' She smiled. 'It was that easy.' Then she frowned. 'Catrin seems to be able to command the weather. I saw her reciting her spells. Is that really possible?'

Meryn laughed. 'Have you never lain on the lawn on a summer's afternoon and watched the clouds and willed one to move?'

Andy smiled. 'Of course.'

'And as a child did you recite, "Rain, rain go away. Come again another day!"'

'Only when I was very small.'

'Did it work?'

'No.'

'Ah, perhaps you didn't have the technique right. It is an art as old as man himself. The weather can make or break a harvest; it can destroy with fearful power. To be able to harness it is magic indeed.'

He glanced at his watch and then climbed to his feet. 'I'm going to call Rob Vaughan at the local garage and get him to collect my car. I think four flat tyres is beyond even my magic powers to fix. I'll ask him to pick me up on his way by.'

'I am so sorry. That was all my fault. If it hadn't been for me, you would never have met Rhona.'

'I haven't actually met her yet.' He gave a rueful smile. 'Let's hope I don't have that pleasure! Just make sure you don't let her get near you.' He looked stern. 'I sense that her power is growing. I suspect she may have absorbed some of the energies of this house. I don't know if she knows it, but there seems to be something in her psyche which is badly out of balance. So, I need you to surround yourself with protection. That will give you a head start over her schemes, whatever they are. You know the psychic techniques already, I'm sure you do. But beyond that, always check your car before you get in it, in case she's played the same trick on you, and never ever forget to lock it. I know up here it's probably something you don't bother with, but for the time being, lock everything always.'

* * *

'Have you told the police?' Rob Vaughan from the garage whistled angrily through his teeth as he looked Meryn's car over. They had found deep scratches on the doors, and a huge quantity of earth wedged into the exhaust pipe as well as the lacerated tyres. Rob phoned back to the garage for the low loader to come and take the car away and then joined Meryn in his kitchen. As he spooned sugar into his coffee he leant on the dresser. 'You do know my brother is one of the cops down in Hay,' he said conversationally.

Meryn shook his head. 'I didn't know.' Rob was an old mate. His father, Gareth, owned one of the hill farms nearby. It had been Gareth who had come to Andy's aid with his pony on the mountainside. Never a man for a quad bike, Gareth.

'Dai's been away in Birmingham, so you might not have met him, but last month he finally managed to transfer to the Dyfed-Powys force and get a posting nearer home. He can be discreet,' Rob went on, reading volumes into Meryn's silence about how the vandalism had come about. 'He could drop in on his way home tonight. Unofficially, if you'd prefer.'

'Then I think that might be a good thing. If he doesn't mind.' Meryn picked up his own mug. 'I have no proof who did this. I didn't see her, that's the trouble, so I can make no accusations. But I can guess. I'm not easy in my mind about this. It's not my quarrel, but maybe this' – he waved his arm towards the window and, beyond it, the car – 'makes it my business.'

'I should say so.' Rob took a gulp of tea. 'Do you want a lift down to Hay?'

'No thanks. I've a lot of writing to do. I can wait till the car is sorted.'

Later he watched as his poor old car was carried off, then he turned back into the house.

Andy had fed Pepper. She opened the back door and stood on the doorstep for a few minutes, watching him wander off into the garden. A heavy mist hung round the trees and drifted over the herb beds and the small tabby shape was swiftly swallowed up. Was Catrin's ability to influence the weather so powerful that the mist had lingered?

Abruptly she went back indoors, closed the door behind her and turning the key hung it on the hook before heading for the staircase and her bedroom. Her bed was unmade; it looked inviting, but more inviting still was the thought of going back into the past and seeing what was happening between Catrin and Edmund. Fully dressed though she was, she climbed in and pulled the covers over her head.

'Joan has gone down to the market,' Catrin said as she came in. Edmund was sitting at the kitchen table, chopping vegetables for the pot. He held the knife awkwardly because of the pain in his arm and chest, but he had made a good recovery. 'I've given her some money and a list of things we need. She won't be back until evening. It is a lovely day further down the hill.' She gave a little smile.

They both looked out of the door where the mist drifted up the valley, winding round the trees.

Edmund grinned at her. 'I won't ask how come the clouds came down so conveniently low.'

'Don't.'

'And Betsi and the other girl?'

'Have gone with her.'

'The Lord Owain has a magic stone,' he said as he set aside his knife. 'It gives him the gift of invisibility.'

She smiled. 'Useful.'

'Very.' Pushing back his stool he stood up unsteadily. He held out his arms and Catrin went to them, clinging carefully, avoiding the right side of his chest where the wound was still painful. She looked up and gazed into his eyes. 'It isn't often we have the place to ourselves,' she whispered.

She took his hand and led him towards the staircase.

He hesitated. 'Cat?'

She put her finger to her lips. Together they crept up to her bedroom and went in. She pushed the door closed behind them and turned to him with a smile. '*Rwy'n dy garu di, cariad*. I love you, my darling,' she whispered.

It was later, as they were dressing, that she pulled away from him distracted by something in the doorway.

'What are you looking at?' He caught her to him again.

'The ghost.' She laughed. 'I am sure this house is haunted.'

Edmund smiled. 'If it is, it doesn't matter. The ghost is hardly likely to tell your father or Joan.'

'It's a she. And no, she won't.'

She reached up and kissed him again. 'Where are you going to go when you are better, Edmund?' They both knew he could not stay much longer. The risk of him being seen was too great. 'You won't go to your father's, surely.'

'I'm going back to Prince Owain.' He held her close. 'He needs me now more than ever. Things have not been going well for his cause. Support is falling away. The French and the Scots promised to help but the help didn't come. Men are tired of war and he can't give them what they need. And the king is sending in ever more powerful forces against him. You do understand?'

'But not yet.' She clung to him again. 'Don't go yet. You're not strong enough, Edmund.'

He grinned at her. 'That's not what you said just now.' He tightened his arms around her.

When she drew away again she looked up into his eyes and sighed. She would not try to dissuade him from leaving. He was a soldier. This was his life. She held his gaze fondly. 'I want you to promise me one thing. If ever you need help you will come here. And if ever you change your mind and need to come into the king's peace you will tell me. I will somehow find the money to pay your fine.'

Later, while he slept, she crept into Dafydd's study and

closed the door behind her. It would do no harm to check how much there was in her father's secret hoard. She managed to push the coffer aside and knelt to lift the stone. There was nothing there. She stared down into the empty hole in dismay. But of course he hadn't trusted her. He had probably moved the money the same day she had first seen his hiding place. She sat back on her heels in despair. Where would he have hidden it, and where had he gone? She had heard nothing of him since he had left in the spring and Edmund had brought no news of him. Was he in South Wales with Prince Owain? Had he heard of the terrible losses at Usk and Grosmont?

Wearily she stood up and dragged the coffer back into place. When she went back into the hall Edmund was asleep on his pallet by the fire. She put another log on, gently, so as not to wake him, then went through into the kitchen and out into the garden. It was a long time since she had gone into the cave. It smelt as always damp and fusty, of bat droppings and rotting leaf mould. She made her way to the back where it was almost dark and sat down on the tree stump she had rolled there long ago to act as a seat. It took no time at all to shut out the rust-lings of the small animals, the sound of the wind in the dried leaves as they stirred in the draught, the thoughts of Edmund or Joan. She needed to find her father.

Andy crept closer, watching the narrow entrance, holding her breath in case Catrin heard her. The garden was wet with mist. She reached out to the ivy which hung over the opening and eased it back. She was concentrating so hard she did not hear the footsteps behind her.

'Who are you!' Edmund's voice was harsh in her ear. She felt his hand on her shoulder as he swung her round. 'Why are you spying on us? Answer me!' He shook her arm. She screamed at the pain as his hand closed over her bandaged wound.

Catrin appeared at once, her eyes huge with fright. 'What is it? What is happening?'

'This woman was spying on you.' Edmund turned to Andy. He stepped back in obvious confusion. 'Where is she?'

'What woman?' Catrin peered past him. The mist hanging over them eddied back and forth but it revealed only the empty garden.

'The one you talked about. The one you called a ghost.' He was staring round wildly. 'She was no more a ghost than I am. She was solid. Real.'

'She's not real, Ed,' Catrin said softly. 'She is from another time.'

'She is real. She was following you. She was peering into the cave.' The colour was fading from his cheeks and he clutched at the cliff wall as he began to sway.

'Oh, Edmund, you shouldn't have come outside.' Catrin took his arm. 'Come back into the kitchen and sit down. You will make yourself ill again.'

'She was here.'

Catrin sighed. 'Well, she's not here now.'

'I am,' Andy whispered. 'I am here.'

She took a deep breath and clicked her fingers. Her fingers were wet with moisture from the misty garden, the dripping plants and trees all round her, and nothing happened. She was still there, standing outside the cave as Catrin and Edmund made their way past her and back towards the house. 'Wait!' Andy cried. They didn't hear her. The wind whisked a vortex of leaves up into the air and it whirled past her. The mist was clearing. Behind her the brook was cascading over its rocks with an angry roar. She watched as they disappeared inside and closed the door behind them.

Trying to ignore the pain in her arm she raised her hand and brought finger and thumb together again. There was blood on them now, as well as moisture from the dripping plants and trees. She still couldn't make her fingers click.

'It doesn't matter,' she muttered to herself. 'They don't want me here. I need to go home. Wake up. Please wake up!'

*   *   *

Bryn had parked beside Andy's car. He shivered. The sun had gone in and a thick white mist had drifted up the valley to hang around the house, wrapping everything in damp heavy moisture. He climbed the steps and walked round into the gardens. He wouldn't have come if he had known the weather was going to close in like this. He went round to the kitchen door and knocked. There was no reply so he reached for the handle. The door was locked. He stood still and stared round the garden. She must have gone for a walk.

Slowly he walked up the path towards his shed. He might as well do a bit of pruning while he was here. He opened the door and went in, selecting a pair of shears from the row of hooks on the wall.

He had been working for twenty minutes when he turned to look back at the house. He had begun to feel strangely uneasy. Surely Andy wouldn't go for a walk in this mist? She wasn't in the garden as far as he could see, but he searched again in case he had missed her, glancing into the cave, the greenhouse, the drying shed, going down to stand by the brook. 'Andy?' he shouted.

There was no reply. The garden was silent, his voice muffled by the mist. Slowly he walked back towards the house. Pepper was standing on the windowsill inside the kitchen, meowing frantically. Bryn looked at him for several moments then he reached a decision. He stooped to find the spare key, inserted it in the lock and, kicking off his boots, he stepped inside. 'Andy?' he called. Pepper leapt off the sill and came to wind himself round Bryn's legs, still meowing. There was an untouched cup of tea on the table. A cold milky skim lay on the surface. Really worried now, Bryn walked over to the door into the hall and opened it. 'Andy? Are you there?'

Pepper ran past him into the living room, then on up the stairs. Bryn hesitated then he followed him.

He found Andy in her bedroom. She was lying fully clothed in bed, one of her pillows clasped in her arms. Her right arm had been bandaged, but the dressing had been torn off and the wound under it was seeping blood onto the sheets.

'Andy?' Bryn shook her shoulder gently. 'Andy? Can you hear me?'

She lay without stirring. She was breathing evenly, her face relaxed, but something about the depth of the sleep worried him. 'Andy!' He shook her harder this time. 'Come on. Wake up!' He turned and walked through into her bathroom. Grabbing the flannel which was hanging with the towels on the rail he wrung it out in cold water and took it back into the bedroom. Carefully he sponged her face. She still did not wake. He hesitated, wondering what to do, then he put the cold flannel over the wound on her arm and pressed it firmly in place.

Downstairs in the kitchen he rummaged in the cupboard. Sue always used cayenne pepper for closing wounds. One of the best herbal first aid tricks he knew. He found the jar, grabbed it and ran back upstairs. Once the bleeding had stopped he retied the bandage over the wound, then went down to the kitchen again and grabbed the phone. 'Sian? Thank goodness you're there. I need you. I'm at Sleeper's Castle.'

Sian arrived twenty minutes later. 'How long has she been like this?' she asked after she had examined Andy.

'I arrived about an hour ago I suppose.'

'Did you ring Meryn?'

'There's no reply. I'm sorry to call you, but I thought it better if there was someone else here.'

Sian sighed. 'Do you think she's there? In the past?'

'I would assume so.'

'What happened to her arm?'

'It looks as though she's been stabbed. Someone has done a good job of tidying it up. There were even steri strips, but she seems to have torn them all off in her sleep. It was bleeding badly when I came up.'

'You've done a good job then. Do you think we should ring the doctor?'

'No.' Bryn was adamant. 'She will sleep it off in the end and wake naturally.' He sounded authoritative. 'This is Sleeper's Castle stuff, Sian. I expect she will wake herself when the time is right in her dream, but it does seem odd that she can't hear us.'

Sian glanced up at him. 'This is spooky. She's genuinely somewhere else.'

'But she's breathing normally.' Bryn reached for her wrist. 'And her pulse is steady.'

'If she was dreaming you would expect her to be moving about, and maybe talking, maybe flinging her arms around. I mean, if something awful was happening, she would be screaming, like a nightmare. Wouldn't she?' Sian murmured.

They both stood watching her closely. 'There's no rapid eye movement,' Bryn commented after a while. 'That's interesting. If she was dreaming, there should be.'

'It feels intrusive, watching her like this,' Sian said after a moment. 'As if we were spying on her.'

'Well, we can go downstairs. She seems calm enough and I'm pretty sure she's not in any immediate danger.'

Sian glanced up at him. 'As long as she lies there and doesn't decide to get up and walk about or drive the car or something.'

'Well, that's easy. We'll hide the car keys.'

'She's not drunk is she?' she said suddenly.

Bryn stared at her. 'At this hour of the morning?' He sniffed. 'No smell of alcohol. This happened to Joe, didn't it,' he went on as they walked down the stairs. 'This is what made him leave?'

Sian stared at him. 'I suppose so.'

'It freaked him out so much he left the next day.'

'But Sue stayed.'

'Sue is a tough cookie.'

'But now she's gone away for a whole year. Did you ever wonder if she was planning to come back?'

Bryn followed her into the kitchen. 'I did, yes.'

They sat down at the table.

'The strange thing is, I don't find this house scary,' Sian said. 'There are one or two houses near me at home which I find really spooky and cold and I wouldn't spend the night there if you paid me, but this place has always seemed so friendly, somehow.'

'I'm not so sure,' Bryn replied quietly.

They both turned at a sound behind them.

'What are you both doing here?' Andy was standing in the doorway.

'You're awake!' Sian cried.

'What do you mean, I'm awake? Of course I'm awake.' Andy had changed her sweater, Bryn noted, and brushed her hair. There was no sign of the new bandage under the long sleeves of her jumper. Her face was pale and tired.

'Are you OK?' he asked.

She glared at him, irritated. 'Of course, why shouldn't I be?' She eyed him. 'You weren't out there earlier were you? In the cave?'

'No. I was weeding.'

'Strange. I thought I saw you there.' Andy shivered and rubbed her arms. When her hand ran over the bandage she flinched.

'You've hurt yourself,' Bryn said gently.

'I must have caught my arm on something.'

'I know. I saw the blood.'

'You saw—'

'I'm sorry. I wasn't prying. I was worried so I rang Sian and we rebandaged it for you.'

She gaped at him. 'What are you talking about? Why on earth didn't you wake me?'

'Because we couldn't. We shouted and we shook you and we even tried a cold flannel. You were too far away in your dreams. I'm sorry. I shouldn't have been in your bedroom, but

I was worried when I couldn't find you and when I saw the blood I thought that wretched woman had tried to kill you.'

She rubbed her face wearily. 'It wasn't Rhona. I was dreaming.' It was coming back to her slowly. 'I was in a panic. I had to get out of there. I tried to snap out of it like Meryn showed me, and it didn't work.' Her teeth were beginning to chatter. 'You grabbed me,' she glared at Bryn. 'You were angry. You thought I was a ghost.'

Bryn caught Sian's eye and raised his eyebrows. 'I didn't touch you, Andy, except to feel your pulse and make sure you were all right. Sian was there. She'll tell you.'

'So how do you think this happened?' She was becoming more and more confused. 'You grabbed my arm and reopened the wound. You were so angry. You thought I was spying on you.' She couldn't stop shivering.

Sian went over and put her arm gently round Andy's shoulder. 'Come and sit down. Let me make you a hot drink,' she said firmly.

Andy didn't protest. Sian busied herself with the kettle and mugs and a few minutes later put three cups of tea on the table.

Bryn sat forward. 'Andy. Who do you think I am?' he asked.

'What do you mean?' She stared at him. She cupped her hands around the warm mug, still shivering.

'Was I in your dream with you?'

She screwed up her eyes as though she were trying to focus. 'I don't understand. Of course you were.'

'I was there, with Catrin and with you, in the past?'

'I, I don't know.'

'It wasn't Bryn there, was it,' Sian put in quietly. She leaned across and put her hand over Andy's wrist. 'You're confused. Bryn couldn't have been there, could he.'

'Edmund. It was Edmund,' she said at last.

Bryn gave a sigh of relief. 'Well, at least we've got that straight.' He glared at her. 'I hope this Edmund is a fine upstanding fellow,' he added sharply.

431

'He is.' She smiled wistfully. 'He's very good-looking actually. I am sorry I muddled you up.'

Sian laughed. 'You're blushing, Bryn!'

'I am not!'

'Please, ring Meryn,' Andy looked from Bryn to Sian and back. 'I need to talk to him.'

They tried Meryn's phone again. 'It's still switched off,' Sian said, worried. 'And it's not taking messages. Oh, he is so irritating, that man! He might have known we would be trying to contact him.'

'Try the landline,' Bryn suggested.

'It's dead.' Sian stared at the phone accusingly a minute later. 'It's completely dead.'

'Do you think Rhona cut the line?' Andy put in quietly. The tea seemed to have revived her. 'Oh God, it's the sort of thing she would do. You know she punctured all four tyres on his car.'

'She did what?' Bryn stood up, pushing back his chair.

'She was up there wandering around spying on him.'

He stood up. 'Listen, Sian, you stay here with Andy. I'm going to drive up to Meryn's and make sure he is all right.'

27

Half-hidden amongst the trees near Meryn's gate was a small red convertible. Bryn pulled up sharply and stared at it. Rhona was here.

He climbed out to investigate. Her car was locked, the bonnet cold. She had obviously been here some time. He shivered. He glanced round, taking in every possible hiding place, every hollow in the landscape, every small, knotted tree. A thrush was working in one of the thorn trees, industriously collecting haws from the brittle twigs. It would not be there if there was anyone hiding nearby. He looked round one final time then he climbed back into his van, reversed and drove back up the track, slowly, keeping his eyes skinned.

Meryn's car wasn't there. When Bryn knocked there was no reply. He made his way around to the back and knocked again then he glanced round the garden. It was open, windswept, the bushes and shrubs low-lying and bent against the force of the west wind even though the cottage huddled into a low bank in the hillside which acted as shelter. If Meryn were there he would see him.

Bryn went back and surveyed the front of the house and it

was then he spotted the phone line. It had been cut through near the wall and the loose ends had been neatly tucked into the creepers so that they didn't dangle on the ground. He heard a distant yelping cry and glanced up. A pair of buzzards were wheeling on the updraughts from the hill, high up, almost out of sight above the ridge, their huge wings no more than black dots against the heavy grey of the clouds. They probably knew where Meryn was.

He took out his mobile. Sian answered at once.

'I can't find him but Rhona is up here somewhere. Her car is parked at the end of his track and his phone wires have been cut. Don't say anything to Andy. We don't need to worry her at this stage, but be careful.' He switched off the phone. The buzzards were closer now. They were circling the high common. He could hear their mewing calls, sounding ever more urgent on the still, cold air.

Sian had gone upstairs with Andy and helped strip the sheets with their drying bloodstains off her bed, throw them in the washing machine and put her discarded jumper in the basin to soak. Then she had gone back down to the kitchen while Andy had a shower. It was as she was sitting at the kitchen table that Bryn had rung.

The call ended, Sian went to check the locks on the front and back doors with a shudder. She glanced upstairs. All had been silent up there since she came down. Bryn and Meryn would be back soon. No one could get in. All she had to do was wait.

Upstairs Andy had wandered into her bedroom wrapped in her dressing gown and only then did she allow herself to recall her dream.

She could remember it clearly now; Edmund had turned on her. He had walked towards her angrily and grabbed her arms. He had seen her, reacted to her as a real person. He had hurt her. Hurt her, Andy, in the twenty-first century.

Or had it been Bryn?

She sat down on the edge of the bed. He had looked uncomfortable, embarrassed even when she accused him. Surely he could not have been there in the dream. Or was Edmund here in real life in her bedroom? She felt a wave of heat sweep over her. She wasn't sure what she was thinking, but she had made that mistake only once before, muddled up the past and the present, and then too, it had been Bryn and Edmund who had confused her.

She closed her eyes with a shiver.

'Catrin stop it!' Edmund had his hands on her shoulders. He shook her gently to stop her screams. 'She has gone. I don't know who or what she was, but she has gone.'

Catrin was still shaking with fright. 'I have never seen her so close. She is a ghost, Edmund. The woman with buskins.'

He clenched his jaw with pain as she pressed against his chest.

'Oh, Edmund, I am sorry.' She drew back.

'No. No, don't be.' He pulled her close again and bending, kissed the top of her head. 'She was more than a ghost. She was solid flesh!'

'Her name is Andy,' Catrin said as she nestled against him, more careful of his wound this time. 'I have heard her friends talking in the echoes of the house and that is what they call her. She means me no harm.'

Andy watched, her heart thudding, aware that she had drawn back, hidden amongst the bushes, not wanting to spy but unable to look away as he bent and kissed her again, properly this time. At last he pulled away and, catching Catrin's hand, he pulled her with him back towards the house. It was deserted, there was no one there. She watched as they ran through the kitchen and up the stairs to Catrin's bedroom – Andy's bedroom – and fell together onto the bed. Then she turned away.

* * *

Bryn had climbed back in to his van, not sure what to do next when there was a knock on the window. When he recognised Meryn he slid it open with relief.

Indoors, Meryn listened to Bryn's account of what had happened. They were both looking out, watching the drive, concealed by the curtains. 'She's almost certainly capable of coming back to finish the job,' Bryn muttered, switching the subject back to Rhona. It appeared Meryn had been walking on the hill. His buzzards had called him back.

'You're right. I don't think common sense is one of the lady's main attributes,' Meryn said with a sigh. 'At least if she's here, she's not down at Sleeper's threatening Andy.'

'She must be here somewhere,' Bryn murmured, 'but where is she and what is she doing?'

They turned back to the window.

'Rob Vaughan's brother turns out to be a policeman,' Meryn went on after a moment. 'I know Andy doesn't want the police involved, but this situation is escalating out of hand. The woman is dangerous. He's going to drop in to see me, off the record, about six. When we've talked, I'll get him to drive me back to Sleeper's Castle on his way home.'

'It might be as well.' Bryn rubbed his nose. 'This scares me. All of it. Quite apart from Rhona, I don't think we can trust Andy. Not that she is doing it deliberately but, with all due respect to your techniques, I don't think she is strong enough to fight the dreams.'

'You may be right. Sian is there with her now you say?'

Bryn nodded.

'Good. She shouldn't be alone.' Meryn stiffened as he peered through the rainswept glass. 'There's someone out there now.'

'Oh no!' Bryn peered over his shoulder. 'Where?'

'She's ducked down behind your van.' Meryn grinned.

Bryn was at the door in seconds. He pulled it open and strode out into the rain. 'Mrs Wilson?'

436

Rhona stood up. There was a clasp knife in her hand. She didn't seem flustered.

'Don't you think you've done enough damage for the time being?' Bryn called. 'You may as well come inside. Let's talk about this.'

'I don't think so!' He could see the expression on her face, gleeful, excited like a naughty child, then she ducked out of sight. When he ran round the van to look for her, she had disappeared. He turned full circle, scanning the garden, his eyes narrowed against the rain. There was no sign of her.

'Leave her,' Meryn called. 'We can't hold her against her will anyway and we'll never find her.'

The mist was hanging over them now, dropping lower, filling the hollows and spaces on the higher ground. Meryn came out to stand beside him. 'Did you stop her in time?'

They surveyed the van. The tyres appeared to be intact. 'A good job you spotted her,' Bryn said with relief. 'Did you see the size of that knife?'

'I suspect that in itself would be a reason to arrest her,' Meryn said as he led the way back inside. He closed the door behind them. 'That woman's vandalism will be top of the list of the things I want to discuss with Dai. You're welcome to stay, if you wish.'

Bryn was looking increasingly anxious. 'Don't you think I should go back to Sleeper's Castle? She might go straight there next.'

Meryn frowned. 'You're right, they shouldn't be alone. But be very careful. My gut feeling is that she didn't bring that knife in order to slash car tyres, that was just a fun thing to do as she was passing.'

'You saw her face.' Bryn pushed his wet hair back from his forehead. 'She was like some kind of evil Puck figure. Gleeful. Not the least bit guilty or frightened at being caught.'

He hesitated for a moment. 'I've seen people who look and act like that before. It's not a good sign. Meryn, for personal

437

reasons I've never told anyone round here much about my past, but I trust you to keep this under your hat. I used to practise as a psychologist.'

Meryn glanced at him. 'Indeed?' he said thoughtfully. 'And it's your professional opinion that she's mad?'

'I think she may be, shall we say, dangerously unbalanced.' Bryn chose his words with care.

Meryn raised an eyebrow. 'Interesting.'

'This is more than just spite.'

'Are you going to tell the police?'

'There is nothing to tell at the moment. Everyone who meets her must realise that there's something wrong. First things first. I would like to know if your policeman thinks we have cause to have her arrested now we've caught her in action with a knife bending over my tyres. Your car is a startling piece of evidence, I would say.'

'Irrefutable. Except for the fact that neither of us actually saw her do it.' Meryn whistled through his teeth. 'This is very different to my normal line of enquiry. I'm usually called in because people have been disturbed or possessed by unhappy or vengeful spirits. Not, as a rule, a police matter.'

'Obviously not.'

'But,' Meryn went on, 'as we both have Andy's interests at heart, I would say we need to recognise our overlap of skills.' He went to stand with his back to the fire. 'I have always sensed you are not entirely unsympathetic to my areas of, shall we for the sake of argument call, expertise.'

Bryn smiled. 'You deal in ghosts and dreams. They were part of my training, believe it or not. And as for ghosts, well, I work at Sleeper's Castle.' He grinned. 'But Rhona is something else.'

'Not entirely. Andy isn't our only dreamer. I think there is more than jealousy or resentment or even mental instability motivating Rhona's behaviour. From what I sense of her aura, she is herself a sensitive. I suspect she was motivated to come up here by some kind of a psychic link to Andy and I suspect they're both being fed by the currents of energy that wash around Sleeper's Castle.' Meryn was staring down at the rush matting at his feet. He glanced at Bryn's face. 'Scientist or not, you feel all this too.' It wasn't a question.

'Which is probably why I gave up practising psychology and became a gardener.' Bryn gave a wry grin. 'I couldn't work at Sleeper's Castle and not believe it.'

'Fair enough.' Meryn nodded. 'We should work together, then.'

Rhona scrambled into her car, soaked to the skin and pulled the door shut behind her. She sat back, her head against the headrest and began to laugh. That man's face! He had caught her about to slice the tyres on his precious van and he had been calm and polite and called her Mrs Wilson! What a weak fool! She forced her wet hand down into her clammy raincoat pocket and brought out the knife. It was seeing that chisel in the old man's hand that had done it, the blood, dripping from the blade. At the mere sight of it she had felt such a surge of power and excitement she couldn't contain herself.

She looked up. The inside of the windscreen had steamed up; she could hear the rain pattering on the fabric of the roof. She was in a world of her own. She unfolded the knife and ran the blade gently against her thumb. It was sharp. It didn't take much pressure to draw blood. She stared at her hand exultantly as the hairline of scarlet appeared. The feel of the handle against her palm was glorious. She laid the knife reverently down on the seat next to her and sucked her thumb before groping for the ignition key.

She was tempted to return to Sleeper's Castle and see what had happened. She had been a fool to run away, but it was too late to change her mind now. Instead she would drive back to the pub where she was staying in Brecon before those two had the nous to call the police. She leant forward to wipe the windscreen with the back of her hand and began to turn the car.

Dai Vaughan arrived at ten past six, shortly after Bryn had left. Meryn showed him in and the two men sat down on either side of the fire.

'I want this to be entirely off the record, at least for now,' Meryn started. 'I'm not at all sure of my ground in this and I'm going to make some pretty forceful accusations. I just want your opinion and, if we can think of anything sensible to do about it, your cooperation.' He glanced at the younger man's face and was reassured by the strength of character he saw there. 'I suspect someone is planning a murder.' He had promised Bryn he would keep his name out of it for now. 'She has tried once, and she will try again.'

Meryn went through the events of the past weeks systematically. He mentioned no names, but he was pretty sure Dai knew he was talking about the woman at Sleeper's Castle. Even more so when the policeman grinned and said, 'We're not talking about the ghosts here, I take it?'

Meryn shook his head. 'That's another story and one we can ignore for the moment. No, this woman is all too real.'

Dai frowned. 'I know we agreed this was off the record, but I can't ignore the information that there is a psychotic woman walking around with a knife the size of a scimitar, you know I can't!'

'I don't want you to ignore it, but I want you to be very sure before you do anything.' He sighed. Mentioning Dafydd ap Hywell and his bloody chisel and the energy generated by his fury was not going to be any kind of corroborative evidence. 'I personally suspect the slightest thing could set this woman off on a killing spree, but I have no proof. Even Andy wonders if what happened to her on the mountain was a hallucination of some sort – she was, after all, in the first stages of hypothermia. And Mrs Wilson is cunning. You can bet you wouldn't find the knife on her if you stopped her. There'd be no point arresting her and then bailing her, or giving her a warning and letting her go. That would be the worst possible scenario – and that's what would happen, isn't it? Assuming you'd even be allowed to arrest her in the first place if you tell your colleagues down at the station that the mad wizard on the hill gave you this information based on his gut feelings.'

Dai sighed. 'I'm afraid you're not wrong there.'

'And if you were to drive past Sleeper's Castle a couple of times a day that would only excite her. She would be thrilled to know we were taking her seriously.'

'So, what do you want me to do?'

Meryn shook his head grimly. 'I don't know. Maybe just keep your eyes open. Maybe check her name. See if she's been in any kind of trouble before. We have her car number if that helps.' He was impressed that Bryn had had the foresight to write it down. 'It's a red sports car. Pretty distinctive.'

'The number helps a lot. We can check it against various databases.'

'Not just Swansea?'

'Not just Swansea. I have noted your concerns, I promise. Leave it with me.' Dai tapped the side of his nose.

In the kitchen at Sleeper's Castle, Bryn and Sian were quietly talking. Upstairs Andy slept.

Time had passed again. Glyndŵr's fortunes had waned even further. Edmund had returned to Owain's court, which was still safely based at Harlech, frequently leaving on missions to help in a quest for allies, but his job was becoming harder all the time. Support was falling away as fast as, in 1400, it had built. Several times Edmund had come back to Sleeper's Castle and to Catrin's bed. Joan knew they were lovers, but she said nothing. Sufficient that he was safe. Until now.

Edmund had returned, late at night. Once more he was

injured, though not so badly this time. His arm was swathed in dirty rags where a sword had caught him and he brought the worst of news. Harlech Castle had fallen; Margaret Glyndŵr and her family, including her daughter Catherine and the Mortimer grandchildren, all had been captured and taken to the Tower of London.

Joan and Catrin listened, white and anxious as he told them what had happened. Owain himself, his only surviving son Maredudd and a few others had escaped, and Edmund had gone with them.

'And *Tad*?' Catrin cried. 'Where is my *tad*?'

Edmund shook his head. 'He was with us earlier in the month in the castle, but he had gone, Cat, before they tightened the siege. I haven't seen him for a while. Please God and all the saints he is safe somewhere.'

He gulped down the goblet of ale they had given him.

'If the Lord Owain had asked me, I would have followed him to the ends of the earth, but he did one of his disappearing acts.' He gave Cat and his sister a sad smile. 'You know as well as I do that when he does that no one can find him until he chooses to be found. Before he vanished he told me to come back here and look after you; he told me to seek the king's peace.' He gave a rueful grimace. 'I am not important enough to warrant being held for ransom; my reward would be a noose if they caught me. Better I hold up my hands. I am not alone. His followers are falling away fast. They have no choice. This war has been terrible for Wales and her people. Whichever side has rampaged through the countryside, the result has been the same: farms laid waste, crops burnt, houses destroyed, churches and abbeys pulled down, castles captured and recaptured, ruined and rebuilt over and over again. Everyone is too tired and too hungry.' He took Catrin's hand and raised it to his lips. 'And yet, after all that, if he calls me again I will go.'

'How much money do you need for the fine?' she whispered.

He scowled in anger. 'I don't know. I am going to plead with my father for my life. Maybe he will have a change of heart.'

Before he left, as they kissed one last time, Catrin pressed a small linen bag into his hands. 'My necklace and my bracelet, and my mother's rings. They will help pay your fine.' She made to pull the silver ring from her finger but Edmund stopped her. 'The prince himself gave you that. I would never take it.' She did not remind him the prince had given the necklace and the bracelet too. Her father's treasure, if it still existed, was hidden away and she had never found it.

The four armed men arrived unannounced at dawn. They kicked in the back door and dragged Joan out of her bed. When she screamed one of them punched her on the side of her head and left her unconscious on the floor. The other three ran up the stairs. They found Catrin in her chamber asleep and dragged her out of bed and down the stairs. They roped her wrists behind her back and threw her across one of their horses. The whole arrest had taken only a few minutes.

When Joan awoke the house was empty, the doors hanging open. Betsi was cowering in the barn. 'They took her away without a word. When she screamed they tied a rag over her mouth.' She was shivering with terror.

Joan stared round the house, her head still thumping with pain. Nothing had been taken or damaged as far as she could see, only the back door. The latch had been broken, the bar splintered and the bolts wrenched off with the force of the blow that had thrust it open.

She ran upstairs to Catrin's bedchamber. The sheets were trailing off the bed where they had dragged her across the room. They hadn't touched the coffers. 'Who were they?' she turned to Betsi, who had crept timidly up behind her.

'Bedell's men. From the castle.'

'What?'

Betsi was pleating her skirt nervously between her fingers. 'I recognised one of them. They have taken her as a witch.'

Joan stared at her. 'But—' she broke off. 'Why?'

Betsi looked at her shoes. 'She magicked the weather. And she helped the rebels.'

'Did you do this, Betsi?' Joan turned on her with such a look of fury the girl flinched. 'Did you betray her?'

Betsi looked terrified. 'No, not me. I would never.'

'Then who?'

'Megan has gone,' Betsi whimpered and she burst into tears. 'I don't know if it was her.'

Joan stared about her in despair. 'Go. Get out of here!' she shouted.

Betsi fled. Joan waited until the patter of the girl's shoes died away downstairs then she went over to the corner of the room. Catrin's keys were hanging on the beam where she always put them at night. Joan went over to the coffer and knelt before it, inserting the key into the heavy padlock. She pushed back the lid against the wall and rummaged through the contents. There were rolls of parchment covered in small neat writing, three books, Catrin's most treasured possessions, the tiny, exquisitely illuminated book of hours and though Joan did not know it, not reading either Welsh or English, a collection of the poems of Taliesin, the inheritance from her long-dead mother. With them was the small book Edmund had given her, inscribed by their author, Iolo Goch. Also there was the vellum folder containing dozens of loose pages of notes on herbs and cures. Catrin's jewellery had gone. She sat back on her heels and thought. She hadn't seen Catrin give the bag to Edmund, but maybe that was what she had done.

Climbing to her feet she turned and ran downstairs. Snatching up her cloak she went out. It took only minutes to catch the pony and saddle it. Climbing on its back from the gate she set its head towards her father's farm.

She breathed a quick prayer to the Blessed Virgin that Edmund was still there. He would know what to do. She didn't let herself even think about what would happen if he wasn't there, if their father had thrown him out again.

They untied Catrin's wrists and pushed her into a small chamber at the top of the gatehouse tower. As she tore the rag from her mouth she heard the door slam behind her and the huge old lock clank into place. She ran to the narrow window and peered out. She could see the town of Hay huddled below, beyond the castle walls, parts of it still ruined and burned, other parts rebuilt. It was market day and already the stalls were in place and the market vendors setting out their wares. She and Joan had planned to go today. She felt her eyes flood with tears. She was still in shock, still unable to work out what had happened. Why was she here? The man-at-arms had hissed at her that she was accused of witchcraft. That couldn't be.

She was shivering violently and she hugged her arms around her body in an effort to warm herself. There were no shutters at the window and the ice-cold wind filled the chamber. She was still wearing nothing but her linen bed gown. Her feet were bare. She stared out again miserably. Beyond the town walls the river was hidden below its steep banks and overhanging trees, but beyond it she could see the once fertile valley, its fields laid waste by the last raid of passing soldiers. Had they been the Lord Owain's men or the king's? She wasn't sure now. Both had rampaged up and down the valley so many times over the years.

Beyond the meadows the country rose steeply on the far side of the Wye Valley towards the bleak uplands of Elfael, shrouded now in heavy cloud.

She turned away from the window and went to sit in the corner on the floorboards. At least up here the floor wasn't of stone. The room was bare, completely empty. There wasn't even a pile of straw to burrow into like an animal. She pressed herself against the stone of the wall, hugging her knees, as the tears continued to flow.

She must have dozed. When she woke she could hear the noise of the market below in full swing through the window. The sky was blue now although no sunlight shone in to warm her. There were heavy footsteps outside the door she realised. That was what had woken her as they tramped up the stairs. She heard the key in the lock and watched as the door swung open. Two men stood there. One she recognised as the man-at-arms who had carried her from her bed at dawn.

'On your feet. The constable wants to speak to you,' he said.

She managed to stand up and pushed her hair back from her face. There was little dignity in being taken before anyone in your nightgown, hair uncovered, feet bare, but that was the way it was. She raised her chin a fraction and followed them down the spiral staircase.

As she stood before him she recognised John Bedell, the rich merchant and landowner, and a fair man by all accounts, who had known her father and even had them sing in his house. The man was her grandparents' neighbour in the Wye Valley, but what use was that knowledge now? Her grandparents had never shown the slightest recognition that she even existed. No doubt their judgement and lack of interest in their granddaughter's fate would be justified when they learned of the charges against her.

Even in the warmth of the great hall beside the huge fire she found she could not stop shaking. Bedell was sitting at a table which was covered in documents and as he looked up she saw a flash of compassion before his eyes hardened again. 'Find her a cloak and shoes or she will die of cold before she can be brought to trial!' he snapped at her guards. One of them bowed and hurried away.

'You know why you have been brought here?' he asked.

She didn't reply.

'A warrant has been issued for your arrest on charges of treason, witchcraft and of . . .' he looked at a parchment which was lying on the table in front of him, 'being one of the tempestarii, that being a practitioner of weather magic. It has been stated that you were in league with the traitor Owain Glyndŵr and taught him the art of calling down rain storms and lightning and fogs to the detriment and consternation of the king's men, causing the weather in Wales to conspire against him.' He looked up at her for one second and she thought she saw a flash of humour in his eyes. 'These are serious charges, Catrin.' He sighed. 'You have been dealing with the devil.' He crossed himself piously. 'I am not able to deal with them here in Hay, so you will be taken to the assize. Until an escort can be arranged, you will stay here as my prisoner in the castle.'

He glanced behind her as the man-at-arms reappeared. He had a warm cloak over his arm and a pair of slippers. He handed them to her. The shoes were far too big, but at least they were warmer than standing on the bare flagstones of the great hall. The cloak was heavy and thick wool. She pulled it round her gratefully and at last she managed to speak.

'You have known me most of my life, John Bedell. How can you look me in the eye and charge me like this? I am your neighbour! I was coming to the market today.' She pointed towards the great doors, which were closed. Even through the walls they could hear the shouts from the street below, the bellowing of cattle and even the cheery notes of a flute and a fiddle. 'Who made this charge?' She fixed him with a steady gaze.

He glanced down at the document in front of him. 'There is no word of who made the charges, Catrin. I am sorry, I can tell you nothing. The warrant came from the bishop. His office deals with accusations of Satanic practice, the king's assize deals with treason. You should know,' he paused, 'that these charges carry the death penalty if you are found guilty.'

She gasped.

'I will see that you have a bed and food while you are here,' he went on. 'It will be some time before they send for you. There is much distraction in the countryside, as you know, and

447

the next assize is not until Lent next year.' He looked at the man-at-arms behind her. 'Take her back to her cell.'

They brought her clothes and a truckle bed with a mattress and blankets, a stool and a small table. There was a chamber pot and a pitcher of water and a pewter mug. Later they brought her a bowl of pottage and a lump of fresh bread.

'I need to speak to your constable again,' she said to the man who brought the latter. 'Will you tell him, please.'

'He's gone home,' the man replied.

'Home?' she echoed.

He gave a grim smile. 'You don't think he lives here, do you? This castle has a garrison under his command, but my officer is in charge. The constable goes home to his comfortable house when his duties here are done. He has left you in our care.'

She shrank back at the words. His eyes were all over her. 'Then I must speak to your officer,' she said as strongly as she could.

He gave a small bow. 'Yes, my lady.' The words were heavy with irony. 'I will convey your message. But I doubt he will find time before tomorrow. He has gone to the inn. One of them. Maybe all of them.' He laughed.

It was a relief when he turned away and left her alone, locking the door behind him.

'Catrin!' Andy whispered her name. 'I am here with you. Can you see me?'

Catrin was huddled on the bed miserably. She had tasted the pottage, which was cold and greasy, and pushed it aside. She had nibbled the bread and then turned to the bed as the only place where it was possible to get warm. As night fell the room grew darker and more and more chilled.

'I'll stay if you like,' Andy whispered again. She moved closer to the bed and put out her hand. 'Maybe I can help.'

Catrin did not move but Andy sensed she was listening. 'I wish I could get you out of here,' she went on. 'But maybe I can fetch help. Maybe I can find Edmund for you.'

Catrin made a little moan. She huddled down under the blankets, pulling them over her head, and Andy heard her beginning to cry.

She could do no good here.

Raising her hand she tried to click her fingers. Her hands were stiff with cold. She could make no sound. Panicking, she turned towards the door. The wood was iron-hard beneath her hands; the walls as solid as the stone they were built of. She pushed and battered at them for a long time before she gave up. She was as much of a prisoner as Catrin.

'Andy! Andy, wake up.' The voice was gently persistent. 'Can you hear me? Wake up.'

She had been hearing it for some time, ignoring it, too panicked to pay attention.

'Andy! Come back to me. Listen.' It was becoming sterner now, more insistent.

She had stopped beating on the walls of her prison. Part of her didn't want to leave Catrin. It was unfair. It was horrific. That locked door was Catrin's death sentence. And, dear God, perhaps it was hers as well.

She sniffed miserably, wiping the tears from her eyes, and sniffed again. There was a strong sweet pungent smell in her nose. It was finding its way into her dream, into her brain. It was bringing her back. Illogically she was fighting to stay asleep, yet she wanted to escape, she wanted desperately to leave that cold cell and come home.

The urge to stay asleep was growing less compelling, it was lifting.

Slowly she opened her eyes.

Meryn was standing over her. He looked at her sternly. 'Why did you not come back when I told you?'

'I didn't want to.' She waved her arm wildly, knocking something which was lying on her chest. 'What is it? What was that?' She pushed herself up on her elbows, confused and shivering. She was lying in her own bed.

'Rosemary.' He stooped and picked up the large piece of the herb, which he had held under her nose. He brushed it again, releasing more of its bitter-sweet scent. 'The next best thing to smelling salts, and I'm sure I don't have to tell you rosemary has a reputation for warding off bad dreams and night terrors. While you may choose not to listen to your ears, your nose transfers the message straight to your brain.'

She stared at him blankly, trying to make sense of what he was saying. She could see Sian by the door behind him with Bryn beside her. Meryn was forcing her to think, to come back and to remember. She leant back against the pillows and looked at her hands. They were bruised and bleeding.

He noticed at the same time she did and reached out for them gently with a sigh.

'Did you remember nothing of what I told you?' he asked.

She shook her head miserably.

'Don't touch anything; don't let anyone touch you. You anchored yourself in the past, Andy. You chose to stay there.'

'A prisoner with Catrin.' She was crying now. 'I didn't want to leave her alone. She's locked up in Hay Castle. They want to charge her with witchcraft and weather magic.' A tear trickled down her face.

'You cannot help her, Andy,' Meryn said firmly. 'Nothing you do will affect what happens to her.' He studied her face intently. 'Now, I want you to stand up.'

She gave a little whimper.

'Now, Andy.' He bent and picked up the branch of rosemary, crushing the leaves between his hands. The scent filled the room again.

'You used that to force me to wake up?'

'And it's clearing your head, whether you want it to or not.'

'Catrin has been arrested and dragged off to the castle as a prisoner.' Andy reached out and stroked the rosemary. The scent filled the air, heady, warm. 'Did you get this from the pot on the terrace? I had to help her. You do see, don't you? I had to do something. I couldn't leave her.'

'You cannot alter history, Andy.'

'But if I am there, I am part of history.'

'If you are a part of history, Andy, then the outcome is out of your hands and you must accept whatever happens, not only to Catrin, but to you as well.'

She felt herself grow cold. 'What are you saying?'

'I am saying that you must not let that happen.'

28

Bryn had three new emails waiting when he finally arrived home that night, one from London and two from the States. Sian and Meryn were spending the night at Sleeper's Castle. They didn't need him. He pushed the memory of Andy's distraught, tear-streaked face firmly out of his mind and, sitting down with his laptop, he opened the inbox and started to read.

He had sent the emails the day before. He had been mulling over Andy's mention of the fact that Rhona had spent time in the US and it was obviously worth asking. The name Rhona Wilson had drawn a blank with the first. Opening the second he sat forward with sudden interest. Chemically dyed scarlet/crimson hair was the last thing he expected to turn up in the database; who in their right mind would walk around with something so immediately recognisable? But she wasn't in her right mind, was she, and there it was. The vicious murder of a man called Abner Schmitt had happened in Massachusetts and a warrant had been issued but never served. Psychopathic was the word his former colleague in the forensic department in Boston had used. The name of the suspect was different but the description fitted exactly.

His own six-month stint in the US had been one of the most informative and exciting parts of his former career. He had nearly decided to stay out there and make it his permanent residence, but his wife had had a sharp attack of home sickness – what in Wales they call *hiraeth* – and he had come back. But he had kept in touch socially with some of his former colleagues; that much at least of his connection to his past life had held strong.

He looked back at the email. Psychopath, sociopath, what did it matter? A woman answering Rhona's description was chief suspect in a gruesome killing which was still on the books as unsolved. The victim had been a US citizen who had been resident in the UK for some time. He looked at the date. It could fit Andy's recollection. He sat back and thought for a long time. Was it too great a coincidence? He moved on to the third email, this one from a former colleague at the Maudsley Hospital in London, and there she was again, roots growing out this time, which was strange. He would have thought, given Rhona's controlling personality, that she would have ensured she was immaculate at all times. The name was Sally Smith and a note had been made that it was almost certainly an alias. Her true name had never been discovered, or more accurately, probably no one had had the time to follow it up. He looked at the dates and made a note. One killing had occurred seven months after she and Graham Wilson had split up, the other two years before their marriage. Nothing seemed to have come up in either country in the last ten years, but then, who knows, she might have discovered wigs, or taken a temporary liking to another colour or maybe she had just gone quiet, waiting for something to push her over the top again; something like the death of her husband; or even, if Meryn was right, the atmosphere of a place like Sleeper's Castle.

That thought made sense. To anyone remotely sensitive or spacy the energy at Sleeper's Castle could be overwhelming. Its history was self-evident. He remembered how he had felt when he first went to work there. In the early days the place had exhausted him; when he had started to get attuned it had become more and more energising and then at last he had begun to see things himself. Figures, shadows in the mist. Occasionally he had heard voices, snatches of conversation. He fetched himself a lager from the fridge. To someone who was already unstable it could act as a touchpaper.

He took a swig from the bottle. At least for tonight Andy was safe from the woman. Tomorrow he would go to the police.

He glanced doubtfully back at his inbox. The trouble was, unfortunately all this was purely circumstantial. There were no fingerprints, no forensics, not even what Matt in Boston described as a strand of her 'goddam hair'.

Slipping from the pony, Joan tied its reins around the gatepost and scanned the forecourt of her father's farm. There was no one about. Even the dogs were missing. She walked across to the door and went in. Her sister-in-law Elizabeth was sitting by the fire, stitching. She looked up in astonishment. 'Joan? What are you doing here?'

'I came to see Edmund. Is he here?'

She waited, holding her breath as Elizabeth stuck her needle into the soft linen coif she was sewing and stood up, dropping the work on the cushions of the settle behind her. 'Yes, he's here,' she said haughtily. 'If he wanted to endear himself to father-in-law again he couldn't have thought of a better way of doing it. Arriving as a shabby outlaw, covered in blood and dirt! He and your mother were beside themselves with worry and fear when they saw the state he was in. He told them he had forsworn Glyndŵr and your father opened his arms and forgave him everything.'

Joan came to stand closer to the fire. She was soaked through after the ride. 'Can I see him?'

Elizabeth looked her up and down. 'That won't be possible. He has gone out with your father and Richard to ride the bounds.'

'To ride the bounds?' Joan echoed. 'Is he well enough to ride?'

'Yes, he seems to think so.' Elizabeth glanced at Joan again. 'You look worried.'

'Of course I am worried. He promised he would let us know what happened after he had spoken to Father.'

Elizabeth sighed. 'I doubt if he would have wanted to remind anyone of where you work and who you work for.'

'He told you how we saved his life on more than one occasion, I trust?' Joan retorted tartly.

Elizabeth sneered at her. 'Oh yes, he did that all right.'

'And what did Father say?' Joan was becoming impatient. She and Elizabeth had never seen eye to eye.

Elizabeth shrugged her shoulders eloquently. 'He was too thrilled with the return of the prodigal son,' she said coldly, 'to think about you. Father has been celebrating ever since. Naturally, he killed the fatted calf and tonight there will be a feast.'

Joan heaved a great sigh of relief. 'And has he paid the fine?' She folded her arms under her wet cloak, trying to stem her shivering. Elizabeth had made no move to offer her a change of clothes or even ask her to sit down. She was still standing dripping onto the rush matting where she had been since she walked into the room.

'What fine?' Elizabeth looked shocked.

Joan bit her tongue. Obviously the woman hadn't been told everything.

'I hope it is not something he wants paid by his father!' Elizabeth was growing more indignant by the second. 'The income from this farm has dropped to almost nothing since these wretched wars.'

'No, nothing like that.' Joan gave up waiting to be asked. She untied her cloak and dropped it on the floor where she stood, then she moved closer to the fire and squatted down on the hearthstone, holding out her hands to the fire. 'I'll wait to see him now I'm here,' she said tartly. 'Where is my mother?'

'She's resting upstairs. You can go and see her later.' Joan's mother had never been a strong woman; she had handed over the reins of the house to her daughter-in-law with what seemed to be alacrity as soon as Richard had married, retiring to her solar upstairs where she sewed and wove and dreamed her days away, appearing only for meals.

'You had better sit down.' Elizabeth was finally shamed into action. She called two of her maids and bade one of them fetch a warm shawl for her sister-in-law and to take her cloak away to dry in the bakehouse, then she told the other to throw more logs on the fire. Joan took the proffered stool, with its comfortable cushion, reminding herself that for all her airs and graces her sister-in-law had married into a yeoman family, albeit a wealthy one, and was no better than Joan herself. It was a comforting thought.

As though picking up on Joan's reverie Elizabeth leaned forward from her seat on the cushioned settle and addressed her with a supercilious smile. 'So, you still work for the Welsh poet and his daughter?'

Joan tightened her lips. 'I do.'

'They don't make you speak the devil's language, do they?'

Joan clenched her teeth. 'If you mean Welsh, I speak it, as do many of your neighbours, living on the border as we all do,' she said shortly. 'As does Father. And Edmund. I am surprised you have not learned it yourself after all these years married to Richard.'

It was with some satisfaction she saw Elizabeth's face colour.

It was nearly dark when the three men came home. Joan stood up nervously as her father appeared. Raymond of Hardwicke stopped in his tracks, staring at her, then he gave a curt smile. 'So, Joan. Have you come to see how Edmund does?'

She nodded.

Edmund stepped forward. He was very pale and he looked exhausted. 'How are you, Joan? Is everything all right?'

'No,' she whispered. 'I need to talk to you urgently.'

Edmund glanced round. The rest of his family were talking together loudly, and fussing over one of the family dogs, which had torn its paw on some brambles while they were out.

He caught Joan's hand and led her into the far corner of the room. 'We'll have to talk here. Hurry. What is it? What's happened?'

'Catrin has been arrested. She is being held in Hay Castle on charges of witchcraft and treason.' Her eyes filled with tears. 'They dragged her off at dawn.'

Edmund stared at her, aghast. 'I don't believe it.'

'It's true. Betsi went down to the market to see if she could find anything out. They are talking about nothing else. They say she will be taken before the Lent Assize. They say . . .' she paused and looked up at him miserably, 'they say she will be hanged for treason or burned as a witch.'

'Edmund?' Elizabeth's voice was sharp. 'Come over here near the fire. I am sure Joan can't have any news she can't share with the rest of the family.'

They glanced at each other and reluctantly moved closer to the fire. Edmund was white with shock.

'So, Joan, how is life with the poet and his daughter?' Her father looked at her critically.

'My life with them is busy, Father,' she replied. She met his eye boldly. 'As you know we looked after Edmund and dressed his wounds on more than one occasion before he rode on here. I came to see how he was as no one had seen fit to let us know.'

Raymond looked at her in irritation. 'Didn't Elizabeth send a maid over to inform you?' He glared at his daughter-in-law.

She looked slightly discomfited. 'I am sorry. I meant to arrange it. I must have forgotten. There was so much to do with celebrating Edmund's return.'

Joan said nothing. Her withering glance at her sister-in-law spoke volumes. 'Soldiers raided Sleeper's Castle this morning,' she said defiantly. 'They knocked me out and took Catrin away.'

Her words were greeted by a stunned silence.

'Why should they do that?' Elizabeth spoke first.

'I don't think they need a reason,' Joan snapped. 'There is hardly a farmstead or manor in the whole Wye Valley which hasn't been visited by one side or the other over the last half-dozen years. She has been charged with treason.' She glanced at Edmund.

'And her father?' Edmund asked.

'Wasn't there, naturally!' Joan couldn't keep the bitterness out of her voice.

'It sounds like a trumped-up charge,' Edmund said firmly. 'And if Dafydd is not there to help her, then we must.'

Elizabeth snorted derisively. 'I don't think so. It is none of our business. From what I hear about Mistress Catrin, it's far from a trumped-up charge. That girl has been dabbling in the devil's arts for a long time. I'm not surprised to hear she is a traitor as well. That was why we were so against you working there from the start, Joan. If you hadn't been such a stubborn little—'

'Enough, Elizabeth!' Raymond roared. 'Joan has decided to work for these people, so she is part of their household. We should at least make enquiries as to what the situation is.'

'I will do that,' Edmund said.

His brother stared at him. 'You will not. You are under suspicion yourself.'

'He's what?' Raymond stared at him.

'Oh come on, Father. You know where Edmund has been for these last few years.' Richard glared at him.

Raymond did not reply. He turned away from them. 'My son has been in the army,' he said, his voice tight. 'It has not been possible to keep track of where he has been and I have not enquired.' He rubbed his hands together slowly. 'He returned to us wounded and we have cared for him as any family would. That is all I need to know. Hopefully he will stay with us now and help to run the farm.'

Richard scowled. 'So, the prodigal son returns,' he said coldly, unwittingly echoing his wife. 'How nice.'

'And why not?' Raymond said angrily.

'Meanwhile,' Joan said, long accustomed to inserting herself between her warring brothers, 'what of Catrin?'

'A Welsh woman,' Elizabeth said coldly. 'Don't forget the sanctions the king has laid down against the Welsh. No English man may marry one, for a start.' She glanced at Edmund with something like a spark of triumph in her eyes. 'If he does, he forfeits everything. And her father is a poet and such men are forbidden to ply their trade ever again.'

'The English king and his parliament are punishing Wales sorely,' Edmund said softly.

'Of course they are. They are a nation of thieves and rebels, and as such, however much you may feel we should sympathise with Catrin and her father,' Elizabeth went on, 'we are in no position to help them. It is against the law.'

She turned as two serving men staggered in carrying a huge basket of logs, which they put down near the fire. 'Set up trestles and tell cook we have one extra for our meal.' She looked at Joan. 'I suppose you will be staying the night?'

'Oh yes, I'll be staying the night!' Joan straightened her shoulders.

She did not get a chance to speak to Edmund alone until much later that evening. Elizabeth had retired to the nursery to say goodnight to her children, Richard had gone out to make sure the men had settled the stock for the night and Raymond was sitting at his desk in his study, his account books in front of him.

Edmund beckoned Joan into the corner by the fire. 'When did they take Catrin?' he asked urgently.

'This morning, before I was awake. I told you. Betsi saw it all. They kicked in the door and dragged her away.'

'And you have no idea who informed on her?'

Joan shook her head.

459

Edmund caught her arm and made her face him. 'Are you sure you don't know, Joan?'

'You think it was me?' She wrenched her arm away.

'I don't know. Sometimes I have thought you disliked her. I thought you resented her. At other times I thought you were close friends. I could make no sense of your relationship.'

'She supports Glyndŵr and I don't.' Joan raised her chin and glared at him. 'And we don't always get on, I admit it. We are very different people. You know that. She is . . .' she paused, trying to think of the right words to explain. 'She is educated, a lady, yet not a lady. She is a dreamer, she is an independent spirit who does not like to abide by the rules. She is the woman her father made her, but she is loyal to me. She and I are friends, Edmund. We talk together, we sit and sew together, we laugh together and it was my choice to take a position with her and serve her. I would never, never, never betray her, no matter what the law says. Everyone in the whole valley, everyone in the whole March is torn, Edmund. We English have friends who are Welsh and we are told to despise them; the Welsh have friends who are English and they are told they may not treat us as friends. It is a sad time to be alive.'

There was a long silence. At last Edmund put his arm round her shoulders and gave her a hug. 'My eloquent sister! So, my question remains. Who has betrayed her?'

'Betsi said she thought it might be Megan, but it could be anyone in the valley, anyone in Hay. It could be a passing drover, a pedlar, a rival poet who is jealous of Master Dafydd's talent, or hers. She is a poet in her own right, as you well know.' She paused. 'Her own father is jealous of her.'

'It wouldn't be him.'

'Why not? He and she do not get on any more. Sometimes I think he actually hates her. Where is he? He has been away since they had that terrible quarrel. I assumed he had gone back to Glyndŵr's service, but you say that is all over and everyone has fled. She doesn't know where he is. She thought he was at Harlech with you.' She fell silent, then she went on, 'Will Father give you the money to pay the fine and come into the king's peace, Edmund?'

'I think he will. But Richard mustn't know.'

She gave a small nod. 'Nor Elizabeth. She is still as unpleasant as ever, I see. Why on earth did he marry her?'

'She brought land with her. Father had ambitions.' Edmund gave a wry smile. 'You and I are a complete failure in that respect.'

Joan gave a little snort.

Edmund sighed. 'Poor Cat. She must be so frightened.'

'You can do something, can't you?'

'I'll do my best.' He gritted his teeth. 'Of course I will. I am not going to let her rot there and I am not going to let them drag her off to the assize.'

He rode back to Sleeper's Castle at first light while the rest of the household was still asleep. He needed to see for himself what had happened there. The house was empty, the doors unlocked. He went in and looked round. All the fires were out. There was no sign of Betsi or Peter. He walked through the cold house slowly, room by room. It was undamaged apart from the back door. No one appeared to have been in since Joan had left. The place already felt damp and uncared for. He walked through every room downstairs, aware that he was moving as silently as possible. Dafydd's study was as Joan described it. His desk was empty, his candlesticks assembled on a small table, the candles burned down into pools of cold beeswax, his coffer pushed back against the wall. There were no papers or books. It was as if when Dafydd left he had taken everything he still possessed.

Edmund pulled out the coffer and searched for the loose flag. It was there, easy to spot as it stood proud of its neighbours. The space under it was empty, as he had known it would be. He left the coffer where it was and walked back into Catrin's parlour. That too looked bleak and uncared for. When he reached the bottom of the stone staircase, he stood looking up, listening. He could not see round the bend in the stairs where it curved behind the chimneystack. He put his foot on the bottom step and began to climb. Halfway up he stopped. Some sixth sense told him there was someone up there. He put his hand to his belt and pulled out his dagger, then he went on up. He went into the room on his left first. It was Dafydd's bedchamber. Small, it was furnished with an oak bed and two large coffers. One or two garments still hung from the pegs on the wall, but otherwise the room was empty. He walked across the floor, hearing the creak of boards beneath his feet as he did so. He lifted the lid on one of the coffers. It contained bedcovers and blankets. When he pulled them out they gave off a smell of dust. The other coffer was all but empty. A few old clothes, two spare sets of braies, a torn shirt, otherwise nothing.

He turned and went into Catrin's bedroom. There were signs of her everywhere. The bedclothes pulled from the bed and still trailing across the floor, her shoes tossed to one side, her gowns hanging from their pegs, her coffer, the lid open, full of shifts and girdles. He took out one of her shifts and buried his face in it longingly. Her harp stood on a low bench by the wall. Her combs lay on the table near the window with her mirror and a dish of trinkets. He stared round. The soldiers had touched nothing. In spite of himself, he was impressed.

As he stood looking out of the window he sensed that someone was standing behind him. He tensed, his fingers tightening on the hilt of his dagger, then he spun round. It was Peter. His eyes widened and he turned to flee, but Edmund lunged forward and caught him by the collar. 'Stand still! I won't hurt you,' he exclaimed. 'What are you doing here?'

'Everyone else has gone,' Peter cried. 'Even Betsi. I didn't know where to go. I stayed to feed the hens.' A tear rolled down his face. 'I heard you and I ran up here to hide. I didn't do no harm, I swear.'

Edmund released him. 'Of course you didn't. That was the right thing to do, to feed the hens and keep an eye on the place.' He scrutinised the young man's face. 'You know who I am, don't you? I am Dame Joan's brother. I was here for a while when I was ill and you've often seen me visit.'

Peter nodded.

'Do you know where Master Dafydd is?'

The boy shook his head.

'Did you not go with him last time he left?'

Peter shook his head again.

'And Mistress Catrin?'

His eyes grew even larger. 'They carried her away on the back of a horse. Her hands were tied.' Another tear followed the first.

'And we have to rescue her.' Edmund swallowed the wave of impotent rage that swept over him. He stared round helplessly. The least he could do here was save Catrin's possessions so they would be there for her once he had thought of a way of getting her out of Hay Castle. 'There are things I need.' He looked at the young man thoughtfully. 'Is there a cart or a trap here?'

'The ox-cart is in the barn.'

'And the ox?'

'In the back field.'

'Can you drive it?'

The young man nodded.

Edmund gave a grim smile. 'Then let us collect Mistress Catrin's belongings and put them in a coffer and load them onto the cart, plus anything else you can think of that might be useful. And we will put the hens in a coop and take them with us and you shall drive the cart to my father's farm where you will find a place at our hearth until Master Dafydd and Mistress Catrin come home. Does that sound good to you?'

The young man wiped his nose on the back of his hand. 'It's good.'

Edmund sent him to find something to lever the padlock off Catrin's locked chest, then while he went out to organise the ox-cart he carefully packed up her harp and a selection of her clothes. He forced open the second coffer and took out all her writing materials, her pens and the rolled poems, and her three precious books. He held the book he himself had given her for a moment, dropped a quick kiss on its cover then, wrapping them in a shawl he placed them in the larger chest with her clothes and shoes. Closing it, he tied it shut with a cord.

'And is there anything special of Master Dafydd's we should take to keep it safe for him for when he returns?' Edmund asked when they had piled everything they could save onto the cart.

He watched Peter's face. It was completely without guile as he replied. 'Master Dafydd hid things in the Dreamer's Cave,' he said. He met Edmund's eyes trustingly. 'He didn't know I saw him going in there.'

'Show me.' Edmund tried not to betray the wave of optimistic excitement which swept over him. He followed Peter out of the house and through the garden. In the cave nothing had been touched as far as he could see. He could smell the bat droppings and see the dusty bracken piled against the back wall. He stopped, unable to see in the darkness after the sunlight outside. Peter made his way surefootedly to the back and felt his way along the cave wall. There, high up in the fissured rock, was a hole, invisible in the darkness and probably invisible even in candlelight. Peter pulled himself up onto the log which had been left there and reached up on his toes. After a moment's scrabbling Edmund heard the drag of something heavy and the chink of metal. He closed his eyes and breathed a prayer of thanks to the Blessed Virgin as the boy pulled down one and then another heavy bag. He jumped down from the log and looked at Edmund expectantly, his face barely visible in the twilight which seeped in from the fern-covered entrance. Edmund smiled at him. 'You have done well. Master Dafydd

464

will be so pleased we have rescued these. Now run and harness the ox and we will go together. My horse is in the paddock at the back.'

One bag was full of coin; the other contained four of Dafydd's most precious small books, their pages gilded and illuminated, wrapped in soft leather oiled to ward off the damp.

When they left the house their menagerie had been increased by three: the two short-legged cattle dogs which followed Peter unquestioningly, and the house pig which squealed frantically as it was lifted into the cart. The sheep they left behind. They would wander on the hill and join another flock. The barn cats would look after themselves.

Edmund was pretty sure, as he rode behind the cart, that Peter knew as well as he did that it was unlikely they would ever return.

Neither of them saw the woman watching from the house doorway as the ox slowly plodded down the track.

Andy stared after them. She hadn't wanted to see Edmund and the farm hand. She had wanted to be with Catrin. To find herself drifting alone round the deserted house was bleak and frustrating. She turned into the kitchen and stared round. One of the little brindled cats peered in at the doorway. She made an involuntary movement towards it and it fled.

Slowly she climbed the stairs and looked round. Inexplicably, night seemed to have come between one moment and the next. How much time had passed? She had no way of knowing, save that the wind which whistled through the rooms seemed to be colder than before. It smelt of snow. There was someone else there now, in Catrin's room. Her room. She tiptoed along the short passage and peered in through the doorway. Catrin's father was standing there, looking round. Andy stepped back slightly into the shadows, watching as he walked across to Catrin's chest and threw back the lid. It was empty, the black iron hasp hanging off. He stood staring down into it for several seconds then he turned away. Andy stepped hastily backwards out of sight. She followed him towards his own bedchamber, into which he glanced perfunctorily from the doorway before turning back to the staircase.

His next port of call was the cave. He walked across the garden without looking left or right. She was correct about the change of season. The leaves had fallen from the trees and the garden was bleak and cold. So, what had happened to Cat? She stopped in her tracks. She wanted to be with her, to know how she was, but still she felt compelled to follow Dafydd as he ducked into the cave.

His howl of fury several minutes later told it all. His hiding place was empty. She heard him crashing around inside the cave and imagined him searching for other fissures in the wall in case he had made a mistake about where he had left his precious bags, searching the floor beneath the dried leaves and bracken in case they had fallen to the ground. It was a long time before he emerged. His face was white with shock and anger. He stood still outside the cave entrance and looked round. It seemed to dawn on him at last that the place was deserted. The only animal was the horse he had ridden into the paddock and left hitched to the fence. The hens had gone and the dogs; there was no sound from the pigsty or ox pen.

Watching, Andy wondered where he had been all this time. His clothes were mud-spattered, the roll on the back of his saddle appeared to be the only luggage he had with him. Not once had he called out for Catrin or Joan. He must have known they weren't there.

He was walking back towards the horse now, still looking round. With a sigh he unsaddled the old cob, took the roll off, unhitched a saddlebag, then he slipped off the bridle and turned the animal loose in the paddock where it trotted round, calling in vain for its former companions.

He found the flint and tinder in the kitchen without any trouble and lit the fire in the hearth before opening the door to the pantry. He found himself enough food to throw in the pot and discovered a jar of mead on a top shelf in the stillroom. He stood contemplating Catrin's store of herbs and medicaments then pushed them aside violently, sweeping his arm along the shelf, knocking them to the floor before turning away and slamming the door shut behind him. He took a long swig of mead and smacked his lips, then he pulled up a stool to sit in front of the fire while his food heated.

The wind outside was rising. The sound of the trees thrashing and the roar of water in the brook hid the sound of the approaching men. Andy watched as the kitchen door was pushed open and the first soldier stepped in. He had a drawn sword in his hand.

29

Andy awoke all at once. She was in her bedroom, Cat's bedroom, and it was dark outside. She lay still, not daring to move, listening. The small bedside lamp was on and the room was full of shadows. She was alone. She sat up slowly and swung her legs to the floor, sitting still for several moments as she tried to gather her wits. She glanced at her wristwatch. It was ten past two. She screwed up her eyes and rubbed them. She was so tired she couldn't get a grip on her whirling thoughts. Meryn had been with her. Surely he wouldn't have left her alone in the middle of the night. Then she remembered. Meryn and Sian were downstairs. She was safe. She sniffed. She could smell the pungent scent of rosemary. She brought her fingers to her nose. It was still there on her skin.

So what had she been dreaming about? She tried to remember. Catrin, in the castle? No. No, she had been dreaming about Edmund. He had come back here to try and find the money. He wanted Dafydd's money. Why? Of course, to pay his fine and come into the king's peace. That would mean he was forgiven for his part in the rebellion. Life could go back to normal. Except that his Catrin was gone.

She stood up and went over to the window, pushing it open and leaning on the sill to look out through the old stone mullions. The brook was in spate, so it had been raining up on the mountain. Water was pouring over the rocks and crashing down into the pool below. She heard the owl hoot. The sound sent goose pimples up her arms. There was a movement below in the garden. She caught her breath nervously, then she saw who it was and smiled, reassured. Meryn was walking slowly up and down the terrace in the dark, the light from the kitchen throwing his long shadow out across the grass. She saw the ridiculous shape of a cat, elongated, erect tail monstrously long, approaching him. He bent and picked it up and momentarily their shapes merged into one as he crooned lovingly into Pepper's ear. She smiled affectionately. How could she be afraid of anything when she had good friends like Meryn and Pepper, like Sian and Bryn. But she was afraid. The past like a huge black veil hung over her, threatening her, overshadowing her with its secrets.

Sitting on the bed she reached for the history of Glyndŵr which she had left on the table. She opened it and slowly turned the pages. The last chapter was headed 'The End of the Dream and the Birth of a Myth'. After the capture of Harlech, Owain's wife and family had been dragged away to the Tower, nearly a full decade after the first wonderful excitement of the declaration at Glyndyfrdwy. Owain himself and Maredudd, their only surviving son still free, had escaped to fight on. The rebellion trickled on for another year, then after what turned out to be his final defeat on the Shropshire borders, where three of his last and most staunch supporters were captured and executed, Owain Glyndŵr slipped away into the mountains for the last time and disappeared from history.

Andy put down the book, her eyes full of tears. She had wanted to know what happened in the end, but to read it now that she was involved was just too much. All the dreams, all the plans for a glorious independent Wales had collapsed like a house of cards. How could it have all come to an end so quickly, so completely? She lay back against the pillows for several minutes, her eyes closed.

She ought to get up and go downstairs to find her notebook. She must not stop making her notes. Somehow she had to stand back and maintain some kind of perspective on this incredible story. But it was so hard.

Taking a deep breath she opened her eyes and sat up.

And let out a scream. Dafydd, dripping with blood, his hair matted on his head, his clothes torn and mangled, was standing in the middle of the room watching her.

Meryn was outside on the back lawn, looking up at the stars, lulled by the sound of the water. He had heard the owl and smiled as Pepper nestled closer to his neck as though aware that the night was his domain, but content to stay and cuddle like a housecat for a few minutes more. At the sound of the scream from upstairs Pepper leapt from Meryn's shoulder, leaving a deep scratch across his neck. He fled into the darkness as Meryn ran back towards the house.

He took the stairs two at a time.

Dafydd was standing on the landing.

Meryn stopped in his tracks, panting. He eyed the apparition cautiously. 'So, my friend. You look as though you've been in the wars,' he said after a moment. The figure was standing between him and Andy's bedroom. He took a step forward. 'Andy? Are you all right?' he called.

There was no answer.

'Andy?' He took another step.

Dafydd was looking straight through him, his expression vacant, his eyes black holes in his face.

'Andy? I need you to answer me,' Meryn called again.

There was no response. He moved forward again, closer to the figure. He could sense nothing from it but an intense cold. 'Are you a God-fearing man, Dafydd ap Hywell?' he demanded quietly.

470

He thought the remnant of the man who had once been Dafydd heard him, but the figure made no reaction.

'Did you meet your end here, in this house?' Meryn pressed. He kept his voice even. 'Did you die here unshriven?'

He sensed it now, anger and pain and terror, and somewhere there behind the final act of violence which clung to him like a bloody garment, a deep regret, but the figure was fading. 'I am sure God will forgive your sins, my friend,' Meryn said quietly. 'And whatever happened in this house, whatever violence you suffered here, whatever pain you caused your daughter, it is time to forgive yourself and move on.' He stepped forward into the intensity of cold which clung round the shadow. No more than a shadow now. Then it was gone.

He drew in a deep slow breath. He might have gone for the time being, but he was under no illusion that the problem that was Dafydd ap Hywell ap Gruffydd was solved.

Meryn brushed his shoulders as if to remove a clinging spider's web and hurried into Andy's room. She was lying crouched on the bed, her eyes closed, her fists clenched on the blanket she had pulled over herself.

'Andy?' Meryn sat down beside her and put his hand on her forehead. It was ice-cold. 'Andy? I want you to wake up!' he commanded.

She did not respond.

She was in the castle.

She was holding Catrin's hand.

Catrin was sitting on the edge of the bed, rocking backwards and forwards in her misery. She had been sick twice and she was shivering violently. Andy put out a hesitant hand and touched her forehead.

Catrin shrank back as if she had been burned. 'Who are you? Go away!' she murmured.

Taken aback, Andy stood up and went to the table. Picking up the wooden beaker, she poured a little water from the jug that stood there and passed it to Catrin who took it reluctantly. Andy watched her sip. The cell, high in the tower, facing north across the town and the river towards the hills of Elfael, was bitterly cold. They had brought more blankets and given Catrin more food, but there had been no news of what was to happen to her. She asked the guards again and again when they came to bring her water or bread or pottage. Sometimes they brought her more substantial food. One of the men, more garrulous than the others, told her that was when the constable was in residence. He had ordered she be fed from his own table. He had not forgotten she was there. She sat staring into space and her hand strayed to her stomach. It was an unconscious gesture, gentle, caressing but in that moment it betrayed everything.

Oh God, Andy thought. She's pregnant.

Catrin stared up at her, startled, as if she had spoken out loud. Then she burst into tears.

Andy looked on helplessly, unable to comfort her, unable to do anything.

She didn't know if she slept; Catrin lay on her pallet on the ground shivering. It was at dawn that they heard the tramp of feet on the steps outside the door, the rattle of the key, the creak of the hinge. Andy drew back into the corner as Catrin sat up. A flicker of light played across the stone and a figure appeared in the doorway, a lantern in his hand. 'Hurry! Come!'

The two words were whispered, barely audible.

Catrin scrambled to her feet. 'Why? What's happened?' She was terribly afraid.

'Follow me if you want to get out of here alive.' The man retreated, holding the door open and waved her past him.

Catrin grabbed the cloak from her bed and ran towards the door. The candle flame guttered in the lantern and the shadows flickered up the walls, then she was gone. The door swung shut and the key turned in the lock.

Andy followed her to the door expecting to be there on the winding stair with her, running down towards the bailey. She put her hand out. It met the solid wood of the door, then the stone wall. She turned round desperately in the empty cell. She was locked in.

The rosemary had worked before. Meryn had retrieved the branch from the shelf where she had left it and held it under her nose once more, crushing the soft needles in his fist. 'Come on, Andy!' he commanded. 'We don't need this. I want you back here.' He shook her gently. He could see it was no use. Under her lids her eyes were darting back and forth rapidly, her face contorted with fear, and she was beginning to make swift desperate lunges with her hands.

'Help me!'

'Andy, I am here, wake up.'

'Help me. Let me out!' She was crying now. He could see the tears trickling beneath her closed eyes. 'Please, I shouldn't be here!' She sat up and clutched at the front of his sweater. 'Oh God help me.' He felt her begin to shiver.

Gently he pushed her back against the pillow and pulled the blanket over her again, watching her carefully. They were enveloped by the spicy smell of the rosemary. She was more peaceful now, lying quietly, clutching the bedcovers up to her chin. 'Where are you, Andy?' he murmured. He touched her hand gently. It was ice-cold. He lifted the pile of sweaters from the chair near the window and pulled it over beside the bed. Then he sat down. 'You and I need to talk, Andy,' he murmured. 'I know you can hear me. I want you to listen.'

Downstairs Sian had awakened with a start. In her dream she had heard the scream. She sat up, staring round. Outside the curtains it was daylight. She had been asleep on the sofa in Sue's little parlour, covered in a rug. Staggering to her feet she made her way into the great hall and looked towards the staircase, her heart thudding with fright. She took two steps up, then she heard Meryn's voice from upstairs. It was steady, soothing. Whatever was going on up there he was dealing with it.

She glanced at her watch then headed towards the kitchen. It was just after eight. She had to get back to her dogs.

Bryn had decided it was raining too hard to go to work. His first email had gone off as he was waiting for his coffee to perk; there was little chance of it being read for a few hours yet. However keen the man was it was still the middle of the night in Boston. He pondered the wisdom of getting in touch with Meryn's policeman contact, Dai Vaughan, direct. The police would be necessary at some stage, but in the meantime perhaps he would wait for more concrete information.

It might be too wet to work, but he was too worried about Andy to stay away for long. It took Bryn no time at all to drive to Sleeper's Castle and tuck his car in next to Andy's. He headed round to the back door. It was locked. He knocked gently, then more loudly. Stepping back onto the grass he looked up at Andy's bedroom window in time to see a face in the shadow.

Meryn opened the door and drew him in. 'Sian had to go back to let her dogs out. And Andy's upstairs.' Meryn sighed. 'She promised me she was going to take a shower and come down to breakfast. When she didn't appear I went up. She's gone back to sleep and I can't wake her.'

Bryn stared at him in astonishment. 'I thought you knew all about this stuff.'

'I do, usually.' Meryn pursed his lips. 'This house is so powerful.' He sighed. 'And so is she. She's determined to stay there, in the dream.'

'And you don't want to leave her to sleep it off?'

'I'm not convinced what is happening is good for her.'

Meryn led the way out of the kitchen and upstairs and the two men made their way into Andy's bedroom.

She was lying sprawled on the bed, clutching her pillow to her as if her life depended on it. The room smelt strongly of rosemary. Her hair was tangled across the pillow, her face white, her eyes not merely closed but almost screwed up against the light. As they watched, she began to thrash to and fro, groaning, then she lay silent again.

'Look at her hands,' Bryn whispered as the two men looked down at her. Her fingers were clawing at the pillow, her nails splitting and bleeding as they watched.

'She's tearing at something far more solid than a pillow in her dream,' Meryn said quietly. 'A wall perhaps, or a door.'

'You have to do something!' Bryn said in anguish. 'For goodness' sake! You can't leave her like this.' He pushed Meryn aside and, taking Andy by the shoulders, he shook her hard. 'Andy! Andy wake up!'

She gasped and tried feebly to pull away from him. Meryn put his hand on Bryn's shoulder. 'Leave her. She can't hear you.'

'But we have to do something.' Bryn looked round. 'Supposing we take her out of the house?'

Meryn frowned, then he understood. 'Because the house is making her dream? It's worth a try.'

Between them they pulled her off the bed. Bryn draped her arm around his shoulders and with Meryn on the other side they half dragged half walked her across the room and down the stairs. Opening the kitchen door they edged her out into the garden, panting, and lowered her onto the bench. 'I'll fetch a rug to keep her warm.' Bryn ran back into the house.

Meryn sat down beside Andy, then he caught her hand and rubbed it. 'You're free, Andy. Wherever you are, you can come home now,' he said gently. 'See, the door is opening. Walk towards it. It's morning. The sun is rising. You are free.'

She grew still at last, shivering. He looked up as Bryn appeared with the rug and they tucked it round her. 'Andy, wake up,' Meryn said again. 'You are free now. Walk outside and come home.' She gave a groan. 'Do you want me to come and fetch you?' He tucked her hands under the blanket. 'Face me, Andy,' he went on. 'And open your eyes.'

After a moment's hesitation as the two men held their breath she seemed to hear him. She turned her head slightly. Bryn breathed a great sigh of relief. 'Oh thank God!'

Meryn leant forward. 'Open your eyes, Andy. Wake up now. You are free.'

30

Roy Pascoe had parked the car a couple of miles away at the bottom of the hill. This was one of his favourite walks, up through the fields following the network of tracks up towards the Offa's Dyke Path which led over the high tops of the Black Mountains towards the south. It had stopped raining and a soft curtain of mist was drifting across the fields. He had dropped Ella off with a friend in Hay and had promised to go and pick her up later. Their boy Friday was looking after the shop. The rest of the day was his. He took a deep breath of fresh air; he felt blissfully light-hearted and free.

He stopped to extricate his camera from his daysack and hung it round his neck. Somewhere above the mist he heard the cronking call of a raven.

The path led up through the foothills behind Sleeper's Castle and gave him a perfect view of the house in the distance. He could see the lichen-covered slates of the roof, the old stone chimney, the clump of houseleeks nestled in the angle of the roofs above the guttering. It was an attractive old building, built in an L-shape around a stone-flagged courtyard, which opened on two sides onto a terrace. He could see the stone walls to one side, now in ruins and photogenically hung with moss and fern. There was a large expanse of gardens around the back and what looked like a couple of paddocks nestling into the side of the hill. As he stood staring down at the house a beam of sunlight broke through the mist, lighting up the lichen on the roof in shades of orange and silver. It was beautiful. He groped for his camera and headed down the field to get a closer shot.

He stopped abruptly. He hadn't realised there were people in the garden at the back of the house. Holding his breath, he edged closer. Andy and Bryn and Meryn. It was peaceful down there and very private and suddenly he didn't want to intrude. All he wanted was a photo of that lovely roof.

He moved closer. He would take the picture from the hedgerow and then turn back without disturbing them. He was placing his feet carefully amongst the litter at the foot of the hedge so as not to make a noise when he glanced away from the scene in the garden and realised there was someone standing near him. He turned to look and found himself face to face with a woman wearing a belted raincoat. She was only a few feet away from him and in her hand there was a large knife. He had no time to cry out, no time to think. The last thing he did was click the shutter on the camera as he fell forward into the bushes.

Bryn sat down on the other side of Andy, drawing the rug more tightly round her. 'You're fine, Andy. Safe now.' He groped for her hand and held it tightly. 'Stay with us. You're awake. It was only a dream.'

Meryn was standing beside them, distracted, staring beyond the lawn towards the hedge. 'Take her inside, Bryn.' He had heard the raven's warning and now he felt the surge of visceral fear on the air, sensed the blood. He had seen the agitated sway of leaves and branches. This was not part of Andy's dream.

Bryn looked up, hearing the urgency in Meryn's voice. 'What is it?'

'I think we have a visitor.'

Bryn didn't hesitate. He threw his arm round Andy and pulled her to her feet. 'Can you walk or shall I carry you?'

She was too confused and exhausted to argue. She staggered a few steps, and then leant towards him as he swung her up into his arms. Staggering under her weight he half ran with her towards the kitchen door. Inside, he slid her onto a chair. 'Will you be all right there? Let me go and make sure Meryn is all right.'

She was pale, dishevelled, scented with rosemary. 'What is it? What's happened?' she stammered, but he had already gone back to the door. He stared out. Meryn had disappeared.

Turning towards Andy he watched for a fraction of a second as she sat, her hands spread out on the table in front of her. He grabbed the key from the lock, pulled the door shut behind him and locked it. At least she was safe. He ran across the lawn towards the far hedge seeing now where Meryn had forced his way through, breaking branches as he went.

'Don't try and come,' Meryn's voice emerged from the undergrowth. 'Call an ambulance.'

'Are you OK?'

'I'm fine. It's Roy Pascoe. He's been stabbed.'

Bryn froze. 'Is he alive?'

'Yes.'

'Rhona?'

'No sign of her. Stay with Andy till they come. I'll wait with him.'

Bryn could see them now through the criss-cross of hawthorn branches, Roy lying sprawled amongst the thorns, his camera discarded beside him. Meryn was crouching by his side, pressing a pad of something over his chest.

Bryn groped in the pocket of his jeans for his phone, then turned and sprinted back to the house. He found the key and let himself back into the kitchen, terrified for Andy, but she was still where he'd left her, sitting at the table. She raised her head wearily as he came in. 'Is she safe?'

479

'Is who safe?' Bryn closed the door behind him with his shoulder. He was barking instructions into the phone.

'Catrin of course.'

'I don't know.'

Andy stared at him uncomprehendingly. 'Why do you want an ambulance? What's happened?'

He switched the phone off. 'Roy Pascoe's outside. I'm afraid he's had an accident. Don't worry, we're safe in here.'

She stared round the room, slowly taking in what was happening. 'Was it Rhona? Where's Meryn?'

'He's with Roy.'

'But Rhona might hurt him.'

'If it was her, she's gone now.' Bryn went to the window and peered out. He was torn. He wanted to go out and help Meryn, but he wasn't going to risk leaving Andy alone a second time. She climbed to her feet and came to stand beside him. 'This is all my fault. That wretched woman. She's completely mad.'

'I think she probably is.' He put his arm round her shoulders. 'The ambulance won't be long.'

'You should call the police.'

'The operator has already done that.'

Andy stood up and staggered over to the sink. She picked up a glass off the draining board and filled it with water. She was waking up fast. 'She won't have gone far if it's me she's after.'

'She might. If she thinks she's killed someone,' he replied grimly.

'You don't mean he's dead?' She dropped the glass into the sink. 'Not Roy!'

'I don't know how he is. Meryn is with him.'

'Supposing she comes back. Meryn is alone out there.'

'And you're alone in here,' he said softly. 'The police will be here soon. Until they come, I'm staying here with you.' He managed a smile. 'I'm stubborn like that.'

'You're stubborn in a lot of ways.' She went over to the rocking chair and sat down. 'But thank you.'

The police were there within minutes. Bryn and Andy heard the siren in the distance. When the car arrived Bryn was at the front door to let them in. He led them through the house to the back door and pointed across the yard towards the hedge. 'The air ambulance is on its way.'

One of the policemen stayed with Andy, the other followed Bryn across the grass. After that, it was all out of their hands. The helicopter landed in the paddock behind the garden and the paramedics examined Roy, put him on a stretcher and loaded him. The police searched the premises, the outbuildings and the cave. There was no sign of Rhona. What they did find was Roy's camera and the last picture taken, which showed her, knife raised, eyes staring, teeth bared as she attacked him.

The patrol car left soon after the ambulance; Meryn had given them Ella's phone number and they headed down to Hay to pick her up and follow the ambulance to the hospital. Another, unmarked, car arrived. In it was Dai Vaughan, looking very serious. 'We've lost track of Rhona Wilson,' he reported. 'Her car was seen parked behind a pub in Brecon yesterday, but she checked out last night and there's been no sighting since. She seems to know her way around. There's a warrant out for her arrest, so it shouldn't be long before she's apprehended.' He looked from one to the other. 'Can I suggest that you, Miss Dysart, move out until then. You're very isolated up here.'

'I'm not going anywhere!' Andy retorted. 'It's nice of you to be concerned, and obviously you have to be, but I can keep the doors locked. She hasn't perfected the art of walking through walls yet.'

She glanced at Meryn with a rueful grin.

Dai intercepted the exchange between the two of them and raised an eyebrow. 'Should I be worried by that remark?'

'No!' Meryn replied. 'No, Rhona Wilson may be many things but a ghost she is not.'

Bryn walked with Dai back to his car. On the way he told him about his research into Rhona's possible past.

'But I was told you were the gardener!' Dai had stopped and extricated his notebook.

'One man in his time can be many things!' Bryn retorted. 'Ambitions change and I opted for a life tilling my native soil. It suits my temperament better.' He folded his arms.

Dai shook his head. 'You should have told me this when you first suspected who she was.'

'I didn't have any proof. I still don't.'

'And your boss up there doesn't know any of this?' Dai gave him a quizzical look.

'My boss? Oh, you mean Andy?' Bryn shook his head. 'No. She doesn't know.'

'I see. Well, I suspect you ought to tell her. And Meryn.' He studied Bryn's face. 'Ah. Meryn knows.'

Bryn grinned. 'You're not a bad psychologist yourself.'

'Maybe not.' Dai climbed into his car. 'Ring the hospital this evening. They'll let you know how your friend is. I gather from control that he was stable when they left. I'm afraid we can't spare a full-time police presence to leave with you here at the moment, but if there's any sign of the woman we can be back within fifteen minutes, so call us immediately. I'll give you the priority number to put into your phones, and 999 will always get us. And we will be looking for her meanwhile, have no fear of that. There is already a call out for her vehicle registration – shouldn't be too difficult to spot a red sports car.'

Andy was stunned into silence after Bryn had finished explaining. 'So, you are telling me that Rhona has a long history of insanity, and you have a whole secret life!' she murmured eventually.

He inclined his head in a rueful nod. ''Fraid so.'

'We should be grateful for Bryn's knowledge,' Meryn put in firmly. 'So, does it help us?'

Bryn shoved his hands deep into his pockets. 'It could go

two ways. She's either so fixated on Andy she will never give up, so we can expect her back here at some point – probably sooner rather than later – or she will decide to cut her losses, as she must have done in the States, and go to ground for a while. Of course you know where she lives, Andy, so we can make sure the police are waiting for her if she returns to Kew.'

'My guess is she won't do that,' Meryn put in. 'She seems to be a clever lady. She's not going to walk into a trap. I am not happy with you staying here on your own, Andy. It's too isolated and she's too good at finding her way around. And my cottage is even more isolated, so I won't offer to have you up there. She knows where I live and we already know she's capable of cutting phone lines.'

'I doubt if she's learnt to intercept a mobile signal yet,' Andy retorted.

'The weather can do that all by itself,' Meryn replied dryly. 'As anyone round here knows. What about your place, Bryn? Does Rhona know where you live?'

'No!' Andy interrupted. 'Don't talk about me as if I'm not here! I am fine where I am. I can lock the doors. And I am not leaving Pepper.' She paused. 'Where is Pepper? I haven't seen him for ages.'

'I wouldn't worry about him. He can look after himself.' Bryn smiled tolerantly. 'The offer is there if you change your mind. My place is only tiny; it's in the town and easily defensible. You would be safe there.' They looked at each other and Andy looked away first. She could feel herself blushing. 'Thank you. I'll bear it in mind.'

Meryn and Bryn exchanged glances. 'If you won't go there, Bryn will stay with you here,' Meryn put in firmly. 'It's the obvious answer.'

It was amazing that people still hadn't learnt to lock their cars. Rhona had tucked her own into a corner of the main car park in Hay, where it was partly hidden by a large camper van. To

keep suspicion at bay if someone was checking, she purchased
a ticket and stuck it to the windscreen then walked back towards
the road, carrying her bag, trying to appear casual, which was
hard when she was fizzing with adrenaline. There were a lot
of cars parked here but very few people walking about. As she
touched the occasional driver's door handle she expected alarms
to go off, but none did and the fifth car she tried allowed her
entry. The driver of the neat silver Honda had even left the key
in the ignition. The idiot had probably left it unlocked because
he had only nipped into the public conveniences or to buy an
ice cream or something and didn't feel he was letting it out of
his sight.

She climbed into the car, started the engine, engaged first
gear and put her foot down. The car was nice and nippy. She
drove up the car park, threading her way through the neat
rows of vehicles, turned left at the exit and left again, heading
back towards Brecon. She was surprisingly hungry after her
early start and on her previous drives up and down the road
she had noticed a pub which would allow her to park round
the back, out of sight of the road while she had an all-day
breakfast. She gave the man she had stabbed less than an hour
ago no thought whatsoever.

'I have to go to sleep!' Andy was arguing with Bryn. Meryn
had left half an hour before. He had borrowed Andy's car. He
and Bryn had quietly agreed to take turns in staying with her
until Rhona was caught.

'I'm exhausted,' she went on crossly. 'Are you expecting me
to stay awake for the rest of my days?'

Bryn was exasperated. 'No, of course not. But you've had
enough sleep for now, Andy. Quite enough. And I don't want
you to sleep again in this house. Not for now. For goodness'
sake, you know why. Even Meryn couldn't wake you last time.
You were trapped, Andy.'

She was too tired to argue. She watched resentfully as Bryn

heated a tin of soup on the Aga and came to sit at the table when he called her, realising she barely had the strength to stand.

He put a bowl of the soup in front of her and found a loaf of bread in the crock. 'At least eat that. If you don't you will probably pass out!'

'Is that your medical diagnosis?' she snapped. 'Fascinating that you have somehow metamorphosed into an expert psychologist! So, now I'm supposed to do what the gardener tells me!' She pushed the soup away.

'Yes.' He was losing patience fast. Perhaps he should have told her the truth about himself earlier, but then again it was none of her business what he'd done in his former career. 'Yes, you should.'

He sat down at the end of the table, tore himself a wedge of bread and buttered it vigorously. 'If you want to sleep we'll go back to my place in Hay. You can sleep there for as long as you want.'

'What makes you think I won't dream there?'

'I don't know. I'm not sure you won't, but I never have. Not about Catrin, anyway.'

She stared at him, shocked. 'You mean you've slept here? You've dreamt here too?'

'I have done, yes.'

'When?'

'When I house-sat for Sue.'

'You never said.' She was still staring at him. 'What did you dream about?'

'Dafydd and Catrin. Quarrelling. Shouting.'

'Why didn't you say?'

'I've grown used to keeping my counsel. And I rather hoped you would stay here. I was afraid you would be off the moment you realised there was something sinister about Sleeper's Castle.' He glanced up at her and then away again.

'I assumed the last thing you wanted was for me to stay. You

485

seemed to resent my presence here.' She picked up her spoon, and then dropped it again.

'I am by nature a bit of a grumpy sod, I'm afraid.' He gave her an apologetic grin. 'I didn't want to get to like you and then find you were off at the first sign of trouble.'

She stared at him. 'Well, you certainly convinced me that you didn't like me!'

'I'm a good actor.'

'That too?'

'Sorry.'

'It would've been helpful if I had known. I could have talked to you.' She looked up wearily. 'You weren't driven away by your dream?'

'No, but I haven't got involved. And I'm not afraid of the paranormal.'

'Neither am I. I thought you would've understood that by now.'

He grinned. 'You may not be afraid, Andy, but you're unable to control it. You're too susceptible; too sensitive.'

'Then fix me so I can control it. I take it you can do that?'

He shook his head.

'Why not, if you're a shrink?'

'Oh, Andy.' He sighed. 'I don't practise any more; I'm not allowed to practise any more, my licence has expired. And even if I did, I couldn't fix this. It's not in your head. It's not a disease or a mental condition. You're not on some strange autistic spectrum. What you are doing is picking up on an ancient story which is somehow imbued in these walls. I've thought about it a lot and I've discussed it with Meryn. This house is as old as the ground it sits on. The echoes of the past are trapped here, as are, I suspect, the echoes of everything that ever happens here, including what we are saying now. All those echoes are trying to find expression. If anyone can cleanse this place of its past and its present – and for all I know, of its future – it's Meryn, not me.'

'Meryn! With his sprig of rosemary!' Her voice was heavy with scorn.

'Don't knock it,' he said sharply. 'It worked!'

She sat forward. 'The dreams will go on until the story is told,' she said. 'You realise that, don't you. I may not know as much as you or Meryn, but I can work that much out. Even my father had worked that out. Catrin wants to tell her story, and so does Dafydd. Their quarrel has soaked into the air here, the stones, the vegetation. They're vying for attention, looking for someone to listen to them.'

He sat back. 'I think you're right there.'

'So, if I listen, then maybe it will stop. I have to know what happened. I wasn't here after Catrin left her cell. I couldn't follow her. I was locked in, but now I'm free. I can come back, I can see where she went, see if she and Edmund ever got back together. See what happened to them all.' She reached out and put her hand over his on the table. 'You can help me, Bryn.'

He looked down at their hands and smiled, shaking his head. 'It's too dangerous.'

'Why?' She fixed him with a piercing gaze. 'What could happen to me?'

He clasped her hand gently and turned it over, then he spread out her fingers, exposing the torn nails and the bruising on her fingertips. 'You tried to claw your way out of a cell in the castle. You got stuck in the past, you could get stuck again, and in your dream you could come to harm,' he said patiently. 'This is dangerous, Andy. You are identifying with your dream, you are entering so completely into it that you are manifesting indications of the events about which you are dreaming. Maybe it is some sort of self-hypnosis. You're exhibiting sympathetic wounds as people do in spiritual trance who develop the stigmata, the wounds of the nails from Christ's cross on their own hands and feet.'

She shuddered. She pulled her hand away and hugged herself deeper into her sweater. 'That's creepy.'

'Even now people don't know how it happens, but it does.'

'But I'm not identifying with Catrin. She hasn't been hurt. It was me! I was locked in and I couldn't dream myself out of that cold stone cell. The guard locked the door with a key. I heard it close. I heard him turn away and stamp down the stairs until the sound died away. I couldn't get out. The stone was solid.'

'Exactly!'

'But then I did escape. The door didn't open. Someone didn't come and rescue me. I woke up.' She glared at him.

Bryn sighed. 'All I know is that this could damage you emotionally and psychologically, not to mention physically. Try to use a bit of common sense, Andy. It must be obvious to you that this is extremely dangerous.'

He stood and picked up her soup bowl. 'Let me warm this for you again. I don't want to quarrel with you. I just want you to be safe.'

She managed to eat the soup without any further argument, casting the occasional malevolent look at him across the table. He ignored them.

'If you want me to stay awake,' she said as she pushed the bowl aside, 'you'll have to walk me up and down for the rest of the time you're here. I can't keep my eyes open.'

He laughed. 'Perhaps we should go for a walk outside.'

'And risk Rhona finding us?' She stood up. 'I need the loo. Are you going to follow me in there?'

'No.' He smiled. 'I will have to trust you.'

She snorted derisively.

He sat where he was as she walked out of the room. A few seconds later he heard the cat flap. He turned to see Pepper peering at him. His tail was twitching nervously. Bryn smiled. 'So, where have you been, old chap? Do you want food? You missed your breakfast, so I hear.' He walked over to the dresser and poured a handful of biscuits into a saucer. Pepper stalked over to it and sniffed them critically. He gave Bryn a pained look as though to point out the standard of service was not up to scratch, but he sat down in front of the bowl and began to pick at the biscuits nevertheless.

He had crunched his way through the first dozen or so when Bryn glanced at his watch. 'Andy?' he called. He went out into the hall and stood outside the cloakroom. 'Andy?' he tapped on the door. There was no answer. He pushed the door open a crack. There was no one in there.

He let out a furious oath and ran to the bottom of the stairs. He glanced up. 'Andy?'

There was no reply.

She was in her bedroom, asleep on the bed, the cover pulled up over her head. He shook her by the shoulder. 'Andy!'

There was no response.

Catrin couldn't see the identity of the man who guided her across the darkened bailey. It was pouring with rain as he pushed open the postern gate and gestured her through, then he closed it softly behind her. She stood still, confused. There was a movement beside her and she felt an arm go round her. 'Cat, thank God! I thought I had lost you forever.' Edmund hugged her, then he released her, caught her hand and dragged her forward. They ran down the ramp from the main gate towards the market place. It was deserted at this hour and they hurried, splashing through puddles and mud, until they could duck between houses into the narrow empty streets.

He had two horses waiting in an alley nearby. Without a word he boosted her onto one of them, leapt on the other and, grabbing the rein to keep her close to him, he set off at a canter. They had not gone far when he pulled to a rearing halt and slid from the saddle: someone was waiting for them in the shadow of the town wall. There was a chink of coins as he passed the man a small bag. The gate opened and they rode through.

They galloped without stopping for a couple of miles on the

potholed, muddy road, before he allowed the blowing horses to slow down. 'Are you all right?' he called softly as he saw her swaying in the saddle. The shock of being outside, of riding again after so long in a confined space, was hitting her now.

She was clinging to the horse's mane. 'How did you do that? How did you make them let me go?' She was crying and laughing, her cold hands slippery and wet on the leather reins.

'I'll explain when we are safe.'

'Where are we going? I must go home? Where is *Tad*? Is he all right?' Her teeth were chattering.

'Sweetheart, don't you understand?' He edged his horse closer so he could lean across and put an arm round her shoulders. 'It was your father who betrayed you.'

She pulled away from him. 'No. That is not true.'

'It is true. I have been making enquiries. Your father betrayed you to the constable. He bought his own peace and told them you were a witch!'

'No! No, I don't believe you!'

'It is true, Cat. I swear it.'

She straightened in her saddle and kicked her horse on. 'I am going home. I am going to see him for myself!'

'Cat, don't.' He urged his own mount after her. 'You will only put yourself in danger again. He is a vindictive old man. He was jealous of you, don't you understand? Don't go back there!'

He bent across to catch her rein, but she hit out at him desperately. Tears were pouring down her face. 'I don't believe you! I have to see him. I have to ask him myself!'

He gave up. He followed her along the road, more slowly now, and turned after her up the track towards Sleeper's Castle. As the shock of what had happened sank in, she was growing less certain. She was slumped in her saddle, clinging on.

He came up beside her again. 'Sweetheart, please. He's not there. I don't know where he has gone.'

'No!' She pushed his hand aside. 'Why would you say such awful things about him?'

'Because it's true.' They were shouting at each other as the wind grew stronger. The horses slowed to a walk in the lashing rain as the lane began to climb.

Sleeper's Castle lay in darkness. They pulled up near the paddock and Catrin half slid, half fell from the saddle. 'Where is Joan?'

He dismounted and came to stand beside her. 'Joan has gone home to my father,' he said gently. He put his arm round her. 'Betsi is there with her and Peter and the animals. There is no one here now. I have been trying to tell you. Last time I came, the house was empty.'

'He's not here?' Finally it was dawning on her what he was saying.

'No. The place is deserted.'

'And his money?'

'I found his money, Cat, hidden in the cave. That is how I managed to get you free. I bribed one of the guards.'

'All of it?' Her eyes were wide.

He smiled. 'All of it. You were a valuable prize. And I must get you away. When the constable finds out you have gone, there will be a hue and cry.'

She walked forward towards the house and he followed her. A thin line of watery daylight was beginning to show behind the hills to the east. Even in the wind and the splashing of the rain the place was very quiet. Unnaturally quiet. Catrin paused and shivered. She could smell it now. Fire and the stench of death. She reached out her hand and Edmund took it. He squeezed her fingers tightly. 'Wait here, Cat. Let me go first.'

She shook her head. 'I have to see.'

There was enough light now to see their way across the herb beds towards the house. The kitchen door hung off its hinges.

Catrin crept inside, Edmund close behind her, still holding her hand.

They found Dafydd, or what was left of him, lying in front of the hearth. The rooms were all in ruins. Someone had lit fires in several places, the front door too was hanging open, the ceiling beams charred beyond recognition, the roof in places gone.

They stood side by side, looking down at Dafydd's body.

Catrin let out a whimper. 'Blood, fire, death,' she whispered. 'It was his own end he foretold, not Owain's.' She looked up at him piteously. 'Who did this?'

Edmund pulled her away. 'We will find out. Come outside, let me sort this out.'

'How?' She stared at him, her eyes huge in the semi-darkness, her cheeks sodden with tears. 'How can you sort it out? How can anyone?'

He didn't know. 'People will be looking for you, Catrin,' he said at last. He gazed at her in confusion. His heart was aching for her. However evil Dafydd had been, even though he had betrayed her, his own daughter, he was still her father and she had loved him. 'We should go,' he said gently. 'We haven't got long. They will have discovered that you have gone when they find the cell empty.'

'He has to be buried, Edmund,' she whispered. 'We can't leave him here.'

He stared round the ruins of the room. 'I will do it. Come outside. I will bury him in the garden.'

It took him a long time. He found a spade lying outside the barn. The ground mercifully was soft and wet. He would not let her help and he would not let her watch as he dragged the charred, mangled body outside and lowered it into the makeshift grave. Only then did he let her toss some winter flowers in on top of her father's corpse and murmur prayers for his soul. He shovelled the earth back into the grave, and watched while she transplanted a clump of marigolds into the angry red soil.

As it began to rain they went to find the horses in the paddock. When they left they had Dafydd's old cob with them.

On the way up the track towards the mountain Catrin insisted they stop. She left Edmund holding the three horses as she scrambled down into the *cwm* and across the brook to say goodbye to Efa.

The cottage had gone. There was no sign of it ever having been there. There were no burnt scars, no tumbled stones, nothing but wisps of mist which clung over the clumps of wild herbs and came curling and caressing round her skirts. She smiled and raised a hand in farewell then she made her way back to Edmund.

Once more they stopped, to look for the last time towards the ruins of Sleeper's Castle below them in the valley, then they urged the horses on and rode forward up into the clouds that cloaked the mountains.

'Wait!' Andy called. 'Wait, let me come too.'

They didn't hear her.

Bryn stood up. He had been dozing in the chair in the corner of the room. He stood looking down at her for several seconds then he touched her gently on the cheek. 'Time to wake up, Andy. It's over now.'

He had watched her sleep, watched her murmur and cry out, watched her sob with Catrin as she stood at the edge of her father's grave and looked down with her at her father's body as she whispered the Latin words of the Mass.

The whole time Andy had lain in her bed, barely moving.

'Andy?' he called again.

Her eyes opened. 'I know what we have to do,' she said almost to herself. She sat up slowly, slid out of the bed and walked towards the door.

'Andy?' he called again. 'Are you awake?'

She didn't hear him. She pulled open the door and walked slowly, barefoot, down the stairs across the hall and into the kitchen. Halfway across the room she hesitated. Pepper had been sitting on the table. He looked at her and Bryn saw his fur rise on end as he fled out through the cat flap.

Andy didn't appear to see him. She reached for the key,

turned it and pulled the door open. Stepping outside, still bare-foot, she walked over the icy flags towards the lawn. There, almost at the first of the herb beds, she stopped and looked down. 'Here,' she called over her shoulder. 'Dafydd is buried here. He will not rest until he is given Christian burial some-where away from here. He doesn't want to be here any more.'

Bryn came and stood beside her. 'Are you sure?' She was staring down at the ground. 'Andy?' He took her arm. 'Andy, can you hear me?' He pulled her against him gently. 'Andy, your feet are freezing. Come inside. We will deal with the grave later.'

'Where did they go?' She turned to him and for a moment he thought she was awake. Then he saw the fixed gaze; the dilated pupils were still there.

'We will find out where they went,' he whispered. 'I promise.'

'They never returned to Sleeper's Castle,' she said. She let him lead her back towards the house. 'They never returned to the valley. The house fell into ruins. No one would live here. People thought it was haunted.'

He managed to guide her into the kitchen and he closed the door behind them, turning the key. Perhaps now she would sleep and wake normally. He led her through into the hall. 'Shall I light the fire?' he asked. He pushed her onto the sofa and covered her with one of the rugs, tucking it carefully around her cold wet feet.

'That would be nice,' she answered him. She lay back and closed her eyes.

He waited patiently, watching her, but she lay still. He piled up kindling and logs and lit the fire in the hearth, the hearth which had stood on that same spot for six hundred years. He watched it spark and crackle, saw the flames lick across the logs. The room filled with the scent of burning oak and apple.

He threw himself down in the old leather armchair in the corner and set himself to watch her.

*   *   *

494

Secrets can be kept by hundreds, perhaps thousands of people and yet not divulged. Edmund was one of those who knew the greatest secret of all: where they needed to go for help.

He did not take Catrin home; he left her hidden in the woods above his parents' farm while he collected a few of her belongings, packed by Joan, and the old mule she and Betsi had brought with them with the pony from Sleeper's Castle. His father's horses might have been remembered as they passed through the countryside; her father's old cob and the pony might have been recognised. He said goodbye to his mother, explaining he was going to seek his fortune in London and would one day return home a rich man, bade her tell the same to his father, and then he slipped out into the cold dawn and headed south, leading the mule.

In the event they were not going far. They travelled on byways and drovers' roads, keeping to the high hills, off the beaten track, following the line of the Golden Valley southwards, cautiously skirting farmsteads and villages, avoiding all signs of habitation. This was true border country, the hills of Wales to the west and the valley and the verdant fields of Herefordshire to the east. It wasn't far, their journey, perhaps twenty miles in all, but it took them four days, four days where they met no one.

They slept at night huddled together in barns and sheepfolds, sharing the space with the mule to help keep them warm. And still Edmund had not told Catrin where they were going.

She was very quiet, still shocked by everything that had happened to her and by the death of her father. Sometimes she clung to Edmund and sometimes she walked apart, following behind or wandering off at an angle away from the track to sit beside a pool staring into the peaty waters, or under a tree. While she was doing this, slowly recovering her strength, he allowed the mule to drift to a standstill and graze the grasses and herbs along the track while he sat and patiently waited. Sometimes he dozed, sometimes he whittled a piece of wood.

Sometimes he would go and sit beside her, and when she didn't move away he would put his arm round her and let her nestle into his shoulder. He knew that they had to discuss her father's treachery, so she would understand how Dafydd's jealousy of her talent had been allowed to fester until it had grown into a bloated, irrational canker inside him. Once she understood why he had done it, once she faced the truth of his terrible betrayal, maybe then she could put her memories to rest.

Edmund had chosen the man to whom he had paid the bribe well. Many people in Hay had sided with the Lord Owain, many had rejoiced when his cause was in the ascendant all across Wales, but when the prince disappeared into the mountain mists for the last time their support was replaced by pragmatism and many quietly returned to their previous lives. A wise and intelligent king chose to pardon all but a few. He could not wholly defeat a nation, but he could encourage them to follow him. The vicious laws which so damaged the Welsh people were still in place but where the local administrators were sensible and sympathetic they were set aside or forgotten. John Bedell's men-at-arms in Hay had been hired for their competence and ability to man the castle walls. He had been no happier than they to single out a lonely young woman merely on the word of the bitter old man who was her father. Fathers do not condemn their own daughters to almost certain death.

The bribe had been accepted, carefully shared out where necessary, and the door to Catrin's cell opened and closed again. If enquiry was ever made into her whereabouts by the authorities it was greeted by bewildered incomprehension and denial.

Who it was who murdered Dafydd ap Hywell ap Gruffydd and burned Sleeper's Castle was never established and never would be. The house was to lie in ruins for decades, sleeping. Biding its time.

Edmund told her of her father's duplicity as they sat by a small fire in a clearing in a forest on a lonely hillside. She listened in silence, hugging her knees as she gazed into the flames.

'I think I had guessed as much,' she whispered. 'As I sat in that cell I had plenty of time to think. He came to hate me, I never knew why. I did everything I could to look after him.'

'But the one thing he couldn't forgive, you couldn't do anything about,' Edmund said. 'Your poetry was better than his, your voice was lovelier than his and your playing of the harp was like the sound of angels.'

She gave a sad little smile. 'I did not go out of my way to make it like that.'

'I know.' He hugged her closer. 'You couldn't help it. You were blessed.'

She didn't speak for a long time. 'I miss my harp,' she said at last.

He grinned. 'We have it with us.'

She pulled free of his arm so she could turn and look at him. 'Where?'

'What did you think was in that pannier which bumps so uncomfortably beside the others on the mule's back?'

She stared at him, speechless, then her face broke into an incredulous smile. 'I thought it must have been burnt with all my books.'

He shook his head. 'Joan rescued much from your coffers and I brought the rest after you were captured. Anything that was left in the house must have been destroyed or looted, but your books and your most precious things are here with us in the packs.'

She stared into the darkness beyond the fire where the mule's harness and the bulky panniers were piled in the lee of the crumbling stone wall which was sheltering them from the wind.

'I am not sure what condition everything is in, to be honest, but you will be able to sort it out I am sure.'

She was smiling for the first time since they had started their journey. Scrambling to her feet, she went over to the packs and felt carefully for the soft leather bag that contained her little harp. She took it out and unwrapped it. Bringing it back to the fire she sat down and set it on her knee, pulling it back against her shoulder. She touched a string and scowled. 'Poor thing, it is sadly out of tune.'

Edmund smiled. 'I should think so, after the adventures it has had.'

Two strings were broken and the wooden frame was split, but still it was able to sing. After several minutes of tuning and gentling she stroked the instrument into a soft lullaby. Edmund looked round. Were the trees themselves listening? He thought so, and the wind had eased for a while to pluck an accompaniment from the bracken and heather on the hillside above them.

She played two tunes and then she set the harp aside. 'There is something I have to tell you,' she said.

He frowned at her, sensing her change of mood.

'When I was in the castle my ghost came with me. Andy, the woman from Sleeper's Castle.' She hesitated. 'She guessed before I did.' She paused nervously. 'I sometimes wonder if she was left behind, a prisoner in that cell. I hope and pray she wasn't.'

'Guessed what?' He leant across and took her hand again. He wasn't interested in the ghost.

'I am expecting a child, Edmund. Your child.'

There, she had said it. She held her breath, not daring to look him in the face.

He couldn't speak. He didn't realise how tightly he was holding her hand until she pulled away with a yelp of pain, then he smiled. 'Cat! My darling. My *cariad*!' He pulled her onto his lap and kissed her. 'We will be a proper family. We will be married as soon as we can.'

'But the law will punish you if you marry a Welsh woman,' she protested.

'Then the law is a fool.' He kissed her again.

'Will you tell me now where we are going?' she asked when she could get her breath back.

'Tomorrow you will see, I promise.' He smiled. 'Until then it is a surprise.'

* * *

'Bryn?'

Andy's voice in his ear startled Bryn into wakefulness. He stared round, trying to get his bearings. He had been dreaming of an open hillside with a small campfire in the lee of a wall, and the music of a harp.

He cleared his throat and sat up. 'I'm sorry. I dozed off.'

She smiled. 'And so did I, and I didn't dream at all, or not that I remember. I rang the hospital,' she went on. 'They said Roy was stable. We're to ring again in the morning.'

'And Ella?'

'Her phone went to voicemail.'

He looked down at his hands, still trying to clear his head. 'You said you didn't dream. Maybe that's because the dream was mine.'

She came and sat down near him by the hearth. 'What does that mean?'

He ran his fingers through his hair. 'I dreamt about Catrin and Edmund. She worried about you, you know. She realised you were left behind in the castle. She said you told her she was pregnant.'

Andy was staring at him, open-mouthed.

'They escaped together down the Golden Valley and they had a mule with them with panniers on its back and Edmund had brought her harp.' He hesitated, still trying to remember. 'She played it on the mountainside in the dark. It was magical. Edmund told her again that it was her father who had betrayed her.' He thought for a moment. 'And this time she believed him. He had a grisly end but he deserved it after doing something so despicable. What a jealous old git! His own daughter!'

Andy was beginning to smile. 'And that's the story?'

'That's the story.'

'Where did they go? What happened to them?'

'I don't know. Someone woke me up!'

She looked crestfallen. 'I'm sorry.'

'Perhaps we will find out one day.'

They sat for several minutes in silence, staring into the fire as it crackled in the hearth. The air in the room was heavy with the scent of the burning logs. Andy reached out and took his hand. 'Thank you for staying with me. And for rescuing me from the castle.'

'Meryn did that.'

She gave a little grimace. 'You were both there for me. I am so grateful. I'm sorry I was such a grumpy bitch.' She was silent for a while. 'Has Dafydd gone now?'

Bryn sighed. 'I don't know. I feel if he is still buried out there in the lawn he should be moved. Maybe that's what he wants. Maybe that's what he always wanted.'

She nodded. 'Until he's buried properly he can't rest. And maybe not until Cat forgives him.'

'How do you know she hasn't?'

She gave a wry smile. 'I don't.'

'But once he is at rest, then perhaps we can forget about all this. You can get on with the rest of your life.' Bryn stretched and stood up.

'Once they've caught Rhona,' she murmured.

'Once they've caught Rhona,' he echoed. He glanced up at the window, and was immediately intensely aware of the emptiness of the garden outside. It was so easy to imagine the woman out there watching them. He shuddered. Walking across to the window he pulled the heavy curtains across on their wooden rings.

Over the sound of the rattle they made neither of them heard the scream of the cat in the dark outside.

31

Sian was at home with the dogs when the phone rang. She groped in her pocket for her mobile.

'Sian. It's Ella!'

'Ella? What's wrong?' She could hear the tears in Ella's voice.

'It's Roy. He's been stabbed.'

Sian stood up. 'What do you mean, stabbed? Where are you?'

'Abergavenny. They brought him here in the air ambulance. He's in surgery.'

'Oh, Ella. What happened?'

'The police won't tell me anything. Just that he was stabbed. He was walking on the hill behind Sleeper's Castle.'

'It was Rhona, wasn't it?' Sian was pacing up and down the carpet. The two dogs were watching her anxiously.

'I suppose so. Meryn warned us about her. Oh, Sian!'

'Is there anyone there with you?'

'Yes. Don't worry. My sister is on her way.'

Sian could hear her sniffing. 'If you need me, Ella, I'll come.'

'No. I'm OK. Just pray for Roy. Please.'

Sian had only just put the phone down when it rang again. She picked it up. It was Sue.

For a moment she couldn't grasp what Sue was saying. Sue in Australia. Sue who had no clue that the world around her home had just fallen apart.

Sue was laughing. 'Listen, Sian, I have some news.'

Sian walked slowly into her kitchen and sat down at the table, listening. It was impossible to get a word in edgeways even if she wanted to. Her dogs followed her in. One of them came and rested his head on her knee.

'I'm getting married!' The Australian voice was ringing round the kitchen, full of excitement. 'Joe came over to find me.'

'Sue!' Sian found her voice at last. 'Congratulations! How wonderful.'

'Isn't it, though?' Sue was positively bubbling. 'I'd missed him so much, the old bugger.' She laughed, then she sobered again. 'We're going to live out here, Sian. It's perfect. I'd forgotten how much I love it here with the family nearby and everything. This is home.' For the first time she hesitated. 'So, you can guess why I'm ringing.'

Sian's mind had gone blank. 'You want me to come?' she hazarded blindly.

Sue laughed. 'Of course I want you to come, but there's something else. Sleeper's Castle – I'm going to sell it.'

There was a long pause.

'Sian? Are you there?' Sue's voice echoed down the line. 'Did you hear what I said?'

'I heard,' Sian said slowly.

'The thing is, I don't want to drop Andy in it. I know she's in a difficult situation, but then I need the money. And she hasn't actually got an official tenancy agreement. Do you know how things are with her by any chance? Has she got her act together yet? I know I gave her the option of staying there for a year, give or take, but obviously things have changed.'

'Obviously.' Sian was reeling with the effort of trying to get her head around all this. 'Sue, can you leave this with me for a day or two? Let me speak to her.'

'Sure.'

'It's a bit of a shock!'

'For me too!'

'We'll miss you.' Sian took a deep breath. 'Sue, what about Pepper?'

There was another silence. When Sue spoke again it was with a slight catch in her voice. 'Don't ask me, Sian. I can't bear it. I'm going to have to find him a home. I can't make him come all the way over here, it wouldn't be fair. I thought I'd ask Bryn. If he can't have him then maybe he can think of someone who would. He knows so many people.'

'And the herb garden?'

'Sleeper's Castle has survived hundreds of years without me, Sian. It will manage.'

Sian put down the phone, went into the sitting room and sank into a chair, staring into space. Both dogs followed her anxiously. They sat down, one on either side of her.

Andy, Roy, Rhona and now this. She held out her hands and two warm muzzles pushed into them comfortingly. 'What on earth am I going to do, boys?' she asked.

When she climbed into her car half an hour later the two dogs were in the back.

She headed up to Meryn's house and drew up beside his car. Her dogs were first in through his door.

'Did you hear about Roy?' she asked. Meryn kept a tin of dog treats on his windowsill. Both dogs sat pointing at it expectantly while she threw herself into the chair by the fire. Suitably rewarded, the dogs lay down to bask in its heat.

Meryn nodded. 'I found him.'

'I just spoke to Ella. He's in surgery. Do you know who did it?'

'It appears he took a photo of her as she jumped him. It was Rhona.'

'Oh God.' Sian slumped back in her chair. 'Does Andy know?'

'Yes. Bryn's with her. They're locked in, I trust, until the police find the woman.'

Sian sighed. 'This is just awful. Meryn, something else has happened.' She took a deep breath. 'I have just spoken to Sue on the phone. You remember that guy Joe we were talking about? He's gone out to Australia after her and they're getting married out there and not coming back.' She rubbed her face hard with her hands. 'She's going to sell Sleeper's Castle and find a home for Pepper. She wants me to tell Andy.'

Meryn whistled. 'I certainly wasn't expecting that.'

'No.'

They both sat in silence for a while, staring into the fire.

'I suppose Andy is secure. It looks as though she will get her house in Kew back. She won't be homeless. Maybe she would take Pepper with her?' Sian said at last.

'He couldn't live in a town. He's a country cat, used to his own acres.' Meryn smiled fondly. 'I wish I could have him. The trouble is I'm away such a lot.'

'I hoped Andy would stay,' Sian wailed suddenly. 'I like her so much. We don't want a stranger at Sleeper's.'

Meryn leant back in the chair and stretched out his legs. 'I like her too, but we have to acknowledge that she may not want to stay, Sian, after everything that has happened. She's had a pretty rough ride. Maybe it would be better if someone came to live there who was impervious to the other dimensions.'

'Like me.'

'Like you, dear.' He smiled fondly.

'I wish I was pervious.'

'No, you don't. Look at the pain and confusion it causes people.' He sighed. It seemed only a few hours ago that Andy had told him that she would buy Sleeper's Castle 'if Sue wants to sell' and now, as if on cue, Sue had made her decision. Andy loved the house, of that there was no doubt – look how she had refused again and again to leave even for one night – but she had made that one telling proviso: 'only if you can sort out Dafydd'. He stood up. 'Right, my car is outside and all mended, so why don't we drive down the hill together and see how Andy and Bryn are getting on.'

They piled into Meryn's Fourtrak, with the dogs in the back barking happily as they bumped down the track and onto the mountain road.

They didn't recognise the mud-splashed silver Honda Civic parked in the field gate a hundred yards up from Sleeper's Castle.

Rhona had pressed herself flat against the wall beside the window as Bryn appeared and looked out. He was silhouetted against the lights for a brief moment, then he had drawn the heavy curtains across, leaving her in total darkness. Temporarily blinded she had virtually fallen over the cat who had let out a terrifying screech before fleeing into the darkness. She swore under her breath and waited. The curtains didn't move. Either they hadn't heard or they didn't care. She smiled. Finding a way of getting into the house was a challenge, but it was the sort of challenge she enjoyed and tonight she had no reason to leave at any particular time. She hadn't checked in to a hotel or B & B, and the car was tucked away discreetly where no one would find it even if it had by now been reported missing. She had all the time in the world. She had her knife. She had matches.

'Bryn? Are you asleep?' Andy touched his shoulder. She piled another couple of logs on the fire and sat down beside him to find he had dozed off again. He had spent a long time in the garden calling Pepper, but there had been no sign of him anywhere and eventually he had given up and let himself back into the house, locking the door behind him again.

Rhona had watched from a safe distance, a grim smile on her face. So, the cat was called Pepper. If she came across it again she would deal with it as well.

'He'll turn up.' Andy had tried to comfort him. 'He's a feisty animal. I'm sure he wouldn't have let Rhona get near him.'

They sat down together near the fire, all the curtains drawn, both doors securely locked and Andy had pulled the rug over her knees, but for the first time in a long time sleep had eluded her. She lay back with her eyes closed, listening to the crackle of the logs. It was some time later that she noticed Bryn had dozed off. She stood looking down at him, her back to the fire.

'Are you with them?' she asked softly. 'There in the Golden Valley?'

There was no reply.

They loaded the mule at dawn and began the last long trek downhill towards their destination. Edmund still hadn't told Catrin where they were going and she grew nervous as they approached the lower slopes where sheep grazed and the field strips had been tilled. They saw people more often now and had to duck down behind stone walls and into woods several times as they saw men working in the farmsteads.

Their destination was a fortified manor house in a lush valley below Garway Hill not far from the village of Ewyas Harold. They stood in front of the gatehouse and looked up the broad driveway.

'You mean we're going in?' Catrin was nervous.

'We are expected.' Edmund put his arm round her shoulder and led her forward, the mule plodding on its long leading rein behind them.

The place was busy; servants and estate workers were coming and going, but no one paid them any attention. They stopped outside the entrance and only then did a stable boy come to take the rein from Edmund's hand to lead the mule away round the back. The door opened and a woman stood there, her face wreathed in smiles. 'Catrin! Edmund! Welcome to Kentchurch.'

It was Alys, the daughter of Owain Glyndŵr.

The knock on the back door woke Bryn. He sat up with a start. 'Who is it?'

Andy sighed. 'I don't know. I am sorry it woke you.' They went through into the kitchen and tiptoed towards the door.

'Who is it?' Bryn called again.

'Meryn and Sian.'

They all went back to sit around the fire. 'I take it there have been no further sightings of Rhona?' Meryn said as he leant against the cushions.

'Not a word,' Bryn replied.

'And Catrin?' Meryn smiled at Andy. 'How are things with her?'

Andy shook her head sadly. 'She left Sleeper's Castle in ruins. Someone had tried to burn the house down and her father's body was inside. There was nothing for her here. So, after they buried him in the garden, she went with Edmund.'

'The archer?'

She nodded. 'He seemed to have been reconciled with his family.'

'And?'

Bryn put in. 'And, we don't know what happened next.'

'So there's another dream pending?'

'You could put it that way, I suppose.' He glanced at Andy. 'It seems I've joined in the dream fest. I've had two dreams about Edmund. Or at least, taken the story on from Edmund's point of view.'

'Because Catrin herself didn't know what happened while she was imprisoned in Hay Castle,' Andy added.

'But they both ended up free.' Meryn leant forward, looking from one to the other. His arms were folded across his knees.

'I suppose so.'

'And you're feeling more relaxed about the whole story of Sleeper's Castle now?'

Andy was staring into the fire. 'There is still Dafydd.' She shuddered. 'He's still here, Meryn.'

Bryn cleared his throat. 'We thought' – he glanced at Andy – 'that perhaps we should dig and see if Dafydd is still buried out there in the garden. Might he not rest more easily if he had a proper Christian burial, somewhere away from here?'

The question seemed to hang in the room. If they were hoping for an answer, none came.

'I think it would be the right thing to do,' Andy went on quietly, 'if this house is ever to be at peace.'

She and Bryn had talked as the logs had blazed and then burnt down to ash; their antagonism too had died as quickly as it had flared. On the subject of Dafydd's reburial they agreed totally. He caught her eye and smiled.

She stared at Meryn. 'What?' She had intercepted the glance he had exchanged with Sian.

'I think that's a very good idea,' Sian said. 'Andy, we've got some rather unexpected news,' she added. 'I had a call from Sue a few hours ago.'

Sian and Meryn left at last. Rhona watched them make their way round the side of the house and disappear down the steps. Meryn had offered to drive Sian and the dogs back to his cottage to pick up her car, then he was going to return.

Rhona was perched on the outspread branch of the old rowan tree at the back of the house, swaying perilously amongst the rustling leaves. The berries had been stripped bare by the birds and the leaves were dried now and scattering below the tree at every gust of wind. Neither Meryn nor Sian had glanced up as they walked beneath her unsteady hiding place. She smiled to herself, exhilarated by the feel of the wind and the rain spattering her cheeks in the dark. She had spotted the open window as she crept around the outside of the house and noted the tree, conveniently close.

It was all too easy. Perhaps in her next life she would be a cat burglar. She leant forward, for a second her full bodyweight suspended in mid-air, and clutched at the windowsill. The shot of terror that poured through her was magnificent. She gripped the sill, swung forward and managed to grab at the open window frame. Half the windows in the house still had their old mullions, which she would have found hard to squeeze through, but this window was square and, mercifully, open. It took only a moment to jiggle the stay off its hook, pull the casement fully open, wriggle through and jump to the floor.

She found herself standing in a bedroom. Neat, tidy, attractive, with a double bed but no personal effects. Obviously a spare room. It was very quiet after the roar of the wind in the leaves and the rush of the water in the brook outside. She could feel the house holding its breath. The atmosphere was electric. She crept across to the door and opened it a crack.

Her heart was thumping and her hands sore from the tree branches. She was a bit old for this kind of malarkey, she thought, gleefully pleased with herself as she put her ear to the gap and listened. There was no sound from outside on the landing. Bryn and Miranda must be downstairs.

She tiptoed to the next door. It stood half open, the room beyond it dark. She pushed the door back against the wall and waited for a few seconds before turning on the light. This was clearly Miranda's bedroom. It smelt curiously pungent, not unpleasant but spicy, even herbal. She spotted some sprigs of rosemary lying on the bed which explained it. Rhona looked round curiously. The woman's belongings were scattered over every surface. There was a photograph of Graham on the dressing table and she picked it up, surveying it critically. It must have been taken relatively recently. He looked much older than she remembered him and disgustingly healthy, considering he must have been near to death. She let out a small spiteful cry and threw it down on the bed. She continued her tour of the room keeping half an ear open for sounds behind her in the rest of the house.

There were cosmetics on the chest of drawers, with a hair brush, a box of sticking plasters, several pencils, a small sketchbook and a couple of history books on the bedside table and two books on herbs on the windowsill. Miranda's clothes were mostly in the cupboard – the door was hanging open and she pulled it wide to have a look. What a supremely unglamorous woman she was. Nothing here but sweaters and jeans and shirts. Socks, for goodness' sake! She pulled a face and went on with her tour. There were bloodstains on the carpet; at least she thought they were bloodstains. Perhaps that was why she needed the plasters.

There was a creak from the landing and the door moved slightly. Rhona swung round. The cat was standing there, glaring at her. It must have followed her in up the tree and through the window. She felt in her pocket for her knife and opened it. She had a score to settle with that animal. It eyed her disdainfully and then turned and fled down the stairs. She gave a silent humourless laugh. Give her time and she would deal with everyone in this house, cat included. The handle of the knife settled comfortably against her palm. It was warm, solid, the kind of knife that vicious old man would have relished. Her fist tightened round it.

She followed the cat out of the room and cautiously made her way down the curved stone staircase after it, finding herself in a large living room at the bottom. A fire was burning gently in the hearth; the room was in shadow, lit only by one table lamp in the corner. Several doors led off it. She tiptoed across the room and pushed the first. A small sitting room, as far as she could see in the dark. Another door opened onto yet another living room, which, judging by the table and chairs, was an unused dining room. Beyond that she came to the front door, heavily curtained against the draughts. She lifted the curtain and looked at the ancient oak door. It boasted a huge rather crude iron lock, a heavy circular door handle and two antique bolts, both of which had been shot home. She dropped the curtain quietly and continued her tour to the far side of the room. The door there led to a passageway and signs of life. At the end of it there was a closed door, the shape outlined by the bright lights behind it, and now she could hear the sound of voices. She tiptoed down the passage. Like the large room behind her, it was paved with uneven flagstones. Pushing gently, she opened the door a crack.

There was a movement beside her as the cat flew past her, hurled itself at the door and disappeared into the kitchen.

'Pepper!' It was Miranda's voice. 'Where have you been?' Rhona heard the sound of a scuffle and the rattle of the cat flap, then Miranda's voice again. 'What was the matter with him? He was terrified.'

There was a moment's silence. Rhona could imagine her staring towards the door. Then she heard a chair leg scraping on the floor. 'Stay where you are, Andy. There's something wrong.' It was the gardener's voice.

Rhona smiled. So the moment had come at last. She pushed open the door and stood there looking at them, her knife ready in her hand. Miranda was seated at the kitchen table, Bryn standing opposite her. They were both looking straight at her as she appeared. To her delight she saw Miranda blanch. She was not so delighted to see that she had a mobile phone in her hand. 'I thought we got rid of that thing,' she commented acidly.

'I got a new one,' Andy replied. 'And I have just pushed the button that connects us directly to the police. They will be here in less than ten minutes.'

Rhona gave a snort of laughter. 'It won't take me ten minutes to do what I've come to do.'

'And what's that?' Bryn put in.

'Kill.' Rhona sounded almost smug. 'You've left me no choice.'

Bryn laughed. 'Oh, you have plenty of choices, Mrs Wilson. Are you sure this is the path you want to take? Remember, in Sleeper's Castle there are so many people watching you.'

She hesitated. 'There is nobody else here. I checked.'

Bryn hadn't moved or taken his eyes from her face. 'That's where you're wrong. Dafydd ap Hywell ap Gruffydd is here, and his daughter Catrin, and Joan and Betsi and Peter. And there are others outside. Killers, far more accomplished than

511

yourself.' His voice had taken on a soft, hypnotic lilt as he recited the names.

He could see her hesitating. Andy stayed completely silent. 'You can feel them, can't you?' he went on, his tone conversational. 'Clever lady like you. You know I'm telling the truth.'

'You mean the ghosts!' She managed a sneer. 'That old man!'

'Ah, so you have met him.' Bryn nodded, satisfied. 'Dafydd. A more experienced purveyor of evil than you, Rhona. And he's not alone. There are others here. Many others.' He was silent for a fraction of a second, then went on, holding her attention, his voice even and thoughtful: 'You probably don't know this, but I used to practise as a criminal psychologist. I was in the States when you were there. I recognised you immediately, of course, from the mugshots.' It wasn't true, but she wasn't to know that. He was watching her carefully. She didn't move. 'I emailed a friend of mine over there to say you'd turned up this side of the pond. They're arranging an extradition order as we speak. I don't fancy your chances over there, Rhona. They still have the death penalty.'

She gave a small frozen laugh. 'I don't believe you.'

'You don't believe me? Which bit don't you believe?'

In the total silence of the room they all heard the distant siren of a police car.

Rhona ran past them, grabbed at the door handle, wrestled with the key and pulled the door open. 'I'll be seeing you again,' she said. Her face was hard and very white. Then she was gone.

They would never find her in the new car. She leapt down the front steps two at a time, ran up the road twenty yards, then scrambled up the bank. Forcing her way through the hedge she found herself tangled in some loops of rusty barbed wire but managed to drag herself free, hearing the sound of her coat tearing as she almost fell into the field. Her stolen car was parked out of sight in her usual gateway further up the lane. She glanced over her shoulder. The police car was silent now. There was no sign of its lights. It had obviously reached its destination. She would gain valuable time while they ran up to the house and discovered what had happened. She followed the line of the hedge, eventually spotting the silver car tucked into the hedge. She scrambled over the gate, unlocked it and threw herself in. Pushing the key into the ignition and turning it she swung out onto the lane, speeding up towards the mountain road.

She hit the cattle grid at about 80 mph, rattling the car so that it almost took off. She turned off the lights now she was on the open road. It would only be a matter of time before the police worked out that she must have come this way. There was just enough light in the sky to see by and she had to reach the turning back down towards Hay before the police emerged and saw her on the open mountainside. If they did that, there would be nowhere she could hide.

When Meryn let himself back into the kitchen at Sleeper's Castle an hour later he found Andy and Bryn seated at the table. One glance told him all was not well. 'Rhona came; the police chased her away,' Bryn said quietly. 'Then we had another visitor.'

Meryn glanced round. He could feel him there, the angry vengeful husk of a man who was Dafydd ap Hywell.

'I can sense him,' he said quietly. 'I hoped he might be content now we know his story, but it appears not.'

'We don't know his story,' Andy put in, her voice a whisper. 'We don't know who killed him.'

Meryn was watching the doorway through into the great hall. Shadows flickered on the wall of the passage as a log slipped in the hearth and lay smouldering in the ash. The shadowy figure was cowering there, watching something they could not see.

'This story has always been about him,' Meryn murmured. 'His dreams, his terror, his visions of blood. The poor man had to live with that for his entire life and even now he's haunted by it still.'

With a sigh he took a step or two closer to the doorway.

Dafydd didn't seem to see him. 'It is time to rest, my friend.' Meryn spoke out loud now. 'How can we help you forget?'

'Catrin loved you,' Andy said softly. She tiptoed over to stand beside Meryn. 'She never forgot you; she forgave you everything.' She spoke with complete certainty.

He turned towards them slowly, scarcely more than a shadow in the darkness of the hall. They could see the flickering light of the fire through him.

'The Lord Owain was grateful to you for your help, I am sure he was,' Andy went on.

'You may not have died shriven, with your sins confessed and forgiven by the Church,' Meryn's voice was firm, 'but they were forgiven by Catrin. Your daughter was a loving child and she learnt that love from you.'

'And we can bury you in a place of sanctity, if that is your wish. Somewhere you can rest in peace,' Andy went on.

The shadow had faded now, but they could feel him still, a presence in the shadows.

Meryn turned to Bryn. 'Can we arrange to have the bones removed and placed somewhere in a churchyard with a blessing?'

'If we can find the bones, I am sure we can,' Bryn said.

There was no sign of the police behind her as Rhona reached the signpost and swung right, locking the car wheels in a violent skid. The lane almost at once left the open common and dived back between steep banks with hedges almost touching overhead as it threaded its way down through the foothills to the valley below. She had to turn the lights back on in the near pitch-dark as she shot down the narrow muddy road. Thankfully she met no one coming the other way and emerged on the road below with no sign of any other cars in pursuit.

She made her way back towards the main road gleefully. Those stupid people couldn't catch a fly on their own backsides. She leant forward and turned on the radio. Music blared inside the car and she let out a whoop of delight. She was high on excitement.

It took her several minutes to realise there was another car behind her on the empty road. She glanced up at the mirror several times. It was staying behind her. No flashing lights. No sirens. She put her foot down a bit more. Yes, it was staying behind, keeping up but at a discreet distance.

The road was straight here with no turnings off it. She eased the throttle down a bit more, feeling the power of the car respond. She had made a good choice with this baby. She glanced up at the mirror again. The car behind had gained on her if anything. She smiled. She knew what she was going to do. She had got to know a little about these roads in the last few days. A turning was coming up soon which led to a byway through one of the small stone-built villages which were scattered through the foothills of the mountains. With luck the police car would be past the turning before they had time to react. Even if they stopped and reversed, it wouldn't matter. She would have gained a precious few minutes and maybe lost them altogether in the network of small streets.

She was enjoying this, pitting her wits against a carful of plods. She circled through the little town a few times, cautiously approaching every turning, creeping down sleeping streets where all the houses seemed to have darkened windows.

When she regained the main road there was no sign of them. With a small laugh of glee she turned the music up and headed on towards the Brecon bypass. She would take the road on towards Cardiff. Once there she would be safe.

She turned onto the A470 without noticing the car sliding out of a lay-by to follow her south. When she did notice, it was very close behind.

She let out a curse. Was it another police car? If so it was unmarked too. And it wasn't trying to overtake. She put her foot down slightly, watching to see what it did.

It dropped back. She smiled and relaxed, her hands tapping the wheel in time to the music.

The road was running between bleak mountains now, winding along the side of one range, above a narrow valley. She glanced sideways. Down to her left the hillside dropped steeply away out of sight with only the occasional post to mark the narrowness of the verge. She pulled the car into the middle of the road. This was like driving in Switzerland, hair-raising, exciting, dangerous.

Then two things happened at once. She glanced at the petrol gauge, something she hadn't thought to do so far, and saw that it was registering empty, then she raised her eyes and saw the car behind her had turned on its blue flashing lights. The gap between them was closing fast. She licked her lips. Problem.

She would never know whether it was a conscious decision. She was on a high. Life was perfect. Maybe it was better to call it a day now. There was no thought; no plan. She swung the wheel hard to the left, felt the tyres leave the road, heard the scratching and splintering from the small bushes which had clung to the rim of the ravine and she felt the car take off. It swung out in an arc, music blaring, and dived gracefully into the valley below.

'They will catch her, won't they?' Andy sat staring down at her mug of coffee. It had grown cold long since. The shadow of Dafydd ap Hywell had gone for now, but the threat of Rhona still hung over them.

'I think they will this time.' Bryn was reassuring.

They had just had a phone call from Ella. Roy was out of surgery and had regained consciousness. He was going to be all right. Bryn stood up to put the kettle on again. That at least was one piece of good news.

Until now they had not mentioned Sian's visit and the bombshell she had dropped.

'Do you think Sue means it?' Andy spoke again after a long silence.

'I always liked Joe,' Meryn put in. It wasn't really an answer.

'But you weren't surprised when Sue said she wasn't coming back. I saw your faces.' Andy looked from one man to the other.

It was Bryn who finally admitted the truth. He was making a fresh pot of coffee. He carried it over and put it down on the table. 'To be honest, I did wonder. She didn't really fit here. She had lots of friends, and the herb garden was very special to her, but she belonged in the sun. I could always tell when she'd been Skyping the family back home, or when she had had news from old friends; she'd get very wistful. And when she left, it was with almost undignified speed.' He smiled fondly.

'And then I appeared.'

'And then you appeared.'

'And stirred up a hornet's nest.'

'You did, didn't you.' Bryn gave a mischievous grin.

She glared at him. 'Sue must have seen them too: Catrin and the rest,' she persisted. 'Surely?'

'She did have nightmares sometimes,' Bryn conceded.

Andy stared up at him. 'Why didn't you say?'

'She told me not to tell anyone. She swore me to secrecy. I caught her on a particularly bad day once when she was feeling very blue. She poured out her heart to me.'

'So you've been playing the faithful retainer and keeping schtum? Oh, Bryn!'

'She also told me that you would fit here. That the house would like you.'

Andy opened her mouth to reply, then closed it. She couldn't think what to say. 'But you didn't,' she said at last.

'Didn't what?'

'Like me.'

He was thoughtful. 'No.'

It was like being slapped in the face. For several seconds she said nothing then she stood up and walked over to the sink to pour her coffee away.

Meryn was watching them in silence. He stood up and came over to put his empty mug next to hers on the draining board.

'I'm off home now, children,' he said quietly. 'Bryn, I assume you will stay here tonight, to keep an eye on Andy? I'll see you in the morning.' He reached out and gave Andy's arm a squeeze. 'Ring me if you need me.'

She watched as he let himself out into the cold darkness. Almost at once she heard the owl. Meryn's watchdog was on duty.

'I suppose that's that, then,' she said bleakly.

Bryn went over and turned the key in the lock behind Meryn. 'What do you mean, that's that?'

'If you don't like me.' Her voice was very quiet.

'I said I didn't like you at first. I didn't say I don't like you now.'

He came to stand behind her and put his hands on her shoulders, turning her to face him. 'I thought you were going to be a pushy, snobby Londoner who would give me the sack.' He smiled.

Their faces were very close. They looked at each other, then he turned abruptly away. 'Would you think of buying Sleeper's Castle?'

She turned back to the window without replying. Her reflection showed the misery and exhaustion on her face.

'I gather the house in Kew is yours, now they've found a will,' Bryn went on cautiously. 'If you didn't want to sell that, maybe you could still buy this as a second home. Will you have lots of money?'

'No. No, I won't have lots of money,' she whispered. 'Graham wasn't rich. Apart from the house. He'd inherited that. And no, this ought to be a proper home.' She sounded fierce. 'And this is Pepper's house. Whoever buys it would have to keep him.'

Bryn smiled gravely. 'He would approve of that notion.'

As if on cue, the cat flap rattled. Pepper pushed through, stopped just inside the door and looked round apprehensively.

'It's OK, old boy. The nasty ghost man has gone for now,' Bryn said gently. 'And so has the nasty red-haired lady.'

Pepper sat down and now they could see him clearly they realised there was mud on his face and one of his ears was matted with blood.

'What's happened? Oh Pepper!' Andy stared at him in horror. She bent to pick him up, everything else forgotten for the moment. 'He's been hurt. Should we take him to the vet?' She carried him to the rocking chair and sat down with him on her lap. He pressed against her, shivering.

Bryn knelt before her, and reached out gently to run his fingers over the cat's head and body. 'I don't think he's too bad. It's only a scratch. Ears bleed easily. I'll get you some cotton wool and warm water. Let's give him a sponge so we can see how bad it is.'

He was right. The ear appeared to have no more than a superficial scratch. Having removed the mud and dried blood, Andy left Pepper to wash it again himself, which he did, purring, still sitting on her knee. She glanced up at Bryn with a sheepish smile. 'I've hardly dared sit on his chair before.'

It was ten minutes later that they heard a car draw up below the house.

Dai Vaughan came to the back door. He looked exhausted. 'I'm sorry to come so late,' he said. 'I saw the light on so I reckoned you were still up.' He hesitated. 'I have a bit of news and I wanted to tell you myself. I'm afraid it will be all over the TV news tomorrow.' He looked from one to the other grimly. 'Rhona Wilson has been killed in a car crash. She was driving down the A470 near the Storey Arms and the car went off the road into the valley.'

Andy closed her eyes, numb with shock, and hugged Pepper close, her face buried in his fur.

'There will be an enquiry as there was a police car in pursuit,' Dai went on, 'but the whole thing was caught on their cameras. The car didn't skid or swerve or anything as if a tyre had burst. It turned off the road at right angles and accelerated over the edge.' He paused. 'It was almost as if she meant to do it.'

He turned back to the door. 'I'm sorry to be the bearer of such shocking news, but at least you can sleep easy in your beds tonight. She won't be threatening anyone else with her knife.'

They sat in silence listening to his footsteps outside, then to the sound of his car engine as his headlights flared then disappeared down the road into the dark.

'It was my fault,' Andy whispered at last. 'If I hadn't provoked her, hadn't visited the house in my dreams.'

'It would still have happened one day,' Bryn said. 'She was a deeply unstable woman and if it's confirmed that she killed someone in the States it proves she was already seriously disturbed before you ever met Graham. You mustn't blame yourself. This was exactly the kind of exit she would have planned for herself if she thought about it,' he went on sadly. 'It was dramatic, quick, exciting. I doubt if someone like her would've been able to face the rest of her life behind bars.'

Andy gave a small half-smile. This was the psychologist talking, not the surly, taciturn gardener.

'So you think it was deliberate?'

He put his head on one side. 'As Dai said, there will be all sorts of tests on the car, but my guess would be yes: deliberate.'

'I can't believe it's over.' She sighed. Leaning back in the chair she closed her eyes. Pepper settled himself more comfortably on her knees.

'You don't have to stay now, Bryn,' she said after a moment.

'I suppose not.'

'Pepper and I will look after each other.'

'OK.' Bryn hesitated, studying her face. She didn't open her eyes. With a sigh he reached for his jacket. 'I'll see you in the morning then?'

'I expect so.'

'Are you sure you'll be all right on your own?'

'I'm sure!' She opened her eyes. 'Rhona has gone and Dafydd

has gone at least for now. The house is at peace. I need to think.'

'OK.'

It was only as she heard the sound of his van disappearing into the distance and realised that she was completely alone that she started to cry properly. She was crying for Rhona and for Graham and for Roy; for Catrin and Dafydd, and for Sleeper's Castle, which would soon be on the market, and at the last for herself. She climbed the stairs with Pepper still in her arms and crawled into bed. As she pulled the covers over her head he snuggled in beside her and started to purr.

In the solar behind the great hall at Kentchurch Court Alys had introduced Catrin to her husband, Sir John Scudamore, and their family. It was a while later that she took Catrin by the hand and pulled her away from the crowd round the fire. 'There is someone else here who wants to see you.'

She led her out of the hall to the great tower and up the winding stair. Two sconces threw wildly dancing shadows on the walls as they climbed. Catrin glanced up nervously as she followed Alys. 'Who is it? Who's here?'

Alys glanced back over her shoulder. 'Wait and see.'

Halfway up the stairs, Alys halted and pushed open a door in the wall. They entered a comfortably furnished chamber with a large fireplace and windows shuttered against the night. A warm fire burned low in the hearth. Wall hangings and cushioned settles added to the room's comfort. The room was empty. Catrin stared round but Alys had walked across the floor. She pulled aside one of the hangings. Under it was a small door in the stone wall. Catrin followed her through it and they climbed a narrow staircase which led up inside the wall, into the room above. This was furnished as a bedroom with a large bed, the tester and hangings richly embroidered. By the fire sat a hunched figure wrapped in a heavy cloak.

'I have a visitor for you, Father,' Alys whispered.

521

'So, my little friend, Cat.' Owain Glyndŵr looked up and smiled. He was pale and looked ill and much, much older than when she had last seen him.

Catrin gasped. She stared at him in confusion.

'Come here.' He beckoned. 'You knew, didn't you. You saw truly what would happen to my ill-fated cause. Your father told me of your dreams and nightmares when he told me of his own. He would speak of glory but then he would warn of defeat and ruin to follow and I silenced him. I was angry. It demoralised my troops. It demoralised me! So, he would change his mind and speak what I wanted to hear.' He sighed. 'I chose to ignore his warnings and to believe the men who foretold nothing but triumph. Forgive me.'

She was speechless.

He held out his hand and, still bewildered, she stepped towards him and put her hand in his. This man had been, was, the prince of all Wales, her idol, her father's lord.

He looked down at her fingers and ran his thumb over the silver ring she still wore. 'I gave you this?'

She nodded. 'I have never taken it off,' she whispered.

'You are a good woman, Cat. My daughter tells me that you are going to stay with us; that your father died. I am truly sorry for that, but pleased that we shall have the pleasure of your company.' He leaned back in his chair. 'Go now, my dear. Alys shall take you downstairs. I am tired. But we will speak again soon.'

As she followed Alys back down to the lower chamber Cat found her voice again. 'I thought he was a fugitive in the mountains! Or even—' She stopped and put her hand to her mouth. 'People think he's dead,' she whispered. 'Thank the Blessed Virgin he is safe with you.'

Alys gave her a mischievous grin. 'My father is always safe. He will recover his health and return to fight again. You'll see.' She caught Catrin's hand. 'But please, Cat, remember he is in hiding here. No one knows about him. And no one can ever know. Our English neighbours don't even know that the daughter of Glyndŵr is John's wife. It is too dangerous. Only a very few servants wait on him.'

Catrin bit her lip. 'Does he know what has happened to Catherine, to your mother? Is it true they took them to London?'

Alys's eyes flooded with tears and she dashed them away angrily. 'They are in the Tower. All we can do for now is to pray for their safety.' She sniffed bravely. 'Come, let's go back down to the others. They will be wondering where we are.'

Catrin caught her hand. 'Does Edmund know?'

Alys smiled again. 'Of course Edmund knows. That is why he brought you here. He has been a true and faithful servant to my father.'

Two days later Catrin and Edmund were again summoned to the tower chamber. This time Owain Glyndŵr was in the lower room, sitting at a table, a pen in his hand. He put it down when they were shown in to him.

'It is good to see you again, my Cat.' He smiled. He glanced at Edmund standing behind her. 'And you, my most loyal friend.'

Edmund blushed.

The Lord Owain leant forward. 'I know you have come into the king's peace and your father paid your fine. I would want it no other way, Edmund,' he said. He paused for a long time and they waited in silence. A gust of wind shook the windows and the candles on the table guttered. 'I had such dreams for Wales,' he went on. 'We could have been a great nation. We will be a great nation one day, but my people have suffered too much. I could not ask them to do more. I want them to eat; I want them to prosper. I want them to have a fair and peaceful life. I couldn't do that for them.' He leaned back and blinked away tears. There was a long pause before he sat forward again in his chair. 'So,' he went on, his voice regaining its strength. 'You are looking after Catrin?'

'I would like to marry her,' Edmund said. He didn't look at

her. 'Lord Owain, if you would act in her father's stead, we would dearly like to have your blessing.'

Catrin gave a little whimper of joy. She reached out to grab Edmund's hand.

Owain's face was weary and sad but when he smiled his eyes lit with their old sparkle. 'And are you agreeable to this plan, Cat?'

She nodded. 'Oh, yes. Please.'

And so, three days later, Catrin *ferch* Dafydd and Edmund, son of Raymond of Hardwicke, were married in the porch of St Mary's Church. She was given away by a man huddled in a heavy homespun cloak which effectively disguised the fact that he was Owain, Prince of Wales and Lord of Glyndŵr.

As a wedding present Sir John Scudamore, Alys's husband, was prevailed upon to give them a cottage on the estate. Later he was to make Edmund one of his bailiffs.

In the spring Catrin was delivered of a baby son. They called him Owain.

Bryn rifled through the box of papers which he had pulled out from the cupboard under the stairs in his cottage. His father had left them to him with strict instructions to keep them and hand them on to his son. Bryn gave a grim smile. If he ever had a son. His father had not seemed to consider the fact that it might never happen. He found old letters and copies of the deeds of the family farm, the farm which he, Bryn, had sold. His dreams of the fifteenth century had awakened strange memories of stories he had been told as a little boy by his grandfather, sitting by the range in the old farmhouse on the hill. Stories of Owain Glyndŵr.

The legend of what happened to Glyndŵr had lasted since the days of his last defeat. He had disappeared into the hills, as he had done so often before, hidden by the mists and clouds of Wales that had come to his aid so many times in the past. Where he went to ground no one ever knew.

Stories abounded, one of which was that he went to the home of his daughter Alys at Kentchurch Court and that she and her husband shielded him for the rest of his days. To this day no one knows where he died; no one knows where he was buried. The story goes that, like King Arthur, he is not dead but merely asleep, hidden deep in the caves beneath the mountains of Wales, waiting to come again in her hour of need.

Bryn picked up one of the letters his grandfather had written to him when he was at Jesus College, Oxford – the Welsh college. 'Do not forget your roots, boy,' he had said. Bryn smiled. He could hear the old man's voice, the light lilt of the Welsh hills always there in the background. 'Do not forget that Glyndŵr gave us this house.'

Bryn sat down on the sofa and leant back, exhausted, the letter in his hand. He had always thought of his grandfather's stories as so much romantic nonsense, but now he was wondering.

For the first time he had heard Edmund's full name. He was Edmund of Hardwicke. Andy kept saying how like Edmund he, Bryn, looked. Edmund had been his grandfather's name. And his great grandfather's name. An English name, going back a long time, that in itself strange, in so passionately Welsh a family.

He leant down to the box at his feet and pulled out the large folded sheet, which contained his family tree. Standing up, he spread it out on the table. To his shame he had barely looked at it in all the years he had kept it.

He traced his finger up the generations of names until he reached the top.

Edmund Hardwicke married Catherine Davidson in 1410. They had three children: Owen, John and Alice. It all looked very English.

He, Bryn, was the direct descendant of that Owen who in his turn married a girl called Margaret. They called their eldest son Edmund.

He paused, his finger still pointing at the top of the page. Catherine Davidson. Catrin *ferch* Dafydd. *Ferch* Dafydd meant daughter of Dafydd. David. People in England didn't call their children 'daughter of'. He smiled quietly. Was it possible he was a descendant of Catrin and Edmund? Had he inherited one or two look-alike genes from Edmund after so many centuries? It was probably all nonsense, but it was a thought.

More to the point, had he inherited the farmhouse that Owain Glyndŵr's daughter and son-in-law had given them as a wedding present? And then he, Bryn Hardwick, had sold it.

Was it possible that some indignant fate had, in response, guided him back to Sleeper's Castle to dream of the past and realise his folly? He bent over the box again. At the bottom, under a pile of old typed letters was a large, much-folded Manila envelope. As he pulled it out he realised it contained books. He opened it and extricated them. There were three, very small, chunky and heavy, bound in leather. He opened one, hardly daring to touch it in case the leather fell to pieces in his hands. It was handwritten, the vellum pages thick and crackling slightly as he touched them. It was an illuminated book of hours. Dear God! He found himself a mass of goose pimples. He recognised them. These were Catrin's books, the books Edmund had saved for her and packed and carried down the Golden Valley on the back of a mule.

He sat staring at them for a long time, then he put them down with meticulous care on the table in front of him, stood up and went to help himself to a bottle of lager from the fridge.

If only he could he afford to buy back the family farm to appease the shade of Owain Glyndŵr.

Three days later Bryn and Meryn dug up the bones of Dafydd ap Hywell. They were almost exactly where they had guessed they would be, only a foot or so down under the grass of the lawn. They told no one. Sian had declined to be there. This was ghostbusting stuff, and not for her; instead she went to visit Roy.

Bryn put the bones reverently one by one into a wooden chest he had discovered in one of the outbuildings. He had carried it up to the bedroom which Andy now used as a studio and she had painted it with medieval scrollwork and wreaths of flowers. When they brought it down again they laid it on two makeshift trestles in front of the hearth in the room which in Dafydd's day had been the great hall of the house, the room in which he had died. With his bones they put in a reproduction of a medieval book of hours which Andy had found in the Pascoes' bookshop in Hay and a copy of *The Mabinogion* which contained, she was sure, some of the stories he had loved.

Meryn told their story in confidence to a local clergyman, a friend of many years, who, as he'd hoped, agreed to help with a quiet interment in a private, shadowy spot beneath an ancient yew in the corner of an isolated churchyard in the mountains above Sleeper's Castle. There were only the three of them there as mourners to lower the box into the ground as the priest spoke the age-old words.

Requiem eternam dona ei, Domine,
Et lux perpetua luceat eis.
Requiescat in pace.
Lord grant him eternal rest,
And let perpetual light shine upon him.
May he rest in peace.

Behind them the shade of Dafydd ap Hywell stood for a few moments staring down at the box that contained his earthly remains, then with a gentle sigh he was gone.

When they left there was no sign that a new grave was there. There had been no witnesses save the yew tree, which scattered her needles and berries gently on the grass.

In the end they came up with a plan. It was tentative and optimistic and probably mad, but as they drank to Dafydd's memory that evening it seemed as good as any. As soon as she got legal possession of the house in Kew, Andy would sell it; its memories, happy as they had been, had been tainted by Rhona's malevolence and without Graham there the house was no more than a pile of bricks.

With part of the proceeds she would then proceed to buy Sleeper's Castle; she would illustrate Meryn's book on herbs, a book that had nothing at all to do with botany and everything to do with magic, and Bryn would continue to be the gardener, though no longer paid by direct debit. They exchanged a comfortable, humorous glance when this point was mentioned and agreed to negotiate further at an unspecified future date. One thing would not change. Pepper would still be in charge.

Meryn raised his glass first to Andy and then to Bryn. 'One thing needs to be said,' he announced fondly. 'You may not be ready to hear this, but I feel I am in loco parentis, so I give you both my blessing. I too can sometimes see the future, probably better than you, possibly better than poor old Dafydd.' He took a sip from his glass. 'I see quarrels ahead, and regrets and sorrow for Dafydd and for Rhona, but I also see laughter and banter and much happiness . . . and after all that, I see a descendant of Catrin *ferch* Dafydd living in this house, and I see you two as his parents.'

He chuckled at the sight of their faces, both shocked and indignant, in Bryn's case incredulous, in Andy's embarrassed. He put down his glass and stood up. 'With that thought for you to ponder, my children, I shall bid you both goodnight.'

Author's Note

Catrin and her father did not exist but I am certain people like them did. Wales was and is a land of isolated houses and remote valleys where writers and poets and their ilk quietly practise their trade. Glyndŵr was famous for his patronage of poets and seers and bards. If Catrin and Dafydd had existed, I am sure he would have sought them out.

There were women poets; the names of at least two famous ladies have come down to us, Gwerful Fychan, who was writing during the fifteenth century and her namesake, Gwerful Mechain, who was writing towards its end. (She is the lady famous for her 'Ode to Pubic Hair'!)

This novel was first inspired by Hay Castle itself. Having written about its building by Matilda de Braose in *Lady of Hay* I thought it would be interesting to write about the castle's destruction. Possibly bad timing in view of the fact that, at the time of writing, a programme of restoration is beginning, preceded by an archaeological and 'geophys' investigation of the site. At long last, but not alas in time for this book, perhaps we will know the answer to all those questions about a moat, drawbridge, curtain walls, etc. and what is under the 'mansion' which today takes up so much of the original site.

When I started to look up accounts of the castle's destruction, I found so many different dates given for the dastardly deed, I was utterly confused. I was aiming to set my novel in the years when the country was torn apart by the rebellion of Owain Glyndŵr, that is between 1400 and about 1410. He was an incredibly charismatic and interesting character, but he is also credited with destroying almost every old building in Wales. Hay Castle was one of them – or was it?

I consulted a few websites. One, which had better remain nameless, claimed that Glyndŵr destroyed the castle in 1353 (for shame – he was a small child then, if even born). Others gave variously 1400, 1401, 1402, 1403, all possible as it turned out. I turned to books – far more reliable. Yet one gives three different dates within the same book. Other sources differ again. Some official records give the date when it was 'ruinous', others when it was once again defenceable. The conclusion to be drawn is that, either Glyndwr came back several times – which, given its strategic position on the border and between other places he is known to have visited, is perfectly possible – or that he never destroyed it at all, just gave it a bit of a fright. I gather the latter view is beginning to prevail. This is a novel, I'm allowed to be vague!

I hadn't intended Owain Glyndŵr to be a character in the novel at all. He was going to lurk off stage, but he muscled in almost at once. He was a forceful personality. And a wonderfully mysterious one. His magical reputation is almost as legendary as his final disappearance. I couldn't not include him.

I was given so much unstinting help with the writing of this novel. Thank you once again to my son Jonathan who on this occasion introduced me to the wonderful tool of the dashboard camera; fantastic aide memoire for research purposes. And I must acknowledge the many people who we met as we visited the various sites mentioned in Catrin and Dafydd's tour of the border March. I don't know who they were but at the first glimpse of my camera and notebook they materialised with their dogs and their gardening gloves and their shopping to give me their views on Glyndŵr, his battles, his successes and his failures, historians every one.

I want to mention Annie McBrearty as well, who I first met all those years ago when I was looking for an expert on medieval Welsh when writing *Lady of Hay* and who has been a friend and inspiration and translator-in-chief of all matters Welsh ever since. And thank you Sheila Childs for your encouragement and help as honorary researcher. It was Sheila who introduced me to Jan Lucas-Scudamore. Thank you, Jan, for showing us Glyndŵr's rooms in beautiful Kentchurch Court and for introducing us in turn to Professor Gruffydd Aled Williams and his colleagues. I shall long remember that wonderful evening we all spent at the Garway Moon. I am not sure if Aled realised the kind of books I write, but I thank him for his enthusiasm and knowledge and for a sprinkling of academic stardust over the project. Thank you too to Séza Magdalena Eccles for her masterclass in weather magic. I'm not sure if we got it right, but it was fascinating and inspirational.

In fact, I'm not sure if I got anything right. All the mistakes and inaccuracies in this book are mine alone with the excuse once again that I write novels, not history books.

Thank you above all to the people of Hay who have been so consistently supportive over the thirty years since *Lady of Hay* was published and who helped and encouraged me in the ten or so years even before that, when I was researching the book and publication was only a dream.

Which brings me full circle to my agent and friend Carole Blake. Thank you Carole for so many years of brilliant agenting and friendship and thank you to the team behind this book. Susan Opie, Anne O'Brien, Kim Young and all the wonderful people at HarperCollins.

Historical Note

When preparing to write a historical novel one does masses of research, consulting dozens if not hundreds of books, documents and websites, visiting museums and buildings, castles, abbeys and battlefields, all the time making notes and taking photographs. Much if not most of this research is not used as such in the book, but it is there in one's head, forming a background, a scenario, a flavour of the times. Below I have included a selection of these notes, which I hope will interest you and which cover topics which fascinated me.

Edmund is fictional. He is a typical example of a younger son, forced to find a living beyond the family farm which, like the whole country and indeed the whole of Europe after the Black Death half a century before, was still depleted and unable to support the family. Many young men, trained since childhood in the use of often primitive, home-made weapons, sought their fortune and the excitement of war in the service of their local lord and in the case of talented archers, in mercenary bands. Glyndŵr attracted many such to his service. His own experience of war in France and Scotland in the service of the Earl of

Arundel as a young man had taught him to be a talented soldier and it is believed he learned some of his skills in guerrilla warfare from fighting the Scots who were experts at it.

At the start of the story Catrin has left to her by her mother some precious notes on medicines passed on from a family of healers who lived on the far side of the mountains. I found my first copy of *The Herbal Remedies of the Physicians of Myddfai* in a bookshop in Hay back in the early 1980s. It is described as a collection of ancient and Celtic remedies associated with a legend of the Lady of the Lake. The book had everything that I love. History, herbs and folklore. Myddfai is a small village in Carmarthenshire on the far side of the Brecon Beacons. Nearby there is a hidden lake, called Llyn-y-Fan-Fach and local legend has it that in the late 12th or early 13th century a mysterious Lady of the Lake (yes, possibly that one) passed on to a local family the secrets of the – mostly herbal – remedies. It is a complicated, Druidic story and may just hide the fact that generations of a family of physicians were the first to write down what had up to then been an oral tradition. The legend was first collected in 1841 and published by the Welsh Manuscript Society in the 1860s with an English translation. The 'recipes' are wonderful and sometimes truly awful to read! The herbs are good and usually tally with a double check in a modern herbal. Some of the other ingredients are formidable though; the brain of a red cock, verdegris, dung of mice, 'some newts, by some called lizards, and those nasty beetles which are found in ferns during summer time, calcine them in an iron pot and make powder thereof . . .'. I am sure Catrin exercised due caution!

Re-enactors are a wonderful source of information on the period in which they specialise; they do masses of research and put their findings into practice. It was at a medieval fair at Hay Castle that I first came across the form of knitting called nalbinding. 'Proper' knitting came from Islamic roots probably entering Europe through Spain in the 13th century and made its way only slowly into popular use, but the ancient Viking form of nalbinding had been around for thousands of years and was universally used. The wool is pulled into shorter lengths (not the 'ball' used in knitting) and is threaded through a bone needle which is used with the thumbs in a form of crochet which is worked in the round for stockings, caps etc. The lengths of wool are joined together by felting.

Hence the origins of the 'Monmouth Cap', a warm and practical head covering worn by sailors, by soldiers under their helmets, by men and women, by all classes. It was usually brown (white for women) and sometimes red. The felting process makes them waterproof. Very few have survived from the early period but they are often seen illustrated in medieval manuscripts.

Weather magic, was, like all magic, above all practical. Rain was needed for crops; sunshine at the right moment for ripening. There were two parts to magic (say my books): the spell, which involved a formula of secret words; and the rite, a set of actions by which the spell conveyed to the object the desired effect. For example, to get rain, sprinkle water on the ground; to make corn grow, jump up and down in a field. There are dozens of ways to divert bad weather – one of the commonest, planting stonecrop on your roof to ward off lightning. It is harder to attract bad weather and then direct it towards someone else. That would be classed as black magic if used for malicious purposes, but perhaps not if you are using it to fight against your enemy! Weather witching was one of the most commonly used forms of magic – and still is! Even I have whistled for the wind when out sailing. I found two books especially helpful with this part of my research. Ella Mary Leather's *Folklore and Witchcraft of Herefordshire* and *The Silver Bough* by F. Marian McNeill, the first volume of which deals with folklore and folk belief in Scotland. Not Welsh, admittedly, but Celtic all the same.

The ending of Glyndŵr's story is full of mystery and that of his surviving family is also uncertain. After the fall of Harlech Castle, his wife and two of his daughters, one of which was

535

Catrin (in the novel I called her Catherine to differentiate her from my heroine) were captured, together with Catrin's son Lionel and her daughters, and taken to the Tower of London. There is a record in the Exchequer Rolls:

> *To John Weele, Esq. In money paid to his own hands, for the expenses of the wife of Owen Glendourdi, the wife of Edmund Mortimer, and others, their sons and daughters, in his custody in the city of London, at the King's charge, by his command – £30*

This record is dated 27th June 1413. By December they were all dead. What happened is unknown, and deemed in some quarters then and now to be suspicious, though one view seems to be that they succumbed to the plague. We don't know where Margaret was buried, but we do know what happened to Catrin. After she and her daughters died in 1413 there was an entry in the Exchequer rolls of a payment made to the valet of the Earl of Arundel:

> *'for expenses and other charges incurred for the burial and exequies of the wife of Edmund Mortimer and her daughters, buried within St Swithin's Church London – £1'.*

There is no mention there of poor Lionel. St Swithin's church was in Candlewick (better known, later, as Cannon) Street in the City of London. There is a poignant coda to their story. St Swithin's was bombed in the Blitz of 1940 and not rebuilt at the end of the war, but its churchyard has been turned into a tiny garden, dwarfed by the enormous steel and glass buildings that now surround it. There, a memorial to Catrin, the daughter of Owain Glyndŵr has been erected. This was also dedicated to the suffering of all women and children in war.